NIGHTCLUB SINS: COMPLETE SERIES

A BAD BOY BILLIONAIRE ROMANCE

MICHELLE LOVE

CONTENTS

✼ Created with Vellum

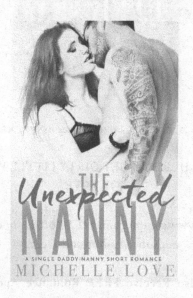

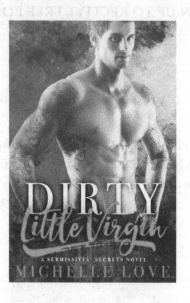

THE FORBIDDEN SITTER BOOK 1

A Billionaire Holiday Romance (Nightclub Sins 3)

By Michelle Love

A two-year-old. A best friend with a little sister who'd love to babysit. And one hard-on that refused to go away...

When in a bind who else would you look to for advice?
Your best friend, right?
And when this best friend tells you his little sister is majoring in child development then you know you gotta use her, right?
He only has one damn rule.
Do not touch his virgin baby sis...
Now how hard could it possibly be to keep a promise to your best bud when you're in desperate need of a babysitter, because you're clueless when it comes to kids?
Let me tell you the answer to that simple question.

Very f-ing hard!

From the moment I met her, everything became hard. And I soon found it was only going to get harder, since she was determined to keep me a secret.

Me!

Was I really gonna let her get away with hiding what we'd found?

A little boy needed me. A grown man needed me. And I needed to let go of my V-card ...

Excitement and sadness are a rare combination, but that's exactly how I felt when I went to work as my big brother's best friend's babysitter.

Tossed away by his horrible mother, the two-year-old needed me desperately.

I could be there for the poor boy.

But I fell in love.

With both the son and the father.

My overprotective family wouldn't mind my love for the child.

But my love for the man who wasn't supposed to be touching me at all?

Well, no one was going to be okay with that.

So I told the billionaire who was used to getting his way that we'd have to hide our relationship.

Keep the steamy sex a secret.

I found out billionaires do not like to be kept hidden.

So how long would I get to feel his phenomenal touch before we had to end it all?

1

CHAPTER 1

Gannon

The first day of November and a chilly wind tore through our fair city of Los Angeles at ten in the morning. The first cold front of the fall season had arrived, bringing with it an enthusiasm for change.

I stood, looking out the floor-to-ceiling windows of my fifteenth-floor office. In the distance the waves coming in off the Pacific Ocean took my attention as I waited for my personal assistant, Janine Lee, to let me know when my video conference was up and going.

My job was CEO of Forester Industries; a business passed down to me by my father. He'd inherited the company from his father and had turned it from a million-dollar company to a billion-dollar one.

Was I born with a silver spoon in my mouth?

That would be a yes. I had never known hardships, poverty, or the feeling of going to bed hungry. I had only known the world of the super-rich. A world where you asked for something and you got it. And it all happened very quickly.

Maybe all that instant gratification wasn't healthy for me, because I was impatiently waiting for the first time in my life. At thirty, some might say I hadn't even begun to live my life yet, but waiting for my dream to be built felt like an eternity to me.

At a prestigious nightclub in Vegas one night a few months ago, I met a couple of fellow billionaire's at Hakkasan, a nightclub for the extremely wealthy. One could blow a hundred grand with ease at the place. And it was there that a plan was hatched to build a nightclub comparable to that one.

Hakkasan was number one on the top-ten chart of high-status nightclubs around the world. The men I met that night wanted to build something even better than that. And right here in L.A., the place we all called home, coincidentally.

It took us no time to find a place and get construction going on the club. Currently, we were bantering about the name of the place—hence the conference I was waiting for. We were at the stage where the name was necessary to order insignia and other things that would carry the nightclub's name on them.

I turned away from the window as my office door opened. There stood Janine, all four-feet-five-inches of her. Her short hair hung in dark-black, silky strands around her round face. Thick-framed glasses housed her chocolate eyes. One hand on her hip, she jerked her head in gesture. "Mr. Forester, your Skype conference is up in the conference room. August Harlow and Nixon Slaughter are ready and waiting for you, sir."

"Excellent." I strode across my large office, following her

to the room at the end of the hallway. "Do you think you could find me a coffee this morning? Something that says fall is here?"

"I'm on it, boss." She flipped her hair and turned, heading off to find what I'd asked for. The woman was amazing. At nearly forty, she was adept at making things happen for those she worked for. I was lucky enough to have found her when her old boss had passed away a few years back.

She and I had something in common, we found out, as we accidentally met at the funeral home where her boss' memorial was taking place and where my father's body had just arrived.

It was in the hallway that we both went for the same box of tissues. And in that tragic moment, we found each other. She told me about her boss and her lack of a job as a personal assistant. I told her about how I was —now—with the loss of my —father—the CEO of a large business and could use a personal assistant. And in that sad moment, a partnership was made that would make us both feel better about life in general after suffering from our losses.

My mother had passed on several years prior to my father. Breast cancer took her from us. Being an only child, my father's death left me utterly alone in the world—something I wasn't real crazy about being.

But with Janine's appearance right at the time I felt the most alone I'd ever felt, came hope. Perhaps things wouldn't always feel the way they did at that time. One day, things would get better. One day I wouldn't be the only member of the Forester family. Or so I hoped anyway.

Not that I was looking for a wife or anything. I was a bit on the busy side to be doing that. But once I had things the way I wanted them, the nightclub included, then I would slow down and find time to date more and find Miss Right. Instead of what I had been doing—settling for Miss Right Now.

Currently, I wasn't even messing with Miss Right Now. I was involved in my work as the CEO and my work with the club. There just wasn't time for anything else.

Stepping into the conference room, I found my partners faces on two of the large screens that ran in a circle around the room. Some conferences for the business took up all seven screens at once. We were global, after all.

August and Nixon greeted me with wide smiles as I came in and took a seat. "Morning, gentlemen. And I do use that term lightly," I joked.

August smirked. "So the time has come for us to put our bickering behind us and agree on a name for this nightclub.".

Nixon picked up, "Let the record show, I like the name, Club X."

I threw down, "And I've told you before, that name is much too common."

"Yes," August agreed. "But, Gannon, you have yet to come up with a name. You've shot down all the ones we've come up with, though. So I am throwing you into the middle of this debate and challenging you to come up with a name on the fly so to speak. You have one minute."

"What?" I looked back and forth at the screens, finding two earnest faces. "I'm not that creative. You guys are ..."

"You're wasting time, Gannon," Nixon reminded me.

August's arched brow told me he was completely serious as he looked at his watch. "The time is ticking away. Thirty seconds, Gannon, or we're sticking with Club X."

"No! Wait—give me one more minute—I'm terrible

under pressure." I pinched the bridge of my nose as I tried to inject some creativity into my business brain.

August wasn't giving in and was not about to give me any more time. "Nope, no extra time, and we're coming in on ten, nine ..."

One word popped into my head, and I blurted it out, "Swank!"

I looked back and forth at my partners and was shocked to see smiles curling their lips. August nodded. "I like it."

Nixon chuckled. "Me too. Swank, it is, then." He looked at August through the other screen. "Seems we've had a productive meeting, August. Time to get back to our real jobs. Catch you guys later in the week. Nixon, out." The screen with his face on it went black.

August gave me a nod. "Back to work, buddy. Let's get together on Friday evening for dinner and drinks."

"You got it." I had to laugh as he ended the call. My friends knew I worked best under pressure, and they were, as always, expert manipulators

Walking out of the conference room, I heard Janine arguing with another woman, "No, you may not go looking for Mr. Forester, Miss!"

"Out of my way, you midget!"

I headed in the direction I heard the voices coming from and found my assistant trying her best to stop a tall, skinny redhead with a small boy at her side. He huddled against her leg, eyes wide with dismay at the shouting.

The irate woman's dark-brown eyes caught mine. "Gannon Forester, there you are."

"And you are?" I inquired, giving the boy what I hoped was a reassuring smile. Not that I knew the first thing about kids. Surprisingly, he ducked his head shyly and then looked back up, offering a sweet gap-toothed grin.

The woman cleared her throat impatiently. "Cassandra Harrington. Surely you remember me." Her thin lips pulled into a smile. "Club Acapulco on the strip?"

Not a clue ...

I had the feeling I didn't want to talk to the woman in the hallway with so many people's ears leaning our way. "Would you mind stepping into my office, Mrs. Harrington?"

"Miss. And that's where I wanted to talk to you at in the first place, but this little troll ..."

I took her by the arm and ushered her and the little boy into my office. The way she shoved the kid forward, like he was a sack of flour, irked me for some reason. As I closed the door behind us, I rolled my eyes apologetically at Janine and she winked, ever-unperturbed. Her husband was a lucky man, and he knew it.

I turned back to Miss Harris and watched as her face twisted in what looked like disgust as she let the boy go and gave him a nudge—really more like a shove—away. "Stop clinging. Gannon, this is Braiden Michael Forester. Your son."

My brain froze. My eyes shot straight to the little boy. He hovered uncertainly between the woman—his mother, presumably, poor kid—and my desk, before picking up courage. Walking around my desk and briefly disappearing, his tiny body dwarfed by its huge breadth and height, he reappeared moments later climbed up in my office chair. Leaning back in it, he kicked his feet and spun in a circle. Something tugged at my heartstrings—and let me tell you, up until then, I didn't know I *had* heartstrings.

"Gannon?" the harpy snapped. "Did you hear me?"

I refocused my attention from the boy onto Cassandra, even as he began to play with my stapler. My automatic instinct was to take it from him, so he didn't staple his little fingers. Which was bizarre, because ... since when did I have automatic instincts when it came to anything except women and business?

Still buying time, I offered Braiden a box of paper clips in exchange for the high-powered electric stapler and liked when he didn't fuss at all, switching gears seamlessly to playing with the colorful, little metal clips.

"Gannon!" Cassandra finally exploded.

Yes, he was a really nice kid.

But he wasn't mine. That, I knew for sure. I didn't know this crazy bitch. "Look, lady," I informed her coolly and calmly. "I don't know you."

"Oh, but you do." Her snarl transformed into an equally unpleasant smirk, stretching her thin lips into a wide rictus. "You and I went back to my place after drinking too much at that club that night, a little under three years ago. I ended up pregnant, something I didn't bother you with for nearly three years. Your son is two, just so you know. And I've done all of the mothering I care to. I want out. I'm not cut out to be a mother."

As she spat the words at me, I couldn't help but marvel at how utterly unattractive she was in every way, way beyond just her witch-like exterior. Her voice was like nails on a chalkboard. I'd heard the expression, but had never actually seen it come to life until just now.

For some reason, the bombshell she'd dropped kept getting replaced with other thoughts. Maybe I was avoiding it. Or maybe I just couldn't believe I would've had anything to do with a shrew. I had a type when I looked for female company—a very, very specific type that was more personality-based than physically-based, honestly. Gorgeous was hot, but fun to spend a long evening with was even better—and she didn't fit it in the slightest.

"I don't know you," I repeated. "And he's not mine."

Cassandra didn't even notice that the kid was reaching for scissors, or if she did, she didn't care. I cut him off at the pass and handed him a stack of Post-Its instead.

Aggravated, she snarled, "I don't care if you believe me. I just wanted to let you know you have a kid, and I can't do this anymore. He's yours or social services. Choose. Now."

"Wait. What?" For the second time that day, I was being forced into an instant decision, but this time the stakes were infinitely higher. "Social services?" I echoed in disbelief, grateful that the boy was clueless about what he was hearing as he giggled and decorated himself with sticky papers. "What the hell is wrong with you? He's your child!"

"And yours," she retorted. "I'm not mother material. Are you listening to me at all, Gannon Forester? I'm tired of talking. I'll just take the kid and dump him on social services' doorstep. I can see you're not going to be a father to him." She started toward the boy, who dropped his newfound papers toys and shrank back into his seat. I felt a jolt of electricity shoot through me.

"Hey, wait a minute." I stepped in front of her and the desk. The words that came out of my mouth didn't even sound like mine. "Listen, give me time to get a DNA test done. If he's mine, then I want him."

Wait—what did I just say?

"One week. You have one week, and that is it, Gannon Forester." She stalked around me, picked up the boy, whose big eyes were suddenly filled with tears, and left my office in such haste that I had to run to catch up to her.

"I need your phone number and address." I grabbed a notepad off Janine's desk and a pen as I hurried after her.

She stopped then and dumped Braiden—that was his name, right?—on top of the desk while she scribbled those things down on the paper. As she scrawled, pressing hard enough to undoubtedly indent the whole notepad, I hesitantly leaned in to check on the toddler. His dark hair did look a lot like mine, but plenty of kids had dark hair. And his wide blue eyes, gleaming with unshed tears, well, they kind of looked like what I saw in the mirror first thing every day, but still ... just ... not a possibility.

"Hey, buddy." I smiled at him and handed him a fresh pad of Post-Its, these far more colorful than the ones from my own office. "How are you doing?"

Braiden sniffed and smiled back shyly, his pudgy little hand scrubbing across his eyes in a way that made those newly-discovered heartstrings twang once again.

SHOVING the paper and pen back in my hands, Cassandra picked Braiden up like a sack of potatoes. "He can't talk, you idiot. He's only two."

Stifling my anger, I straightened. "I think toddlers can usually talk. Mom just used to say that by the end of the evening, she'd have no ears left from my chatter."

"Well. He's stupid," Cassandra informed me, and it was all I could do to keep from reaching out and wringing her scrawny neck. "I better hear from you by the end of the week, or it's off to foster care for your son."

And with that, she left my office with my potential son looking forlornly over her shoulder, one small hand stretched out to me.

CHAPTER 2

Brooke

The first day of November had a chilly breeze washing over our city of Los Angeles. Wearing a light sweater over my t-shirt and blue jeans, I was ready for autumn to take over for a while, leaving the heat of summer behind us.

My heels clicked along the sidewalk as I made my way to meet my brother, Brad, for lunch at Pitfire, a pizza joint my brother and I loved.

A whistle caught my attention, and I looked around to find Brad getting out of his brand-new Lambo, the fire-engine-red exterior sure to capture everyone's attention. "Hey, show off."

His hand ran over the hood of the car as he made his way to me. "You like my newest ride, baby sis?"

"It's awfully bright. Did you really have to go all out and get fire-engine-red, Brad?" I crossed my arms as I stood there, looking at the high dollar piece of machinery.

My brother had struck it rich when he went to work for Forester Industries right out of college. From there, he jumped off into his own business venture, procuring investments overseas for wealthy people.

Brad came up to me, holding out his arms for a hug, which I gave him. "That's not fire-engine-red, little sis; it's called Rosso Mars, and that particular model is an Aventador Coupe."

"Fancy." I kissed his whisker-covered cheek. "So, you're sporting a beard now. How fashionably progressive of you. But it needs more conditioner; it tickles my lips."

His eyebrows wiggled as he grinned. "That's what she said."

I punched him in the arm. "Eww! Nasty!"

"I didn't mean anything dirty by it, kid." He looped his arm through mine, leading me into the eatery. "Get your mind out of the gutter."

I rolled my eyes and leaned into him, not about to say I'd missed him while away at college, even though I had.

After being seated in what used to be our usual booth and ordering a blistered cherry tomato pizza and some root beers, my brother and I started catching up. I had been away, staying in the dorms at Berkeley for the last year. With my first year of college behind me, I was excited about my future and the new semester that I was a couple of months into.

Brad had been gone all summer, having to work overseas, and had only been back a couple of weeks. He told me he was eager to talk to me and find out how my schooling was going. "So, how did you like your first year?".

"I loved it, Brad!" I informed him, over a mouthful of lusciously buttery breadstick. "Mmm. I missed these. I mean, I knew I would love it. But it's even better than I thought. The teachers, the campus, just ... everything is amazing. And the classes. They're all theory right now, but I'm more convinced than ever that teaching little ones is where I want to be."

"No surprise there. What were you when you first started babysitting? Three?" The tiny wrinkles that etched the sides of his grin reminded me that he was in his early thirties. That age group of people who had kids, even though he didn't have a wife and kids yet, himself.

"No, seven. I watched Lainey Bradshaw down the street while her mom took piano lessons in the next room." Our conversation was briefly interrupted as our drinks arrived.

He gave the waitress a nod as his eyes roamed up and down her body. "Thanks." He leaned forward, steepling his fingers while resting his elbows on the table, obviously trying to look distinguished. "You doing okay this afternoon," he looked at her nametag that was strategically pinned just above her left breast, "Meghan?"

Gag me with a spoon. I groaned, kicking him hard under the table.

Her pretty green eyes lit up as she smiled at my brother. "I'm doing fine. You?"

"Pretty damn good." He winked at her. "Thanks, sweetie."

With a tiny wave and flushed cheeks, she left us alone as he watched her go. I rolled my eyes.

"Some things never change. So, Brad. Have any of your friends had kids since I left? I've missed working with kids who aren't just textbook studies. And I want to try out some of the things I've learned."

. . .

"NONE of my close friends have kids, kiddo. Sorry." He reached into his pocket and pulled out a set of car keys. "I have a surprise for you."

"No way," I mumbled, staring at his palm without touching the silvery keys. "Brad ..."

Brad only had the most badass automobiles. He'd given everyone in the family one of his used ones at one time or another. Brad's used cars weren't like normal ones. Bentleys, Mercedes, Beemers—you name the expensive car, he had owned one or more at one time or another, and my big brother had always been generous with his hand-me-downs around his friends.

He jingled the keys playfully. "Say please ..."

"Brad," I repeated, just as our pizza arrived and we had to wait till everything was settled in front of us. When Megan sauntered away, I turned back to my brother. "Tell me you didn't."

He placed the keys in my outstretched palm. "You need transportation now that you're back here. Taxis eat up way too much spare cash. You are now the proud new owner of a gently-used Carpathian Grey, Jaguar F-Type."

Automatically, my fingers snapped shut around the keys. Even so, I had to protest. I mean, how did it look for a brother, even one as wealthy as mine, to be doling out hundred-thousand-dollar cars to his sister? I was no mooch. "You really shouldn't have. I mean it, Brad. And I can't even promise to pay you back, because that would take me 5,000 years on a teacher's salary."

He winked. "I'll figure out some way for you to repay me." Lifting a dripping cheesy slice, he dug in, grinning around his huge bite.

A little in a daze, I got up and hugged him hard before

sitting back down. "You are crazy," I informed him, reaching for my own slice. "But thank you. Wow. Thank you, thank you, thank you. And don't even start about insurance and crap. I'll find a way to pay for it."

I had no idea how, but I would, I promised myself.

CHAPTER 3

Gannon

Only three days after having the DNA test done on the little boy, I held the envelope in my hand.

Janine was by my side in my office as I pulled out the sheet of paper that would either change my entire world or leave me free. "Before you read it, tell me what you're hoping for, Mr. Forester."

I'd been turning it over in my head ever since the bitch had stalked in and out of my office in less than five minutes, steamrollering my day and leaving my mouth close to hanging with her news.

"That he's mine."

It wasn't that I wanted the responsibility of a kid. Far from it. But Cassandra had been such an obviously awful mother. And Braiden looked like such a nice kid. He deserved better. Way better.

With a nod, Janine placed her hand on my shoulder. "Then I'll pray that way for you, sir."

Closing my eyes, I finished pulling the paper out, then I

opened it, wanting to surprise myself. "Ninety-nine percent." I blinked and felt the strangest shifting in my newly-discovered heart. "He's mine."

We remained in silence for a long moment as I stared blankly at the page full of cryptic scientific info, with two bolder words standing out above everything:

Probability of Paternity: 99%

"I have a kid," I whispered.

"Congratulations, daddy." Janine squeezed my shoulder. "I know it's not what you expected, but you'll be a great father, Mr. Forester."

Father. The fact that the word now applied to me didn't feel even close to sinking in.

"Janine." I cleared my throat and sat back. "Get my lawyer on the phone and let him know to proceed with the custody paperwork. I want it today, so I can take it to her when I pick up my ... son."

Son??

"Oh God. I'm a father ..."

Janine touched my shoulder once again and started for the door. "I'll get on that right away."

After she left, I sat in dumb silence for who knows how long before I took out my cell and made the call.

"Finally," she answered. "Well? What do you want?"

"I received the results—"

She didn't bother to let me finish. "He's your son."

"Yes, he is." I had to put my cell down on the desk and press the speaker button. My head was aching and spinning with the news. I was both happy and deathly afraid at the same time.

I don't know one damn thing about kids.

"Then come get him."

I'm a father. And she's his mother! Jesus.

"Cassandra, aren't you going to miss him at all?" I demanded. "How can you treat a kid that way? Any kid. Much less your own."

"When will you be here?" she replied without answering. "I'll have him ready to go."

Shock had me numb inside. As if on auto-pilot, I moved forward with the horrible conversation, "My lawyer is drawing up papers you'll need to sign. I want full custody. And I don't want to wait through court proceedings to get it. Cassandra, you do realize you will never see your son again if you sign the papers, right? I'll want to make a life for the boy. One without a mother who seems to hate him."

"Yeah, whatever. Cry me a big old river. So hurry up and get your paper and I'll sign it. I want to get rid of the burden your unprotected cock put on me."

BITCH.

"Fine. I'll be there just as soon as my lawyer tells me the documents are ready. Goodbye." I ended the call, feeling as if I'd just had a conversation with the devil.

The intercom buzzed. "Brad Moore is here to see you."

As protective as she was of me, Brad was likely one of the few men Janine would have patched through at this stage.

My head was still reeling as I leaned back in my chair. "Send him in, please."

When my best friend opened the door to my office, he could tell immediately that something was wrong with me. "What the hell happened to you?"

I just shook my head, numb.

He made his way to my desk, taking the seat across from me. "You look like a Mack truck just ran over your dog or something. You don't have a dog though, right?" The words weren't coming to me. How in the hell do you tell someone this kind of news? Bluntly, apparently.

"I'm a father, Brad."

His blue eyes went wide. His jaw dropped. He jumped up and slammed his palms on the desk, making a loud slapping noise. "The fuck you say!"

Yeah, he took it the way I thought he would.

"I have a two-year-old son. His name is Braiden Michael." I got up and walked over to the minifridge to grab myself a bottle of something with alcohol in it. Picking out a bottle of beer, I tossed it to Brad then got myself one.

Brad just looked at his without opening it. "You know it's like nine in the morning, right?"

Twisting the metal top off the bottle, I nodded. "And your point is?" I looked at him with no expression at all on my face.

With a shrug, he opened his bottle and took a swig. "So day-drinking it is, then." He went back to sit in his chair, looking as if he was as lost in thought as I was. "Who's the mother?"

"A redhead from a strip club who I don't remember in the slightest. If DNA hadn't confirmed the evidence, I wouldn't believe it."

"So, what?" he asked, taking a long pull of the cold brew. "She hitting you hard for custody and cash?"

"No, actually."

I made my way to the sofa. I needed to lie down for a minute. Let my body catch up to my scattered mind. "I'm taking him."

"What?" Brad spun around in the chair to face me as I plopped down on the overstuffed black leather. "You can't just take him away from his mother, Gannon!"

Pressing my forehead to the cold beer, I shook my head.

"She doesn't want him. She was going to give the kid away if I didn't take him." I looked over at him.

Brad's face went from stunned to horrified. "She *what?*"

"She's a real bitch, Brad. Like the meanest woman I've ever met. And somehow, I don't know how—I don't know what got into me about three years ago—but I fucked her without using a condom, apparently." More beer went down my throat as I tried to drown the anxieties that were bubbling up inside of me. "Brad, I need help. Like permanent help, dude."

"Do you really not remember sleeping with this woman?"

"Not at all." I jerked my head toward the paper on the desk. "But I had a DNA test done, and the boy is definitely mine."

Brad walked over to the desk and picked up the paper, staring at it as he spoke. "Well, at least you did the smart thing and had that done, instead of taking this woman's word for it. So what now?"

I took another chug, "As soon as my lawyer calls to let me know the documents I need are ready, I'll go get him." I closed my eyes. "Brad, what am I going to do? I don't know the first thing about raising a kid. I don't know how to take care of one. Like what do two-year-olds eat? Drink? Do? Can they bathe themselves? Can they dress themselves? Cause I don't know how to do that for him."

"You need a nanny, Gannon."

"And fast," I agreed. I put the bottle to my lips but found it was empty. "Fuck!"

Brad reached out, taking the bottle away from me. "Fathers don't day drink. I don't think they do, anyway. Not the first day they're meeting their kid."

"I met him already," I informed him. "A few days back.

She treated him like a dog toy. He was a really nice little boy, Brad. Quiet. Calm. Friendly. No tantrums or anything. But ... he wasn't my son, then. Oh, and he can't talk, she says. Can't two-year-olds, I don't know, babble or something?"

He shrugged. "No idea, man. None whatsoever. But if you make me a promise, I think I can help you out."

I cracked an eye and watched as he hauled up a chair and sat down beside me. "Yeah? How?"

"You have to mean what you promise me, Gannon. I'm dead serious about this. Lethally serious."

"Anything." I sat up and rubbed the back of my neck. "What do I have to promise?"

His light blond brows scrunched together. "You remember my baby sister?"

I knew of her in passing, even though we'd never met. "Yeah?

"She's in her second year of college, majoring in early child-hood development. She was just asking me about possible jobs she could take to pay bills and practice what she's learning in theory, since the school won't let them handle actual small humans yet. She'd jump at the chance to take care of this kid for you."

My eyes popped. "Brad, that would be fantast—"

"Hold on there, Gannon." He leaned in close, eyes flash-ing. "If I do this for you, I don't want you to so much as lay one finger on Emily."

I started to protest, and he cut me off. "Because if you do, then I'll have to reach into your chest." He pounded his fist on my chest just once. "And I will pull your beating heart out and feast on the fucking thing. You got me, bro?"

"Leave your little sister alone." That would be more than easy. "Got it!"

"As long as you understand me, repeat these words, and we'll have us a deal. Oh, and you have to pay her pretty well too. That's a given, dude." He thumped my chest once more.

"Chill on that shit, Brad. I can only take so much, bro. Tell me these magic words you want me to say to make you believe that I will never lay a finger on your little sister."

"I, Gannon Forester, do solemnly swear never to flirt with, fondle, or otherwise sexually harass my best friend's baby sister, the apple of his eye, and the sweetest and most innocent girl on the planet."

Who is this chick?

All I could do was nod as I recited his words, sealing our deal and getting me the babysitter I needed. "And can she move in with us too? I'll need her twenty-four-seven."

"I'll check with her, but I'm guessing that'll be fine. Fewer bills for her to pay."

I almost sagged with relief. I now had a kid and a babysitter to go with said kid. Things might just turn out okay after all.

CHAPTER 4

Brooke

Only three days before, I'd told my big brother I was looking for a babysitting job and here he was with a huge one. "So, you'll be a live-in. It'll be a full-time job, Brooke. The little boy is two, and his father has no clue what to do with a kid. This whole thing just fell in his lap. You'll have to go in and take complete charge of the little boy. Is this something you think you can handle?"

Sitting on the bed in my dorm room, I chewed on my lower lip. "What about school?"

"You said most of your classes this semester will be online," he reminded me. "And living-in will save you money on room and board, since you won't let me pay for those. He'll pay you well enough that you'll graduate debt-free, Brooke."

"Wow." I nodded slowly. This was not a gift horse whose mouth I was going to look too deeply into.

The father will hardly ever be there," he went on. "He's

hardly ever home now. It'll be you, the kid, some servants, and that's it most of the time." He looked back at my absent roomie's bed and took a seat on it after pulling the blanket up to cover the mess of sheets.

"And which one of your friends is this, Brad?"

One hand stroked his beard as he looked off to one side, trying to look nonchalant. "Gannon Forester, the man who gave me my first job."

My eyes must've been bugging out. Not only was Gannon the worst of the bad boys my older brother hung with, but he was a billionaire to boot. And I knew that meant he got whatever he wanted. "Him?"

Brad just nodded as he cut his eyes to look around the small room. "You'd be able to say goodbye to this little rat hole. That would be a blessing in and of itself."

I'd never actually met Mr. Forester. But I'd overheard Brad telling stories about how much of a womanizer he was. Could I handle a man like that? "Um, he's kind of known for being a major ladies' man, right?"

Brad's blue eyes leveled on mine. "Not to worry, Brooke. I told the man you are not to be messed with. He made me a solemn vow he'd never do a thing to you. Not so much as one word of flirtation. If he does, you let me know, and I'll properly beat his ass for it."

It wasn't that I was anti-flirtation. I was just ... shy. And totally inexperienced. And if I was going to live-in, I needed to know I'd be safe, obviously. "And this poor kid, his mother was just going to turn him over to social services? That's so terrible." My heart hurt with the thought.

"Yeah," Brad got up and went to look in my closet. "Is this all the stuff you have here?"

"That's it. So, this job would start today, then?" I shoved my feet into my sneakers and leaned over to tie them.

"Yes, it would. I think you should come with me to meet him and his kid before you make the decision." He turned around to face me. "If you think it's something you'd like to do, then we can come back for your things. You can even leave them here, and I'll pay the room and board for the remainder of the semester, in case you ever decide you want to back out."

I never let my brother pay for anything, but he had a good point for once. And I was definitely struggling to make ends meet. "He's around your age, right?" I got up off the bed and followed my brother out of my dorm room.

"Yeah, he's thirty. He's a decade older than you are. Surely you won't find him attractive in the least." He stopped and took me by the arm, looking me in the eyes. "Right?"

"Pish ...yeah, right. I'm not into old dudes, Brad." Call me old-fashioned, but in my twenties, I was still a virgin. My sum total of experience was a few kisses and a little basic groping. I was waiting for the right guy to come along.

About an hour later, we pulled up to the sprawling mansion Mr. Forester lived in.

"Wow, Brad. This is bigger than your place in Malibu." I couldn't believe how beautiful the place was. I adored the rustic look. The home looked like a huge log cabin with a covered front porch that spanned only one part of the humongous home. Tall pine trees lined the asphalt drive. The lush green grass was well kept, making the whole place look almost fake.

"Yeah, Gannon likes his little slice of wilderness out here in the sticks." It wasn't really the sticks—just the Hollywood Hills.

At the door, we were met by the butler, who introduced himself to me as Ashe.

"Who in this day and age has a butler?" I hissed to Brad

as we walked through a dizzying maze of rooms until we came upon one that had cartoon sounds coming out of it.

He just shrugged.

Ashe gave me a smile. "Mr. Gannon is in there with his new son."

With a nod, he left us to enter the room on our own. My brother pushed the door open. "Here she is, Gannon."

The back of the man I might soon be working for was all I saw. Dark hair that was kept short and neat gave way as he turned, and the darkest blue eyes looked at me as he got up.

"Brooke, it's a pleasure to meet you." He came toward me, and a small boy with huge blue eyes and a tearstained face immediately jumped off the couch and scurried over to stand beside him, sliding a pudgy arm around the man's long legs. It was obvious the poor little guy was bewildered at having lost his mother and gained a stranger for a father all in the same day, so he was terribly anxious.

"Hello, Mr. Forester," I greeted him, then smiled at the toddler. "Hi there."

Thumb wedged firmly in his mouth, the boy attempted a small smile around it.

"Please, call me Gannon. And this is my ... son, Braiden."

"Hey there, Braiden." Brad hunched over and stuck his hand out. "I'm your Uncle Brad. It's nice to meet you." My brother took the little boy's hand and shook it, making the kid giggle before he pulled his hand back.

His giggle was every bit as adorable as he was.

His father chuckled in a way was anything but adorable. Deep and husky, it was sexy as hell.

I wasn't sure what was wrong with me. I didn't think this way. I didn't find older men attractive. So what was happening here?

Sure, Gannon Forester was tall. Like six-foot-three or

something. Sure, he had broad shoulders and the rest of his torso tapered elegantly to a waist that wasn't exactly narrow, but smaller than his wide chest. Long legs, covered in blue jeans that clung to some pretty great looking muscular thighs, made my gulp. The man was a masterpiece in a white t-shirt and faded blue jeans. And bare feet.

Even his feet are gorgeous.

It was then I realized I had looked the man over, all the way down to his naked feet. I quickly snapped back and pointed to the sectional the two had gotten off of. "Should we discuss the arrangement?" Someone had to take over this interview, and it might as well be me.

"Of course," came the words from Gannon's chiseled lips. Yes, even his lips looked as if they were cut from marble. His features were sharp, yet soft around his gorgeous eyes. Blue pools that were surrounded by thick, dark, lush lashes. Any girl would die to have those natural lashes. Lashes the little boy had, too, I noticed after another glance. The boy finally disengaged from Gannon's leg and wandered back over to the couch, where he had a battered children's book and a sippy cup.

"You and your son are nearly identical," I found myself saying. "He'll be a real lady-killer one day." Then I found Gannon's eyes on mine. The slightest hint of a sexy smile was on his lips. I realized what'd I just said. Ahhh ... crap ...

I looked away, feeling shy as Gannon began my interview, "So the job pays whatever you want it to. You'll have a bedroom that will adjoin the one I've had set up for Braiden. It's right across the hallway from mine."

My brother interrupted. "A bit close, don't you think, Gannon?"

Those blue eyes raked across me as they swung to meet the lighter blue eyes of my brother. "It's for the boy, Brad. I want him to feel safe. After all he's been through, I want him to feel safe, secure, and loved."

When my brother scoffed, I felt offended for the man immediately and came to his defense in a heated rush, "Brad! Don't act that way. It doesn't matter what he's done personally, all these years. He's a father now. He's just thinking of his little boy."

"Sorry, sis." Brad still looked suspicious, even as he apologized. "You're right. Sorry, Gannon."

Gannon chuckled lightly. "Wow. A real tigress you've got there, Brad. And one I'd love watching over my little boy." His eyes fell on me once more. "Please tell me you'll take the job. I'm being totally serious when I say you name the price and I'll gladly pay it. I have no idea what the going rate is for sitters, but I want you to be the highest paid one in the history of nannies."

"I have to have Tuesday and Thursday mornings off until eleven," I told him, in case Brad hadn't. "I have class for one hour each of those days, and it'll take me until then to get back out here. Will that be a problem?" I chewed my lip, nervously hoping that would not put me out of this once-in-a-lifetime job opportunity.

"Not at all," came his quick reply. "I'll adjust my work schedule to go in a bit later on those days. Any other accommodations I need to know about? Oh, and you'll have a car to use too. You can take it to school and anywhere else you want to go."

"I have the car my brother just gave me a few days ago. I don't need your car. And I don't need a boatload of money either. Five hundred a week is fair, since you're also providing room and board."

Gannon shook his head. "No. No way to only five hundred. I tell you what; how about a thousand a week and you let me pay off any student loans you have and pay for the rest of your college? It's only fair to you. You're going to school to learn how to take care of kids after all. I want to help you do that."

My brother answered for me as he jumped up, "Deal!"

I looked between handsome father, adorable son, and my beaming brother. My senses reeled, and suddenly so were my deliriously happy finances. Things looked very, very good.

CHAPTER 5

Gannon

After Brad and Brooke left to go get her things, Braiden and I waited for her to return, still watching cartoons. He asked me to read him his book in between episodes, plopping the book in my hand and smiling up at me in a hopeful way that left me weirdly warm and soft.

Is this what being a dad is really like?

Tuckered out by his earlier tears and the total upending of his life, Braiden eventually feel asleep on the sofa, so I let my mind wander to the young lady who'd be living under my roof. From the moment I'd seen her, I'd known things were going to be rough for me.

Why couldn't she be a female version of Brad?

That is what I'd pictured when he'd said he had a sister who could take this babysitting job, after all.

She had his most basic of features—blonde hair and blue eyes. But that's where the similarities ended. Her long hair had golden strands that caught the light. The blue in her eyes were like lipid pools of sparkling blue water. Her rosy cheeks were full and plump, just like her strawberry-pink lips.

I knew I shouldn't allow myself to think about her like that. I knew Brad would have my heart in his meaty fist in no time if I didn't get this little fetish under control.

She's your best friend's baby sister, Gannon Forester. And your son's babysitter. Stay away from her in all ways, sexually speaking!

So I sat there, staring blankly at the cartoon cat who chased the mouse on the big screen television that usually had some kind of sports game playing, instead of animated characters.

Slowly, Brooke seeped back into my brain. I saw it all in my head; her cute little curvy frame. The top of her head came to my shoulder. I could see myself wrapped around the beautiful girl. Her tits were full d-cups, I was sure. Her hips were round and her ass ...oh, my God, her ass!

Braiden mumbled something in his sleep, and I snapped out of it, catching him before he tumbled off the couch. "Easy, buddy," I murmured, picking him up and starting for the room that I'd designated as his nursery. I'd sent Janine out to get the most basic things, like a little boy's bed and a few toys, but Brooke would need to help me really decorate it.

As I tucked my son gently under the covers and hesitantly brushed his forehead, Brooke came to mind again. I flipped the night light on and slipped out of the room, leaving the door ajar in case he cried again.

My cock thumping, I walked a few doors down to my own room and sprawled out on the bed, reaching for my engorged cock and freeing it.

I was already fucking up, and I knew it.

I should call Brad and tell him I can't keep my promise.

But I wasn't about to actually do that. Braiden needed her. And I could allow myself to have sexual fantasies about the girl, couldn't I? What would be the harm in that, so long as there was no touching?

My eyes closed as I thought about her sweet lips on mine, and I fell headfirst into a sexual fantasy about the beautiful woman who was about to move into my home with my new son and me.

My fantasy jumped several pages past the start, beginning as though Brooke and I were already tangled in one another, our clothes scattered every which way.

Standing over her, I looked down on her blonde head as she took my hard cock all the way in, bobbing her head up and down eagerly. Her soft moan vibrated over my dick, and I groaned with desire.

When I couldn't take it anymore, I lifted her up, pinned her to the wall, and caught her lips in a searing kiss as her hips wrapped around me. "You want me, baby?" I whispered, stroking my hands over her smooth, lithe body.

"Please, Gannon ..." she moaned as I guided myself home and thrust hard, reaching the deepest parts of her. "Ahhh ... baby ..." Her moan made me insane, her hot breath tickling my ear.

"You're tight, honey. So tight," I groaned, cupping her ass and seating myself even more deeply. "I'm not hurting you, am I?"

"No." She kissed me hard, her arms wrapping around my neck, gorgeous breasts pressing into my chest. "Fuck me, Gannon. Hard.

So I did, taking her harder and higher until she shuddered and cried out in ecstasy, her head falling back. I bit her throat gently and came hard myself, filling her with my seed.

"Ahhhh, Brooke," I groaned over and over, holding her tightly to me, my hips jerking with each driving release. "Baby. Yes ..."

Her hands moved all through my hair as she tried to catch her breath, just one word on her sweet lips. 'Fuck.'

Fuck, yes, the sweet little thing would curse, even though I was sure the word would never leave her lips outside our bedroom. She'd be a saint in front of others, saving her naughty sexual side only for me.

I stared up at the ceiling, barely starting down from my high when my cell rang. "Gannon," I answered the call without looking at who was calling.

"Hi, Mr. For—uh, Gannon."

I jolted with another spasm of unexpected pleasure at hearing her sweet voice. "Hi, Brooke. Everything all right?"

"Yeah, it's fine. You sound winded. Is Braiden wearing you out already?"

I grabbed a pillow and muffled a hungry groan in it, desire already rising in me again at how sexy that sweet, innocent voice sounded. "Yeah, he's a little rascal We were, uh, playing tag."

"I just wanted to call before I leave town. Do you or Braiden need anything from town? I mean, like does he have milk and pull-ups or diapers or whatever he's wearing?"

How damn sweet is she?

"Oh, that's a great idea. I know we have milk. Um, I don't know about the pull-ups or diapers. His mother just gave me him and nothing else. I did have my personal shopper bring some clothes for him earlier today. Do you know if he has a diaper on?"

She chuckled a little. "Mr. For—Gannon, have you not even looked to see if he has on underwear or a diaper?"

I got up and started cleaning myself up. "No. How do I do that?"

"Just pull the back of his little shorts out a bit and see if he's got on underwear or a diaper."

"Oh, yeah. I saw like some white, thick fabric when we were running around. Is that a diaper?"

"Pull-Ups at this age, more likely, but who knows. Okay, I'll pick up some stuff. I don't suppose you know if he takes a bottle at night, do you? You know, to help him fall asleep," she added, before I could ask why.

"He didn't need one just now to fall asleep," I remarked. "So maybe he doesn't use one."

"Asleep?" she asked, sounding confused. "I thought you guys were just playing. That's what had you all out of breath, right?"

Shit ...

"Yeah. Um, well I told him to go sit and watch cartoons, and he did, and he fell asleep."

"Huh. I guess it makes sense. The poor little guy's worn out after everything. I'll grab some stuff and then head over there. Brad helped me pack my car up ..."

"Okay. See you soon, Brooke." I ended the call, then beat my head against the wall, glaring down at the rampant evidence of my desire for my new nanny. "Stupid. Stupid. Stupid."

Then a little voice sobbed just down the hallway and I was forced to pull my act together, pull some clean pants on, and go comfort my small, scared son, patting his back and singing, really not knowing what I was doing, but giving it my best. That was what counted, right? That I was trying?

CHAPTER 6

Brooke

Unpacking in my new bedroom a couple hours later, I couldn't help but look out the large windows that overlooked the back part of the vast property. More tall trees spotted the hilly terrain, and I could see it all through the creamy sheer curtains.

A light knock had me turning to see who was at my partially-closed door. And there was my handsome new boss, carrying my adorable new job in his strong arms. He might have been a new father, but he looked like he was meant for the job.

"Come in."

Gannon put the little boy down, and he briefly clung to his father's leg before starting to curiously look around my new living space.

I took out the little firetruck I had bought for him when I stopped at the store to pick up the diapers and wipes. "Come here, Braiden." I smiled and crouched down. "See what I have for you."

Without an ounce of shyness, he made a B-line for me and the toy I held out to him. I got on my knees to get on his level. He took the toy out of my hand and looked it over, then his eyes went to mine and his tiny arms went around my neck as he hugged me.

I smiled in total surprise and hugged him back. "Hi, sweet boy," I murmured, kissing his hair and then his plump cheek. "I know you've had a really rough day, but we'll make it better," I promised him, sitting back and showing him how to push the tiny truck back and forth.

"You're really great with him," Gannon said, taking a seat on the floor, but not before I caught his eyes roaming over my body. A pop of warmth burst inside me, along with a nudge of worry.

Uh oh ...

Leaving the two to play with Braiden's new toy, Gannon making vrooming sounds while Braiden, who was oddly not verbal yet, tried to imitate him and mostly blew raspberries, I rose and went back to unpacking my bags. An uneasy feeling was washing over me—one that told me I had to be careful with the charismatic playboy who I now not only worked for but also lived with.

I was sure women who had even less to do with the man had a hard time keeping their heads straight where he was concerned. My work was really cut out for me.

Picking up a handful of panties and bras out of my suitcase, I held them close to my body, discreetly covering them with my hands as I took them to the dresser. Dropping them inside the top drawer, I folded them, making sure to keep them out of sight.

When I turned back around, I found Gannon sitting back, watching Braiden zoom his new toy all over the walls and carpet. "Can you believe his own mother could turn her back on him the way she has?" He had a dazed, kind of sad look on his face that made me want to go over and put my arms around—

Uh, no! Hello? Bad, bad idea! What's the matter with you? Self-control has always been Brad's problem, not yours!

I shook my head and returned for more clothes. "No, I can't believe that. Brad told me about all of it. I just can't imagine what sort of person does a thing like that. He doesn't seem like he's a problem at all. And certainly not a piece of trash to discard so easily." Picking up several pairs of shorts, I turned to walk back to the dresser, but Gannon's hand on my arm stopped me.

Oh, the spark that shot through me wasn't good at all. My eyes were wide as I looked at his large hand, wrapped around my wrist. My eyes traveled up my arm until they found his. His thick lashes fell as he blinked, then I saw those blue eyes once more. "The truth is that haunts me. I don't understand how anyone could do such a terrible thing. And I'm glad he has you now. I mean, I can try my best to be what he needs as a father, but a kid needs a mom more than anything, I think. I don't know how I would've turned out if I hadn't had a loving mother."

But I wasn't the boy's mother. I was merely his babysitter. "Mr. Forester ..." His eyebrow arched. Oh. Right. "Gannon. While I will do my very best to be what your son needs, please understand that a babysitter is no replacement for a mother. You'll have to be both mom and dad for the poor little guy."

He let me go and looked down, the powerful image briefly slipping as the weight of this new burden obviously settled home. "I don't know if I have that in me, Brooke."

Putting my clothes down on the bed, I ran my hand through his dark hair, before I could stop myself. I was honestly just trying to convey my compassion for him and his desperate situation, but ...

He raised his head, locking eyes with me, and I realized I had to pull myself together for all of our sakes. "Gannon, I'm here to help you get through this hard part. You'll be great at being a father, just like you're great at everything else you've ever done in your life. My brother has told me all about you. You may have been born wealthy, but you've done plenty on your own as well. You should be proud of your accomplishments and sure in your ability to raise your son."

I was much too close to the man, our faces only inches away from each other. *What the hell am I doing?*

Taking a step back, I broke our eye contact. Out of the corner of my eye, I saw him shaking his head slowly. "Thanks, Brooke. I needed to hear that, badly."

Gathering my shorts once more, I headed to the dresser, knowing I needed to get some space between us. My body wasn't acting right. It had some kind of electric current fizzing through it, leaving me giddy.

Turning back around, I found his eyes sparkling at me. There was no more lost, young father in them. *Oh, no. Here we go ...* I had to set things straight right from the start or I'd lose myself to the man. The *womanizing* man, I had to remind myself.

"You know, Gannon, Brad told me about your success, your driven personality, and your problem with finding help with your new-found son." I stopped as he leaned back on my bed, resting his muscular body on bent elbows and gazing at me as if I was the most interesting person in the world.

I swallowed hard, watching him sink onto my new bed, and tried not to imagine being beside him. Beneath him ...

"Brad also told me about your escapades with numerous women."

That seemed to get to him, and he sat up, looking appropriately sheepish. "About that. You should know guys kind of exaggerate about matters of that nature. I'm not quite as bad as some make me out to be."

With a light laugh, I grabbed my clothes and went across the large room to put them away. "I'm sure you're not. But I'm also sure you're very adept at seducing the female gender. I'd like to warn you, though. I won't pull punches. I'm ... inexperienced, Gannon. Deliberately so."

While I hoped he would infer the message in my words —I don't know what I'm doing, so cool it—the heated look that suddenly filled his eyes suddenly told me my words had had the opposite effect.

"So, you've never ..." His dark brows raised as he looked directly into my eyes.

"That is none of your business," I replied as calmly as I could, even though I was the one who had broached the subject in the first place. "Let's just say we're both new at certain things."

"But I'm willing to learn," he drawled softly, his own implication crystal clear.

Oh, the man is danger wrapped in a gorgeous package.

Done with my unpacking, I took a seat on the floor next to where Braiden was busily pushing the firetruck around. I took a turn, marching it over his head and belly and loving how he doubled over, laughing.

I found my eyes going to Gannon's once more and decided the best policy would be honesty and bluntness. Surely he'd respect that. "I'm a virgin, Gannon. Try to keep that in mind when you find your flirtatious tongue taking you over, please."

I saw his cheeks flush. I had no idea what that meant, but at least I'd gotten everything out in the open between us. Now to see if he could pull his bad boy ways in a bit, for the sake of both our sanities.

CHAPTER 7

Gannon

For the first time since I was a kid, I felt my cheeks heating as I blushed. *She actually made me blush!*

A deep laugh came out of me as I ducked my head. Then I remembered who the hell I was and stood. "I'm sorry if you saw anything I said as being flirtatious. I certainly didn't mean to make you think I'm flirting with you." That was a blatant lie, but she didn't have to know that. And if she reported anything like that back to her older brother, he'd snatch her away from me in a heartbeat.

I had to exercise my self-control, even if it wasn't a thing I was used to doing, so it wasn't easy.

But I would get them.

Now she was the one ducking her head in embarrassment. "I'm sorry if I misread you, sir."

Not back to sir!

I took the same position she was in, sitting cross-legged on the floor next to my son, and chuckled to let her know I wasn't trying to be a jerk. "Come on, let's not go all the way back to calling me sir." I reached out and pulled Braiden to sit on my lap, hoping like hell that made me seem more approachable and less like a male whore. The way Braiden immediately snuggled into me made me feel a little like a heel for having the hots for his nanny when that was the last thing he needed. What he needed was a father who could keep it in his pants and keep from losing the new woman in both our lives, who was going to be instrumental to helping us figure out the father-son thing.

"This is going to take some getting used to by all of us. We've all been thrown into this thing. This very-similar-to-being-a-family thing. And you're the female in this thing we're in. The mother-figure." She shook her head, but I didn't let that stop me, "Shake your head all you want, Brooke. It won't change the fact this little boy needs a mother, and that that will be your job for the foreseeable future. At least until he's in school. And maybe even after that."

With a sigh, she looked at me. "Yeah, I guess you're right. I'll get used to it. I guess we all will get used to our new roles. You as a father and the boy as a cherished son, a thing he must've never been. Poor baby." She reached over and touched Braiden's soft hair where it was nestled into my shoulder. "And me as the female lead in his life."

"Okay, then." I felt better about the whole thing. "Are you ready to take over your babysitting duties, Brooke?"

"Sure," her tone was chipper and her smile bright. "I've got this, Gannon. Go do what you need to do. Braiden is in good hands with me."

Placing Braiden back on the floor, I got up and roughed up his mop of dark hair before kissing him on top of his little head. "I'll catch you guys later, then." Heading out of her bedroom, I found myself looking back, finding her and

Braiden playing with his truck. My heart did an odd little pitter patter thing, and I sighed inwardly.

When did I get so damn sappy?

After a quick change of clothes, changing into a suit for dinner, I headed out to meet up with August and Nixon for dinner and drinks. It was our usual Friday night thing to do since we'd met in Vegas.

The other two men had already been seated, as I found out when the maître d took me to their table. A small table for four near the back of the seating area is where I found them, snickering about something. "Good evening." I took a seat as they both looked at me with curious expressions.

It was August who had to ask, "So an hour late. What gives?"

My grin was sly as I saw the waiter making his way to me. After ordering my drink, I let them in on what was happening in my life. A good half-hour and two drinks later, I had them thoroughly mesmerized by how my life had taken such a sharp turn.

Nixon shook his head slowly as he muttered, "That's fucked up, man."

"What a bitch," August added. "I've never heard of anyone doing such a horrible thing." His eyes were filled with compassion. "That poor little kid."

Taking a sip of the twelve-year-old Scotch, I nodded. "Well, he was a poor kid. He's finally going to have a good life now. And the woman I found to babysit him is sure to make him happy too." I placed the glass on the table. "She makes me happy too, unfortunately."

"And why would that be unfortunate, Gannon?" Nixon asked as he waved at the waiter.

"Because she's the baby sister of my best friend. And he's threatened me about doing so much as flirting with the young thing." I had to close my eyes to conjure her in my mind. "The absolutely gorgeous young thing."

"Excuse me," Nixon told the waiter. "Can you get us something to eat. Some finger foods. I'm thinking maybe something with shrimp in it."

"Oh, and cheese too," August added. "Something maybe we can dip chips in."

"I'll be right back," the waiter assured us, then made his way toward the kitchen.

Both turned their attention to me once more. August raised one dark brow. "So how young is this girl?"

"Her brother told me she's twenty." That earned me critical stares.

"And you're thirty," Nixon pointed out. "Ten years older than she is. But my guess is that's not too much of an age gap to put you off, is it?"

I'd never been attracted to anyone as young as Brooke. The thought of being older by any amount of years than a female conquest hadn't ever occurred to me. "It's not her age that matters to me. It's her brother's friendship that matters. He and I have been friends since our college days. We roomed together since freshmen year. Our bond is tight."

August thoughtfully stroked his beard. "So you have known this girl since she was a kid, then."

"No." I eagerly eyed the platter the waiter placed in the middle of the table. "Looks great." I grabbed a chunk of bread and dipped it into a thick white cheese concoction, brimming with tiny shrimp. "I've never met any of Brad's family before. He and I never were those kinds of friends— the kind who go to each other's family homes."

Dipping his own bread into the gooey dip, August nodded. "That's good. It would definitely be weird if you knew her as a little kid and still wanted to bone her."

Nixon nodded in agreement. "Yeah. Since you just met her, I guess it's okay. But you still can't go for her. Not if it would mean losing someone who's been your friend for such a long time. Find someone to take your mind off the girl." He jerked his chin toward the table to our right. "There are four nice-looking ladies right there. Take one of them home with you, screw the hell out of her, and see if that doesn't help you deal with your little problem."

Looking over at the table of women, who were most likely available, I checked each one out. And nothing. Not even the slightest thump in my cock came.

With a sigh, I admitted defeat, "It's no use. I'll just have to get over the fact that she's going to be around my house all the time and I have to treat her like a kid sister." Even I knew that wouldn't be an easy thing to do.

My two friends cracked up.

"What? I can do it. I can!" I protested, admittedly uncertainly.

"Sure you can," Nixon taunted me.

August wasn't about to be left out, "It'll be so easy to turn off that wolf who rules your libido."

More raucous laughter had me clenching my jaw. I could do it. I'd show them. I'd show everyone. Especially myself.

Brooke Moore was nothing more than a beautiful girl, and I'd known lots of them.

I could change my ways a bit. I could look at her for what she was to me—my kid's babysitter. That's all she could be to me.

That and the youngest sister of my best friend. Yeah, there it was. I had it all wrapped up in a neat little box.

In the beginning, though, I thought it might be best to spend as little time with her as possible. Just until I could get my head wrapped around the idea that she wasn't someone I wanted, sexually speaking.

She was my employee. My son's nurturing nanny. A person I needed to regard much like I did the women who worked in my office.

One does not shit where they eat, after all—a rule I had practiced my entire life. Brooke was right there at the table. She'd be there all the time. No, I wouldn't have any trouble at all putting her into the same category I did with all the female interns and admin aids I worked with all the time.

"I should take off soon. This day has kind of taken its toll on me." Bidding my business partners goodnight, I left to head home and get some much-needed sleep.

And, hopefully, my dreams wouldn't end up the way my little daytime fantasy had gone.

I was almost thankful when I got home and Braiden woke up suddenly, maybe hearing something in his sleep. I had to spend thirty minutes soothing him back into dreams. Brooke volunteered to do it, but I wanted to spend some time with my son. It served a triple purpose—letting her get some rest, giving me some quality time with my boy, and keeping my fantasies firmly in check.

By the time Braiden drifted off to sleep once more, curled up in my arms on his little bed, there was nothing else in my mind except making him feel safe again after his world had been ripped from him so suddenly.

"I ...love you, son," I whispered as he snored softly, and I knew immediately that it was true, even though we'd barely met. He was my blood, but more importantly, he had become my heart from the moment he smiled shyly at me the first day that Cassandra walked in.

I'd move mountains to keep him happy. And that included keeping my libido firmly in check.

CHAPTER 8

Brooke

Nearly three weeks into my new job and I was beginning to lose patience with my new boss. I knew he had never been a father before, nor thought about being one, but damn it, the man wasn't spending enough time with his little boy. He'd initially been really good about it, making time in the mornings and coming home at reasonable times in the evenings, so he could spend at least a few hours with Braiden before he had to leave again.

But, recently, Gannon had become like a ghost in the house. He was hardly ever there, but when he was, he caused quite a stir. In his son and in me. I both hated and loved it.

My heart would speed up with just the sound of his dress shoes clicking across the marble floor of the foyer. Braiden had a similar reaction to hearing his father come home. He'd rush on his little legs to get to his daddy, and I'd have to rush right behind him to make sure he didn't get lost in the massive one-story home.

He'd be grabbed up into his daddy's strong arms as I tried not to be jealous of that fact. I would've liked to have been pulled into those strong arms too. But I knew what I felt was wrong.

I'd been pretty frank with the man, letting him know I was an innocent little virgin who could easily be broken. I kept wishing I hadn't told him.

Ever since that conversation, I noticed he barely looked my way. Oh, he was very nice and cordial, asking how my day had gone and asking how his little boy had behaved. It was all very nice.

Nice. Proper. Boring.

But my rising interest in him aside, he wasn't being the father he needed to be for the little boy. Not once in a week-and-a-half had he been home to put the child to bed.

The last thing I wanted was for the boy to bond with me more so than with his own blood—his father. But that was already occurring, as Gannon just wasn't around enough.

Putting Braiden to bed, I read him a story and kissed him goodnight once he'd fallen asleep. Then I went to my bedroom, leaving the door wide open to make sure I caught Gannon before he went to bed.

Time kept ticking by and still no Gannon. Finally, at midnight, I closed my bedroom door, put on my sleeping shorts and a tank top, and climbed under the blankets, giving up for the night.

Just as I closed my eyes, I heard his door opening, and I shot out of bed, trying to get to him before he went to sleep. Just as I threw my door open, I saw he'd only partially closed his. "Gannon?"

"Yeah," came his deep voice from inside the room.

"Can I come in?" A sudden onslaught of nerves filled my stomach with enormous butterflies. Was I really about to tell this grown-ass man what he needed to do as a father?

"Sure. Come in, Brooke."

I guess I was.

So in I went and stopped as soon as I stepped through the door. There he was, taking his shirt off, revealing the body I had only been able to daydream about.

Perfect abs ran, ladder-like, across his tone stomach. More perfection ensued as my eyes traveled up to his tattoo-covered pecs. "Tribal?" I should have acted like I hadn't noticed, damn it. I should've acted like he was dressed in a business suit, not half-naked!

His hand moved over his left pec as he looked down at that tat. "Yeah."

His biceps were bulging, and one had another gorgeous tat that I had a very hard time pulling my eyes away from. "They're, uh, nice." Sexy as sin, was more like it. I found myself imagining kissing them ...

"Thanks." He looked up at me with an easy smile on his handsome face. I could tell he'd been drinking. He wasn't drunk or anything like that—just relaxed. "Did you want something?"

You.

I shook my head to get that bad thought out of it, and he laughed. "No?"

Stopping the movement, I nodded instead. "I mean, yes. Yes, I'd like to talk to you about your time."

"My time?" He stepped out of his shoes and sat on a nearby chair to take his black dress socks off too. And there were his gorgeous bare feet.

Who has such nice-looking feet? I thought again.

Pulling my eyes back to where they belonged, I gave

myself an internal berating for ogling my boss. *So unprofessional!*

"Yes, I know you're new to the parenting thing. And I know you must not even be thinking about this, but you're neglecting Braiden." I put my hands on my hips, shifting my weight as I watched to see his reaction to my words.

His brow furrowed in obvious irritation. "Neglecting is a strong word, Brooke. I talk to the kid every day. I scoop him up every evening when I come home and give him my full attention." He shook his head. "That's not neglect in my book."

"You give him about twenty minutes of your time out of each day. You were doing much better a week and a half ago. What happened, Gannon?"

He shrugged. "Business hours can be erratic. That's why you're here. To provide stability when I can't be home on time."

I scowled. My temper was fairly mild, unless my core beliefs were in question, and they certainly were now. "I've waited for you to get into some kind of a pattern on your own, but you haven't done that. That's why I'm intervening now, before too much time passes and things become difficult for you two." I tried to think of how to say things the best possible way to avoid putting the man on the defensive. "Certain rituals are good for kids to help build a bond that will last a lifetime. Like putting your child to bed, reading him books until he falls asleep, then kissing him goodnight. You should be doing that with your son every night that you possibly can."

"Okay, I can do that." He tossed his socks toward his shoes. "What's his bedtime?"

"Eight."

His laugh made me frown as he shook his head. "That's

way too early. I'm almost never home by then. I tried to be early on, as he settled in, but it's difficult. Find something else for us to bond over. You can do that ritual with him each night yourself."

Fire began to ooze through my veins, building up heat inside of me. "Gannon, this isn't a joke. And just what is so important that you have to go out each and every night?"

Those blue eyes landed on mine with a blue flash of anger. "Business meetings, often. I work with a lot of companies on different time zones, where my night is their morning. And dinner, Brooke. Yes, I sometimes go out to eat dinner with my friends. It's not a crime."

Now I was irate. "Gannon, your son is a lot more important than your friends are. He needs you a thousand times more than any of them do."

Gannon folded his big arms over his broad chest. "Braiden seems to be doing just fine with the limited time I'm spending with him."

I could see I needed to put things in black and white for the man. "It's what you did before you had a son to think about. Now you have one, and he needs to be your number one priority. Not a bunch of over-privileged, spoiled rotten, rich jerks!"

I earned another frown, which I didn't much like seeing on his handsome face. But I'd put it there, and now I had to deal with that fact.

His tone was low, his voice quiet, "Brooke, you're paid to make him your number one priority. Tell me if that's not the case."

Shaking with raw anger, the likes of which I'd never felt before, I lit into his selfish ass, "He is your son, Gannon Forester. Not mine! His mother threw him away as if he was nothing more than a piece of trash. He definitely is my top priority. And as that, I will make sure his father does right by him. If I have to nag you, beg you, or bribe you to become the father that child deserves, then I will do that."

With his head cocked to one side, he looked at me with no expression on his face. "Do you realize how you're speaking to me?"

I could feel my brows raise in surprise. Had the man never encountered an angry female before? Had he no instinct for self-preservation?

Although I wanted to dart across that large room and smack the man upside the head to get him to snap out of this master-of-the-manor bullshit, I stayed put and took my hands off my hips to avoid the negative stance I'd been in.

Using my soft-but-firm voice, a thing I'd learned how to use when dealing with rambunctious and bratty young children, I forged ahead, "Braiden needs more from you. I'd like to see you at breakfast each morning. I can have him at the table each morning at whatever time is convenient for you. And dinner in the evening is another good way to establish time you will be spending with him each day—times he knows he'll see his father, a person he absolutely adores."

A smile pulled his chiseled lips up at each corner. "He does, doesn't he?" Crossing his long legs, he touched his whisker-shadowed chin as he looked up dreamily. "I can see it in his eyes every time he runs to me when I come home. Pure love for no reason at all. He barely knows me, yet we share such a deep and instant connection. It's unlike anything I've ever experienced."

With his words, my heart started to fill with something close to hope.

Maybe he can be the man Braiden needs in his life after all.

But then his hand moved and his eyes met mine. "I think

the time he and I share when I get home is enough. For now."

And just like that, he pissed me off once more. One hand flew to my hip; the other pointed a finger at him as if it was a pistol. "Now you listen to me, and you listen good. He needs more from you. A lot more than twenty minutes of your precious day. Let me lay this out for you. Breakfasts, dinners, and bedtimes are now added to the time you will spend with your son. Make it happen, Gannon. Or I will." And with that, I turned and left his bedroom.

And prayed I hadn't just lost my job.

CHAPTER 9

Gannon

S itting in stunned silence, watching Brooke stride out of my room, I didn't know how to take the way she'd talked to me.

I wouldn't call it a verbal assault, but I did feel as if I'd been knocked around a bit. And that wasn't anything I was used to, after years of being one of the most powerful men in business. I'd earned respect, including how people addressed me. I didn't like being told what to do. I never had.

Walking into Braiden's room, I stood there for a while, watching him sleep. Brooke had told me he was gradually sleeping more hours without waking from the bad dreams that had plagued him when he first arrived. Still, he occasionally still missed his mom, even if she hadn't loved him.

"I love you," I said quietly, kissing his soft cheek. "I'll do better, Braiden. Somehow. I promise."

Drawing the covers more securely around him, I left the

room and headed for the shower. I always liked to rinse off the day before hitting the sheets.

The hot water ran over me as I wrestled with feelings of desire and guilt. The guilt was because I knew Brooke was right. I'd fully intended to be a better dad to Braiden, but a combination of trying to do the right thing and keep my hands off Brooke and old habits had waylaid those initial good intentions. I found myself staying out later just to keep away from her, even when I did miss my little boy and thought of him frequently throughout the day.

I'd have to do better, somehow, I acknowledged to myself, letting the water sluice over me. Starting tomorrow, I'd be a better dad. Some tension dissipated with that decision, but another remained firmly in place. Very firmly, as I thought about how cute Brooke had looked in her little shorts and tank top. Pink always looked good on her. The color accentuated her naturally-tan skin tone. Blondes always looked cute in pink. But Brooke took that cuteness to a whole new level.

I noticed her toes and fingernails had a light pink color on them too. I had to wonder if she painted them herself or had them done.

Lathering my hands with soap, I ran one down the length of my shaft that was growing stiff as I thought more about Brooke than I'd allowed myself to in the last two weeks.

Closing, my eyes, I gave into my need. Stroking my cock, I thought about her. My imagination had her coming into my bedroom with a different agenda.

'Gannon, can I come in?' her soft voice called to me.

I was lying in bed, naked, the sheet tented from my hard-on. 'Come in, baby. I've been waiting for you.'

Walking into the room, she gave me a warm, sweet smile, the kind that always left me half-liquid when it was paralleled with the heat in her eyes.

Drawing back the sheets, she raked her eyes slowly down my naked body, making me impossibly harder with her gaze. Then she climbed onto the end of my bed and crawled on her hands and knees toward me. Moving in between my legs, she eyed my cock as she licked her pink-stained lips.

For a moment, she looked at me. Our eyes met as she slowly moved down until her lips touched the head of my dick. She puckered just before her mouth touched me and it was the sweetest kiss I'd ever felt.

With a soft groan, I took her head and gently urged her to take more of me in. The heat of her mouth moved over my cock as she moved her head nice and slowly.

Humming, she took me higher and higher. Finally, I drew her back and looked into her beautiful eyes. "Next time it'll be my turn to make you crazy like that," I promised, lifting her over my rigid shaft. "Right now, though, ride me, baby."

A smile pulls her plump lips into a half-moon as she moves up my body, straddling me and easing down my shaft. "Ahhh," she moaned, leaning back and rolling her hips, making me groan. "Ohh ..."

She moved up and down as I held her by the waist, watching her tits bounce with each stroke she made. Her golden hair fell over her narrow shoulders and over her tits, only allowing peeks at her pert pink nipples now and then.

"Lean over me, baby," I urged, and moaned with delight as she did, her nipples now in range of my hungry lips. I drew one soft rosy nipple into my mouth and nipped it, making her moan delightfully. Then I sucked hard, knowing the combo of tongue and teeth that she liked so much.

Her body moved in waves over mine while I sucked and sucked, switching from side to side in an increasing frenzy and *reveling in the sounds we both made and the marks I was making on her perfect body, until she convulsed and cried out.*

I didn't come yet, letting this pleasure be all hers as I continued to suckle and nip and lick.

"Please, don't stop," she chanted over and over, holding my head against her delicious breast.

Rolling over with her, I fucked her slowly, making her wait just a little bit before I really give it all to her, whispering dirty words that made her blush prettily.

Her legs wrapped around me. Her soft feet moved up the backs of my legs. Once I was in, balls deep, I let go at last. "Oh, yeah, baby. Now I'll give it to you hard," I whispered, kissing her hard and imitating the thrust of my cock with my tongue.

She stayed with me all the way, crying out, begging for more, trembling, and clawing at my back like the sweetest she-cat.

"Do it, baby," I finally urged, as we both fell over the edge." Come for me."

Her body convulsed around my cock as she let it all go, shuddering right along with me, like we were one body. When it was over, I held her close and kissed her soft lips endlessly.

My cock erupted in my hand, bringing me out of the fantasy. Panting hard, I leaned my forehead against the tiled shower wall.

Bewitched.

That had to be it. The girl had bewitched me. There was no other explanation. No one had ever gotten so embedded in my brain. No woman had ever affected me the way Brooke had. And in only two weeks' time at that.

As I got out of the shower, grabbing a towel and wrapping it around my waist, I looked at my reflection in the mirror over the sink. "What the hell are you letting happen to you, dude? She's just a chick. There are plenty of them you can have. Forget about her like that. Don't you remember that you made your best bud a promise about that girl?"

Sighing, I made my way to bed and prayed I wouldn't have any dreams about the girl who was sleeping just across the hallway.

CHAPTER 10

Brooke

The very next morning, I was in the kitchen taking inventory of what kinds of food were available for Braiden to eat. The sounds of expensive dress shoes clicking on the tile floor made my heart do a little dance.

"How's daddy's little man today?"

Yes! It seemed my boss might have listened to me last night.

The chef, Consuela, was the first to greet our employer, "Good morning, Mr. Forester. Will you be having breakfast here this morning, sir?"

Without looking back at him, I tried my best to act as if I was still taking stock of the food, but my ears were keened, waiting to hear what I hoped I would.

The legs of the chair scraped the floor—a good sign he was taking a seat at the table where Braiden was sitting in his high chair. "I will be having breakfast here this morning." He chuckled. "Good morning to you too, son."

The tenderness in his voice melted me completely. God. He really did mean well, in spite of his arrogant tendencies.

"And I'll be eating breakfast here every morning, Consuela. How about some eggs? I don't care how you make them. Surprise me."

Making her way to the fridge that blended into the darkly-paneled wall, she got out a carton of eggs and got to work. I put my clipboard down and finally turned to greet my boss. "Morning."

Looking over his shoulder at me, he pointed at the chair across from him. "Tell our chef what you would like to eat this morning and join us over here, Brooke. I want this little bonding time to have you in it too."

"Oh, I don't ..." I couldn't get it all out before one of his dark brows raised, and I went to him without saying anything further. "You can make me the same as what he's having, Consuela. Thank you."

Smoothing out my knee-length skirt, I took the seat opposite him at the small breakfast table. Braiden took a fresh strawberry out of his bowl and held it out to his father. "How thoughtful, son. Thank you." He took the fruit and ate it in one bite. Then his eyes turned to me. "Coffee?"

I went to get back up to get him some, as that's what I assumed he meant. "How do you take it?"

"Sit down," he said with a chuckle. "I meant, do you want some coffee? Not that I wanted you to get up and get me some."

"Oh." I felt stupid, but shook that off. "Yes, I think I'd like one cup."

Overhearing us, Consuela was already sending one of her kitchen helpers to us with cups and the pot of freshly brewed coffee. Placing the cups in front of us, she filled them, then left us alone.

Looking at the steaming cup, I thought about the fact I liked sugar in mine and some cream too. Gannon took a sip of his, then he looked at my untouched cup. "Sarah, cream and sugar please." He looked up from my cup to me. "You know you're allowed to ask for things you want here, right?"

Letting out a breath I didn't even realize I'd been holding, I nodded. "I'm just a little out of sorts this morning. Our exchange last night has left me a bit shaken. I hope I didn't overstep my bounds. "Gannon ... I have no idea where my lines are with you. Could you please help me understand them better?"

Sarah placed the cream and sugar on the table and a small spoon on a white linen napkin next to my cup of untouched coffee. "Here you are, ma'am."

"Thank you, Sarah." It was only then that I realized how the rest of the staff was regarding me. Not like one of their own. No, not at all. I was treated the same way Gannon was. *Only I* was allowed to call him by his first name. *Only I* was sitting down to eat with him. *Only me,* and they all saw it. But why only me?

Gannon took another sip of his coffee as I fixed mine up and Braiden offered his father a fat blueberry. "How about you eat that one, Braiden? Daddy wants you to be nice and healthy." I caught Braiden's wide smile as he popped the fruit into his mouth, chewing it happily.

The kid was happy almost all the time. He wasn't whiny or moody or demanding. It didn't make any sense why his mother wanted to be rid of him. He was a joy to be around.

Gannon turned his attention back to me. "Brooke, I don't know how to do this father thing, and I'm looking to you for guidance. When you came into my bedroom last night," I caught the kitchen staff stopping to look at us, "and told me I was neglecting my son," Consuela's face contorted as if she had a stomach cramp, "I wasn't too pleased."

Sarah nodded. I knew what they had to be thinking--*this girl is an idiot.*

Trying my best to ignore our small audience, I tried to speak as if no one was listening. "Yet, here you are at the breakfast table as I asked you to be." I tapped the silver spoon on the inside of my cup to rid it of the drop of coffee that had settled into the scooped bottom before placing it back on the white napkin. Pulling the cup to my lips, I blew the steam off the surface and took a sip. *Much better.*

Gannon's eyes danced as he grinned sexily at me. "Yet here I am." One large hand rubbed his dark beard that he kept neatly trimmed. "You made me think. I'm really not used to being told off that way, you know."

"I did it for the sake of your son." I leveled my eyes on his before I turned them to his son. "I'd do anything for him."

"I can see that." Trickles of electricity moved through my hand as I had laid it on the table. When I looked to see just why that was, I saw his hand on top of mine.

I looked up to find his eyes filled with emotion. "Brooke, I know you'd do anything for him. And that's why I listened. I'm not used to admitting that I can be stubborn. And I hate being told what to do. But what you told me last night changed me a tiny bit."

I was mesmerized by the man. His soft, smooth, deep voice. His handsome face. The way he looked at me. I was lost in him. "Oh, yeah?"

"Yeah." He smiled, making soft lines crease around his mouth and eyes. "Women don't talk to me the way you did last night. And not many men have dared to either."

I must've been insane to have spoken to him in a way

others didn't dare to. But I'd had to do it, and I'd do it again if necessary. For Braiden, I'd do whatever I had to, to give him the father he deserved.

Gulping back some highly-charged emotions, I pulled my hand out from under his, as his touch was freaking me out a bit. "I hope I didn't offend you with anything I said last night."

Shaking his head, he ran one hand through his dark hair, disheveling it just the tiniest bit. "Not at all. You just stirred me up a bit. Made me think. And you're right. Twenty minutes a day isn't enough to be spending with my son."

Sarah brought our plates to us, and we both sat back to allow her the space to do that. I looked at the gorgeous plates, heaping with fluffy scrambled eggs, bacon, and toast. "My goodness, Consuela, you certainly can come up with something that looks amazing very quickly. Thank you."

Gannon took a bite of his eggs and moaned. "So much better than the crap I grab on my way to work. Thanks, Consuela."

"You two are more than welcome," came her reply.

It was Friday, and I knew that meant Gannon would be out late. The breakfast was nice, but I wanted him to give Braiden more than breakfast and twenty minutes after work. "So, it's Friday. Any plans?"

"Many plans." He bit into his toast.

I waited to see if he'd tell me about them, but he took a sip of coffee instead, prompting me to ask, "Wanna tell me about them?"

"Sure do." He gave me a grin that told me he was pretty happy with himself. "I'm taking off at lunch today. I want you to make some plans for us. Bonding things. Since I have no idea what kinds of things those are, you have carte blanche. Go crazy. I want to do something with Braiden. And I'm not going out tonight. Not at all this weekend. I want to get into the habit of putting my son first. Just like you said to."

"Oh, Gannon," I exclaimed, barely preventing myself from hugging him. "That's fantastic! I can pack him all up and get him ready for you. How about a trip to the zoo today? I'm sure he's never been. That witch would never have done something like that for her baby."

He shook his head. "I'm sure she didn't. But he's not hers anymore. He's mine. And, by default, yours. You have to come too, Brooke. You're an important part of this little family." He chuckled as he shook his head. "I never knew I even wanted a thing like this, but now that I have it, the idea is growing on me."

It was growing on me too.

CHAPTER 11

Gannon

My mind couldn't stay on work no matter how hard I tried. Just before lunch, I got a call from Brad. "Hey there, Gannon. Wanna do lunch?"

It took me a moment to answer, as I had no idea how to tell him that I was going to have lunch with his little sister and my son. There just didn't seem to be a way I could find to put that out there that I saw him taking well. In the end, I had no real choice. "I'm taking Braiden to the zoo. I figure we'll eat there."

"On your own?" came his surprised question.

"No." I chuckled. "Of course not. I still don't know a damn thing about actually taking care of him. Brooke will go too. She is his babysitter. And she's really good with him too. Thanks for lending her to me," I decided to throw that in.

After yanking off to her for a second time, I wasn't sure how much my best buddy would see through me. I was nearly transparent to him at times. And I figured with his overprotective nature where his little sister was concerned, he'd be able to see right through me. I just couldn't allow to happen.

I couldn't lose her.

"The weather today is great for a trip to the zoo." He didn't sound as if he was reading anything into it. I breathed out a silent sigh of relief. "Brooke loves the zoo too. Especially the monkeys."

Without meaning to, I made a mental note to buy her a stuffed one while we were out that day. "Good, then she'll have a good time too."

"As long as you get her some ice cream she will." He laughed. "I recall a certain trip to the zoo when she was about five, and we were on our way to the exit, leaving after a long day there. She saw the ice cream shop and wanted to get some. Dad wasn't about to let anyone eat in his new car, so he told her she could have some at home. She threw the biggest fit any of us had ever seen."

"Noted. Get the babysitter ice cream to make sure she doesn't throw a fit." I laughed as I picked up my jacket, heading out the door. I was eager as hell to get home and get things going.

"Yeah, I'd hate to have her teach your little boy how to throw a real fit. Have fun man. Maybe we can meet up later tonight. I'm thinking Monaco's for dinner, then clubbing. You?"

"Making a home night with the boy. You know, trying to make him the most important thing in my life. That's what your sister says to do. I've never even thought about being a parent, so I'm following her sage advice." Giving nods to Janine and several others who were in the reception area, I walked out the door and headed to the elevator.

"So she's doing well, then?" he asked.

Pushing the down button, I waited for the elevator as I thought how to put it into words how well she was doing. I couldn't help but gush. "Dude, she's amazing with him. I swear she's already falling in love with him. She looks at him with just as much adoration as I do. It's crazy how fast she's become completely devoted to him."

"She's always been a real kid-lover. That's why she wanted to make a career that has them at the core. Brooke's a natural with kids."

The elevator finally came up, and I stepped in amongst the other people who were heading to lunch. "That she is. Thanks again for letting me borrow her. I'll talk to you later, bro."

"Later."

Ending the call, I kind of felt terrible, but also great at the same time. I was keeping my hands to myself, right? Mostly? What I did alone didn't count, I promised myself.

The thought came to me that it had felt good to place my hand over hers while we were talking at breakfast. I honestly hadn't meant it in any way except in thanks for the lesson she had taught me, but the jolt that shot right through me shocked me. Literally.

It felt like I'd accidentally put my hand on a live wire. Nothing like that had ever happened to me. And by the look on her face, the wonder in her blue eyes, I thought she might have felt the same thing.

The ride back home took way too long, as I was anxious to get to them. My little family. It had just been so damn long since I'd had one. So long since I had anyone other than myself to think about or come home to.

As soon as I came through the door, I heard Braiden's screams of delight, and he ran around the corner, flying into my arms. As I grabbed him up, I couldn't help but notice

Brooke smiling away at us. "Good, you're here. He's been dying for you to show up so he can go see the animals."

"Oh, I thought he was happy to see me." I wanted to ask Brooke if she was happy to see me too, but the smile on her face told me she was.

"He's happy about that too, daddy." She laughed and hooked her thumb in gesture to the door behind her. "I've laid out your clothes on the bed. I was pretty sure you wouldn't want to wear a suit to the zoo, so I laid out proper dad attire."

No one had laid clothes out for me since I was ten. I wasn't exactly sure I liked that she did that. But I was nice about it. "Thanks. I'll get changed, then we can leave. Did you guys eat lunch yet?" I put Braiden down and headed out of the room.

"No, I thought we'd eat with you." She took Braiden by the hand. "We can eat at the zoo if you want. Whatever you want to do."

A smile plastered on my lips. I said, "Okay, we'll eat at the zoo then."

As I went into my bedroom, finding my clothes laid out on the bed, I thought about her going through my closet to find the clothes. At first, I was incensed the tiniest of bits. Then I was turned on as I thought about her hands flowing over my things, picking out what she wanted me to wear— what she wanted to see me in.

My cock jerked, and I stopped the train of thought instantly, warning myself sternly, "Quit it."

The ride to the zoo was full of laughter, as we both adored Braiden and his silly antics. And strolling through the zoo, me pushing the stroller that I'd rented that looked like a golden cage that Braiden loved, I felt like a real family.

Brooke walked at my side, pointing out each animal,

saying its name, and making the sound it made. Braiden tried to mimic her, something she said was good, as he didn't talk at all yet. At two, he should be saying a few words, she told me.

I assured her if anyone could have him talking soon, it would be her. We passed a small gift shop, and I saw stuffed animals inside. "Hey, can you take over with him while I do something really quick, Brooke?"

"Of course." She took over for me, pushing the stroller to keep him moving. "And that's a monkey over there, Braiden. It says, hoo hoo."

I heard a chorus of similar sounds as the monkeys in the cage called out to her. Inside, I purchased a stuffed monkey for her and a stuffed tiger for my son.

Heading back out, I caught up to them, as they'd stayed nearby. Giving Braiden the tiger first and receiving a fantastic smile from him, I handed Brooke the monkey. "I saw this and thought of you."

She laughed, and the sound was beautiful. So fresh and innocently happy. One perfectly-arched brow arched a bit more as she took the monkey out of my hand. "So you think I look like a monkey, Gannon? Thanks."

That didn't come out right at all.

"No, I don't think you look like a monkey at all. You're gorgeous." I stopped, as that last part wasn't supposed to come out. It was meant to sit silently in the back of my mind. And the blush that covered her cheeks as she quickly ducked her head shyly told me she totally caught my little slip. "Your brother told me you like monkeys."

"Oh." She shook her head. "Of course he did. Did you talk to him today? Tell him where we were going?" She held the monkey like a baby on her hip, and it was ridiculously, over-the-top cute, to where I wanted to kiss the breath out of her.

"Yeah, he called, and I told him. He also mentioned that I had better buy you an ice cream before leaving here or I'd face a tantrum from you that would end all tantrums." I laughed and watched a smile crack her lips too.

"Man, I guess I'll never live that down." She swayed a bit as we continued walking. "In my defense, I was four. I'd missed my afternoon nap and had a sugar rush from cotton candy and lemonade they gave me earlier."

"Oh, well that explains it all." I fought the urge to wrap my arm around her narrow shoulders and pull her close, kissing her cheek. Man, how I wished I could just do that.

"Gannon, can I ask you something that's a bit personal?" She looked at me, and we stopped underneath the shade of a tree. Giant goldfish swam to the surface of the pond that ran underneath the little bridge we'd stopped on. Gulping air at the surface, it was plain to see zoo patrons would feed them from this spot.

I put a quarter in the machine that released a handful of what looked like dog food pellets and tossed them to the fish. Braiden laughed and clapped as he watched them frenzy over the food. "Sure you can, Brooke."

"Why haven't you found someone to settle down with?" She eyed me as if gauging if I was going to be truthful with her or not.

I found I was going to be honest as I opened my mouth and the words poured out freely. "I've been busy building a successful business, for one. And once I got that largely completed ... I realized I don't want just anybody. I want a woman who has it all. And I've never met one."

"Never?" she asked as she hugged her little monkey.

The honesty just kept on flowing, "Well, I wouldn't say never. You see, I think you just might have it all, Brooke."

She blushed and had to look away. "Gannon."

I had to save myself. "The guy who gets you will have more than just your brother to answer to. You're my number one girl, so he'll have to answer to me too. I don't envy the poor soul."

Her eyes cut back to me. "I'm your number one girl. What does that mean, exactly?"

My smile was crooked, I could feel it. "You can figure that out, I'm sure."

I moved on, pushing the stroller and feeling good about what I'd told her. A bit of how I was feeling about her was out there. Not enough to get my ass handed to me by her older brother, but just enough to let her know I thought a hell of a lot about her. It wasn't a crime. Right?

CHAPTER 12

Brooke

The trip to the zoo was fantastic. The dinner together later that evening was, too, as Braiden had his first ever pizza. Then we gave him a bath together, to deal with all the tomato sauce and cheese, and got soaked. Finally, Gannon read a bedtime story to Braiden and made me sit on the other side of the bed as he read. He told me he wanted me to be a part of this with his son too.

Part of me knew it wasn't the right thing to do, and that Braiden and I both might get hurt when Gannon finally met some woman he wanted to marry. Then she'd be the boy's mother.

Even though that stayed in the back of my mind most of the time, I couldn't help what was happening between the poor little boy whose mother abandoned him and me. I loved him, and he loved me. It was simple, and there was no way to stop it from happening.

And what I was feeling for Gannon was just the opposite. I knew it was wrong. I knew I had to stop it. And it was far from simple. No, it was the most complex situation I'd ever been in.

I was falling hard for a man who was ten years older than me. And the fact that he was a bad-boy womanizing man who was used to getting what he wanted didn't make things any better. When you added in the fact my brother would kill us both, you had a recipe for disaster.

So I knew I had to keep my thoughts to myself and try to keep Gannon from catching me when I looked his gorgeous body up and down. And most of all, I had to try hard not to let any of the staff see me drooling over the man who was our boss.

After Braiden had fallen asleep that night, after the long day at the zoo, Gannon and I stepped out of his bedroom and into the hallway. There was the adjoining door between my bedroom and Braiden's, but I wanted to walk out with Gannon—walk by his side just one more time before I went to bed.

"Did you have fun today, Brooke?" He stopped after closing the door and leaned up against the wall.

Why does he always have to look so damn hot?

"Yes, I did. Thank you for taking me with you guys. Did you have fun too?" I leaned up against the wall opposite him, folding my arms in front of me.

His eyes sparkled as he nodded. "I did have fun. More fun than I ever remember having. And I want to do this all weekend. What do you say? Think you can handle all this fun I'm dishing out?"

Oh, the things I'd love to try to handle ...

"I'll try to keep up with you." Rolling my shoulders, I moved off the wall and headed toward my bedroom—the one that was just right across the hallway from his.

He caught up to me, his shoulder barely brushing mine

as he walked next to me. "Night, then. See you at breakfast."

"Night." I went into my room and closed the door, leaning against it, sighing, and wishing like hell things could just be simple and easy.

As I went through the drawer with my nightclothes in it, I spied something I didn't realize I had taken from the dorm in the small box of feminine toiletries I'd packed.

In a brand-new package, unused, there was a pink vibrator. My college roomie had gifted it to me when I moved out of the dorm, teasing me that I might find it handy, living with someone as hot as Gannon.

As I pulled it out of the box that was pushed into the far back corner of my nighty drawer, I felt my stomach tighten. My inner thighs pulsed and I went damp inside.

"Hmm." I walked from one of the bedroom doors to the other, making sure they were both locked. Then I went to my bed and tossed the package on it. Undressing, I kept looking at the thing.

Stripping all the way down, I got under my blanket and took the long pink thing out of the package. Pushing down on the end, I found it buzzed to life and was even getting warm.

"Okay, here we go then." I pressed the tip of it to my pussy and found my eyes closing all on their own. "Oh, yeah. I can see why people like these things now."

Moving it around, I pretended it was Gannon's mouth on me down there. I moved it through my folds, up and down the slit, and pressed it to my sensitive nub. "Oh, yeah!"

Holding it there, I let Gannon's body fill my mind. Those muscles, those tats, those eyes ...

As I shuddered, feeling pleasure roll steadily over me and build with astonishing speed, my mind kept drifting to the man who was in bed just across the hall. A man who'd bought me a monkey and some ice cream. A man who'd made my cheeks hurt as we laughed more than I ever had before. A man who could look at me almost the same way he looked at a little boy who he openly loved.

My hips lifted and pumped hard and fast, grinding myself against the toy, urging me higher until I had to grab a pillow to muffle my scream. Finally, I put the vibrator aside and lay there, as stunned by the orgasm as I was by the realization.

Could Gannon Forester actually be falling for me the way I was for him?

Was that even possible?

I'd Googled Gannon a few days back, during some free time I'd had while Braiden napped. I'd found more than a few pictures of him with gorgeous, full-grown women on his arm. A few even showed him kissing some raving beauty. But in not one of those pictures did I see the face he showed his son and me.

Not one picture with adoring women gazing at him had him gazing back at them the way I caught him looking at me way more than one time.

Did Gannon actually like me? Did he think of me as more than just a sex object, the way he seemed to have thought about all the other women?

Or was I simply fooling myself about the whole thing?

He was a man with great looks, charisma, money, and power, and he knew how to use those things to get what he wanted.

Did he merely want me and was he using his arsenal of traps and baits to get me where he wanted me--underneath him, in his bed?

Heaven help me, I wanted that man more than anything I'd ever wanted in my life. But I knew I couldn't have him.

CHAPTER 13

Gannon

I stepped out of the shower where, once again, I'd found myself fantasizing about Brooke.

When will I stop thinking about the babysitter that way?

I couldn't help myself, though. As I pulled on sweat pants and headed down the hall to make sure Braiden was still settled where I'd left him after our bedtime story, my thoughts drifted to the day at the zoo and the nice homey dinner of meatloaf and mashed potatoes that Brooke had showed me how to make, in between teaching me to multitask with an active toddler. Everything had been so easy. So relaxed. So utterly wonderful.

And it was all so completely innocent.

Walking side by side along the pathways of the zoo. Sitting across the dinner table from her, both of us giving Braiden bites of various foods. Both of us laughing at his silly faces as he tasted new things.

The funny thing was that I knew Brooke was off-limits. And I tried hard to wrap my head around it. I also tried not to believe I saw in her eyes what I kept wanting to believe I was seeing.

Braiden was fine, and I started back to my room, thinking of how Brooke looked at Braiden with love in her pretty blue eyes. And I could have sworn to the Almighty above, she looked at me with that same look in her innocent eyes.

Could she be falling for me?

And what if she was? Then what?

Was I ready to be the man who deserved such a rare girl? Was I ready to put my roving ways behind me and settle down?

Because that's what it would mean if I tried to make her mine.

I closed the door to my room and leaned back against it, lightly thudding my head against the wood in frustration. I knew Brad would only accept us being together if I made a real commitment to his baby sister. I knew he'd be watching out for her at all times and keeping his eye on me, making sure I wasn't skirting around behind his sister's back, hurting her.

Could I put my past behind me and do right by the young woman?

I wasn't sure about that. Not yet, anyway. And until I was certain, I had to keep my hands to myself.

And what if I was misreading her look?

What if she merely respected me and that's why she looked at me the way she did? What if she was happy to see me doing more with my son and she simply found pleasure in that? What if she thought I was too old for her?

She could think that. Ten years her senior might be too old in her eyes.

With a sigh, I started for the bed, then my cell rang. It wasn't unusual for me to get calls late at night, but seeing August's name on the screen surprised me. "Hey man, what's up?"

"Our club, in flames," came his quick reply.

For just a fraction of a second, I thought he must be joking or that I had misunderstood him. "Flames?"

"Yes, there's been a fire at our club." He paused before going on. "The investigators have to do their thing, but I'm pretty sure someone tried to burn the place down, Gannon."

"My God!" I headed for my closet to throw something on. "Was anyone hurt?"

"Not that we know of. Nixon is on his way there now. The security company called him. Can you meet us down there? We need to assess the damage and make sure the authorities know we all want to press charges on whoever did this."

"Shit," I mumbled as I made my way to my closet to find something to put on. "Yeah, give me half an hour."

AFTER PUTTING MY SHOES ON, I grabbed my keys and headed out. I stopped outside my door and looked at the closed door that Brooke was just behind.

Maybe I should tell her I have to go. Just in case she needs me for anything.

I walked across the hallway and thought I heard something. A low moan.

What the fuck?

My heart pounded furiously in my chest as I leaned my

ear against the door, and then I heard it loud and clear, her soft moans.

"Yes, Gannon! Yes, baby! Oh, yes, Gannon ..."

Ho-ly shit. For two seconds, the fire fled my mind.

Brooke wanted me the same way I wanted her, and now I knew for sure. No guessing required.

I turned and headed outside, hurrying toward my car, even as thoughts tumbled through my head, a clash between worry about the nightclub and worry about Brooke.

Even if Brooke wanted me, I couldn't do a damn thing about that until I knew I was ready to commit to her or her brother would have my ass. I couldn't hurt him by hurting his baby sister. I just couldn't do it. I was a lot of things—womanizer included—but I couldn't stab my best friend in the back.

The whole ride to the club, I went back and forth in my mind, up until I got there and found August and Nixon were waiting for me outside. Only one firetruck remained at the scene. I saw no damage to the outside, which filled me with relief.

Not too bad.

I got out of my Jag and jogged up to them. "Hey. So what's the damage?"

Nixon hooked a thumb behind him. "Come on, let's go inside. It's not too bad. One bar got the brunt of it. Someone had put a very small explosive device under one of the shelves in that bar."

I shook my head as I thought that it had to have been one of our construction workers. They were the only ones with access to the inside of the club. "So we'll have to question everyone on the crew then."

August nodded as we went inside. "I can't believe any of

those guys would purposely try to hurt us like that. Man, we give those men a lot of extras."

We did give the guys lots of perks. Plus, they all were promised free nights at the club a few nights out of each month, forever, if they wanted. Who would do such a shitty thing when we were being so damn good to them all?

CHAPTER 14

Brooke

I woke up the next morning with a smile on my face. Only the sweetest of dreams had crept into my sleeping brain. Dreams of Gannon holding me, kissing me, loving me.

In record time I was showered, dressed, a bit of makeup on and my hair pulled into a high ponytail, ready for whatever Gannon had on the agenda for that Sunday. He'd promised to give us his time all day, and I was over the moon about that.

Hearing giggles, I walked into the kitchen and found Braiden already dressed and seated in his high chair, with Gannon playing with him.

"Morning," I said with a smile, loving the sight of father and son interacting so naturally. "Hi, Brai. Did you sleep okay?"

I'd been talking to Braiden, not that he would answer, but Gannon took the question as meant for him. "Well, not that great actually." I turned to find him taking his seat again then pinching the bridge of his nose in what seemed like aggravation. That was when I noticed the dark circles under his eyes.

Taking a bottle of water out of the fridge, I saw that Consuela was making pancakes. "Yummy. Do you mind making me a couple of those too?"

"Of course not," she replied as she smiled at me. "And for the baby this morning?"

"Oh, I think we should stick to fresh fruit and some oatmeal for him." I went to the cabinet and pulled out one of his sippy cups, filling it with milk before I sat down.

Handing the cup of milk to Braiden, I took a seat across from Gannon. I wasn't sure how to approach the subject of why he'd not slept well. There was something bothering him, that was easy to see. "So, bad dream?"

"Hmm?" He looked at me. "Oh. You mean why I didn't sleep well, don't you?"

"Yes." I took a drink of the water as I waited and tried not to think about how handsome he looked in the long sleeved pale blue button up and the black slacks that fit him much too perfectly. Or the way his hair was slightly disheveled. I knew he'd been running his hand through it. He did that a lot when he was thinking.

"I got a phone call not long after we parted ways in the hall. Just after I was done with my shower, my cell rang. It was one of my business partners, telling me that we had an incident at the club we're building. Someone tried to blow the place up, it seems. It has me wondering who would do that to us." One wrinkle furrowed just above his dark brows.

One chunk of hair was out of place, and I reached across the small table and ran my hand through it to fix it. "No wonder you're so stressed."

His eyes widened as I sat back, and he looked at my

hand. Suddenly, I thought my action might have been unwanted. But before I could apologize, he said, "Thanks. I've been shoving my hands through my hair all morning."

Happy I hadn't offended him, I smiled. "Only one chunk was out of place." I turned to Braiden and ran my hand through his own dark hair. "I'm kind of OCD about keeping my men looking their best." Then I bit my lower lip as that Freudian slip came out all on its own. "I didn't mean ..."

His deep voice broke in, "It's okay, Brooke. I know what you mean. You feel like I need a bit of looking after like my son does. Thanks for that. You're a real angel."

Consuela placed our plates in front of us and the bowl of oatmeal with fresh strawberries next to my plate. "Enjoy, you three."

"Thank you," Gannon and I said at the same time. Our eyes met as we both found ourselves smiling.

"So was there much damage to your club?" I asked, breaking the suddenly sizzling tension between us.

"Only one bar will need to be replaced. So not too much. It won't set us back by much, maybe a day or two." He poured himself some juice out of the carafe that was on the table, filling his small juice glass up, then he did the same for mine. "What really concerns me is who would want to hurt us like that. We're very good to our crew. And it had to be one of them who planted the device. I'm just thankful it didn't work the way they undoubtedly wanted it to."

"So this club." I stabbed a forkful of pancakes. "What kind of club is it going to be?"

His face lit up as he explained it to me. "It's going to be a nightclub for the ultra-rich. I know that might sound egotistical to you."

"Not at all. Why not cater to people like yourself? Who better to do that than people who know what wealthy people want?" I took a sip of the apple juice as I watched a smile curl his chiseled lips.

"That's a progressive way of thinking, Brooke. I'm glad you don't find the idea shallow and selfish." He watched me set my glass down then his eyes moved back to mine. "You know, you could have your twenty-first birthday party there if we're open by then."

My eyes grew wide; I could feel them doing it. "I'm not rich! I don't belong in a place like that. And besides that, my birthday is right around the corner. It falls on Thanksgiving this year. And that means my family throws one big party that lasts a couple of nights as lots of family comes in for the holiday and my birthday."

"Yeah, it won't be open by then. But as soon as it does open, I want you to be my guest of honor." His eyes shone brightly as he offered me what sounded a lot like a date.

"You sure, boss?" I smiled at him then gave Braiden another bite of oatmeal.

"Don't call me that." His hand moved over mine as I'd left it on the table. "Aren't we more than just boss and employee, Brooke? Aren't we friends more so than anything else?"

He was my big brother's best friend. And he and I had something a lot different than a working relationship. And I had fantasized about the man just the night before. I was treading on dangerous ground. But I wasn't about to leave the man hanging. "I guess we are more like friends."

"Good, then you'll agree to be my guest of honor for the opening of the club. That's settled." He patted my hand then went back to eating his breakfast. "You'll be my date for that night."

Date?

Oh, hell!

I tried not to let it show just how much that affected me. And I tried to ignore it as I thought about the holiday that was coming up. "You know, Gannon, you and Braiden will be here all alone for Thanksgiving. Why not come with me to my family's home in Napa Valley? Brad will be there. I'll let you and Braiden sleep in my bedroom. I can bunk with my sister, Brianna."

He shook his head. "I can't impose on your family like that. Thank you, but no. Braiden and I will be okay here. Consuela can make us a nice dinner. It's okay. You can have that time off. I'll take off from work so I can take care of him. But you'll need to show me just exactly how to do that first." He laughed then patted my hand again. "Damn, girl. Looks like I really need you."

My heart flipped, and I had to try hard not to take his words the wrong way. "No, you two have to come with me. Come on, Gannon. I want to introduce Braiden to my family anyway. They love kids too. And you've been friends with Brad for so long, they should know you too. Come on. Please." I gave him my best smile, and he smiled back at me.

"You sure?"

With a nod, I moved my hand to pat his where it was resting on the table. "I'm positive. So that's a yes then. I'll be your date for the opening night of your fancy club and you two guys will be my dates for my birthday slash Thanksgiving holiday."

"Deal," came his quick reply.

I went back to my pancakes, wondering what we'd just done. Had we crossed an invisible line? Or had we just evolved into a friendship?

Either way, something inside of me bubbled, and I felt pleased about it all.

CHAPTER 15

Gannon

I made each weekend all about my son, and Brooke was right there too. I didn't want to admit it, but it was also all about being with her. A few weeks had passed with us settling into one routine after another.

Never had boring things been so damn fun. But Brooke just being there made everything fun, interesting, exciting even.

I had to get past this thing I had for her. I had to do it. I knew I couldn't be something I wasn't for her. I knew I'd end up hurting her and losing her as my son's sitter and her brother as my friend. It was all way too risky.

Being great friends had to be okay with me. Even if she did want me the same way I wanted her.

Each Monday came with work and it would be time to get back to the real world after each weekend that had been filled with more fun than I had known was possible.

August and I had met for lunch to go over a few things that pertained to the club and we'd just parted ways after leaving The Palm in Beverly Hills. On my way to my car, I heard a woman's voice calling out, "Gannon? Gannon Forester?"

I stopped and turned around to find a woman coming after me. I recognized her right away. She and I had had a brief one-on-one. Very brief. One month, brief. And it had ended like all of my one-on-ones did, with me stepping out on her. But there she was, smiling at me.

No hard feelings, it seemed. I was relieved about that and smiled right back at her. "Jasmine, how have you been? It's been over a year since our paths have crossed."

Her arms outstretched, I opened mine too, welcoming her into them for a small hug. "I've been okay. I've missed you though."

Letting her go, I took a step back, wanting there to be some distance between us. And I was also interested in the fact that my body didn't have an urge for hers. She'd been one great fuck. That's what had kept me coming back for more for longer than I did with most of my female conquests.

"Have you, now?" I laughed a little. Jasmine was a real looker. Long dark hair that hung in a silken sheet to the top of her round ass. Long legs peeked out from under a knee-length dress. Red always had been her color. With her dark hair and eyes, the red made her stand out.

Even as gorgeous as she was, she wasn't doing it for me. I found myself comparing her to Brooke. Brooke was a natural beauty while Jasmine was always so made up that I had no idea what she really looked like underneath the makeup. I did know her assets were enhanced. Double Ds made her tits bigger than Brooke's. But Brooke's were real. And so was her ass, a thing Jasmine couldn't say was about her own.

Blood-red lips parted as one slender hand went to rest on her hip. "Yes, I have missed you. So how about we catch up? How about tonight? I've had a bit of a dry spell here of late. I could use a good romp, if you get what I'm saying. You're still up for helping a girl out when she needs it, right?"

I always had been. But I wasn't feeling it now. Not with her anyway. "Jasmine, things have changed in my life."

She looped her arm around mine and led me off to take a seat at one of the outside tables where waiting patrons of the restaurant would sit until a table was ready for them inside. "Tell me about it, Gannon. I want to hear everything."

"I have a son now," I told her as we took seats right next to each other. She made sure our outer thighs were touching, and she didn't let go of my arm either.

Turning just enough so her tit touched my chest, she sighed and put on a smile. "A son! Oh, that's fantastic, Gannon. And how old is he? And his mother is?"

"He's two. His mother is a witch who never even told me about him until very recently. I had a DNA test done when she came to my office and told me she was going to dump the boy if I didn't take him."

"Oh, Lord. She does sound like a bitch." Jasmine waved her free hand in front of her face as if the thought made her hot or something. "So, it's you and this poor boy." One of her perfectly manicured eyebrows rose. "All alone?"

"Pretty much. Well, I had to hire a full-time sitter to stay with him." A sharp stab of pain in my heart made me think I was doing something wrong. Like talking to Jasmine was the wrong thing to do. And pretending that Brooke was just the babysitter was wrong too.

But there wasn't anything wrong with either thing. I was

a free man. And Brooke could never be anything more than my kid's sitter and my friend.

Jasmine's face lit up like a Christmas tree as a thought crossed her mind. "I'd love to meet your son, Gannon. Oh, please, allow me to come to dinner. I just have to meet him. Please." Batting her thick false eyelashes, she was working hard at getting the invitation. "Maybe—after your sitter puts the boy to bed—you could do the same for an old friend. A friend who's been aching for a good old-fashioned fucking for months now. You do recall how great we were in the sack together, don't you?"

How could I forget? The woman had been nearly insatiable. She'd done anything I wanted her to and then some. Fucking her could have replaced a workout, it was so intense and physical. But it wasn't love. It was just fucking.

Why am I thinking about love?

I didn't love anyone. So why not take Jasmine up on her offer? Why not let her come over and take her to my bedroom for the night?

Because you care about Brooke, you dumbass.

Oh yeah.

But I had to put that behind me. I had to do something to make that happen. And if I took Jasmine to my bedroom, Brooke would definitely see that, and she'd start to look at me differently. Not the way she was currently looking at me. Like a nice guy. Like a guy she wanted to lose her virginity to. Like a guy she cared about, and who she thought cared about her in a way.

Looking at Jasmine as she bit her lower lip, deliberately trying to entice me—a thing she wasn't doing in the least little bit—I made a decision. One that might do something that would end this idea that Brooke and I could be anything more than friends.

Even as my brain told me to go forward with this plan, even as I looked at Jasmine and saw her as a big phony fake woman, I knew I had to do something to stop the thing that was progressing between my best friend's baby sister and me. But damn, I didn't want to.

"I don't know, Jas ..."

"Please, Gannon." Jasmine batted those lashes again as she moved her hand along the inside of my thigh. "Gannon, I need you. You left me high and dry, without a word to let me know what I'd done to lose you. I was devastated. I know you didn't know that, as you didn't bother to call and see how I was taking our breakup."

"We weren't really together, Jasmine. We spent some nights together, but we weren't a couple. Both of us were free to do as we pleased. No words of love were ever exchanged."

She held up her hand to stop me. "Oh, I beg to differ, Gannon. I told you on most of our sexual occasions, once you'd made me come like a demon, that I loved the way you fucked me. Words of love were exchanged."

How shallow.

How unlike Brooke.

And how perfect for Brooke to see me as the man I really am, instead of the man I am with her and my son.

"I'm not promising you that you can stay the night or even come into my bedroom, Jasmine. I'm not sure I want that sort of thing going on now that I have a child in my home. I want the kid to grow up respecting me. And having women over just to fuck them isn't a thing I want him thinking is right."

She smiled. "How progressive of you, Gannon. Perhaps this boy is bringing out the man in you. The man I always knew you could be. So, let's take this thing slowly then.

Dinner tonight, and we'll go from there. I think I'll adore this new man you seem to have become. Fatherhood suits you."

"Should I send my driver for you?" I got up, getting ready to leave as I was beginning to feel very uncomfortable about the whole thing.

"No, I'll have mine take me. Around eight?" she asked as she got up too.

"No. Around six. Braiden, that's his name, goes to bed at eight. So we eat at six." I looked up for a moment, asking my parents up in heaven if this was the right thing to do. And just like always, they didn't answer me.

"I'll be there." Then her hands were on my arms, and I looked down at her. She caught my lips with a soft kiss. A kiss that did absolutely nothing for me. "Bye, Gannon."

"Bye, Jasmine."

As I walked away, I couldn't help but feel I'd just made a terrible mistake. But what could I do to fix that? And should I fix it, or leave it like it was? It would probably do the trick. It would probably have Brooke looking at me differently.

Each step I took had me thinking more and more about that. Did I want Brooke to look at me differently? Or did I want her to always look at me the way she did?

CHAPTER 16

Brooke

Braiden and I were sitting in the playroom I'd made him in one of the never-used living areas of the massive home. He and I had gone to the store earlier to find things to put in it. I'd found all types of fun, colorful educational toys to use to help him, and a potty chair too. He was a little behind developmentally, probably because of the total lack of love from his mother, but I was sure Braiden was super smart and would make up for lost time with my help. He was definitely eager, and more than willing to play all kinds of games.

When the door to the room opened, and there stood Gannon, looking at us as we were sitting on the floor playing with blocks that had letters and numbers stamped on them, I looked at my cell to see what time it was. "You're home. I guess the time got away from me."

"Yes, I am." He came to us, picking up his son. "And how have you been today, my big boy?"

Braiden giggled as Gannon rubbed his whiskered cheek

against the boy's smooth one. I got up and made sure my skirt was in place. "I see you found us. I hope you don't mind me making this room into a place where I can help Braiden learn."

"Not at all. In fact, when Ashe met me at the door, I was pleased to hear you'd taken this on all by yourself. You're the expert here, not me, after all." He turned to leave the room, so I followed along behind him.

He was heading in the opposite direction I thought he'd be going in, the direction of the small dining room where we had dinner each night. Instead, we were heading toward a larger dining area. And I found the staff was busily making it beautiful. Fresh flowers were brought in. Nice linen was placed on the table. White linen, a thing we'd found out early on that Braiden was hard on. We'd had it removed from the dining areas we used regularly.

I didn't ask anything about it though. It wasn't my home, after all. When I heard more footsteps coming toward us, I turned to find Ashe leading a woman into the room.

A tall, beautiful, dark-haired woman. And she was looking only at Gannon. "Oh, he's a doll, Gannon!"

Who the hell is she?

Gannon turned his attention to the woman who swept in and kissed his cheek. "You made it, Jasmine. This is my son, Braiden."

She took the little boy's hand and shook it as he looked at her with wide eyes, before burying his face in his father's chest shyly. "Oh, he is sweet, Gannon." She made a point of completely ignoring me.

I was standing right behind Gannon though. My shyness had slipped back in, and I had to step out of his shadow. "Hello, I'm Brooke, Braiden's sitter. And your name is Jasmine?"

She nodded, looking me over once, sizing me up, then looking at Gannon. "You didn't tell me she was so young. Perhaps I should help you find someone to help you with the boy?"

Gannon looked at me with a frown on his face, a thing I worried meant he was thinking about taking her up on the offer. Then he winked at me. "I don't need any help, Jasmine. Her brother is one of my best friends. He recommended her. Brooke's majoring in Early Childhood Development at Berkeley. Who better to care for my son?"

Jasmine's dark eyes took me all in as I stood what must've been too close to Gannon for her comfort. She reached out, taking me by the arm, pulling me to one side. I watched as Gannon put Braiden in his highchair, that had been brought into the more extravagant dining room.

"If you don't mind me asking, just how old are you?" She had the nerve to ask me.

"You first," I threw at her.

"Thirty, dear. Your turn." She batted fake lashes at me as if trying to take over the mother role.

"Twenty. And what does that matter?"

The smile that moved over her face told me she was relieved about my age. Was she there for Gannon? Was she his girlfriend or something?

"It doesn't. Let's sit." She held out her arm, gesturing to the lavishly laid-out table.

When had Martha Stewart stopped by?

There was seating for six at the table, place settings for four. At the end of the table, Gannon sat. Each place on either side of him was open, and one had Braiden's high chair next to it. One can imagine my surprise when this new woman went for that chair.

That's my damn chair!

Gannon's eyes caught mine as she took the seat between him and his son. He shrugged and nodded at the other chair. I took the place, but gave him a scowl.

I wanted to ask him why he hadn't told me he was having company. I'd have left them alone. So I decided it wasn't too late to do just that. "Gannon, I can take my dinner to my bedroom so you and your friend can be alone."

He shot me a look that I'd never seen before. "No."

No? But if she was going to see to helping his son then why did I need to be there?

The woman leaned in close to him, whispering, "Let her go if she wants, Gannon. I can take care of feeding your son, darling."

My blood was boiling. I knew I had no right to be jealous. I had no right to be mad at him for having a woman over. I had no right at all, but fuck, I was livid!

"She's part of my family, Jasmine. She's not some employee to my son and me. She stays." He looked at me once more with a smile on his handsome face. "Dinner wouldn't be the same without her smiling face at my table anyway."

"How nice for you, Brooke," Jasmine gave me a crooked smile as her eyes narrowed a bit, letting me know she didn't really think it was nice at all. "Being treated like a part of an employer's family isn't a thing most servants get."

Servant?

Who the fuck does she think she is? "I should go, Gannon."

His hand moved over mine under the table as I had my hands on top of my legs, clenching my thighs with them so I didn't jump up and smack the bitch.

So unlike me to even think this way!

"No, Brooke. You're going to stay. I've asked Consuela to make us something special for dinner. Something I think you're going to love. I don't want you to eat it in your room. I want to see your face when you taste it."

The touch of his hand on mine, hidden from the woman across the table from me, sent heat directly to my core. And I surrendered to the man as my anger ebbed. "K."

The surprise meal wasn't a thing I'd ever eaten before, Pheasant under Glass, and it was delicious. But I couldn't thoroughly enjoy it, as the woman he'd invited just rubbed me the wrong way.

Gannon had to get up to take a phone call, leaving the two of us all alone, save little Braiden. He was busily munching on some meat she'd placed in front of him. He was getting very messy, and so were his clothes and the tablecloth, a thing I never let happen.

"So, you live here?" she asked me.

"Yes." I didn't want to chat with the woman, and kept eating.

"So, has Gannon had any other women over that you know of?" She craned her head to keep a look out for him.

"No." I took a drink of the red wine we had all been given. I'd had wine before, but no other alcohol.

"Good to hear. So, do you think there's a chance he and I could make it happen?" she asked.

"Make what happen?" I suppose I was clueless.

"You know. Marriage? Now that he has a kid to take care of, the man finally needs a wife. And I could be that. I've lusted after him for over a year. He and I were a thing about a year ago. We got along well. I could make myself available to him, and eventually, he'd see me as a wife and mother." She licked her too-fat lips. *Way too much collagen.*

"Hmm. Who knows." I managed to say it like I didn't care. "I think I need more wine, and this bottle is about empty. Mind keeping an eye on Braiden while I run to the kitchen to grab another bottle?"

"No, of course not. And do you think you could see fit to take the boy and keep him occupied while I work on his father?" My stomach flipped, and I nearly threw up.

"I'll do what I can." I left the room and hurried to find Gannon.

I wasn't about to let some conniving female do a thing to him. He and I collided as we both came around a corner at the same time. "Good. Gannon, we have to talk."

I grabbed his hand and pulled him into the next room to make sure she couldn't hear us. I closed the door behind us, still holding his hand. Then I turned to him as he asked, "What's the matter?"

Looking into his dark blue eyes, I could see he didn't have a clue what she was up to. "Gannon, that woman plans on duping you into marrying her. She thinks your son is the way to get what she's after. She told me she's lusted after you for a year or something like that. That's not love."

"She told you that, huh?" He looked away, then shrugged. "I guess I could do worse, huh?"

What?

"Gannon, how long have you been seeing this woman?"

"I haven't. I saw her about a year ago. We kind of dated for a month before I lost interest. Why? What does that matter?" He looked completely serious.

"What does that matter?" I was shaking my head so much it was making me dizzy, so I stopped. "Gannon, you don't just bring random women around your kid. And you sure as hell don't entertain the thought of letting some woman step in to fill a role merely because it's open. You stopped seeing her for a reason. You have nothing that calls you to her. There is nothing there between you two."

"But that doesn't mean it can't grow with time, right?" His question only served to make me even angrier.

"Gannon, you walked away from her. She's not the right woman for you," I blurted out without thinking.

His eyes softened as he looked at me. I felt one of his fingers move over my hand that was still holding his. "Hmm. You know, you might be right, Brooke. Do you think *you* might be the right woman for me?"

CHAPTER 17

Gannon

I watched her sky-blue eyes dance as she looked at me, trying to grasp what I'd said.

I'd never planned to say that to her. It had just popped out of my mouth. She was so jealous over me that it had me kind of giddy with emotion.

Maybe inviting Jasmine over had been the right thing to do after all. The truth—or a form of it, anyway—was out. And Brooke wasn't running away from me. She was stunned and looked a bit pale, but she wasn't running.

"So?" I urged her to say something.

"Are you messing with me, Gannon?" She blinked rapidly.

"No." I ran my thumb over the back of her hand, grateful that she hadn't let go yet. "I have to ask you that question because, you see, I've been thinking about that for a while now. Like maybe you're the one for me. I didn't know how to go about asking what you thought about that."

"So you invited this woman over for what reason then?" She seemed stupefied.

I was too. "I don't really know why I did that. I bumped into her after lunch with August this afternoon. She wanted to get together; I didn't. But she gave me an idea. A terrible idea."

"Like the idea of seeing if she made me jealous?" she asked me as she cocked her head to one side.

"Well, to be honest, I wasn't sure why I did it. I wanted something to change with you and me. She seemed like a thing that would accomplish that. You know, making you look at me differently, stopping this connection we have that just keeps getting deeper as it grows and grows."

"Or making me jealous and bringing it all out of me?" she asked. Then she pulled her hand out of mine and turned away. "You've manipulated this whole thing, Gannon."

I put my hand on her shoulder and turned her back around. I wanted to see her face. "I know that. I'm sorry. If this wasn't such a hard place to be in, then I'd have done things differently. You see, I value your brother's friendship. That's one reason I didn't let you know for sure how I was feeling about you. But more than that, Brooke, I value you. I knew I had to be the man you deserve before I could ever present myself to you."

"So, what does this mean, Gannon?" she asked, still looking a bit perplexed.

"This means I want you. I want you in the worst possible way. I've never felt like this about anyone. Not ever. I can make you promises I never even thought about making anyone before." I knew I was wearing my heart on my sleeve, and I just didn't care.

"What kinds of promises?" Her eyes went wide as she looked at me.

I knew she was taking each and every word in and storing it in her heart. She'd remember this conversation for the rest of her life. I knew she would. So I was careful about what I said, even as I came to a decision in my mind. Brad was just going to have to deal, because the fact of the matter was, I needed his sister. I ... loved his sister. It was true. I'd fallen for her in way more ways than just the physical. The thought of waking up one day and not having her beside me left me completely gutted. I thought about her as much as Braiden, wanting nothing more than to see her smile. "Brooke, I promise that I will be faithful to you. I will never intentionally hurt you."

"You and I would be exclusive?" She looked like she didn't quite believe me. "Have you ever been that with anyone else?"

I shook my head. "Thirty years old and you are the first girl I've ever asked to be with me in that way. Brooke, I want to be your first love and your last one too."

She stared at me in such disbelief that I wrapped my arms around her and held her in a way I'd only dreamt of. Her body melted into mine and I took in the sweet scent of her mint-scented shampoo.

"Love?"

"Love, Brooke. I love you." It felt good to get that out. "I love you so much that if you tell me that you don't want this, you don't want me, then I'll let you go and never fault you for it. Above anything else, I don't want to lose your friendship."

Her head was pressed against my chest; her heart was pounding so hard I could feel it. "I want it all, Gannon. I have for a while now. I've dreamt of this moment." She raised her head to look at me, and I found tears glistening in her pretty eyes. "I love you too. I have for quite some time. The way you are when you're with Braiden and me—I've fallen in love with that man. But I know how my family will react. We'll have to keep this a secret."

"No. I can talk to your brother. You don't have to worry." My lips were quivering, wanting to kiss her so damn badly. "Brooke, can I kiss you?"

She grabbed my biceps as she licked her lips and stared into my eyes. "Please. I've wanted this for such a long time."

Slowly, I moved my head to reach her lips and when they touched, something inside of me woke up just as something else exploded, shattering me in a way I didn't know was possible.

I knew then that I would move heaven and earth for this girl; I'd do everything I had to, to keep her with me and only me.

When our mouths parted, I looked at her, her eyes still closed. "Was that how you thought it might go, baby?"

"Better," she murmured. Her arms went around me as she hugged me tightly. "Can we do more?"

I nuzzled her hair and kissed her neck, moving up to her ear. "We can do anything you want to. But I'm not rushing you."

"Can we start tonight?" Her words came out so quietly that I almost didn't hear them.

"We can." My heart was soaring. My mind was reeling. And I had something I had to take care of. "I'll go get rid of Jasmine. Can you take Braiden and bathe him while I do that? Then I'll meet you in his room to read to him until he falls asleep. Then you and I can go to my bedroom. If you want."

She looked up at me with eyes that were filled with a

nervous excitement I'd never seen before. "Gannon, is this really happening? Or am I dreaming again?"

"It's real, baby. This is the most real anything has ever felt to me. And I don't want you to worry about a thing. I'll be so gentle with you, I promise." I kissed her again as her lips begged me to do it.

One more sweet kiss, the second of what I prayed would be billions upon billions. Never had I known love like this. I had fallen in love with my son and somehow also opened my heart up in a way it had never been.

Between him and Brooke, I now felt love overflowing inside of me. And things could only get better from here.

"Gannon, I know you said you could talk to Brad and make him understand. But I don't want you to do that. Please promise me you'll keep this a secret. I don't want the staff to know either. Please." She looked at me with pleading eyes.

"But ..." I had to protest. She had to let me be honest and open about this. She was the best thing I'd ever found, outside of Braiden. I wanted to shout that from the rooftops.

"Please, Gannon. Promise me. This will be our secret and ours alone."

With a sigh, I dropped my forehead to hers. "Okay. I promise you that. For now."

Only for now ...

CHAPTER 18

Brooke

My dreams were coming true. Gannon felt the same way I did. A little over a few weeks had passed before he'd been able to admit his feelings for me, but he'd finally done it and I had too.

Watching him as he read a book to Braiden made me melt even more than it usually did.

Knowing he and I were in love made this all that much sweeter.

I could see it all in his eyes. He'd meant what he said when he had told me he loved me. I'd known that for a while. His eyes had told me that long before his mouth did.

I glanced at Braiden as his eyes closed and his breathing slowed. "He's out." Gannon kissed his son on top of his head, the way he'd done every night since that first one.

I'd seen Brad a few days back, and he'd told me he'd never seen Gannon so happy and full of life. He credited Braiden for that. I knew that was a part of it, but so was I.

If only I was older, then maybe we could be open with

this. But I was still a child in my family's eyes. I knew we'd have to keep it a secret. Probably for a very long time.

Putting the book back in the bookcase, Gannon looked my way, catching me as I watched him. "You ready?"

A wave of shyness took me over, but I fought it back. I nodded and got up from the other side of Braiden. He waited for me then scooped me up into his strong arms, carrying me out of the bedroom and across the hall to his.

My stomach was a mess. Butterflies had given way to rabid bats. I laid my head on his broad shoulder to try to steady myself. He was going to see me naked! "God, I'm nervous."

"I'm glad you're admitting that. You wouldn't be human if you weren't nervous." He kicked his door closed behind us then took me to his bed. Laying me down gently, he stood over me, looking down at me. His large fingers went to work, unbuttoning my shirt. He pushed it open then climbed on the bed next to me and kissed the tops of my breasts that spilled out of the bra. "How I've wanted to taste you, Brooke."

My stomach tightened with my shyness. But I had to admit something to him too. "I've wanted to taste you too, Gannon."

He pulled his warm mouth off me, looking up at me. "You have?"

I nodded. There was so much to explore on one another. I found myself lacking patience, wanting to do it all right away, despite my irrational fear of him seeing my naked body. "How about you let me ..."

He didn't let me finish. "No. You're going to let me do things to you. Then we'll see about letting you do things to me. I want to show you things you've never felt, first. I've been dying to, baby."

My heart stopped, my body quivered, and I tried to ready myself for the adventure he was about to take me on. "Okay."

Easing my clothing off, inch by inch, he was going so slowly that I was about to cry out with the impatience I was feeling. It came right along with the unbearable feeling of anxiety at him looking me over. I just wanted him inside of me. I wanted to feel his weight on my body. I wanted to feel his cock spreading me and filling me.

But he was slow with me, kissing every inch he uncovered. My body was on fire as he finished his kisses, ending at my toes. Then he pushed my legs apart, spreading them. His eyes were on my cunt, and I was heating with raw embarrassment.

God, what's he thinking about it?

He growled as he made his way back up the bed, his still-clothed body in between my legs. His hands ran up the insides of my thighs.

I watched as he eyed my crotch. His hands pushed my thighs open even more as he leaned over me, his lips barely touching my innocent ones. His tongue eased through my folds. "Ahh ..." I couldn't suppress the moan he'd incited. And all my feelings of embarrassment and shyness started to ebb.

His fingers kneaded my inner thighs as he moved his tongue all over my sex. I groaned with the sensation it sent through me. He was incredible. And he was all mine. He'd given me his word on that.

His hands moved around to my ass; he pulled me up as he darted his tongue into me with a slow rhythm. In and out, in and out. I was going higher and higher inside my head. My body didn't feel as if it was mine at all.

No. It was his. It belonged to him and only to him. I'd made the right decision, waiting for him. I knew it then.

I fisted the sheets as he moved his tongue out of me, running it up my slit, and then his mouth was on my clit.

He sucked it a bit, then tapped it with the tip of his tongue. Back and forth he did that, until I felt a wave start deep inside of me, filling me with desire, lust, and utter passion. The vibrator didn't hold a candle to the talented man. I nearly screamed with the orgasm. "Yes, Gannon! Yes! God."

The way he kissed my intimate lips after that only served to take me higher. Then he stood up and undressed in front of me as I gasped for air, writhing with pleasure that took me over, destroying any shyness I had left in me.

He could look at me all he wanted, just as long as he made me feel that over and over again for the rest of my life.

I couldn't take my eyes off his body as he undressed. I had known he was built, but my God!

"Oh, baby. Oh, Gannon ..." I let out a moan as ecstasy filled me. Looking at his ladder-like abs and his massive pecs, his biceps that bulged, made me even hotter and wetter for the man. His legs were just as chiseled as the rest of him. "It's as if your cut from stone, Gannon. Perfect."

"I think you are." He placed his hand on my stomach, and my legs went completely still.

I drew in a breath as I waited to see what he was going to do next. "Gannon." I stopped and tried to think of how I should say it.

"What, baby? We don't have to ..."

I stopped him. "No. And we do have to. We most definitely have to. I've never wanted anything so badly in my life. It's just that; I don't know how to ..."

"Is this about birth control, Brooke?" He smiled at me, then winked. "I've got condoms."

I didn't want to use them though. And I didn't know how to tell him that. So I just closed my eyes and went for it. "I'm on the Pill. I have been since I was sixteen. And as long as you know you're clean, sexually speaking, then ..."

He moved his body over mine. I could feel his throbbing cock press against me, but he wasn't attempting to put it in. I arched up to him, wanting it inside of me, a thing he wasn't doing.

Wrenching my mouth away, I found myself begging, "Please, Gannon. Please, I want it."

"Oh, baby ..." He made a low, growling noise. "You don't know how badly I want to be inside of you. But I don't want to hurt you."

"Stop worrying about that," I moaned. "Please, just do it, baby. I need you."

He sighed and kissed my neck, which made me insanely crazy and hot as hell. I arched up to him even more, wanting it so damn badly. "Gannon. Fuck me. Please."

"Oh fuck, baby. I knew you'd be like this. Keep talking to me like that. Tell me what you want. What you need," he growled at me. "Show me the person you'll only be with me. The one no one else will ever see."

"Please, fuck me, Gannon. Make me yours."

"You're already mine, sweetheart," he murmured, taking my face in his hands and kissing me so softly that I could have cried at his tenderness. "You always have been. Then his body raised up, and he placed his hand on his cock, guiding it to the edge of my quivering vagina. He looked into my eyes as he lined it up, then he thrust it into me fast and hard.

Heat tore through me as I spread for him. My nails gouged into the flesh of his arms as I cried out, "God!"

He went perfectly still, both of us panting like animals. Then he began to move slowly. "You did great, baby."

"Did I?" I had to ask as a couple of tears escaped, as it still hurt pretty badly.

"The hard part's over. It only gets better from here." He kissed me then, and I wrapped my arms around him, letting it all sink in.

The pain went away as if by magic and I moved my body with his, knowing I'd waited for exactly the right man.

CHAPTER 19

Gannon

It wasn't like any other experience I'd ever had. Even then I knew I'd never feel this way with another woman. Not ever.

As I moved with slow strokes to get her body accustomed to my girth, I couldn't help but notice the way I was feeling. Light, almost as if gravity had ceased to exist.

We could've been floating on a cloud for all I knew. It was effortless, the love we made. I couldn't tell where I ended and Brooke began. And I never wanted it to end.

Taking my mouth off hers, I kissed my way down her neck then moved all the way down until I had one of her luscious nipples between my lips. Nibbling at first, I couldn't resist the urge to suck it with a hard and demanding tug.

She gasped, and I felt her body shake a little. Her hands went through my hair as her body rolled in a wave-like fashion, undulating with pure desire. "Gannon! God!" I felt her begin to squeeze me inside and was surprised to feel her having an orgasm.

Continuing to suck at her juicy breast, I relished the way her body felt as it convulsed around my cock. It was so fucking tight, and she was moving in a way that had my entire body so on fire that I was helpless against it all and found my own release had been drawn out.

Letting her tit go, I groaned loudly as I shot my load into her. I opened my eyes and looked at her beautiful face as she moaned. Her nails bit into my biceps as she gripped them tightly.

"I love you, Brooke." I leaned down and kissed her lips with a soft kiss. "Thank you."

She ran her hands over my cheeks as she looked at me with glistening eyes. "Thank you, Gannon. I knew it would be you who took me for the first time."

First time?

I wanted every time.

I kissed her again, an easy kiss that conveyed how much I cherished her. "If I have it my way, you'll give me every time. I can't see letting you go."

She smiled, her lips a bit swollen from all the kissing we'd done. I had to take those luscious lips just one more time. Hers opened, the tip of her tongue touching mine. Lightly, they danced, and I felt my cock pulsing back to life inside of her soaked depths.

The taste of her was something I honed in on as our tongues touched with tentative ease. Slowly, I wrapped mine around hers, moving it with soft strokes, actually tasting her. Her teeth were smooth against the sides of my tongue, and then I felt hers running past mine too as she began to moan.

Small pulses began around my cock as her body responded to our kiss. Easing my mouth away from hers, I moved to graze my teeth along the length of her neck.

Nipping at it, I drew in a breath before going to work at the soft spot just behind her ear.

Even the slightest touch she gave me left trickles of pure electricity in their wake. "I've never felt this way before, Brooke." I bit her neck, making her moan as she arched up to me.

Moving slow and easy, I started stroking my cock with her body. I was held so tightly, so completely, by her soft walls. Slick from our orgasms, I moved with so much more ease in and out of her tight little box.

Her soft lips ran over my shoulder as she pulled her legs up higher, allowing me to ease in a bit deeper into her. She moaned with the sensation, "Gannon, this can't be real. It's too unbelievable. I'm here—in your bed—in your arms."

I shivered with her words. "Yes, you are. I feel like you've always belonged here. With me, here, like this." I kissed my way to her cheek then tasted her lips for one brief moment before I pulled away to look at her. "You're beyond beautiful, baby."

The blue of her eyes sparkled like jewels as she smiled. Her cheeks were already red from my whiskered face, but they went a bit more scarlet as she blushed. "Gannon, stop."

Shaking my head, I rubbed my nose against hers. "No, I will not stop. You're amazing. And I've never felt so fucking happy in my entire life."

She giggled as she arched up to me. "Gannon, you're too good to be true."

I was so not too good to be anything. I was lucky as hell that she had let me into her heart, into her body, into her life.

There was so much to show her, to learn from her, to feel with her. Even as I moved my cock inside of her, I knew there was so much more I wanted to do. But I had to get some patience. There would be time to do all I wanted with her.

"This is real. We are real, Brooke. A real live, walking, talking, fucking couple." I took her lower lip between my teeth and tugged it, making her moan.

"Why does everything you do to me feel so fucking good, Gannon?" She ran her legs around me, holding me tightly to her. "Ugh! I could live like this right here with you forever, if it was possible."

"But it is," I growled as I went at her a little harder and a little faster. An eagerness to show her how it felt when things got a little rough filled me, taking me over as I made thrusts so hard, I could feel the air exit her lungs through her mouth.

I rolled over to put her on top of me. But when I went to push her to sit up so I could watch those size Ds bounce while she moved her tight cunt over my hard dick, she hung on tightly to me.

I rolled back over, pinning her to the bed underneath me and looking at her. Furiously, I thrust into her as I kissed her. Then I pulled her arms above her head, holding her down while I looked into her eyes and fucked her for all I was worth. "Keep looking at me, Brooke. I want to watch your face when I make you come all over my cock."

Her eyes went wide as she bit her kiss-swollen lip. She nodded and kept her eyes on mine.

Grinding into her soft core, I made sure my body was moving over her clit each time I was deep inside of her. She bit her lip harder as her body began to tremble.

I felt her insides clamping down on my cock and fought back the growl as long as I could. But then it erupted as she came all over me and I had no choice but to climax too.

Her face contorted as she found her release. She tried so

hard to get me to release her hands, but I held them down as I watched that perfectly sweet face go from shyness to one of desire and scorching hot sexiness.

I lifted my body up more so I could see her breasts as she gasped for air.

Gorgeous.

Absolutely amazing.

"Yeah, baby. Feel that. Take it all in. That's what it's all about. Getting to that place where nothing else matters but you and me." I kissed her once more before I released her hands.

Falling to one side of her, I tried to catch my breath as I listened to her trying to do the same thing. In a harsh, breathless whisper, I heard her sweet words. "Gannon, I fucking love you."

"Yeah, you do. And I love you, honey." The words, which I'd never said to any other woman until today, came totally easily. I clasped her hand tightly, intertwining our fingers. Bringing them up, I kissed hers. "We can sleep for a little while. Then I'll wake you up and make some more of your dreams come true."

She turned her head, and I saw a look I wasn't quite happy with on her face. "Gannon, I have to go back to my bedroom to sleep. Braiden's monitor is in there and ... well ... I don't want anyone to catch us like this."

"But ..."

She kissed me softly then pulled away, climbing out of my bed and grabbing her clothes, pulling them on as I laid there and watched her in utter confusion.

"But nothing, babe. I can't stay in your room with you. I don't want the staff to figure out what we're doing. You do remember what we talked about earlier, right? Keeping this a secret?" She picked up her bra and hid it underneath her shirt. "I had a great time. And I'm really glad we did this. There's no one else who could've ever been better. Night, babe."

"Brooke, I want you to stay. I don't want to hide this from anyone." I found my voice sounding too pleading. So I cleared my throat. "Brooke, baby, I love you. I want you with me. Here in my bed. A bed I hope you'll call our bed."

With a light giggle, she shook her head, making the golden waves bounce around her. "No, silly. Night. I'll see you at the breakfast table in the morning." She blew me a kiss and then she was gone.

My door closed and there I was alone and wondering when in the hell I had lost the upper hand.

CHAPTER 20

Gannon

T he next morning, my heart had never felt so light and full at the same time. I had had no idea love felt this way. My initial instinct was to head straight into Brooke's room and wake her with a long, sweet kiss, but I knew she had to be exhausted and so I managed to somehow resist.

As I straightened my tie, I noticed my cell lying on the nightstand. There was a message that I'd somehow missed.

It was from a number I didn't have in my contacts.

My eyes scanned it, and I froze suddenly.

-Drop the nightclub, or we'll kill your son. This is not a threat; this is a promise.-

Dropping, the phone, I ran to check on Braiden. Throwing the door open on the still dark room as the sun had yet to come up, I found him safe and still sleeping. Almost shaking with relief, I tucked one of his legs back underneath the blanket and kissed the top of his head before I left him again. As I strode down the hall, I called my bodyguard and told him I wanted him inside.

Samson had been with me since I was a teenager. He was in his early twenties and had been less than ten years older than me when my father hired him to be my bodyguard. He was adept at staying out of sight most of the time. He lived in a small house on the side of mine. To most, it looked like a toolshed. He liked it that way. Said he had the perfect perspective of both the front and the back entrances from where it was placed. Plus, no one would ever suspect he was right there, close enough to get to anyone who tried to get to me.

My mother referred to him as my guardian angel. Seldom seen, but always there.

He and I passed in the foyer as he came inside. "Stay with them today, Samson." I showed him the text.

"Got it, boss." He looked at me with those dark eyes that I knew had seen many horrors. An ex-Marine, I knew he had some stories that could curl my hair. But he never told me any. He and I weren't friends. He was my protector, and he took that job seriously. "And how about you?"

"They're more important right now." I shoved my hand through my hair. It was a nervous tic that I'd never learned to conquer. "See if you can find someone for me when you get time. I want you watching over them both. I know the threat is with my son, but his babysitter would definitely jump in front of a bullet for him. You'll have to keep her safe too. But don't let them know you're doing it just yet. Watch over them, but keep it covert. I'll talk to Brooke about it when I get back home."

"Yes, sir. I'm on it. They'll never know I'm watching them." He headed out of the room and stopped to look back at me. "You be careful, Gannon. I don't like leaving you unprotected. Maybe it would be better if you called the police and had them come out here."

"I don't want to upset Brooke with this. It might be someone the cops can easily find, since I have a phone number." I turned to leave. "I'll be fine. And I'll be on the lookout for anything out of the ordinary."

I could tell Samson wasn't taking this well, but he walked away to go watch over the people I loved the most in the entire world.

ON THE WAY to the police station, I made the calls to the other men involved in the nightclub. Neither had been contacted, it was just me, but they met me at the police station anyway.

With the vandalism, and now a threat like this one, it was more than obvious that someone wanted to end our nightclub. But for what reason, none of us had even the slightest clue.

We met in front of the police station just as the sun broke the horizon. The place wasn't bustling yet as we went inside. August looked tired, and I knew it was a bit early for him to be up.

"You know, I can probably handle this on my own, guys."

Both shook their heads as Nixon said, "No. We're all in this together. A threat on your kid isn't a thing we can sit back and allow you to deal with all alone. The only reason we weren't threatened is because neither of us has anyone in our lives who they could use to get to us."

August nodded in agreement. "That's right, Gannon. We're all in this together."

After waiting what all three of us deemed too damn long, we were finally able to talk to a detective. We had no idea he'd been assigned to the investigation of the incident that happened at the club. Detective Peterson had been on that case, and nothing had been found out. So none of us were happy with his work or the fact that they were sticking him on this thing too. The one thing he did manage to find out for us was that the number the text had come from was a dummy number, not real.

Leaving the police station, we all decided it was time to hire our own guys to get to the bottom of this.

August muttered, "Can you believe that guy?"

Nixon shook his head. "He's a joke."

We walked back to our cars that were parked in the parking lot, which had now become quite full as three hours had gone by and the day had officially started.

Pressing the key fob to unlock my car, I growled, "Who the hell in Vegas would care enough about what we're building here to go this far?"

The detective had had one idea in his ancient bald head. He had told us he was looking into the other owners of the upscale nightclubs in Las Vegas. He thought it had to be one or more of them who didn't want the competition our club would bring.

The old guy's exact words had been, 'There just aren't that many super-rich people on the entire planet who can afford to go to expensive clubs like that.'

If that's the way the detective that had been assigned our case thought, then we'd end up with nothing if we relied on only him to figure this shit out before something else terrible happened. Something worse, potentially.

"You head home, Gannon." Nixon jerked his head toward the car his bodyguard was in. "My guy will follow you to make sure you get there okay. We're going to have to make some changes here. Let our drivers take us where we need to go. Keep our bodyguards closer than we normally do. We can't underestimate who's doing this."

With a nod, I had to agree, "Yeah, you're right. I mean, we had the entire crew take lie detector tests, and none of them had anything to do with the explosive device that was set at the club. There's someone with some serious connections who has to be doing this."

"Either that," August added, "Or some completely inept person who has no idea what they're getting themselves into."

I had no idea which one it was, but I knew I'd find the motherfucker and make him pay for threatening my son.

CHAPTER 21

Brooke

Waking up the next morning with a dreamy smile on my face, I half wondered if I'd imagined everything. Then I tried sitting up on the side of the bed and groaned "Ow ..."

It definitely was not a dream. Everything hurt. Literally every part of my body, inside and out hurt. I had had no idea that sex used that many muscles in the human body. After last night, I must've burned every calorie I had in my body because I was also starving to death.

Slowly, I got up and hobbled to the bathroom that was attached to my bedroom. A hot shower limbered me up quickly.

After getting Braiden up and getting him cleaned up and dressed, he and I headed down to breakfast. I was feeling a little shy about seeing Gannon at the table that morning and pretending in front of the staff that he hadn't completely rocked my world the night before.

When I rounded the corner to the breakfast nook, I

found myself smiling away, not able to help it as I thought about seeing Gannon for the first time after our first time.

But I didn't see him at the table. I looked toward the kitchen, finding Consuela and the rest of her staff cooking away. "Has Gannon come down yet?"

All I got were a lot of shaking heads before Consuela asked, "What will you and Braiden be having this morning, ma'am?"

Looks like a steaming bowl of disappointment.

The hunger I had had vanished in an instant. "Um, scrambled eggs for us both. And don't forget his fresh fruit." I put Braiden into his high chair and tried not to show how sad I was that Gannon wasn't there.

Had he still been in his bedroom?

I should've knocked on his door and checked. But he always beat us getting up. But maybe last night's activities had him sleeping in. Maybe he was just worn out.

Whatever his reasons were for not being at the table that morning, I was sure he hadn't intentionally meant to hurt me.

Or had he?

Was this his way of telling me that he regretted what we had done? Or worse. Was this what all the other girls who'd ever fallen for his charms had experienced?

Now that he had had me, could it be that he didn't want me anymore?

God!

I sat down and tried not to look as if I was about to burst into tears, which I was on the cusp of. But I swallowed hard and thought about the fact that I didn't want anyone to see me breaking down for what they would see as no good reason at all.

But the man I loved, the man I'd given myself to, wasn't

at the damn breakfast table the one morning when I was positive he would be sitting there, waiting for me.

God, I was so stupid.

Brad had warned me. He'd tried to keep me from doing anything stupid with Gannon. But I'd fallen for the man's deceitful charms anyway.

What a fool!

Sarah came with a carafe of fresh coffee and one cup. One stupid cup!

I was about to tell her I didn't want any damn coffee. I only drank it because it made me feel like Gannon and I had a little connection. A thing I only did with him: drink coffee.

He wasn't there, and so I didn't want any. But I kept my mouth shut and even went so far as to add sugar and cream to the cup of steaming hot coffee like I always did.

I had to keep up the act of everything being perfectly fine. No one could ever know what had transpired between us. And if I acted the least bit off, I knew the people who watched us every morning would know something was going on between our employer and his babysitter.

Moments later, Sarah brought the food for Braiden and me. "Here you are, ma'am."

None of the staff referred to me as anything else other than ma'am. Ashe was the only one who called me Brooke. Everyone else regarded me differently.

Was that because they saw through me?

Was that because they secretly thought that Gannon and I were messing around and always had been?

Was I being foolish to think the people who were around us the most couldn't see how we looked at one another?

Perhaps the staff was aware of how we'd fallen in love

with each other. Perhaps they wouldn't tell a soul. Perhaps we could be open with our relationship within these walls.

If we still had one.

Why isn't he here?

Spooning Braiden's scrambled eggs into his bird-like waiting mouth, I tried not to think all the bad thoughts I was thinking. Gannon had to have his reasons why he had stood me up at breakfast.

He had to.

The familiar clicking of his shoes on the tile floor had me springing to my feet in relief, turning to see him with my arms almost flying open to embrace him, even though I'd ask to keep things a secret. Then when I saw him, I found him flanked by two massive men and took an uncertain step back. I hadn't heard their shoes clicking, only Gannon's.

When I saw his handsome face screwed into a terrible expression, I had no idea what to think. Was he bringing in his goons to have me removed from the premises? That was impossible. He might be a womanizer, but he surely couldn't be so cruel. Could he?

"Brooke, come with me," Gannon barked. "Consuela, see to Braiden. Don't let him out of your sight."

She hauled ass to the table while I stood frozen in place. Gannon's hand caught my upper arm, and I stumbled along with him. One goon stayed with Braiden, who was looking at all the new faces in confusion, close to crying, and one followed us.

My heart was pounding, and my mind had drifted into a hazed panic. *What the hell is happening?*

Gannon opened a door I'd never opened before, and we were inside an office. He closed the door, leaving the giant man on the other side of it. Only then did he take me into his arms. Arms I found were shaking, as was his entire body.

But at least he was holding me. He wasn't pushing me away emotionally or physically.

Thank God.

"Gannon, what's wrong?"

"Brooke ..." His breathing had gone ragged as his arms tightened around me. "I ... I'm sorry."

I had no idea what he was sorry about, but I was feeling much better now that we were in each other's arms again. "Gannon, talk to me."

He eased his tight grip on me, running his hands down my arms and taking my hands. A sofa ran along the far wall, and he took me to it, sitting me down on his lap.

Brushing my hair back, he leaned in and kissed my collarbone. "Brooke, someone has threatened Braiden's life."

The gasp that came out of me was completely unexpected, and the way my heart stopped was actually frightening. "Who?"

He shook his head. "We don't know."

I felt like I might faint. "How?"

He pulled out his cell to show me something. He'd received a text. Someone had sent him a message. Someone wanted him to end things with the club, so much so that they'd threatened his only child's life to make sure that happened.

"Believe me, if I thought shutting the club down would actually stop this then I'd do it in a heartbeat. But I don't think that will end anything." He put the cell back into his breast pocket and pulled me in for a hug. "We have to find this person and put a stop to things."

"How?" I realized I could only come up with one word at a time. My thoughts were all over the place, making it hard to think hard enough to say a whole sentence.

"My partners and I have hired an investigative team to

find whoever is doing this. We're sure it's the same person or people who were behind the explosive device at the club." His lips grazed my neck. "The bodyguards will have to be with us at all times until we find who's behind this. That'll mean no more sleeping together, no more making love if you won't let us go public with our relationship."

CHAPTER 22

Gannon

"N o," came her one-word reply.

"Brooke, you can't be serious. Baby, I need you more than ever now. You have no idea." Cupping the back of her neck, I pulled her close and kissed her sweet lips. Lips I found were quivering. She kissed me back, and I felt something wet move over my cheek.

She was crying.

Pulling back, I found her with tears rolling down her pink cheeks. "Gannon, we can't let my family know about us. We can't. It's for your own good."

"I'm not some kid, Brooke. I can handle your brother." I rested my forehead against hers. "Do you have any idea how I felt when I saw that fucking text this morning?" She shook her head and wiped her eyes with the back of her hand. "All I could think about was the fact that I had finally found love. Love for a son and love for a woman. I had a family. I've been alone for too long, with Mom and Dad gone. And I'm not alone anymore. Don't make me wait any longer, Brooke. Please."

I was pouring my heart out to someone for the first time in my life.

"You don't understand, Gannon."

I couldn't believe what I was hearing. So I pulled her to me and kissed her again. I wanted her to feel what we had. It was new, but it was strong. And it was real. Why couldn't she put her worries behind her and just let me take the brunt of her brother? I could handle him. I knew I could.

The kiss had her melting into me, stroking my hair with one hand and running her other hand along my shoulder.

Letting the kiss end, I rested my forehead against hers. "I have a meeting with Brad later today. Let me test the waters with him, Brooke. You'll see, I can show him that you've changed me. I'm not the man I was before you came to live with us here. And I'm completely and hopelessly devoted to you, just the same way I'm devoted to Braiden." Our lips met once more then I heard her sigh.

"Promise me you won't blurt anything out." She pulled back to look at me, taking my face between her palms. "You'll have to go in easy to make sure he's taking things well. If not, he'll beat the living hell out of you and come get me. I know my brother. He's irrationally protective when it comes to me. My whole family is, Gannon."

She proceeded to tell me some of the over-the top-things each and every member of her family had done for her and I had to admit there were some crazy things. But I was certain they'd all see the love I genuinely had for their little precious baby girl. She was that to me too, in a way.

She was my girl. My angel. I'd protect her the same way they did.

So, with her blessing, I left her and my son under the

watchful eye of Samson and went with my driver and the bodyguard Samson had called in to stay with me. Josh was also a veteran who Samson had a ton of respect for. Heading to the office for the meeting I was an hour late for, I was finding myself nervous over having to leave the two people I loved most behind.

The meeting lasted about an hour, and I asked Brad to go to my office with me. He hadn't noticed my bodyguard until we got to my office and Josh was suddenly there, standing by the door.

Brad jerked his head in a gesture at him as he asked me, "You're keeping him very close, Gannon. What gives?"

"Step inside, and I'll enlighten you." I opened the door and in we went. I wanted to enlighten him about a couple of things, actually, and had high hopes he'd take them both well.

Brooke's stories were kind of scary, but all those people had been nobodies to her family. I was Brad's best bud. He couldn't be that angry with me.

Brad went straight for the sofa, taking a seat. I decided that would be a great place to talk about things. So I took the chair that sat across from him. "Hey, you want a drink?"

He shook his head as he leaned up to rest his elbows on his knees and clasped his hands. "I wanna know why you've got your bodyguard all up on you. That's what I wanna know. And I wanna know if my sister is safe."

"She's very safe. I have my personal bodyguard watching over her and my son. Not to worry." I sat back, taking a more leisurely position. I didn't want him to get riled up in the least.

"So what's up?" he asked, still looking a little on the tense side.

I decided showing him the text would be a good place to

start, so I pulled out my cell. "There was an incident at the nightclub we're building. That, and this little text, are why I've amped up security around my son and me. And Brooke, obviously."

He took the phone I held out for him and read the text. His eyes were almost red, shooting flames out of them at me when he looked back up. "What the fuck, Gannon? I want her out of there right now!"

"Brad, she's fine. Samson is the best. They're in the best place they could be. I'd never let anyone hurt either of them. Brooke's important to me. Just as much as Braiden is. Of course, I have them under the best watchful eyes I have."

He tossed my cell back to me as he got up, towering over me. "Brooke's important to you?" His voice was a roar.

"Chill, dude," I said as I got up too. He wasn't about to tower over me.

"Chill?" his voice cracked as he shouted at me.

Josh opened the door and looked at me, silently asking if I needed his help. I waved him away without saying a word, and he closed the door. "Brad, you're overreacting."

"Overreacting? You have no idea. Something's not right there. You know your place isn't safe and you know you should be sending Brooke home, yet you're keeping her in harm's way. That tells me one thing and one thing only. You've got a hard-on for my baby sister."

My jaw dropped. Not because he was hitting the nail on the head, but because he was talking like I was some kind of a pervert. "Brad, would you listen to yourself? I'm keeping her where she is because she's much safer there. Plus, I still need help with my kid. Whoever is threatening me like this knows she's with me. If I send her off somewhere, then she'll be in danger and so will anyone she's around. Can't you see that?"

All he heard was one part of what I said though. "She's with you? She. Is. With. You?"

Fuck, had I really said those exact words?

"You know," I tried to fix my mistake, "she works for me. For my son. You know what I mean." I felt the fire from his eyes wash over me. He had that much power, I swear. Brook hadn't been wrong at all. Her brother could turn into a raging maniac over her.

"You might be right about her being safer under your guard. But I smell a rat, Gannon Forester. I smell a horny, oversexed, billion-dollar rat who wants to bone my little sister. And I've already warned you about doing so much as touching her." He slammed his fist into the palm of his hand.

I had to admit; he was intimidating. But I tried to play it cool as I lied, "Dude, I wouldn't harm a hair on your sister's head." That part was true, so it came out pretty easily. "I care about Brooke. I genuinely care about her."

He eyed me with a critical glare. "Do you? Do you care about her as an employee, or do you care about her as something else?"

Now I had to lie. "An employee. But also as a friend. I really like her. She's so pure. So real. You know?"

"And she's innocent, Gannon. She's not like the women you fuck around with. She's nothing like them, and she never will be. Not that I would give you the chance to make her into one of your flavors of the week anyway." He took three long strides to the minifridge and pulled out a beer. I watched in stunned indignation as he opened the brown bottle and turned it up, drinking it all down.

Well, he did need to calm the fuck down.

"I can't believe you think I'd hurt someone who means so much to you, Brad. It's kind of shitty of you to think so little of me." Okay, so what if I actually was screwing his sister? I loved her, damn it!

He tossed the empty bottle into the wastebasket and walked right past me. "I'm going to go see her. Ask her some questions about you. You coming?"

Oh, shit!

"Yeah, I'm coming, Brad. You'll see, she won't have anything but nice things to say about me. All this is for nothing. You'll see." I hoped he would see anyway. I hoped Brooke could pull off lying to her big brother.

CHAPTER 23

Brooke

The familiar clicking of Gannon's shoes was heard by Braiden, and he took off, running full speed to find his daddy. I was right behind him, running too. Then I slowed down as I heard another set of expensive shoes. Someone was with him.

I stayed behind Braiden, a few feet back. "Here he comes," I heard Gannon say. "There's my little man. Hi, son." I imagined him holding Braiden close, reassuring him after all the chaos of the day. The poor kid had been through so much already. I only hoped today wouldn't set him back after he'd made so much progress. We were even starting to move away from diapers to big boy undies.

When I made it to the foyer, I saw my brother was with Gannon. And he had that look in his eye that told me he was looking for information. Brad came toward me, and Gannon shook his head as he mouthed that he hadn't told him anything about us.

Fear ripped through me. I'd never lied to my brother

before. It seemed there was indeed a first time for everything. "Hi, Brad. It's nice to see you."

"You too, baby sis." He came up to me, pulling me in for a hug. "We need to talk," he whispered.

"K." I was on pins and needles as Gannon looked at me.

"I told Brad about what's going on here with the threat on Braiden. He was worried about you," Gannon said with a smile. "I told him I have the best man watching over you two and that you're every bit as important to me ..."

Brad butted in. "I need to talk to her alone, Gannon." He pulled me away with him. "Take me to your bedroom, little sister. I want to see where you sleep."

He was onto us. I knew he was. He wouldn't ask me to do such a thing if he wasn't. And the fact Gannon hadn't told him about us told me that when he'd tried to test those waters he had talked about testing, he'd gotten some pretty bad feedback.

Oh Lord, help me lie to my overprotective brother, please!

Leading him to my bedroom, I wasn't sure how I was going to handle things. I decided just to wait and see where he was going to go with this. "I hope you're not worried about me being here with this thing going on. I feel very protected with Samson around. It's so funny, I never even realized Gannon had a bodyguard before today. He stays out of the way so effectively that I never even knew he was around at all."

"Yeah, well, with a client like Gannon, a guard has to learn how to be invisible. Gannon couldn't bag all the chicks he has if they knew someone was right there, watching." Brad stopped just outside my door, looking at Gannon's bedroom door.

My stomach knotted as I thought about Gannon bagging chicks, as my brother had put it. "Um, this is it here." I opened my door, and he walked in backward, looking at Gannon's door the whole time.

"I thought his son would be in this one. I thought you might be in the next one." He turned and saw the door on the side of the room. "That one leads to the kid's room?"

"Yes," I said as I walked over and took a seat on my bed. I pointed at the chair in the corner. "You can sit over there if you'd like."

Instead of taking a seat, he meandered around my room, looking everything over. "So, how's he treating you?"

"Very well. He's very nice to me." I winced when he picked up a scarf I had hung on my mirror.

Gannon and I had taken Braiden out for a walk in the back of his property. I'd gotten hot with the scarf around my neck and pulled it off. Gannon had been feeling playful, and he had taken it from me and wrapped it around his neck. It smelled like him, and I kept it there so I could catch a whiff of him every now and then.

I found myself cringing when Brad pulled it to him, taking a big ole sniff. "Smells like cologne. Why's that?" He eyed me as he came up to me. Standing over me. "You know you can tell me anything, right?"

"Of course, I do." I smiled at him and batted my lashes. "You're my big brother."

"You'd tell me if Gannon did anything to you, wouldn't you? I mean anything. Has he touched you at all?" The way he looked at me told me he'd bolt out of the room and go whip Gannon's ass if I said one word to provoke him.

"No way! He's not like that. He's not the way you said he was with girls. With me, he's not, anyway. He's always respectable. You don't have anything to worry about. I swear that to you. Gannon is so nice to me, but he's not into me." I tried to look earnest even as my insides grew hot with my lies.

"Oh, he is." Brad placed his hands on my shoulders. "If you gave him a shot, he'd take it. So you can't give him that shot. You have to stay on guard. Never let it down. If you do, he'll swoop in and do to you what he's done to countless numbers of other unsuspecting girls."

There it was again, him referencing Gannon's conquests, and my gut twisted once more. I shrugged as if I couldn't care less. But I did care; I cared a lot. "Why would I do such a thing? He's old." I laughed and shook my head. "Yuck, Brad."

He laughed too. Then grabbed my hand. "That's what I needed to hear. Come on, let's go eat dinner."

I thought I had him fooled. I kind of hated that I had done such a great job of lying. But I was happy he believed me, and Gannon was safe. *For now, anyway.*

At least Gannon saw what I was talking about. I knew he had had no idea of how my brother could be over me. Brad must've shown him a bit of the bear he could become.

Finding Gannon and Braiden in the playroom, I smiled brightly at Gannon as I went to pick up Braiden. "Brad's staying for dinner."

"Great," Gannon said as he got up and we all went to the dining room. They hung back behind Braiden and me and I overheard Gannon as he said, "See, I told you. I wouldn't ever do a thing to hurt your sister. I care far too much for you and her."

"Yeah, well, you just keep that care legit, and we'll have no problem," Brad replied.

With an uneasy feeling about never being able to be truthful with my family, we sat down at the table to eat.

With Braiden in his high chair next to me, Brad watched as I interacted with the boy.

"Are you hungry, Braiden?" I asked him. I talked to Braiden all the time as if he was older than he was. No baby talking at all. And when he nodded at me, I was overjoyed with his response and had to hug him and kiss his cheek. "Yes! You nodded."

Brad laughed as he looked at the smile on Braiden's face. The boy was so proud of himself, probably just as proud as I was of him. "That kid loves you, sis."

"And I love him." I tickled the small boy's chin. "Don't I, pumpkin? Brooke loves her little man."

He giggled like crazy, and I caught Gannon gazing at me adoringly— a thing Brad could not witness. So I stopped what I was doing and sat back.

"She's amazing with him, Brad. It's like she and he were cut from the same cloth." Gannon reached over and ran his hand over Braiden's head. "He's lucky to have her. I can't thank you enough for letting us borrow her. But I don't think my little boy will ever let you have her back."

Brad nodded. "He looks at her like she's his angel, doesn't he?"

I blushed as I felt like the center of attention, a thing I wasn't comfortable being. "Come on, Brad."

"No, I won't come on, Brooke. He does. And you look at him like he's the center of your world." He sighed then reached across the table to pat my hand. "One day you're going to make a great mother."

"You think so?" I found myself asking him.

"I do." He moved his hand off mine then winked at me. "But it'll be in the faraway future. With a guy you meet later in life. After you're done with college and well into your career, then you'll meet a guy near your own age." He purposely looked at Gannon, then back at me, a thing Gannon noticed too.

"You're making her blush, Brad. Stop." Gannon reached out and patted the top of my hand in the same fashion as Brad had, trying to seem as if he treated me in a brotherly fashion.

It was hard not to look at Gannon, but I knew I couldn't trust myself to look at the man who had just made me his the night before. All I wanted to do was crawl up in his lap and continue where we had left off before he'd left for his meeting.

And I wanted to be truthful with what we had with my family too. But I wasn't getting much of anything I wanted. And more than anything else, I wanted to know for a fact that Braiden was safe. The threat he was under made my stomach ache.

What kind of a monster would threaten to kill an innocent child over a damn nightclub?

24

CHAPTER 24

Gannon

I had to admit; I didn't know my best buddy the way I thought I did. Brad wasn't Brad when it came to Brooke. He turned into the Hulk over that girl. And I knew we had our work cut out for us where her family was concerned. So I was into keeping things hush-hush for the time being. Just until I figured out what it would take to get her family onboard with us.

The two of us sat on either side of Braiden as I read him a book and watched him drift off to sleep. Closing the book, I looked at Brooke, who was gazing at my son. "The way you look at him makes me love you even more, baby."

Her lashes fluttered as pink stained her cheeks. "I love kids, but I truly love this little boy right here. He has my heart in the palm of his little hand. It hurts me so much that he's being threatened."

Getting up, I went to put the book back in the bookcase with the rest of the children's books that Brooke seemed to get more of with each passing day. She came to my side, and

I watched her breasts heave with a deep sigh. I knew there were so many things weighing on her mind. And all I wanted to do was give her a little time where nothing mattered at all, save she and I.

Taking her hand, I led her through the door between Braiden's bedroom and hers. "We've got two very capable bodyguards watching over us."

She stopped and looked at me as I closed the door to my son's room behind us. "Do you think you should be coming in here with Josh right there in the hall?"

I chuckled at her naivete. Pulling her into my arms, arms that had ached for too long without her in them, I smiled at her. "Do you think he cares, baby?"

"No, but ..." I kissed her to shut her up. She was young, still had an innocence about her, and had no idea what older people cared about.

Her mouth grew supple against mine. She parted her sweet lips to let me come in and in I came. Picking her up, I carried her to the bed, where I finally allowed our mouths to part. I fingered the delicate lace of the collar on her blouse. "You look beautiful today. I know I didn't get the chance to tell you that, but you do. This little blouse and that pale blue skirt look adorable on you."

Her lips quirked to one side. "But you'd like to ruin them as you rip them from my body, right?"

"Are you reading my mind, baby?" I placed two hands on either side of the chiffon blouse, yanking it apart. Small pearl buttons popped everywhere, showering her as she giggled.

I pushed one side of her pink bra up and took one of those delicious Ds into my hand then leaned over and pulled that pert nipple into my mouth, sucking it with a gentle pull. She moaned, and I sucked harder.

Her hands tangled up in my hair as she arched up, wanting me to take more. I ran my hand over the other tit, still covered in the pink silk of her bra. It was soft and smooth, and I massaged it through the fabric and sucked until she was bucking and begging, "God, Gannon, please!"

I stopped what I was doing to attend to her elsewhere, leaving her in that state, one tit bulging out from under the bra, one tit covered. Her face was pink with a desire for more.

Pushing her skirt up, I got on the bed. She watched me, her eyes glued to mine until I disappeared underneath her skirt. One hard yank had her panties breaking at the seams, leaving her pussy bare for me. She gasped with the action, a sound that was quickly followed by a low moan as I kissed her sweet pearl then licked the hooded organ.

Her knees tried to come together, so I had to hold them apart as I licked her over and over, kissing her in between the long licks every so often. When she began to shiver, I knew she was near the edge and inserted a finger so I could feel her close around me.

Heat flooded her and cum seeped out of her as she came, arching up and slurring a stream of curse words as her fists pounded the mattress. I was happy to hear her moans and groans. But I also wanted to hear some soft whimpers too.

Moving off her sweet mound, I got up and pulled the rest of her clothes off her, leaving her naked on the bed. Her body was all pink, flushed with the orgasm, and completely gorgeous. Her plump lips parted. "Gannon, can you teach me how to please you that way too?"

My cock—that was already hard—thumped in my pants, trying to get out. It seemed it was jumping at the chance to feel her soft lips on it. "You sure you're ready for all that, baby?"

She licked her lips and nodded, then sat up. Sitting on the side of the bed, she slowly unbuttoned, then unzipped, my pants. My tight black underwear covered the bulge, and she bit her lip as she pulled them down.

My cock sprang forth with excitement, eager for her mouth. She ran her hands over it then looked up at me. "Okay. Tell me what to do, please."

My stomach went tight with the thought. I'd never taught anyone how to suck cock. This was a first for me. And the idea that I would be teaching the woman I was truly thinking might be the last woman I'd ever have sex with had me feeling insanely happy.

I ran my hand over her head. "First, remember to sheath your teeth with your lips. You can allow them to graze it only very, very gently. But I'd rather you learn how to handle my dick better before you attempt that. This organ is extremely sensitive, as you might imagine."

She nodded then looked at my straining cock again. "Okay. Treat it that way. Treat it like it's fragile."

"Well, not fragile." I kind of hated to think of anything on me as fragile. "Just very sensitive. Give it a kiss, baby. Don't be shy. Get to know it."

She smiled at me then placed her pursed lips on the tip, kissing it with a soft kiss. I knew her lips would feel like satin. She peppered soft kisses all over the head, then up and down the shaft, letting her fingers move over my swollen balls.

Then I felt her opening her mouth, the heat of it flowing over my cock. The wetness of her mouth, the touch of her tongue as it slid underneath my dick, sent chills through me.

"Oh, shit!" I placed my hands on her shoulders to steady myself. "Damn, baby!"

It had never felt better. Not ever. What she did to me was far beyond what anyone ever had.

My fingers were curling into her shoulders, and I tried like hell to stop doing that as I was sure they'd leave bruises. So I moved my hands to the back of her head, threading her silky blonde strands between my fingers as she moved her mouth over me, making me feel like I was floating on air.

"Fuck, baby ... You're so good ..." a moan ended my words as she tickled my balls.

I was on a high I'd never been on before, and I didn't want it to end. But I felt the tell-tell signs that the end was indeed near. My cock jerked once and she kind of gagged with the sudden movement.

"Let me go, baby." I wanted to pull out of her, so I didn't jizz down her throat, even though she had mentioned wanting that in the beginning.

But she held me tight and hummed a little, sucking slow and strong until I shuddered and exploded, barely able to contain a shout that would've been heard all the way to the other end of the house.

Her tongue swirled around my pulsing cock, then she pulled her head back, licking what was left of my cum off her lips. "So, I did good then?"

"Good?" I shook my head as I pulled my shirt off and got rid of my shoes and socks before climbing on top of her. The shocked expression she wore had me laughing. "Great is the word I would use to describe what you did. Good just doesn't cut it." I settled my body between her spread legs, resting my quickly-recovering dick against her hot cunt. "Now tell me the truth. No lying now. Did you do a bit of studying about giving a blowjob?"

She blushed and smiled as she batted her long lashes at me. "I might've. You could tell, huh?"

"Baby, do all the studying you want to." My mouth fell on hers, and my heart pounded in my chest like a base drum.

I had myself the best woman any man could ever dream of having. And I had no intention of ever letting her go. Now how to get her brother and the rest of her family to actually allow that to happen?

CHAPTER 25

Brooke

As he laid on top of me, his cock at half-mast after he had come in my mouth, he looked into my eyes as he brushed my hair back. His lips came to mine, and he kissed me. Our unique tastes mingled together to create something altogether different. Uniquely us.

Love wasn't a thing I'd ever experienced. It was far better than I had ever dreamt it would be. Gannon was a miracle in my eyes.

As our kiss went deep and grew into something passionate, my body yearned for more. His cock thumped and pulsed back to a fully erect state and I pulled my knees up, urging him to press into me. I was sore from last night. But once he was all the way in, deeply seated inside of me, the discomfort went away, and all I felt was pure delight with him locked into me that way.

All day long I'd wanted to feel his body on top of mine again. That weight that made me feel a way I had never known was possible.

He moved inside of me with gentle thrusts that only made me crave feeling him move harder and faster. I ran my heel up the back of his leg and stretched my arm up over my head.

He threaded his fingers through my hand that was stretched above my head and pinned it to the pillow. His mouth kissed me with a hungry kiss then he pulled his head back and looked at me. "God, Brooke. I can't believe how much I feel for you."

My heart filled almost to the point that I thought it might burst as the beautiful man stared into my eyes. Never had I imagined seeing someone look at me with that much love in his dark blue eyes.

"I didn't know this was possible." My confession only made his expression seem even more loving.

"Me neither."

Could he be telling me the truth? How could a man who'd been with so many women say that and it be true?

"Gannon. My brother pointed out a couple of times today how you've had sex with a lot of women. If that's so, and I know it is—" I had to add that part. He had been with numerous women after all—"How can sex with me be something other than it was with any of the other women you had sex with?"

A slow smile burned a path across his chiseled lips. "I suppose because I am absolutely, one hundred and ten percent, in love with you."

And there it went. Even though he'd told me before, my heart now burst completely open.

Before I could utter one word, his mouth took mine again, and he moved inside of me a bit slower.

Arching up to him, I wanted him to give me more. Not be so easy with me. I ran my nails down his back, and he groaned, the sound vibrating my lips. He pulled back and moved his cock into me with harder thrusts.

I looked straight into his eyes and asked him for what I craved. "Will you fuck me, Gannon? Will you show me what that feels like?"

His eyes flashed, dark and hot. "You want me to fuck you?"

"Please." I knew I sounded slutty. But he'd just shown me that he loved me. I could see it and feel it. I knew it. "Take me the way you would anyone else."

He laughed then. "I can't take you the way I've taken anyone else. I love you. I've never loved any of the women I had sex with before you. You are truly my first love, Brooke." He kissed me. "But I can show you more. If you feel you're ready for more."

Oh, how ready I was!

"Please." I bit my lower lip. "Should we have a safeword?"

He rolled his eyes. "We're not going to get that crazy, baby. Not yet, anyway."

When he pulled out of me, I felt empty immediately.

He took me by the waist then flipped me onto my stomach. It happened so fast, I gasped. Then those same hands that had stroked my body with so much careful tenderness took my waist again, jerking me back until I felt his cock back in my pussy where I felt it hit me even deeper inside, stretching new parts of me. The burn that ripped through that virgin tissue made me scream. "Into the pillow, baby," he growled in my ear, biting my neck. "Scream all you want. But do it into the pillow. We don't want to wake up Braiden now, do we?"

His cock slammed into me as he gripped my hips, holding me still as he battered my ass. I could feel his balls as they banged up against my clit. Each thrust felt better than the one before it.

I had my face buried in the pillow, making noises I had had no idea I could make. A high-pitched wail, a tiny whimper, and some guttural sounds I felt were primal in origin.

In mere moments, I was riding an orgasm, and he wasn't stopping. I moaned as he kept plowing into me. That orgasm barely waned when another took me over by surprise. I cried into the pillow. Real tears. I had no idea why I was crying. It wasn't because it hurt.

Nothing hurt.

But every last part of me was on full throttle. I could feel him in every last part of me. My fingertips, the tip of my nose, my elbows, for the love of God!

He was encompassing me as he made me come over and over until I was nothing but a shaking mess. Every nerve ending I had was pulsing with sheer ecstasy. I had had no idea, truly, no fucking idea, it could be this good. This amazing. This emotional.

I could feel his cock inside of me, and I knew when he was near his own end. Somehow—I don't know how—he got harder. Moved faster. Then. Bam!

He made the most awful slash best sound I'd ever heard. It was like complete satisfaction coupled with exhaustion, surrounded by pure agony. It was the best sound I'd ever heard.

And I'd made him make that delightfully agonizing sound.

I was satiated and proud at the same time.

I shivered at the thought. He dropped to the bed beside me, huffing and puffing, and I laid my body on his, panting with satisfaction.

"Oh, how much I love you, Gannon Forester." I kissed his chest.

One heavy hand fell on my head then moved through my hair, pulling it as it went. "And I love you, Brooke."

So that was it. We were head over heels in love. And not a soul could know about it.

CHAPTER 26

Brooke

Although I was beyond wiped out with the most intense orgasm I'd ever had, I managed to kiss Brooke one more time before settling in so I could fall asleep.

One thought was drifting through my mind as I waited for sleep to pull me under and listened to the sounds of Brooke as she laid on my chest. How could I make her family see that I loved her with everything I had in me?

Smash!

Zip!

My eyes flew open as Brooke asked in sharp words, "What the hell was that?"

Another smash, another zip, and I knew what I was hearing.

"Fuck!" I moved us both off the bed, the blanket and sheet coming with us as I let my back hit the floor.

Holding her tight, I moved her onto her stomach as she hissed, "Were those bullets?"

"I believe so." I could only think about one thing. *Get. To. My. Son.* "Stay low and let's get to Braiden."

We moved quickly despite the bulky material that tried to hinder our progress. I had to reach up to open the door, and then I knew for certain that whoever was outside could see us as another bullet ripped through the window. "Shit, Gannon!"

Once I had the door open, Brooke sprinted forward, grabbing Braiden off his bed where he was standing, crying, and pinning him underneath her naked body. I was right behind her and tossed the blanket from his bed to cover her as I shouted, "Josh!"

The bedroom door opened and Brooke yelled, "On the floor. He can see you!"

Without missing a beat, Josh fell to the floor just as another bullet came through my son's window. "Fuck!" He pressed a button on his walkie-talkie. "Samson, where the fuck are you?"

There was no answer, and I felt sick inside. "Shit."

Brooke glanced at me sideways. "I'm sure ..." Another bullet cut her off, and the light in the hallway went out.

We both jerked our heads and saw Josh was still on the floor, so who the hell had turned the lights off?

"Get the fuck out of there, Gannon." It was Samson, and I was damn glad to hear his voice.

Braiden was crying in shock and terror, which only served to infuriate me further. I would kill the person who had frightened my son so badly. I vowed it.

I ducked and cursed as we both hurried to get across the hallway, with Brooke whispering reassuring words to our boy that it was all going to be okay.

The rooms across the hall were all interior rooms, which meant there were no windows anyone could shoot through.

When we made it out into the hallway, we found Samson all dressed in black, with a black ski mask covering his face. Gun drawn, he was moving into Brooke's bedroom.

I wasn't about to wait to see what he was going to do, so I opened the door to my room, and Brooke, Braiden, and I were finally in a safe place as we crawled into my room.

Wrapping the blanket around my waist to cover myself up, I took a hysterical Braiden from Brooke, He looked so tiny and fragile, crying in my arms. "Daddy's got you, baby. You're okay. Shh." I rocked with him and shushed him, whispering words similar to Brooke's earlier, until he finally seemed to calm down a little and burrowed his little face in my neck, clutching my shirt fiercely with his tiny fists, as if to make sure that I never let go of him again. My heart lurched at how much I loved this child. How had I ever existed without him in my life?

When I finally looked up, I found tears streaming down Brooke's face. "Why? Why, Gannon?" she sobbed. "Who would do this?"

"Believe me, baby, if I had the slightest clue, the fucker would be dead already." I held my son and continued rocking. Not really for him, as he'd fallen asleep, but to calm myself.

I didn't see Brooke move around behind me. Her arms closed around me as she hugged her body against my back, swaying with me. "It's going to be okay. I love you both so much. We're going to be fine."

How did I get so damn lucky?

A knock came to my door, then Samson's voice called out, "Can I come in?"

Sniffling, Brooke pulled away from me, made sure the blanket was still covering her up, and she got up to walk around me as I sat on the floor, holding my son. She gave me a nod, and I told him to come in.

Samson's eyes never let either of us know he knew what we were doing. He just looked the same way he always did. "I got a shot in that nicked whoever the hell that was. His right bicep was hit. I've already called the police to inform them of that, so if the assailant goes to any doctor or hospital, he'll be detained and taken in for questioning."

I could only nod. I had no idea what to ask or say. But Brooke had a question. "And how did he get all the way around this huge house and into the backyard to pull this little feat off? Where were you?" She leveled her eyes on him, and I did not envy the man.

He looked down and pinched the bridge of his nose. "The can."

"I see." She looked away. "I'm sorry I spoke that way to you, Samson. I am. It's just that the boy means more to me than you could ever imagine. And we could've ..." She tried so hard not to fall apart, but she couldn't hold it back. "We nearly lost him, Samson." She sobbed and ran into the bathroom.

I looked up at my bodyguard as I nodded. "You did all you could. Thank you. At least you hit him. Now we have something to look for. And you will step up security around here. I want a lot more people around."

"I'm already on it, boss. You guys get some sleep." He left me then, and I looked down at my son as tears filled my eyes.

Brooke was right. We could've lost him.

When she came back out, she had on one of my t-shirts. I kept some in one of the drawers in the bathroom along with some loose-fitting boxers, and I found some black plaid peeking out from under the white t-shirt that told me she had pulled a pair of them on too.

"Can I sleep with you tonight?"

"You both are. I'm not about to let either of you out of my sight, baby."

She came to me, taking Braiden out of my arms, carrying him to the bed, where she laid him right in the middle. "I'll sleep on one side; you sleep on the other."

I went into the bathroom to clean myself up a bit before putting on a t-shirt and boxers myself. Splashing my face with cold water, I looked at my reflection.

A few wrinkles were etched across my forehead, a thing I hadn't had before becoming a father.

I was finding out that with love for anyone came something else. It made a person subject to threats that were different than when they only had themselves to worry about.

I'd barely gotten my son, and already someone had figured out a way to get to me. A coward who didn't want to face me.

I knew it was someone who didn't want the nightclub ever to open. But why?

None of it made any sense.

A lone gunman came to my home. One person had hidden amongst the work crew at the bar to place the explosive under that bar. It didn't sound like the work of anyone who owned any of the upscale nightclubs in Vegas.

Then who?

"Gannon?" Brooke softly called to me.

I went into the bedroom to find her lying on her side, facing Braiden. "His pants need to be changed. He'd been doing so well, but with all the fear ... Do you think you could go to his room and grab some clean pants and the wipes for me?" She cut her eyes away. "I'm afraid to do it myself. And I don't want to leave him alone for one second either."

I gave her a smile as I headed to the door. "Daddy's on it." I stopped and turned back to look at her as she nestled in close to my son.

I kept saying my son. But the truth was right there, staring me in the face. That boy was every bit as much hers as he was mine. They might not have shared blood as he and I did. But they both were so deep inside the other's heart that it made them mother and son.

I had a lot of shit to do. Find this son of a bitch who had gone way too fucking far. And make that woman—the only woman I had ever loved—mine. And once she was mine in all the right ways, then I'd be giving Braiden her as his mother too.

Both of them deserved that. And so did I.

27

CHAPTER 27

Brooke

After not sleeping well at all, I finally gave up on the dozing and pulled my eyes open. When I did, I found Gannon was also awake. Wide awake and sitting up in bed, looking at something on his cell.

"Morning," I croaked out in a whisper.

He looked at me and smiled, then handed me a bottle of water. "Morning, beautiful."

After taking the bottle from him, I sat up and took a long drink while running my hand through my tangled hair.

God, I must look awful.

My first time waking up with the man, and it had to be after a night like last night.

Looking at Braiden, I was glad to see he was still fast asleep, making little snoring sounds.

I laid back down and tried not to feel so depressed about the situation, but it wasn't going to be an easy task to just act like nothing terrible had happened. Gunshots into my bedroom and Braiden's couldn't be ignored.

Thanksgiving and my birthday were mere days away. With some madman on the loose, there was no way we could go to my family's home and put them all in danger.

"I suppose we should tell Consuela to make plans to make Thanksgiving dinner here, Gannon." I rolled off the bed to get up and go pee.

As I passed by him, he caught my hand. Our eyes met, and his were chock full of guilt. "Baby, I'm so sorry I got you in the middle of this. I swear I'll make it up to you. I never intended to make you miss the holidays with your family or your birthday. I really am ..."

I couldn't let him go on, and leaned in to kiss him. When our lips parted, I said, "I know, babe. Don't worry about that at all. There are so many more important things to worry about. Let that crap go."

He let my hand go, and I went into the bathroom. My hair was a wreck. It was absolutely everywhere, and I groaned at my reflection. And I marveled at Gannon's ability not to laugh or grimace at me. Hell, he'd even accepted a kiss from my dry lips and disastrous appearance.

He must really love me!

I needed to go across the hall to my room to shower and get dressed, but I was afraid to go in there. Shaking my head, I looked at myself in the mirror and gave myself a pep-talk. "You cannot be a chicken, Brooke. Go into that room and do what you have to do. Then go into Braiden's room and get him some clothes."

With a bit of courage settling in, I did my business and then went back out to Gannon's bedroom. I found Braiden had woken up and he'd crawled into his father's lap and was watching a cartoon on the cell. "Morning, pumpkin." I headed over and gave him a little kiss on top of his head. "I need a shower. Do you have him for a little bit?"

"I do." Gannon reached out and took my hand again. "Go grab both of you something to wear, then come in here to take a shower. I'll feel much better with you guys close to me."

So he was feeling the same way I was. Like we'd somehow gotten ourselves right in the middle of a warzone. With a nod, I left the room.

As soon as I got into the hallway, I noticed both Braiden's door and mine had been left open. I went into my room and found bits of glass sparkling on the beige carpet when I turned the light on.

It was dark in there even though I knew the sun had to be up already. Looking toward the windows, I found boards had been placed over them. The sounds of the bullets that had ripped through the room came back to me.

I looked from the window to the other side of my room and found holes in the wall where the bullets had lodged. Thankfully, none had lodged in any of us. I went to my dresser and pulled out some underclothes then got a dress out of my closet and a pair of heels.

Being careful not to step on any shards of glass, I went to Braiden's room and gathered him some clothes too. His windows were boarded up too, and I found a lump form in my throat.

We could've lost him.

I shook my head to get rid of the thought.

We hadn't lost him or anyone else. I had to be thankful for that and be aware of the fact that we were also very lucky that no one had gotten hurt.

Well, except the gunman. Or gunwoman.

Who was to say that it wasn't a woman? Maybe some woman from Gannon's past who wanted revenge for being just another notch on his bedpost.

I headed out of the bedroom with my arms filled with our things and went back into Gannon's room, finding him playing with Braiden, wrestling around on his big bed.

"I'll take a quick shower then bathe him." I placed Braiden's clothes on top of the dresser. "Oh, does he need his diaper to be changed before I do that?"

Gannon was all smiles as he nodded toward the balled up white diaper next to him on the nightstand. "I did it already."

I was a little stunned. He'd never changed a diaper before. "Oh. Wow."

"Yeah, I know. It was a little bit of an ordeal, but I figured it out. But honestly, he needs a bath, so changing him was slightly pointless." He chuckled as Braiden crawled over the bed to get to me. Gannon grabbed him by the ankle, pulling him back to him as the boy giggled with delight. "Hey you, stinky man. She has to get into the shower. You're staying here with me."

"I'll hurry." I turned to go into the bathroom.

"No, you take your time. He's fine with me."

Heading into the bathroom, his bathroom, I noticed all the things that were uniquely Gannon inside it. The shampoo was crisp and clean smelling. The soap was spicy-scented. And I ended up smelling just like the man once I was done.

I pulled his brush through my hair, put his toothpaste on my toothbrush, then used his mouthwash too. Nothing was the same as the stuff I used.

At first I felt out of sorts with the tastes and smells being so different from my normal morning rituals. But then I felt just the opposite. I felt like I'd immersed myself in the man.

And I felt sexy as hell too.

Before leaving the bathroom to get Braiden, I started a bath for him. When I went out to get him, I found him cuddled up on Gannon's broad chest, listening to his daddy tell him a story he'd made up.

I couldn't stop the smile that spread all over my face. Gannon was fast becoming the best daddy in the history of daddies. "How cute."

Neither Braiden nor Gannon had even noticed me until I spoke. But when both of their heads turned to look at me, and nearly identical smiles curved their lips, my heart raced.

I had two of the best-looking males on the planet giving me heartbreakingly gorgeous smiles. What had I done to deserve all of this?

Braiden was intent on getting to me this time and made a mad dash off his father's chest to do it. I had to run to catch him before he careened off the side of the bed. Between Gannon and I, we managed to catch the little bugger.

I scooped him up in my arms and shook my head at him. "Braiden! You silly boy. You could've fallen off the bed and broken your neck. You have to be careful with yourself."

Despite my scolding, the boy hugged me, kissed my cheek, and squealed in delight. Gannon chuckled as he watched his son go gaga over me. "Damn, girl. Looks like you have all the Forester men head over heels for you."

I felt the heat in my cheeks as I blushed. "Oh, you sweet talker." I turned away, heading to the bathroom to bathe his son.

The sound of the blankets whooshing let me know Gannon was getting out of bed. Then his hands were on either side of my waist, and his bare chest was against my back. His lips were on my neck, and I heard him taking a big sniff. "Um, you smell like me. I kind of like that."

"Do you now?" I had to giggle as his whiskered cheek brushed mine as he kissed my cheek.

Braiden chided his father for kissing my cheek and placed his hand on his daddy's face, pushing him away. Then he kissed the same place his father had, marking me as his own.

I laughed and put him down to undress him as Gannon went to brush his teeth.

As I pulled off the little boy's clothes and picked him up, putting him into the bathtub that I'd filled with warm water and his favorite bath bubbles, I thought about how domestic this was.

Daddy brushing his teeth, Momma bathing the child. So damn domestic.

But I wasn't Braiden's mother. No, his mother was a horrible creature.

The child wasn't any trouble at all. He was loving, funny, a joy to be around. How could she just have thrown him away?

Or had she actually been throwing him away at all ...

It occurred to me that the first shots hadn't gone into Braiden's room. They had gone into mine. Now, why would someone threaten the boy but take a shot at me?

"Gannon, has anyone talked to Braiden's mother about this?" I looked back to find him staring back at me through the mirror.

"Hmm. No. I mean, I didn't give the police any information on her. Why? Do you think she might have something to do with this? And why would she? She only wanted to get rid of what she called a burden. Why make this threat?" He shook his head. "I can't see her being involved."

"I have this little nagging thing in the back of my mind that says to tell your investigators to check the woman out,

Gannon." I turned back to Braiden, and my heart hurt even more for the kid.

It was bad enough what she'd already done to both Braiden and Gannon. Could she have a plan that was even worse than what she'd already done?

CHAPTER 28

Gannon

We came down for breakfast only to find Samson had cleared out my staff and there was no breakfast. Only he and Josh stood in my kitchen, talking quietly.

I cleared my throat, making them stop talking and turn their attention us. "And my chef and her staff are where exactly?"

Samson picked up a brown paper bag off the countertop and headed our way. "We've turned everyone around at the gate. I think it's best not to have too many people around here until we catch this guy." He placed the bag on the table as I put Braiden in his highchair. "I stopped while I was out and got you guys some bagels and lox. You like that. I've seen you eat it a ton of times."

"Yeah, that's great. Thanks, Samson." Brooke pulled the things out of the bag and looked at me as she put the packaged food on the table. "I can make us something. Don't worry."

She hurried to the kitchen and looked at the coffee machine. I knew it was way out of her league. "Don't worry about that."

With a shake of her head, she looked around until she found something in the drawer underneath it. "The instructions are right there. I'll figure this all out. Don't worry. Just help Braiden eat a bit of that until I get his oatmeal and fresh fruit please." She busied herself with preparing Braiden's nutritious meal as she made sure he always ate things that were good for him. Bagels and lox were not going to cut it for his morning meal. Not by Brooke's standards.

I waved my bodyguards over while she moved about in the big gourmet kitchen with state of the art appliances. I'd written down Cassandra Harrington's address and phone number on a piece of paper. Taking it out of the pocket of my blue jeans, I pushed it across the table to Samson. "That's someone I want you to check out."

I looked around Samson to make sure Brooke wasn't listening to me and found she was so wrapped up in what she was doing that she wasn't paying any attention to us at all. "That's the boy's mother. I doubt she has anything to do with this, but I think she should be checked out all the same."

Samson nodded. "Yeah, that would be best. Leave no stone unturned." He hitched a thumb back at Brooke. "You know it's best for her not to leave, right?"

"Of course." I nodded, and felt tremendous guilt about that fact. All the rest of the staff had been allowed to stay away from the danger, but not her. And all because she and I had fallen in love. It wasn't fair to her, and I knew that.

My cell rang, and I looked at it, finding Brad's name there. "Shit!"

Then Josh's walkie-talkie went off. One of the outside guards said, "We have a Brad Moore here. He's demanding he be let inside."

I swiped the phone to answer Brad's call. "I'll talk to him."

"Hey, what the hell is up?" Brad asked me with a terse tone.

Pinching the bridge of my nose, I got ready to hear a stream of curse words after I said what I had to say. "We're fine. Your sister is fine. She's safe. That's what's really important here."

"What the fuck happened, Gannon?" I'd never heard him sound like that. It was as if he was deflated.

"Someone shot at the house last night." I held my breath, waiting for the explosion.

But all I got was a low groan. "God, Gannon. My God. Are you guys all right?"

"We are." I took a deep breath, knowing I had to tell him more. "The first bullets came through your sister's window. The next ones came through Braiden's."

"Fuck!" His one sharply said word echoed in my ear. "Why her, Gannon? The threat was against the kid. So why her window?"

"I wish I knew. I do know this; my bodyguard got in a shot that caught the gunman in the arm. That's at least something for the investigators to look for. I'm not relying solely on the police. I have a team of private investigators on this as well. And your sister, my son, and I are staying put in this house until the suspect is found and put into custody. I won't be leaving them alone at all."

"Gannon?" Brad stopped, and I knew he was hesitating to say what he had to say. "Fuck. Goddamn. I can't believe I'm fucking saying this to you. I want you to keep my sister right with you at all times. Don't let her be away from you at any time. Even when you guys go to sleep. And don't you dare fucking touch her. You hear me?"

"Loud and clear." How badly I wanted to let him know that I loved his sister and I'd die before I let her get hurt. I did the second-best thing. "She means more to me than you know. I'd never let anything happen to her. I swear that to you, Brad. I'd take a bullet for the girl. The same way I would for my son."

"You better." He sighed heavily. "Fuck this shit, man. All right. I'm leaving. But you keep me posted about what's happening. And you take care of my baby sister, Gannon Forester."

I gulped as I could hear the cracks in his voice. This was killing him. "I will, and I'm so damn sorry, Brad. You can't imagine how sorry I am."

"I know, buddy. I do. I can hear it in your voice. Just take care of her. Please." The desperation that etched his voice was evident.

"You got it."

After ending the call, I saw Brooke coming to the table with coffee in one hand and the bowl of oatmeal in the other, a bottle of apple juice tucked under her arm. "So how's my brother taking this?" She put everything down then took a seat.

I noticed she hadn't brought one thing for herself. And I also noticed Josh had taken off and Samson was on his cell, talking to someone. I hoped like hell they'd find something out today. I was damn tired of the situation and just wanted it over with.

She went straight to giving Braiden a drink of juice then spooned oatmeal into his waiting mouth. "Is my big boy hungry?"

She was so wrapped up in feeding Braiden that she didn't notice me. I didn't know how to cook, not even a little bit. But I knew Consuela kept frozen meals she prepared in advance. She wanted me to have access to food even when she wasn't available to cook for me. Like at night, after she'd left for the day.

I had no live-in staff. My parents had had some of their staff live with them, but I preferred to be alone inside my house at night. Samson was on guard in his house, so I wasn't completely alone.

After heating up a meal of a cheese omelet and some bacon, I plated it and took that, along with a cup of coffee and some apple juice, to her. She'd just about finished feeding Braiden and turned to look at me as I placed everything in front of her. "Here you are, my queen."

Her smile lit me up inside. "Gannon, you didn't have to do that." Then she looked at the meal a bit more closely. "Wait, how did you make this?"

With a chuckle, I shook my head. "I'm not telling you." I leaned in and kissed her cheek. "I'm magic. Now eat. I'll finish up with Braiden."

She looked at me with a wide smile on her beautiful face. "What did I do to deserve you?"

I walked around the table to take the seat on the other side of my son. "You're an angel. I'm the one who has to wonder what I did to deserve you, baby."

She took a bite, then a drink of the coffee. Pointing her fork that had another chunk of cheesy egg on it at me, she said, "You know what, Gannon? I just keep thinking that woman has to have something to do with this. So tell me what kind of a custody agreement you two have."

"I have it; she doesn't." I cut a blueberry in half then gave Braiden a bite of it.

"Okay. In the case of your demise, who gets custody then?" She ate the bite off the end of her fork as she looked at me.

My head swam a bit as I thought about that. I'd read the legal agreement and recalled that it said that in the event of my death, custody would revert to her.

"Brooke, she'd get him. I can't let that happen." I looked at my son and knew I couldn't ever let her get her hands back on him. Then I looked at Brooke. "I have to get that changed. But there's only one person I'd want to leave him with. And that's you."

She looked grim as she said, "That's not what I'm thinking about, Gannon. I'm thinking she orchestrated everything. The fact that she was going to dump him. The fact that she didn't want anything from you. She never wanted just child support. She wants it all. Every last bit of it. With you out of the way, she gets her son back and all of your wealth, as he's your only heir."

My blood ran cold in my veins as I knew she was right.

CHAPTER 29

Brooke

As the day dragged on from morning until noon, I wasn't exactly happy with the results Gannon's investigators had come back with.

They'd talked to Cassandra Harrington early that morning. They thought she acted kind of suspicious, but she had a solid alibi for the night before. A man who was at her place with her had verbally vouched for her.

But that wasn't cutting it for me, even though they said they'd keep her on their radar, whatever the hell that meant.

We were in the playroom after giving Braiden lunch. He went down for a nap, and Gannon was working on his laptop, taking care of his business from home. I got on my cell and started texting my sister.

Brianna was an avid mystery reader and an amateur sleuth. I thought some covert work would be right up her alley. And I was spot on when she responded to my first text that asked her if she'd heard about what was going on with me and Gannon and Braiden. She was quick to reply that I needed to call her. We had to talk.

So I excused myself to go to the bathroom and went to the one down the hallway, leaving Gannon and Braiden in the playroom.

As soon as I knew I was out of earshot from everyone as I closed the bathroom door, I made the call to my sister. "What the hell is happening, baby sis? Brad's called everyone, telling them about you and the ordeal you're going through. Is it true that bullets came into your bedroom last night?" she asked.

"Right through my window." I chewed on my pinky fingernail nervously. "It was the scariest thing I've ever been through."

"You've got to tell me all about it. Every last detail."

I told her all about it, leaving out the little detail that Gannon had been right there with me every step of the way. But I did tell her that Braiden and I had slept in Gannon's bed with him for the rest of the night as he wasn't going to let either of us out of his sight. That was true, after all.

When she responded that she was glad he was taking such good care of me, I felt like a tiny step had been made. At the very least, my family was seeing that Gannon could protect me.

I went on to tell her about Cassandra Harrington, and Brianna looked her up on the Internet and found out there was a park near her house. She could go there and keep an eye out for Cassandra to come out of her house. Then she could follow her and accidentally meet her. She'd get moving and let me know as soon as she knew anything.

Heading back to hang with Gannon while Braiden slept, I found him coming down the hallway as I stepped out of the bathroom. "There you are." His brow was furrowed, and he rubbed the back of his neck. "I know I'm being overly protective, but if anything happens to you ..." He stopped himself as I got to him and ran my arms around him. His lips touched the top of my head, and he wrapped his arms around me, swaying with me. "I see why your family is so protective of you now. You're just so darn loveable." He gave me a squeeze as he picked me up, my feet dangling in the air.

He carried me back into the playroom and took a seat on one of the sofas, keeping me on his lap. Braiden was still fast asleep on his pallet. We were mostly alone, and I saw the gleam in Gannon's blue eyes.

His lips touched my ear. "Wanna fool around very quietly?"

"Gannon!" I smacked his chest as I blushed with the thought of doing anything sexual with the boy right in the same room with us. I didn't care if he was sleeping or not, it felt wrong. My eyes shot to where he was and then back to Gannon. "No way."

He looked at Braiden and smiled. "He's dead to the world, baby. Come on." He pulled me close and nibbled my earlobe. "Even daddies need naughty time."

I had to laugh at his silly ways. And his love bites were working magic on me. "What did you have in mind?" I found myself asking, then quickly added, "Not that I'm saying okay or anything like that. I just wondered what you had in mind."

His teeth grazed my neck, then soft lips pressed the spot just behind my ear. My thighs shuddered as heat swept through me. "That dress will make things pretty easy to get to and pretty easy to hide stuff we might or might not be doing." He turned me around, facing away from him, and spread my dress out where I felt my panty-covered ass sitting on his bulging male member. "See what I mean?"

"I do, but I don't ..." The touch of his mouth on my neck as he reached around, cupping my boobs, had me going silent.

I went so wet, it was insane. "Gannon, no," the words were said, but there was absolutely no conviction in them. "We can't."

"I need you, honey. Please." He could've been manipulating me to get his way, but the fact was, I wanted it to. And I could see in his eyes that after everything we'd been through, this was a reassurance he badly needed to know I was still whole and safe. And I needed to know the same about him.

His hands moved down, and I felt him doing something underneath my ass. Then I felt the warmth of his bare flesh against my cheeks as he pushed my panties to one side. "Sure we can, baby." He moved his erect cock around my ass, and I moaned softly. "Now, I want you to move up a bit and come down slowly on what I have for you." He pulled my hair to lie over the other side and kissed the spot where my neck and shoulder met. "If he starts to stir, you'll see him, and we can stop."

So, with my eyes glued to the sleeping child across the room, I did as he said to and had to hold in the moan that wanted to come out as I slid myself over his cock. We both went silent as he moved me, holding me by the waist as he kissed my neck.

What I felt was crazy. Sort of reckless and very, very bad. I could see what girls saw in bad boys then. They were hot as hell!

I was on the verge of an orgasm from the get-go. With

the threat of Braiden waking up and ending it all, I was ready to explode if he made the slightest movement.

Gannon's mouth was working wonders on me as he went from scraping his teeth over my skin to sucking it in places that had my toes curling inside my shoes.

The way he picked me up with ease made me feel weightless in his strong hands. Before I knew it, I was coming all over him, moaning quietly and then holding down a scream as he came inside of me with a hot burst and a hard bite to my neck.

His tongue trailed up my neck then flicked into my ear. "I love you, Brooke."

I laid my body back, resting it on his. "I love you too. Damn, baby. Damn. I've got to go get cleaned up a bit."

His hands trailed down my arms as he leaned his head on my shoulder. "You do that. I'll be right here. I can clean up in the bathroom right here."

One of his hands moved up, and he pushed my face to the side. Then our lips met, and I felt his cock pulse inside of me. Oh, the man was good.

But we both heard Braiden as he turned over. I hopped off Gannon. "Damn. I'll be right back," I whispered, then ran out of the room to go to my room.

As I ran down the hallway, I thought I heard something, and when I ran into my bedroom, I stopped as I saw someone was inside. A man was fixing my window. "Oh, hi," he said. "Almost done with this one."

Fuck me!

"Oh, great." I tried to act all cool. "I gotta grab something real quick." I opened my top drawer and balled up a pair of panties in my hand until you couldn't see them at all. "Bye." I went into Gannon's bedroom and went to his restroom to clean up and change

Just as I finished up, my cell rang, and I saw it was my sister already calling me back.

"Hey," I answered the call.

"Oh, baby sister. This woman has to have something up her sleeve," she began. "I talked to Brad and got the back-story on Gannon's baby momma."

Oh, I did not like her calling that woman that. Not one bit. "K. First, don't call her that. Call her bitch, or whatever, but not that."

"Hmm." She paused. "Okay. Well, this bitch and I met in the park where I joined her for a run. And it was more than easy to get her talking. Her first and only subject was how much she missed her little boy. His mean old rich daddy stole him from her after she introduced the two. She said she's been a single mother since she found out she was pregnant and that she only recently let the daddy know about the boy. She was feeling guilty about not letting him know."

"No way." I chewed my pinky nail again as I listened.

"Yep. And there's more," Brianna went on. "She said she's been sneaking out there and peeking in the windows. She wanted to make sure her little boy was safe. She found his window and the one right next to his that must be his nanny's. And guess what she said?"

I was shocked that Cassandra knew so much. She had to be involved in this whole thing. "What else did she say?"

"She said that through the sheer curtain, she could see everything. Her son. The nanny. And her baby's father humping the nanny." Her words made my heart stop beating. "So, baby sister, have you and Bad Boy Moneybags been screwing?"

Fuck my life!

CHAPTER 30

Gannon

I t wasn't long before Brooke came rushing back into the playroom. Her face was on the pale side as she gave one sideways glance at Braiden, who was still sleeping on the pallet she'd made for him.

I had my laptop on my lap and closed it as she came and sat next to me, her eyes as big as saucers. "Gannon, Cassandra has been spying on us!" Her words were only a hiss yet they stopped my heart.

No way!

I shook my head. "Baby, there's no way she's been spying on us. Now where would you get a crazy idea like that?"

"My sister." She nodded. "I called her. I told her to try to talk to Cassandra. And she did. She ran into her at the park near her home."

I held up a hand to stop her as she was talking way too fast and making not a lick of sense. "Slow down. Now what the hell are you talking about?"

"How they met doesn't matter. The meat of the story is

that Cassandra told my sister, virtually out of the blue, that she'd introduced her son to his father after feeling guilty about keeping them apart. And the mean old rich man stole him from her."

"Oh, God ..." I gritted my teeth as I could hardly believe what I was hearing. "That bitch!"

"Yes, she is one. A very big one. And I do believe she is behind this whole thing, Gannon. And I think I was right. She wants you dead. That's why the first shots were made to my bedroom." She sat back and smiled as she crossed her arms in front of her as if she was so pleased with herself for solving the mystery. But she hadn't solved it or finished her story.

"More details, babe. I'm a little lost here," I urged her.

Her brows shot up. "Oh! I forgot the best part. She was spying on us. She knows about me and you. And that is why my ..."

I stopped her. "Yes, yes. I get it now. That's why your room was shot into first." I rubbed my forehead as it all sank in. "She was trying to kill me. Not Braiden." That was a relief, but not entirely.

Sure, Braiden was safe, but not fully. If she got her hands back on him, then he wasn't safe at all. She was a monster, through and through. "I'm calling the lead investigator to let him know about this."

"Yeah, you need to do that right away." She got up and started picking up some toys that were scattered around. "When my sister asked me if you and I had really been screwing—I won't tell you what she called you, by the way —I just about fainted."

I paused my fingers over the cell screen and looked at her. "Wait. What? She asked you about us screwing?" My heart pounded.

Were we finally free to be open about our relationship?

"Yes, she did." Her eyes rolled. "It was terrifying, Gannon. I was all like a deer in the headlights when she asked me that."

"And you said?" I crossed my fingers. *Please say you told her we are indeed screwing!*

"I told her no way." My heart plummeted with her answer. "I told Brianna that the crazy bitch must be seeing things. You and I do not do that. We're very close and are friends above having an employer/employee relationship, but it's nothing more than that."

Well, fuck!

"You know that would've been a great opportunity to come clean, right?" I watched her as she put away the toys she'd collected.

Her narrow shoulders moved with a shrug. "I didn't see it that way."

Of course, she didn't.

It was quite obvious that it would have to be me who outed us. I didn't know when or how, but I knew it was all up to me.

After making the call, I had the investigative team heading our way to get all the fingerprints they could from the windows outside Brooke's and Braiden's bedrooms. I hoped against hope that Cassandra hadn't had the smarts to wear gloves when she was being a peeping Tom.

While I was on the phone, I saw Braiden waking up and Brooke going to lie on the floor beside him, stroking his back and talking to him quietly.

After I'd hung up, I sat there, watching them. I knew it then. I had known it for a while, but then at that moment as I watched the two of them as he smiled at her and touched her face so gently and she ran her hand through his dark hair with such tenderness, that I had to make things right.

"So," I said as I got up, "I've got the team coming over, and if they find her prints anywhere at all, she'll be picked up and taken first to be hooked up to a lie detector and then to the police."

I went to sit on the floor with Brooke and Braiden. They'd sat up, and he'd crawled onto her lap. When he saw me on the floor, he kissed her cheek then came to sit in my lap. "Did Daddy's little man have a nice nap?"

While he and I conversed with nods and nose nudges, Brooke glanced at her cell and got up. "I should get to finding something to make for dinner. Care to join me in the kitchen, you two?"

So off we went to the kitchen, just like a normal family, a thing I'd never been a part of but had seen on television. Meals cooked by a mother weren't a thing I knew about. My mother had never cooked a day in her life.

I placed Braiden in his highchair then carried him in it to the kitchen. "I want to help."

Brooke opened the fridge. "Hmm. Okay. What do you know how to do?"

"Not much. But you can teach me." I washed my hands to get ready to learn from her.

She laughed as she pulled out some frozen chicken. "Funny, huh?" She put the bag into the microwave and started it.

"What's funny?" I had to ask her as she didn't go on.

She ambled up to me, throwing her arms around my neck and gazing up at me. "You teach me in the bedroom. I teach you in the kitchen."

I kissed her and picked her up as I did, holding her tightly. "I can teach you some things in here too. Maybe one night—after this shit is over—you and I will head to the kitchen for a midnight snack, featuring you."

"Always the naughty boy," she said with a giggle. "Now put me down. Braiden is looking at us through his fingers. We're embarrassing the kid."

I put her down and went to whisper in Braiden's ear a little secret that only he and I would be privy to. The smile I wore hid so much behind it. But Brooke smiled back at me without a clue as to what I'd told my son.

"You like cabbage?" She pulled out some light green stuff out of the fridge.

"Not sure." I went to smell it. "It doesn't have a smell, does it?"

"When you cook it, it does." She wrinkled her nose. "On second thought, not a good idea. My brother gets very gassy after eating cabbage, and I have to sleep with you tonight."

I laughed and smacked her ass. "Are you insinuating that I would stink you out of the bedroom?"

She laughed and nodded as she put the stuff back up. "I bet you would. My mom made cabbage rolls one night when we were kids. Later that same night, Brad stunk us out of the den a few hours after dinner. We were all watching a movie on T.V. when that cabbage went to work on him." She pulled out a yellow thing and tossed it to me. "There, you chop that up, and we can mix that in with the chicken breasts that you will also chop up, and we'll have us some good old-fashioned stir-fry for dinner."

The smile just refused to leave my face that night as we made dinner and acted like a real family. She was what made us a family. Without her, there would just be my little boy and me.

CHAPTER 31

Brooke

A nother night of the three of us sleeping in Gannon's bed had me waking up with Braiden's feet wedged into my back. As I moved, a groan came out of me as I found my body felt a bit beaten and bruised.

Seems the kid slept on the restless side and I had gotten his feet in the deal while Gannon must've gotten the softer side, his head. I rolled off the two inches of mattress that I'd been forced onto and stood up, stretching and yawning and feeling the most exhausted I'd ever felt upon waking up.

When I turned around, rubbing my eyes, I found the bathroom light was on, and the door was wide open. Then I saw an empty place on the other side of the big bed.

Gannon was gone.

Padding to the bathroom, I thought I might find him in there. But I didn't. What I did find was a wet towel that told me he'd showered and some empty hangers that told me he'd dressed. But where the hell was he?

I went back into the bedroom to grab my cell to see if he'd left me a message, but I found he hadn't. I also found it to be ten in the morning. I had no idea how Braiden and I both had slept so late.

I suppose the night of kickboxing had worn little Braiden out. And my night as his punching bag had done me in too. Gannon must've escaped the battle we had and had gotten up on time and was most likely somewhere in the house, talking to Samson or Josh.

When I opened the door to go across the hall and gather us some clothes to put on, I found Josh in the hallway, sitting on a chair and reading a book. "Morning, ma'am."

Shoving my hand through the mess of my hair, I looked down, embarrassed, as I had on one of Gannon's t-shirts and a pair of his boxers. "Morning, Josh." I headed to my bedroom and grabbed my clothes.

The windows had been fixed, the mess of glass cleaned up. Everything was back to normal. But I still felt anxious being in the room where bullets had zipped through only one night ago. I looked at the wall where the bullets had lodged and saw that the holes were still there. A project for that day, no doubt.

After I gathered all of our things, remembering to grab my soap, shampoo, and conditioner, I headed back to Gannon's room. Braiden was sleeping even harder as he had the entire bed to himself, and somehow the little thing was managing to take up most of it.

Splayed out, he was sleeping extremely comfortably, and I felt I had a few minutes to shower before he woke up. After a speedy shower and pulling on jeans, a t-shirt, and tennis shoes, I put my wet hair in a ponytail and put only a bit of moisturizer on my face. I knew we wouldn't be going anywhere that day either; might as well be comfortable.

As I opened the bathroom door, I found Braiden was just now sitting up, rubbing his eyes and moaning a bit. Probably all the activity of trying to kick me off the bed had him sore too.

"Morning, my big boy." I headed to him, picking him up and carrying him into the bathroom. "Did you sleep well, Braiden?"

He nodded and this time it came along with an "Um-hm."

"Braiden! Oh, good boy!" It wasn't much, just a mumble, but it was something more than a mere nod of the head. It hadn't been long, and he was making progress.

I knew that being away from his mother had to be traumatizing to the young boy. And being in a new place was too. Taking in so many new things, a father, another woman caring for him, all the staff, it had to be hard.

With all of that against him, the little boy was moving forward, taking things in stride and developing, despite all that had happened to him. My heart swelled with an ache as I brushed his teeth for him.

How could his mother do what she's done?

People who hurt other people intentionally didn't make sense to me. So many things happened that were bad, completely out of anyone's control. I could never wrap my head around people who purposely decided to hurt another person. And their own child? Well, that was inconceivable to me.

The boy who sat on the vanity top, letting me clean his tiny teeth, was not only utterly adorable but sweet too. So loveable and kind-hearted.

How could she do this to him?

After bathing him and putting his clothes on, I took him with me to find his father. I found Josh still in the hallway, and he got up when he saw that we were dressed and on the move. Silently, he followed behind us as we went to the kitchen.

When I found no evidence of Gannon having had coffee or breakfast and also saw that Samson wasn't around, I had to ask, "Did Gannon and Samson leave?"

Josh looked at me for a moment as if he had been told not to tell me anything. But then he looked off to the right. "He and Samson went into town."

I was a bit shocked. He'd left us alone, a thing he'd said he wasn't going to do until the shooter was caught.

Had the shooter been caught?

"Did they catch her?" I asked as I set to work making Braiden's breakfast after putting him in the highchair. We'd moved it to the kitchen so we could keep an eye on him while we cooked.

"No." Josh took a seat at the island bar, opening up his book and reading again. "There were no prints found around the windows. No reason to take her in."

He offered no more information so I chatted with Braiden as I cooked his oatmeal. It did little to help me not to think about Gannon and what he was doing.

Why'd he leave without saying a word to me?

He had to be up to something he knew I'd beg him not to do. Probably putting himself into a dangerous situation. I knew that had to be it.

Why else would he leave us alone here?

Well, we had Josh, and I knew there were still guards all around the property and at the gate. But he'd said he would stay with us until it was all over. But it wasn't over, according to Josh.

After getting the oatmeal ready and cutting up some organic strawberries, I fed Braiden, all the while chatting to him. I shut up when it occurred to me that I might be aggravating Josh with all of my mindless chatter.

With my silence, he put the book down and looked at me. "You okay, ma'am?"

The man was at least ten years older than me, so calling me ma'am was ridiculous. I put my hand on my hip and looked right back at him. "Josh, don't you think that calling me ma'am is a bit over the top?"

He shrugged. "What else do you call your boss's girl?"

It hit me hard. He knew about us.

Well, of course, he does, you idiot!

I really was an idiot. The man had seen us practically naked on the floor in Braiden's bedroom the night the shots were fired. What else would he think?

I let it go, nodded, and went to work, cleaning everything up after giving Braiden a wooden spoon to play with, or rather bang, on the tray of his highchair with. It kept him content, so I dealt with the noise.

When I was all done, I got myself a bottle of water from the fridge, picked up the child, and headed to the playroom. I was going to put all of my focus on him and working with him that day.

It would help me get my mind off Gannon and what he was up to.

Josh followed us to the playroom and took a seat in the far corner and got back to reading his book. I pulled out the blocks with the letters and numbers on them and sat on the floor with Braiden.

Holding up a block, I pointed to the letter. "This is the letter B. Do you know what word begins with the letter B?"

Braiden laughed as if I'd told a funny joke and he took the block away from me and threw it down. But then he did something amazing. He looked at me and looked around the room. Then one eyebrow rose as he asked, "Da?"

My heart skipped a beat as I teared up. I grabbed him and hugged him. "Da! You said a word, Braiden!"

He laughed and wiggled, so I had to let him go. Then he asked again, "Da?"

I was laughing as tears rolled down my cheeks. "I don't know where your daddy is. Let me call him, and you can ask him that yourself."

I took out my cell from the back pocket of my jeans and called Gannon. Wherever he was, he was going to love hearing his son talk for the first time.

Gannon answered the call. "Hey, baby."

I put the phone on speaker so Braiden could hear his daddy. "Hi, babe. Someone was asking about you."

"And who would that be?" Gannon asked with a chuckle.

Braiden's eyes lit up, and he came to sit on my lap and look at the screen, expecting to see his daddy there, but not finding him. "Da? Da?"

"Oh my God!" Gannon was overjoyed. "Braiden? Is that Daddy's big boy? Son, I'm so proud of you!"

Braiden was so happy, he jumped out of my lap and started jumping up and down, shouting, "Da," over and over again.

The tears were streaming down my face. "Can you believe that?"

"No. God, I wish I was there to see him." He slipped off into silence.

"So, where are you, Gannon?" I had to ask. It was driving me crazy not to know.

But all I heard was silence on the other end of the line.

Oh, this can't be good.

CHAPTER 32

Gannon

All I could hear was Brooke breathing as I sat there, not knowing what the hell to tell her.

If she knew I'd put myself in the middle of what might turn into a very bad situation, she'd be worried. And she'd stay worried until I made it back to her safely.

As I sat there, dumbfounded, Samson reached over and poked me in the arm. "He's moving."

"Was that Samson?" she asked. "Gannon, what are you doing?"

"It's going to be okay. We're going to put an end to this today, baby. I've got to go."

"No!" she barked at me. "Gannon, where are you?"

"Baby, I have to go. I'll tell you all about it ..."

"He's going in the side door," Samson interrupted me. "You have to call your crew and let them know they have to get out of there."

"Baby, I've got to go. I love you. Tell Braiden I love him too." I swiped the call to end it before she could stop me.

I felt like an ass, hanging up on her that way. But I didn't know what else to do. I knew she'd push me for more and more information. But she didn't need to know about any of this.

If she did, she'd tell me to stay out of it and to let the cops and my investigators handle it. Only I couldn't do that. I had to see it with my own eyes. I had to have the chance to face the woman who wanted me dead and who would use our son to get everything I had.

Calling the crew leader who was inside the building, I found him answering my call. "Yes, boss?"

"Don't panic," I started.

"Oh, boss, that's a terrible way to start a conversation." He didn't laugh; he knew something bad was coming.

"Get everyone out of there. But don't make it obvious. Call out that you're giving them an early lunch. Make sure everyone goes out through the front exit. Someone went in through the side door. I don't want anyone interacting with him. Don't lock the front doors after you leave, got it?"

"Got it, boss." He ended the call, and I sat back to watch.

Samson and I stayed put in his Ford Focus with darkly tinted windows. It was a perfect car for blending into the surroundings. No one ever noticed a bland car that there were so many of on the road. The only difference between the one Samson drove and the ones other people did was that his had one bad ass engine. He could outrun just about anyone with the motor he had custom-made.

He and I watched as everyone walked out of the building. Each one of them looked happy to be taking an early lunch. And when I saw the crew leader come out, I knew he was the last one inside the building. "That's the last one, Samson. Tell them to go inside."

Samson got on his walkie-talkie to send in the

policemen he'd personally lined up to work with us on this. I watched as a couple of unmarked police cars started to move, pulling out from where they'd been parked and waiting.

Samson had people watching Cassandra's every move. When she had been spotted early this morning with a man who had a bandage wrapped around his right bicep, they'd really honed in her. And that's when they saw them coming out of her house. The man was wearing a trench coat, and she was carrying a brown paper bag. It was the way she was carrying the thing that alerted them that something was going down. She was overly cautious with the package as she got into the passenger side of the car that was parked near the side entrance of the nightclub.

When Samson had texted me early this morning about it all, I'd hopped out of bed and told him I wanted to witness it all. I had to see the look on the bitch's face when she went down.

And the time was getting closer and closer as more and more unmarked police cars moved in. One parked in a way that blocked Cassandra's view from the front of the building.

We knew she was the guy's lookout. And now she was blind to see if anyone went inside. Of course, there were policemen heading in through the unlocked front doors.

Wearing business suits, four policemen got out of the cars they had parked on either side of hers. They got out and got together on the sidewalk, right in front of her car. Another unmarked car pulled up behind her, and another police officer dressed in a business suit got out and was calling out to the others, acting as if they were all together and he had no idea where he should park.

Her car was quite effectively blocked in, and there would be no getting away.

Cassandra became aware of that fact and opened her door, stepping out and looking at all of the men. I eased my window down a bit so I could hear her. "Excuse me, gentlemen. I'll be leaving soon." She looked at the man who had her blocked in. "Can you please move? Once my friend comes out, we have to hurry to get to our next meeting."

"Sure, lady," the officer said with a smile. "Can you see any parking spaces from where you're at? I can't seem to find one anywhere."

"No, I can't see one from here." She rubbed her forehead in aggravation. With her head down like that, she failed to notice the other men who were on the sidewalk, moving in on her.

Their plan had worked extremely well. They had her out of the car, where she'd be much easier to get to when the time came to make an arrest. One had slipped around the other side of the car and was coming up in front of her.

Acting as if he was trying to help his friend, that officer said, "I think there might be one over there." He pointed off to one side, and they acted as if they were looking at something.

The other three, who were closing in on Cassandra from behind, were able to get her to step a bit further from the car so they could pass by. One of them pushed the car door closed and stepped in between Cassandra and the car. The other two were right behind her, and she looked a little panicked as she realized she was trapped outside of the car and the other car was still blocking her in.

Then the side door of my club opened up and out spilled her man in the company of two uniformed police officers. "She made me do it all!" he shouted.

Four sets of hands grabbed her as she tried to spin

around. One of them forced her, face first, up against the car. Another officer began reading her rights to her.

And now she was lost for words as she looked around, dazed and confused as hell. "How?"

Her man-friend wasn't through throwing her all the way under the bus yet as he shouted, "She made me do it. Cassandra Harrington made me take the shots at her kid's father that night. She made me set those bombs in the club to lead the police to think it was someone other than herself that was threatening Gannon Forester and their son, Braiden Forester."

"Shut up, you idiot!" she screamed.

"I will not," he yelled back at her. "I took a bullet for you, and you couldn't even be bothered to tell me you were sorry about that. And just so you all know, I could've actually shot that man; I just didn't want to. I began to grow a conscience. And that bomb I made isn't going to go off. I just told her it would. That ticking sound is an old clock I found to put inside of that plastic pipe."

I looked at Samson. "Can we get out now?"

With a nod, he and I got out of the car and made our way over to the officer who had Cassandra. The guy she'd had do all this saw me and shouted, "Hey, Gannon! She had this planned for a year, dude. She wanted everything you had. She knew the kid was her only ticket to getting it."

She turned to look at me then. Her eyes were wide. Her red lipstick was smeared. "He's a liar. He's the mastermind behind all of this. He made me do it all. Don't believe him!"

I shook my head and looked her straight in her dark eyes. "You will never see my son again. I will get your parental rights completely revoked. My son has a real mother now. A woman who loves him and puts him first every single time. And you will rot in prison. I will make damn sure of that."

"Gannon, no! Please!" Her begging only served to piss me off even further.

"My lawyers will meet you officers at the police station, where they will make sure she's charged with every crime they can come up with." I turned to leave, and Samson followed.

It was over. Finally.

CHAPTER 33

Brooke

Not happy with how Gannon had cut me off, I played with Braiden to try to get my mind on anything other than Gannon and what he was up to.

When Josh's cell buzzed, I jerked my head up and saw him taking the call. His voice was very low. "Josh here, boss."

There was a series of uh-huhs and some hmms, but Josh wasn't talking much. I went back to playing with Braiden, knowing I wasn't going to find anything out.

I looked up again when Josh stood up and started walking to the door. "Bye, ma'am. It was nice working for you guys."

My heart stopped. It had to be over.

I got up, picking up Braiden, and went toward him. "Was it her? Did they get her?"

He nodded and went out the door. "Yep."

I had no idea how to act. I wanted to jump up and down and shout about them getting that horrible bitch. But she was Braiden's mother. It just felt like the wrong thing to be doing.

The poor kid. His mother would spend a considerable amount of his life in prison for what she'd done. And I didn't want him remembering that I jumped for joy and celebrated that horrible fact.

Monster or not, she was his mother and always would be.

Josh left, and little by little the staff came trickling in. It was crazy how they just all got back to work. Everyone was nice and asked how we were doing with the whole thing.

I didn't know how I was doing with it. I wanted Gannon to come and tell me every last detail. I could've called, but I didn't want to bother him. I knew he must be very busy, making sure Cassandra was put away for a very long time.

So when an hour went by and then one more, I just took Braiden to his bedroom after lunch for a nap. When I got to his bedroom, I saw men working on the bullet holes in the walls in his room and mine. So I opted for the next bedroom. It was an empty guest room, and I went in to put him down for a nap.

He was tired, rubbing his little blue eyes and leaning heavily on me. Taking off his shoes, I laid him back on the bed and pulled the blanket over him as I sang him a lullaby.

Since he was half asleep anyway, it took no time for him to go to sleep. I went into his bedroom and got the baby monitor. Then I went to mine to retrieve the one I had.

Going back to the guestroom, I plugged in the monitor and headed out into the hallway, not sure where I should go. The door to Gannon's room was open, and I'd seen house-keeping working on it. So I turned and headed to another guest room across the hallway from where I'd put Braiden.

"Where are you going, baby?" I heard his deep voice ask.

I turned and saw Gannon coming my way. Suddenly I was overwhelmed with emotion and ran to him, throwing my arms around him as tears got away from me. "Gannon! You're okay."

I had known he was okay. Josh would've told me if he was otherwise. But it had just been there, that little doubt. But he was okay, and he was home. And it was all over.

His large hand moved through my hair as his lips met my cheek. "I'm fine. It's over, baby. She's going to be in prison for a very, very long time. And my lawyers have already begun the process of stripping her of her maternal rights where Braiden is concerned. If I have my way, he will never know that woman is his mother. He will never know that woman, period."

I didn't know what to say. I was full of mixed opinions about that whole thing. But right then, I couldn't worry about it. He was Braiden's father. It was his decision to make.

"I'm just so happy to have you home, Gannon." I kissed him and felt his lips pull into a smile.

"My room's getting cleaned. Why don't you, I, and the baby monitor step into this room over here?" His hand slid down my arm, taking my hand then leading me to the same room I had been going into before he'd stopped me.

When he opened the door, I found the room to be very much like the one he'd had me in. But there were no windows, as it was an interior room. It was dark once he closed the door, and he had to turn on the overhead light.

I went to plug in the monitor and was bent over to do that when I felt his arms come around me. He picked me up after I had the plug in the socket and then he took me to the bed. "He's down for a nap, huh?"

I nodded as he pulled my shoes off. "He should sleep for about an hour, I think."

"Well, I guess we'll have to make this short and sweet then." He undid my jeans and pulled them off too.

"Oh, will we?" I sat up so he could rid me of my t-shirt and smiled. "Afterward, can I call my mother and tell her to expect us tomorrow for Thanksgiving and my birthday? Everyone shows up the day before Thanksgiving."

It was all over. No more danger. No reason not to go now.

He pulled off my shirt and then my bra, cupping both my breasts. "You better call her and tell her that. I can't wait to meet them all."

I sighed in relief. He was going to come with me. I didn't know why I kept letting doubt into my head, but I did.

He took one of my pebbled nipples between his lips and rolled it, making me moan already. My panties were still on, and they were already getting damp. But he was quick to rid me of them, his fingers moving through my folds.

Slowly, he moved his mouth off my tit and kissed his way down my body. I watched him as he headed to where I knew his mouth would take me away from any thoughts.

His lips touched my clit; his warm wet tongue circled it lazily. His hands caressed my thighs as he kissed and licked me.

My head was whirling with his attention. I had no idea how I'd made my way into this man's heart. I had no idea why he had chosen me over so many. But I was so damn happy he had.

Even if it didn't last forever. At least he was showing me what love felt like.

But as that thought of this not lasting forever filtered into my head, I found my eyes stinging with tears.

I lost all train of thought then as he gripped my thighs then forced them apart. He moved lower, kissing me and licking me in the opposite direction. Then his tongue went into me upside down, and I moaned and fisted his dark hair.

As he moved his long tongue inside of me, my mind went back to the thoughts I'd been having. When would what we have be over?

Maybe when Braiden started first grade. Maybe then it would have to end.

Gannon moved a bit, his tongue inside me still, but now his whiskered chin rubbed my little nub, and I couldn't think anymore again. I could only feel, and what I felt was out of this world.

"Oh, baby, yes ..." I moaned.

He kept going and going, then I came and tried my best to be quiet so no one would hear me. But it was damn hard. I was left panting when he finally came up for air.

Standing up, he undressed in front of me, and I marveled at his ripped body. That was all mine. At least for now, he was all mine.

I held out my arms to him, and he came into them, moving his body over mine, pressing his knee between my legs to part them for him.

He pressed his thick cock against me, then thrust it into me. "Oh, baby, you were made for me." Soft lips found mine, and he took me higher.

Every time he and I were together this way, it felt as if I was floating. I couldn't feel the bed underneath me or the pillow under my head. All I could feel was him and how he was connected to me. A part of me.

My hands ran over his muscular back, and I arched up to him, wanting this to just go on and on.

It was like there was no one else in the entire world. Just us. And we were like one being, complete.

I'd heard people say things like "I don't know where he

ends and I begin," and that was how I felt. Sensations moved through me that defied imagination.

His mouth moved to my neck, biting me, then sucking the same spot. It sent shots of pure heat to my cunt, and I moaned with each bite he gave me.

Higher and higher I went until there was no higher I could go. It all came crashing down on me at once. My body could take no more. I was shivering, groaning, and growling as it all concluded.

His body came with mine in a glorious display of wet heat and the sound of our juices mixing as they gushed from us both.

Relaxed after such an intense rush, he whispered, "You are mine, Brooke. I love you."

I was his. A part of me always would be. He was right about that. But a part of him would always be mine too. At least we both could take that with us when this had to come to an end.

CHAPTER 34

Gannon

If I said I wasn't nervous, then I'd have been lying. I was nervous. But I was something else, even more so than that. I was determined.

We pulled up in front of her family's modest home in Napa Valley. Besides my Jag, Brad's red Lamborghini stood out amongst the other normal cars that were parked in a haphazard way around her family's two-story home.

"Wow, how many people are here, Brooke?" I was trying not to call her baby at all. It was hard, but I had managed to rein that in so far that day.

It was actually Brooke who kept throwing out 'babes' left and right when she was talking to me. "Um, looks like," her eyes scanned the scene as we got out of the car and I opened the door behind mine to get Braiden out of his car seat, "maybe twenty, give or take. Don't let the size of my family get to you, babe."

"K." I picked up Braiden as she reached into the seat behind hers to retrieve his diaper bag. It was a thing she had told me was on its way out, as she would soon have him using the bathroom like a big boy.

We didn't even get to the door before her mother popped her head out the front door. "You made it!" She hurried out to meet us, grabbing Brooke and hugging her. Then she looked at Braiden. "Oh my goodness!" She pinched his cheeks, making him giggle. "You are so adorable!" She smiled at me and gave me a wink. "It's clear to see where he gets that from. Hi, Gannon. It's nice to finally meet you. Brad's spoken about you so often through the years; it's like we all already know you. My name's Barbara, but everyone calls me Babs." She opened her arms up. "Wanna come with Grams, Braiden?" Then she pulled out a cookie from her apron pocket to lure him in. "I have cookies."

I'd lost him to her then. He nearly jumped out of my arms to get into hers. She led the way, and I fell into step with Brooke. It was hard not to wrap my arm around her, I found out, as I reached out to do just that. "Here, give me his bag, Brooke."

She caught what I had almost done and smiled at me. "Here you go, sir."

I winked at her. "Thanks, sitter."

I couldn't help but love how her mother was already telling Braiden to call her Grams. It was a great start.

Inside the home, I found it was bustling with people. Just inside the doorway, her mother stopped, and it was on to the introductions. "All right everybody, hush up and listen," her mother began. "This little guy here is Braiden. His big, good-looking daddy, this mighty hunk of man who's standing behind me, is Gannon Forester. You might've heard Brad bragging about knowing him a time or two."

Some young guy in the corner chimed in, "Or every

damn time anyone talks to him!" Raucous laughter followed, making the living room shake.

Babs went on, "That wisecracker is Brad and Brooke's cousin, Bobby. He comes from my husband's side of the family. They have no filter, so watch out for Uncle Bob, Aunt Lou, their sons Bobby and Kenny, and you also have to watch out for their little dog, Toto. They're all ones to rattle off about things no one cares to hear." Another round of laughter told me they all were pretty thick-skinned and everyone had a sense of humor.

Out of a side room, I saw Brad coming in, followed by what had to be his father as he looked like an older version of my old friend. "Hey, buddy." Brad waved. "You're taking the dare Brooke gave you, huh?"

With a shrug, I said, "I wouldn't call it a dare. I'd call it a very nice invitation to spend this holiday with her large and funny family. And I'm extremely happy she did invite me. This seems like it'll be a fun couple of days."

Brad laughed as he and his father made their way, curving through the mass that filled the living room, to get to us. "Should be fun," Brad agreed.

His father stuck out his hand, and I took it with a firm handshake. "Benjamin Moore, like the paint company. Call me Ben, Gannon. It's a pleasure to finally make your acquaintance." He gave me a wink then turned his attention to my son. "And who is this handsome young man we have here?"

Babs put her hand in her apron and slipped Ben a cookie. "This is Braiden, and he likes cookies, Papa."

Ben held up the cookie he'd been given and smiled at Braiden. "Oh, my! Look what Papa has for you, little Braiden." Without a hitch, Braiden went for that cookie, as he'd just finished the one Babs had given him, and into Ben's arms he went.

Bab's jabbed me in the ribs, talking out of the side of her mouth, "He's going to be fought over more than the turkey's drumsticks this Thanksgiving."

"I think he'll be in heaven here." I looked at Brooke, who was beaming. "Thanks for letting us tag along, Brooke."

With our backs to the door and her mother in front of us, we had a bit of cover, and I felt her hand move over my ass. Then it settled on my back. "You're not tagging along, Gannon. You're family. Can't you see that?"

We were off to a great start. I was introduced to Bab's sister, Leah, and her husband, and Steve. They had two grown kids, Laura and Andrew. Andrew was married with one kid, and then there was another dog who was part of his family.

It was like a circus in their home. Loud, crazy smells everywhere, and wonderful.

We'd managed to get to the middle of the living room. Brooke had said we needed to take Braiden upstairs to her room so she could change his diaper. So we were heading slowly in that direction as Babs introduced me to everyone.

I heard footsteps on the wooden staircase that came down to meet the end of the large living area. "So, you made it?"

I looked up to find an older version of Brooke coming down the stairs. "You must be Brianna," I called up to her. "I'm Gannon. Nice to meet you."

She stopped right where she was, waiting for us to come up. Her eyes never left mine. "I'll help you guys up here." She looked at her father, who still held my son. "Hey, you."

Braiden looked at Brianna, then back at Brooke. He was confused, as they looked so much alike. When Brianna held out her arms, he went right into them. She turned and went up the stairs with him as Brooke and I followed.

"I had no idea she and you looked so much alike, Brooke." I immediately regretted my words as her eyes cut to me and I saw the insecurity in them.

"She's five years older than me. Much closer to your age," she whispered as we climbed the stairs behind her sister. My son looked at Brooke over Brianna's shoulder with a confused expression.

We filed into Brooke's bedroom, Brianna laying Braiden down on the pink comforter that covered Brooke's twin bed. "Aren't you a handsome devil, Braiden? I could just eat you up." Brianna smiled at him as he held her face, undoubtedly wondering what was happening.

I put the diaper bag on the bed, and Brooke quickly opened it to get out a fresh diaper. "Let's get you freshened up, pumpkin."

Brianna stepped back to let Brooke tend to him and looked me all the way up and all the way down. "Hmm. So you're the man who helped our big brother strike it rich." Her eyes cut to Brooke. "And now you've made sure our baby sister is getting her college all paid for and even getting hands-on experience to boot. Some might call you the Moores' angel, Gannon Forester."

"Don't be rough on him, Brianna." Brooke gave her a pleading look as she pulled Braiden up to straighten up his clothes. "Please. I am begging you."

"Rough?" Brianna cackled.

It made me laugh too. "She's harmless, Brooke. No need to worry about her," I joked. "And that laugh tells me a bucket of water is all it would take to melt her anger."

Brianna held her arm out in gesture to the door. "Shall we join the zoo that is our family, guys?"

Brooke nodded. "Yes, I have Braiden all fixed up. Ready to deal with the masses."

With one step forward, my arm was taken, looped around Brianna's, and off we were going. Brooke followed behind us, carrying my son.

I caught the sadness that flowed over Brooke's face and quickly fixed the situation. "Oh, let me carry, Braiden." I untangled my arm then turned to take Braiden out of Brooke's arms. Kissing his cheek, I went on, "I might not get to hold my boy much these next couple days with so many who are wanting his attention. Let me have it while I can."

Brooke beamed with my actions as Brianna headed on out and down the stairs. Brooke's smile was all I needed. I stopped at the top of the stairs before heading down to join her family.

Brooke stopped just behind me. "You okay, Gannon?"

I turned around to look at her. "Your eyes are darker blue, making them much prettier. Your nose has light freckles that dust the top of it that I love to brush my lips over. Her body doesn't hold a candle to yours. Nobody's could. And most of all, she isn't you, Brooke." I spoke just a bit above a whisper, as her family was really loud. "And I love you, baby. Just you."

She blushed. "I love you too."

CHAPTER 35

Brooke

Thanksgiving morning was crazy as Mom, her sister, and her sister-in-law fought over every dang recipe for the afternoon meal. With all the chaos, Gannon was quick to make an offer no one refused. "How about I head out to grab a bunch of sausage and egg biscuits and some other stuff for breakfast?" He had to shout over the barking dogs, the television Uncle Bob had to listen to way too loud, and the bickering women in the kitchen.

We were in the living room, but somehow their bickering made it all the way out to us.

Hell, yas answered Gannon's question, and before I knew it, he and Brad were headed out the door. And there I was, left with Braiden and kind of feeling a little left out.

I wanted to go with Gannon.

Brianna seemingly floated out of nowhere to my side. "Hey, baby sister. While they're gathering sustenance, you and I can start putting together the tables on the back deck. Give Dad the baby."

The last thing I wanted to do was hand off Braiden. "No. I'll take him with me. Grab a highchair out of the basement. I think mine is still down there."

"Are you nuts?" She shook her head and held out her arms for Braiden. He went right into them. Then she went to Dad, who was sitting in a comfy recliner. "Can you entertain the cutest kid in the world for a moment while Brooke and I put together the tables in the back so we can eat when the food gets here?"

"I sure can," Dad said as he held out his hands. "You wanna watch the Thanksgiving parade with Papa, big boy?" By the way Braiden did a nose dive into his arms, I assumed he did want to do that.

Brianna smiled at me as she looped her arm through mine and out we went to fix up the tables on the deck. The morning was still cool, so she lit the outdoor heaters on the deck and things began to become more comfortable right away.

"It's so pretty out here." I looked out over the sprawling vines of the winery that laid out behind our home. Living in Napa Valley, with its dizzying array of gorgeous landscapes, was like living in paradise. When you added in the temperate climate, you really had a little slice of Eden right there in your own backyard.

"Hey!" Brianna's shout took me out of my little break before actually working. "Wanna wake up and help?"

We got to work setting up tables that we kept in a closet off the side of the deck made especially for these big occasions. Once we had the last table done and the last folding chair in place, we took seats. "Man, that's a heck of a lot of work." I stretched my legs out and looked up to stretch my neck too. And then a tall, handsome man walked into my view, looking down at me.

"Whatcha doing?" Gannon asked as he placed two handfuls of brown paper bags on the table next to me.

I regained my composure. "Taking a break after putting all this together. Dad has Braiden."

"Cool." He jerked his head at the car that my brother had pulled all the way to the back. "Brad parked back here. I think he wants his Lambo to be this Thanksgiving's centerpiece."

Brianna got up to go get more bags out of the car. "Can you say show off?"

We both laughed, and I caught him looking off, watching my sister walk away. I looked down. Maybe he was just playing me. Maybe he was still the man he'd always been. Maybe he hadn't changed at all.

His hand caught my chin, and he pulled my face up. His lips barely caught mine with a quick kiss. Then our eyes met. "Sleeping without you—even with Braiden between us —was excruciating. Promise never to make me do that again, baby." He hurried to leave me to go inside to tell everyone that breakfast was here.

I was left breathless.

Maybe he has changed. Maybe he does love me.

The day went on, and as usual, we ate Thanksgiving food at lunchtime and my birthday was celebrated at dinner time.

Brad and Brianna had a special dinner surprise for me, and I had to stay out of the kitchen as they prepared it. That was cool, nice, great, and all of that. But my siblings had pulled Gannon in on it, and the three of them were in the kitchen, cooking things up for all of us on my birthday. I couldn't help but have a little worry that Brianna was winning over the man I loved.

Night replaced day and the outside lights sparkled as we

all sat out on the deck. The heaters kept it nice and toasty, and the ambiance was very relaxing. Not that I was very relaxed.

My sister—who looked just like me—was in the kitchen with Gannon!

Mom and Dad were whispering far more than I ever remembered them doing before. It was weird, and I found myself feeling left out as we all sat around and waited for the meal to be brought out to us.

Everyone was starving as the meal wouldn't be served until eight in the evening. Brianna said she wanted to make sure that we were all hungry after the huge Thanksgiving feast we had had at lunch.

I was starving, and I wanted to see Gannon out there with me!

With Braiden on my lap, I played patty-cake with him, and I caught my parents looking at us. Both wore wide smiles and Dad even nodded at me when I caught them. "You two are in love, kiddo."

I hugged Braiden and kissed his cheek, then he kissed mine. "That, we are. I love you, pumpkin." I rubbed his nose with mine.

He nodded then opened his mouth as he looked at me. "Ma." His tiny hands took my face, and he kissed the tip of my nose. "Ma!"

I cut my eyes and caught a tear falling down my mother's face. I was about to correct him, but she was quick to say something first. "Oh my goodness. He needs a mother so desperately. How wonderful he has you, Brooke. What a godsend you've been to him and Gannon."

There were absolutely no words that came to me. Then the back door opened and out came Brad, Brianna, and Gannon. A cake was in my sister's hands, and all three were singing happy birthday to me. My family joined in, and I found Mom taking Braiden out of my arms.

I hated being the center of attention. But I took it on my birthday and stood up, blowing out the candles. At the end, I heard Gannon ask, "What did you wish for?"

I shook my head as Brianna and Brad moved off to the sides to put the cake down on the table. But Gannon stayed right in front of me as I answered him. "You can't say your wish." But I had wished one thing as I blew out those candles. I wanted Gannon, Braiden, and I to be together forever, even though I knew that was next to impossible.

"Well, it's not my birthday, so I can tell you what I wished for." He took my hands in his and moved me back to sit in the chair that was right behind me.

I looked at what he was doing, touching me. In front of my family. I gulped. Had he forgotten about having to keep our secret?

Then I noticed that he was moving down. Getting on his knees.

Wait! No, not both knees. Only one knee. And he was pulling something out of his pocket.

My left hand was still in his, and I threw my right hand up to cover my mouth.

What is he doing?

"Guess what your brother told me," Gannon said with a soft tone.

I shook my head as an answer. I couldn't speak. I was half afraid for my life and his and half unsure what was going on exactly.

"He told me that your middle name is Madilyn. Did you know that was my mother's middle name too?" He smiled and winked at me.

I shook my head. I still couldn't talk.

"So I see you are rendered speechless. Well, this is a first. I may as well dive on in then." He opened his right hand. A little blue box was on his palm. He flipped that lid with his thumb, and the largest diamond I'd ever seen sparkled in the twinkling lights that hung all over the deck. "Brooke Madilyn Moore, would you do me the great honor of becoming my wife?"

My mouth dropped. I looked at him, then around at my overprotective family and saw only smiles on their faces. And when Braiden threw his little arms out as he looked at me and shouted, "Ma!" as he nodded, well, I lost it all.

I sobbed out my answer. "Yes!"

My hand shook as Gannon pushed that heavy ring onto my finger and I continued to cry as he got up, picked me up in his strong arms, and kissed me right in front of my entire family.

All I heard were claps, whoops, and hollers.

Then I felt a hand on my shoulder just as our lips parted. I turned my head to find my big brother right there. "Now you be good to this man right here, baby sister. He's one in a billion. But you two were made for one another."

All I could do was nod and cry as Gannon hugged me again.

"Let's eat cake!" my brother shouted, and all the noise of my family faded away as Gannon kissed me one more time.

His lips moved off mine, up my neck, and to my ear. Warm breath stirred my hair with his words. "You are mine, and I love you. And I always will."

The End

MASKED INDULGENCE BOOK 2

A Christmas Romance (Nightclub Sins 2)

By Michelle Love

One night of naughty fun turned into one lifetime of responsibility ...
The little beauty caught my eye right from the start.
The naughty negligee she wore enhanced her luscious body, though the mask hid her face from me.
But I took her anyway and I took her as many times as I wanted; she belonged to me that night.
My little slave gave me everything I demanded of her.
My touch became her undoing, making her give me more than she'd ever given anyone.
In the end, she gave me more than I'd bargained for ...

He picked me — out of a ton of sexy women — he picked me!

Right from the start, he took me over, made me do things
that just weren't safe.

I lost myself to him for the matter of one night.

It was only ever supposed to be one night.

But one night would never be enough for us.

I couldn't get him out of my head. He'd made me feel more
than anyone ever had.

And then a surprise came along that brought us together
one more time.

And this time it just might last a lot longer than one hot
night ...

36

CHAPTER 1

Nixon

Halloween Night

A slight chill took over the night air as my driver pulled up in front of the club I'd directed him to. This was where I'd always come to find a bit of relief. The darker side of me often came out around the most sinful of holidays. The Dom in me wanted a sub to play with for one night. That's all I dared to allow myself.

I'd trekked up to Portland, Oregon, to get away from my life in Los Angeles, California, for a speck of time. I didn't dabble in the BDSM realm at home. I saved that for when I came to the club I'd joined when it first opened a few years back. The Dungeon of Decorum was a place I hadn't often visited, only coming up once, or sometimes twice, a year.

I only liked to play at being a Dominant; I wasn't the full-time kind. I had never leased a sub or even paid for more than a night's pleasure. It was just a way for me to blow off steam once in a while, nothing serious.

When I'd received the invitation to the club's first annual

Halloween Ball, I got the itch to have some BDSM fun and made plans to attend what the invitation assured would be a great time.

A red carpet led me from the car I'd hired to the front door of what looked like a shack. On the outside, that's all anyone saw. On the inside, the stairs took you underground, to where a massive structure housed a large main room, several smaller more intimate rooms, a host of private rooms, and even private suites for long-term stays.

Walking into the main room, I found a giant banner hanging over the crowd who'd gathered to take part in the eerie festivities. Cloaks covered most of the men's tuxedos, just as mine did. A plain Lone Ranger-style mask hid my identity. The women were the real stars of the night, decked out in all kinds of sexy, sinister attire.

I must've looked a bit overwhelmed by the plethora of willing women, as a man nudged my shoulder. "See any who are to your liking?"

With a nod, I answered his question. "Many are to my liking. This is by far the sexiest Halloween party I've ever been invited to."

"Me too," the man said then chuckled. "But I'm not here to shop for a new sub; I've got me a permanent one now." He reached out to shake my hand. "Dr. Owen Cantrell."

As I shook his hand, I recalled hearing that name before —then it struck me. "You're that plastic surgeon to the stars. Or you were before that reality show ended. I believe it was titled *Beverly Hills Reconstruction*. I'm based out of Los Angeles too. Nixon Slaughter. I own and operate Champlain Services."

"I've heard of that," Owen said as he nodded. "It's an environmental agency."

To say I was proud of my company was too small a word.

That company had taken a lot of time to build and to make a name for itself. After years of hard work, I'd accomplished more than I had ever dreamed. We worked worldwide, and the best part was that we were helping the planet and future generations.

Shoving my hands into my pockets, I rocked on my feet, pride overflowing inside of me. "So you've heard of my little endeavor?"

"Who hasn't?" he asked with a grin. "I also read something in the *L.A. Times* about you and a couple of other guys building some new club downtown. An exclusive one much like the select few nightclubs in Las Vegas. When do you suppose that'll be opening?"

"We're hoping to have it open for a New Year's Eve bash. That's the target date for the grand opening." I pulled a business card out of the breast pocket of my jacket and handed it to Owen. "Here's my number. Give me a call, and I'll set you and a date up for that, on the house."

He pocketed the card and clapped me on the back. "Cool. We'll be there. Thanks, man." He pulled out a card of his own and gave it to me. "And if you know of anyone who needs my services, you give them my number. And let them know if they say you referred them, they'll get a ten percent discount."

I put away his card as I said, "Will do, partner."

A woman with long, silky black hair, wearing a barely-there teddy and a giant mask with peacock feathers, came to Owen's side. He put his arm around her, pulling her close to his side. "Allow me to introduce you to the woman who'll be my date at your grand opening. This is Petra, my wife."

She extended a long, slender hand and I took it, delivering a kiss to the top of it. "It's a pleasure to meet you, Petra.

I'm Nixon Slaughter. I look forward to seeing you both at my nightclub on New Year's Eve. You'll be my honored guests."

"Oh," she looked at her husband. "That club, I read about it." Her dark eyes turned to mine. "Have you come up with a name for it yet? Last I read, you and your partners hadn't."

Shaking my head, I shoved my hands back into my pockets. "No, we're at an impasse. But we'll come up with something soon—just as soon as we can figure out how to get Gannon Forester to stop shooting down all of our ideas."

Petra's eyes lit up as she said, "How about Club Exclusive? You know, because it's catering to an exclusive branch of society, the ultra-wealthy?"

"I'll run it by my partners." Our attention was then taken by someone who'd gotten to the mic on the main stage.

"Happy Halloween, everybody!" the Master of Ceremonies called out.

Thunderous applause boomed throughout the large room. Owen gave me a nod, and he and his wife moved forward to get closer to the stage. I stood back, watching the crowd move in. I wasn't too keen on being in the midst of a crowd. I liked to be near an exit most times—it was an odd little quirk of mine. Getting trampled in a panicked frenzy was a bit of a phobia I had.

Thankfully, staying on the fringes of any crowd kept me sane. A waiter came by with a tray of assorted cocktails. I picked up a clear drink that had some cherries floating in it. When I took a little taste, I found it was minty and fresh.

Looking back at the stage, I found four people lining up on it. One man and three women—all wearing red cloaks— were getting into position. Chains fell from the rafters, and more men came onto the stage to string the women up.

Playing with ropes and chains wasn't a thing I'd ever

done. Not that I wouldn't like to someday, but I just didn't have the know-how to put all that stuff up in a space. And I couldn't have a room at home, the way a lot of Doms did. My parents visited from their home in Texas and stayed with me about three or four times a year. They'd usually stay for a week each time, and Mom was a nosy little woman. I'd never get away with having a red room of pain in my place.

Not to mention, Malibu beach houses weren't quite the place to practice things that had women screaming. The cops would be called, that was a given.

So I was left with dabbling with my little fetish in another place. A few people knew my sinister secret. My partners, and my best friend, Shanna. My partners thought it was badass. Shanna thought it was freakish and that I'd get over it one day and grow the hell up.

Shanna and I had been friends back in our tiny hometown of Pettus, Texas. When I came out to L.A., she got mad at me for leaving her all alone in the boring town. After I'd established myself, I gave in to her pleas and let her come out and live at my place until she was able to stand on her own two feet. A thing she did pretty rapidly. It was when she was living with me that she found out about my little secret.

I'd brought a woman home with me one night during the first week Shanna was there. I'd forgotten she was there, to be honest. I was spanking the woman, and she was moaning—a lot—and begging me to hit her harder. Shanna knocked on the bedroom door and yelled at me to come out and talk to her. Which I did, reluctantly sending the woman home as Shanna berated me for my unforgivable behavior. She told me *Fifty Shades* sucked and anyone who followed such a mindless plot was a goddamned fool, a thing she knew I wasn't.

I was expecting another berating and a long sermon to

come from her when I returned home from this trip. I'd managed to duck out of town before she could catch me and try to stop me from going to Portland—knowing what I did whenever I traveled there.

"Excuse me, please," came a soft voice as a woman touched my arm to get me to take a step to one side, allowing her to move into the crowd.

She only made it a few steps in front of me before the outer wall of people stopped her forward progression. Even from behind she was alluring.

Long legs, covered in torn black fishnet stockings, ended in a pair of red heels. A black bodice clung to her curves; her round ass gave way to a dip in her back, displayed by a panel of see-thru black lace splitting the silky material right down the middle.

She wore her hair in a long dark braid that she had pulled over her left shoulder. When she turned around, clearly annoyed that she couldn't see anything from where she was, her blue eyes met mine.

Lifting my drink to her, I said, "Hey."

Hey? Really? How lame am I?

37

CHAPTER 2

Katana

Although the night had started out badly, I found myself looking into the most gorgeous set of deep green eyes I'd ever seen. The mask he wore did little to hide the fact that the tall, muscular man was handsome. "Hey," he said to me as he raised his glass.

I needed a drink desperately. A thing he must've noticed as my eyes moved from his gaze to his almost full glass. Just then a waiter walked behind him, and he stopped the guy, grabbing me a drink off the full tray.

Handing me a dark drink with a lime wedge hanging on the rim of the clear highball glass, he smiled at me. "Would you care for a drink?"

"I'm dying for one, actually." I took the drink from him and struggled to be somewhat classy, taking a dainty sip instead of downing it the way I wanted to.

The last week had been hellish. I hadn't paid attention to my schedule and had set up not two or three deadlines for myself, but ten of them. As a freelance book cover designer,

I was self-employed, and that meant I was my own boss, a thing that was new to me. Not experienced in management, things had gotten out of hand. I'd get it down eventually, I knew I would—but the week had taken its toll on me.

One would think going to a BDSM club for a Halloween party would be the last place an overworked woman would want to go. But being able to give my whole self over to someone else was always a relief. So I took the invite sent to me by my friend Blyss. We'd met long ago, when I was just a kid sent to an orphanage after my mother disappeared. Blyss and I were a lot alike. We were both quiet and kept to ourselves. We'd written to one another when I was sent to live with an elderly couple in foster care, and she stayed at the orphanage. We kept in contact just so we both knew there was at least one person in the world who knew we existed.

Blyss had met the man she'd eventually married at this club, and she had encouraged me to check it out by coming to their first annual Halloween Ball. She knew I had little experience in the BDSM world but assured me that didn't matter. I could just watch things this first time. If someone did ask me to do anything, she told me to let them know about my inexperience.

I'd hoped she and her husband, Troy, would be at the club for the big bash, but he didn't want to bring her back to the place for some reason. I thought it was odd that he wouldn't want to come back to a place that had brought them together.

"Do you come here often?" the hunky man asked me, shaking me from my thoughts.

Only then did I realize I hadn't even said thank you. "Oh, jeez!" I grimaced and felt the plastic of my mask gouge into my cheeks. "I'm sorry. It's been a hell of a week. First, let me say thanks for grabbing me a drink. I need copious amounts of alcohol to rid my mind of all the clutter that's been burning through it for over a week. And second, let me answer your question. No, I don't come here often. This is my first time."

When his lips pulled up into one of the best smiles I'd ever seen, I couldn't help but notice his perfect teeth. "First time, huh? Any experience with this type of thing?"

My body tensed. I wasn't used to talking about where I'd gotten my experience, limited as it was. "Well, I had this boyfriend when I was nineteen. He liked to spank me. And that turned into a little more, a little bondage." I hesitated to tell him the rest, as our little playtime hadn't ended well. I didn't want him to think I was scared by what had happened. But Blyss had urged me to be truthful with any man I might consider doing anything with, so I went on, "In the end, the BDSM thing turned into just plain physical abuse, coupled with mental abuse. It ended when he went to jail for beating the hell out of me and leaving me with a broken arm and jaw."

"Damn." His one-word answer had me looking down. I knew he felt sorry for me and probably thought of me as damaged goods. His fingers touched my chin, pulling my face up. I saw the concern in his green eyes. "Are you okay now?"

I nodded. "That was a few years ago. I got over it," I told him.

And I had, for the most part. The only remnant from that horrible time in my life was a nightmare sneaking up on me every now and then, telling me I still had a little damage leftover from the brute.

"You can call me Mr. S. What should I call you?" He shifted his weight as he looked me over.

"Katana," I said, as I hadn't thought of an alternate name for myself. Blyss hadn't told me about doing that. "Katana Reeves."

"Nice to meet you, Katana Reeves." He jerked his head to one side. "I'm not into crowds. You wanna join me in one of the smaller rooms? We can watch a scene together."

After a nod, he took me by the hand and off we went, leaving the large room behind us. A step behind him, I took the opportunity to chug my drink while he couldn't see me. I needed to take the edge off, and quickly.

As he pushed open a door, I heard horrible groans and saw a woman all tied up and bent over some kind of a table. Hushed whispers were heard as a handful of people watched what seemed to be a brutal scene.

Out of the corner of my eye, I spotted a bar and pulled at my hand to get Mr. S to let me go. He stopped and turned to look at me, seeing the empty glass in my hand. He smiled at me, and we headed to the bar first. "What would you like, Katana?"

"Bourbon and Coke, please." I already felt like he was taking care of me, and it felt awesome—exactly what I needed after my hectic week.

"A double shot of Michter's Celebration and Coke for the lady and some of the same for me, straight on the rocks." He set his half-full glass on the bar, and I placed my empty one next to his. His dark green eyes moved to my lips. "I like that black lipstick you've got on. Shame it's going to get all messed up later."

His confident statement took me by surprise, and all I could do was stare at the hot man who seemed to be made of muscles. A shiver ran through me as our drinks were put in front of us. He took mine, placing it in my hand. Then he grabbed his drink in one hand, my hand with the other, and took me to a little table for two at the back of the room.

I gulped as I heard the loud smacking sound of leather meeting flesh and the yell of pain that followed. My eyes closed as I thought about what I was getting myself into.

His arm moved over my shoulder, and he drew me in close. His lips grazed my ear as he said softly, "You're perfectly safe with me, Katana. No reason to worry at all. Just sit back and relax. Enjoy the show—then perhaps you'll think about what you and I can come up with together. I promise you won't feel abused while in my hands."

The way he spoke, the look in his eyes, the way he touched me—it all made me feel at ease. He was a perfect stranger, yet I felt drawn to him in a way I'd never felt with any other man. Another smacking sound had me looking at the couple on the small stage.

Sagging in the ropes, the woman seemed beaten down. My heart ached as I knew how that felt. In more ways than one. Lyle Strickland wasn't the first person to beat the hell out of me and leave me wishing for death to take the pain away. But he'd sure as hell be the last.

When the woman's Dom untied her, he carried her wilted body to a bed and laid her down with gentleness. He got up to leave her, and her arms went out to him as she moaned, "Please, sir."

"Now you want me?" her Dom asked her. "I thought you wanted that other man."

"Only you, sir. I'm only meant for you. Please take me. I am yours."

Since we didn't get to see most of the show, I figured she must've been cheating on her Dom and had gotten caught. My eyes cut to Mr. S's, finding him none too pleased with the scene. A hard line had his lips clamped shut.

He and I both seemed out of place in the BDSM club. The look on his face was different from the look most of the other men who watched the show had. He looked disgusted, while most of the others looked enticed. I had to admit, that particular scene wasn't a thing I liked either.

If someone cheated on you, you let their sorry ass go. No need to whip them into loving you. As if that could even happen in real life.

It came as no shock to me when he leaned in close once more. "I've got a few toys at my hotel. What do you say we ditch this place and head over there?"

My brain interjected. *Um, hello, Katana. You don't even know this man's real name or one damn thing about him except he's into BDSM.*

Cocking one brow, I dared to ask, "Do you think you could give me some identification before I take you up on that offer?"

Without missing a beat, he pulled out his wallet and showed me his California driver's license. "I'm Nixon Slaughter, owner of Champlain Services in Los Angeles." He went one step further and took a business card out of his wallet, slipping it into my hand before putting his wallet away. "That's my number. Feel better about being alone with me now, Katana Reeves?"

With a nod, I agreed to what he wanted. "I'm in your hands now, Mr. S."

"I think for tonight I'd like to be called Master, my little slave girl." He got up, took my hand, and away we went.

38

CHAPTER 3

Nixon

Heading into the lobby of the Heathman Hotel, Katana and I got a few stares as we strolled in. She'd donned a red cloak to cover her little naughty negligee, but we'd kept the masks on. It felt more fun that way.

In the elevator, we rode up to my room with two other couples. They seemed to sense we were up to no good and stayed on the far side, away from us. When we got out, the others stayed inside, and we both laughed as we walked down the hallway.

Putting my arm around her shoulders, I gave her a little squeeze. "Think we intimidated them?"

"Seems like we did." Katana smiled, and it made my heart beat faster. Her smile was amazing. So bright, brilliant, and genuine. "I guess they thought they'd ended up in an elevator with a couple of freaks."

"Didn't they?" I asked as I chuckled and pulled out the keycard to open the door to my hotel room.

I let her go in first, and she looked around at the glamorous room. "I've lived in Portland for a long time now and
have never been inside this place. It's like a Portland
treasure."

"It is. This hotel is where I always stay when I come to
town." I closed the door, locking it behind us.

She turned around at the sound and looked at the door.
"Just so you know, I've never done this."

"I thought you said you had, but it turned into a bad
thing?" Was she getting cold feet? I hadn't even done
anything to her yet.

She pulled off the cloak and draped it over the back of
the chair in front of the small desk. "I mean, I haven't gone
to bed with a man I've just met." She looked at me and
grinned shyly. "Or are you one of those BDSM guys who just
get off on the punishment phase and not the sexual one?"

Stepping out of my shoes, I wondered what she was
thinking about all of this. She seemed calm, but she had just
come into a hotel room with a stranger. She and I had
discussed nothing on the way in. Nor had I tested the waters
on anything yet.

For my part, I felt very unlike myself—and I had no idea
why she would have this effect on me. But I was going to get
past that for sure. Katana had a beauty about her that
intrigued me. She wasn't able to hold eye contact long at all.
And when we were alone in the back of the car on the way
to the hotel, she hadn't spoken unless I'd said something.

It was almost as if I was a virgin teen again with no real
clue as to what to do, and Katana seemed to be having the
same reaction to me. I found myself stumbling over my
words as I tried to answer her question. "I, um, well—let's
see. I don't get off on hitting, if that's what you're asking me.
And I'd like to have sex, if that's okay with you."

She looked down, her eyes glued to the floor. "Okay. I mean, I'd like to have sex too. It's actually been a long time since I've done anything."

"How long's a long time, Katana?" I took my jacket off and went to hang it up.

"A year or so."

I dropped the jacket on the floor and turned around. "Are you shitting me?"

She shook her head, and my heart went out to the young woman. "About a year and a half, actually." She looked up and looked around the room, her eyes landing on the minifridge. "I don't suppose you have any alcohol in there?"

I unbuttoned my shirt, now completely understanding her need for alcohol. The poor thing was pent up. I could fix that. "No need. I know how to quench your thirst. On the bed, on your back. Your Master is about to please his little slave."

"Should I undress first?" She turned one heeled foot inward as she put her hand on her hip.

"No. Just do as I've told you." I stripped down to my tight black boxer briefs and went to the side of the bed where she lay down, waiting for me. "Close your eyes, slave. Relax."

Picking up her foot, I ran my lips up her long leg then grabbed the top of her thigh-high fishnet stocking with my teeth, pulling it down until it was at her ankle. I pulled off her high heel then removed the stocking.

Running my hands up her bare leg, I felt goosebumps as they pimpled her cool flesh. I did the same thing to her other leg before I settled my body between her legs. She was nervous; I could tell from her shallow breathing.

"One of the rules of the club is that everyone is screened for diseases and the females are in charge of the birth control." I leaned in and blew on her panty-covered cunt, her essence already pouring through the thin fabric. "Have you taken care of all that, slave?"

"I have, Master." I watched as her hands moved into fists on top of the bedspread. She was getting tense in anticipation of what I was about to do.

"You have nothing to fear. Our safe word is red. Say yellow if you're beginning to get uncomfortable. Got it?" I blew on her pussy again.

"Got it, Master." She began to tremble, and I knew she was letting her mind get ahead of her, worrying about what she'd gotten into.

Little did she know she had a pretty great guy who'd make sure she got what she'd gone into the Dungeon looking for. "I'm going to rip your panties off and cut your clothes away from your body. Not to worry though, I'll have something sent up for you in the morning. I want you all night long, slave."

She tensed up even more but said nothing. I smiled as it thrilled me to know she trusted me so much, even when she had absolutely no reason to at this point.

With one swift pull, I ripped her panties off and put my mouth on her cunt, running my tongue through her warm folds. She moaned softly then got louder as I kissed her pussy lips. Lips that hadn't seen any action in way too long.

The sounds she made had my cock growing more and more. I knew right then that it would be hard to keep myself under control with her. But I liked a challenge, so I thought only of pleasing her and ignored my straining male member. He'd get what he craved soon enough, and plenty of it, when I stuffed my fat cock into her soaked pussy after she'd come a few times for me.

Moving my tongue inside her and lapping up her decadent taste, I lost control for a bit as my brain took a siesta while my inner sex god feasted on her delicious cunt. Oh, but she tasted like sin wrapped in heaven!

As great as she tasted then, I had to know what an orgasm would do to enhance that. Moving my tongue out of her, I went to work on her clit, which had swollen to three times its original size. Rolling it between my lips, I sucked it then moved my lips up and down it as it grew even more.

Her moans grew louder, and she arched up to me. I could hear her fists pounding the bed, and then she whimpered as her body let go. I moved down, eager to get my tongue inside her to feel how she contracted with her orgasm.

Fluids met my hungry tongue as I shoved it into her tight pussy. She clenched down on my tongue as I moved it back and forth, encouraging her body to keep coming for me. Amazed by everything she gave me, I knew I'd picked one ripe female for the night. I'd make this a night she'd remember for a very long time. A night that she could get off to if she didn't have sex again for a long time.

I pulled my head away from her soaking pussy to look at her. She looked gorgeous as she panted, her eyes closed. The mask was still on her face, hiding her a bit from me. For one moment I thought about taking the masks off. But I shook my head. The masks lent anonymity to what we were doing. That was part of the thrill—fucking someone you didn't have all the information about, and not caring.

Getting off the bed, I saw her gorgeous blue eyes open, and she watched me as I went to get some things. "Thank you, Master. I really needed that. You were right. I didn't need any alcohol to get into this. You're very good at what you do."

"Glad you liked it, slave. Now tell me how much pain you want to feel, and I'll give that to you, too." I pulled some of my favorite toys out of my suitcase and turned around with four sets of fluffy cuffs. "And how do you feel about being restrained?"

She sat up and ran her hands over her heaving breasts. "I haven't been bound in a long time. I've never allowed that after what happened to me." My face must've shown my disappointment because she quickly added, "I trust you, Master. I'm in your capable hands and will do anything you want to." She laid back down. "Go ahead, strap me down. I am yours to toy with."

My cock jumped with her words. *Mine to toy with?*

She really would be a treat!

39

CHAPTER 4

Katana

The only words I could use to describe Nixon's body were totally ripped. The bulge in his tight black underwear left nothing to the imagination. He was hung better than anyone I'd ever been with and my pussy was throbbing with need for his massive appendage.

The last click I heard left me pinned to the bed in a spread-eagled position. My negligee was still intact, but I knew that wouldn't be the case for long as he headed back to me with a knife in his hand. The light glistened off the long blade; my heart sprang into action with the fear the object invoked. I gulped, closing my eyes as I felt the cold blade against my skin.

Soft ripping sounds met my ears as he cut away the flimsy material that barely hid my body from his gorgeous green eyes. Once he had cut away everything, I felt the tip of the knife as he moved it over me. He stopped at one nipple, and I could feel the sensitive tip pulsing. I had no idea knife-play could be so enticing and erotic. Whenever I'd thought about it before, I thought I'd be much too afraid to enjoy it at all.

How wrong I'd been.

The knife went down my side, and Nixon's mouth came to replace the blade at my nipple. He pulled it with his teeth, and I moaned as a slight pain jolted through me in the best possible way. Then he soothed it with some gentle licks before biting down, making me yelp.

His laugh was deep and sinister. He enjoyed making me cry out in pain. The blade moved up and down my side, igniting both chills and heat inside of me. It would be so easy for him to rip me open with that long sharp knife, yet he wasn't going to do that. Something inside me told me that.

Nixon pulled the knife over my stomach then up to the other tit, and he moved the edge up until I felt the sharpness at the base of my nipple. One swift movement and I'd lose it. I stopped breathing.

Shit, have I handed myself over to a murderer?

Sure, he'd given me his card with his name and number on it, but what would that matter if I was dead?

The safe word, red, ruminated inside my brain, but before I could say it the knife was gone, and his hot mouth was on my tit. He sucked it hard and long, and the cold knife came to rest on my stomach as he sucked me. I groaned as the pain from his strong sucks mixed with pleasure deep in my core. I'd never felt anything like it. I'd never had anyone suck on my tit with such aggression and for so long, and the climax that washed over me took me by surprise.

"God!" I cried out with the sensation. My entire body pulsed with a very different orgasm than I'd ever experienced.

Nixon's voice came softly near my ear, "Hush now, slave. We've only just begun."

My entire body quivered. *We'd only just begun?*

I had already ridden two monstrous waves and we'd only just begun?

Did I have the stamina to make it through the night?

I watched him walk away from me, his fine ass moving with each step.

Yeah, I can find the stamina to make it through the night with him!

My arms longed to wrap around his muscular body, and without conscious thought I pulled to test the cuffs holding them. My legs pulled too, wanting to wrap around him, to hold him to me.

My pussy, still throbbing from the orgasm, wanted more. It wanted him buried so deep inside me that it defied possibility. I ached to feel him all the way up to my heart. And I wanted it now. "Please, Master, take me now," the words came out with a whimpered plea.

He stopped and spun around. His eyes were hard and cold all of a sudden. "Are you telling your Master what to do, slave? That's grounds for punishment—surely you know that."

I didn't know that. I mean I did, but I didn't. I thought I'd phrased it in such a way that it didn't come off as telling him what to do, but I must've been wrong.

He went to his suitcase, pulling out a long black leather belt. I gasped as he came toward me and undid all the cuffs. I lay perfectly still. He grabbed me by the waist and pulled me around until I was face down on his lap.

One smack with the belt had me yelping, and he gave me three more in rapid succession. "Are you going to tell your Master what to do anymore, slave?"

I gauged how my body reacted to the spanking and found it was on fire. And not in a bad way. My hesitation to answer him had me getting three more hits, and I moaned as I felt my pussy creaming with desire.

I wanted more.

I kept my mouth shut, and he gave me three more before asking, "Does my little slave like to be punished?"

"Yes," I whimpered. "More, please."

"And there you go again." He gave me three more smacks then reached under me and inserted his finger into me, finding me wetter than I'd ever been in my life. "Ah, I see why you're being so disobedient now." He pumped his finger into me and used his free hand to smack my ass some more.

Insane as it might sound, I was getting off to that in a huge way. His finger kept moving in and out as his other hand smacked me over and over. Then he moved his finger in a come-hither motion, hitting my G-spot—which I hadn't even been sure I had, as no other man had ever found it, nor had I. I burst into an instant orgasm and cried with the release.

Tears flowed from my eyes like rivers as my body let everything go. The tension I had been carrying around for weeks—maybe even months or years—seemed to turn to water inside me and rushed out of my body through my eyes and my pussy.

Before I knew what was happening, he'd moved me to lie on my back and pulled my ass to the edge of the bed. He got on his knees and lapped up the thick cream I'd emitted for him. The sounds coming from deep in his throat made me think he'd never tasted anything he'd ever enjoyed so much. It stirred something inside of me.

Why can this only last one night?

I shook my head at that thought and wiped my eyes. I couldn't go thinking about the future. Who knew, he might come back for more now and then.

When he'd gotten his fill, he stood up, wiping my wetness from his chin with the back of his hand. "Suck me off."

I hurried to get on my hands and knees on the bed, and his erection was right at my level. I eased his underwear off his massive cock and found it was hard as a rock.

Taking it in my hands, I looked at the beautiful thing and licked my lips, anticipating how full my mouth would be. I opened and closed my mouth a few times, stretching my jaw, and then licked the tip and took hold of the base of his cock.

Only the top quarter fit into my mouth, and I used my hands to cover the rest. After only a few strokes I felt the need to give him more. He'd given me so much, after all.

I pulled my mouth from him and noticed the look he gave me, his expression one of confusion. But he quickly understood what I was up to 'when I got on my back and let my head fall over the side of the bed. He smiled and put his cock into my mouth. In that position, I could take him all in, but he'd have to do the moving.

His dick slid into my mouth and hit the back of my throat, making me gag a bit, but he pushed it further down. I closed my eyes as tears began to fall—not because I was in pain, but just a natural reaction to gagging. He moved slowly at first, gradually thrusting faster and faster until he shot his load straight down my throat.

"God!" he shouted as he pulled his cock out of my mouth. "Fuck!" He breathed heavily as he sat on the bed, huffing and puffing. "No one's ever done that for me. I've always been told I'm too big."

I sat up, and he turned his head to look at me. I couldn't help but smile, feeling extraordinarily pleased with myself. "You're not too big; you're just right. For me, anyway."

A smile crept across his face, and he tossed me onto my back and kissed me hard. Our tastes converged, and we both groaned with how well they went together.

When he mounted me, I spread my legs wide for him and he slid right in, his cock hard once more, stretching me to fit his size. It burned, and I moaned with the pain. But then it felt amazing. He was hitting deeper in me than I'd ever been hit. Our bodies worked each other with a force I'd never known.

When we both came at the same time, our eyes locked. I felt it all so deeply. He stilled inside me as we tried to catch our breaths. We just stared at each other, his arms braced on either side of my head, panting like animals. I had no idea what he was thinking. But I had my own thoughts to focus on.

This can't be real!

40

CHAPTER 5

Nixon

O ur time together passed much too quickly. Katana and I did everything I could think of, and not once did she seem the least bit apprehensive about anything I did to her. For a couple of complete strangers, we connected in a way that felt as if we'd known one another forever.

We'd only had a couple of hours of sleep before the driver I'd hired was expected to arrive to take me to the airport, where I'd hop on the company jet back to L.A. I had work to get to.

When I rolled over to wake her, I saw her mask had come off as she slept. Mine had stayed on, but I pulled it off as I gazed at her.

Katana's face was just as gorgeous as I'd thought it would be. I'd pulled her dark hair out of the braid at one point during our night, and the long strands were everywhere. She looked like an angel as she slept, her lips swollen from all the kissing we'd done. I pushed a lock of hair off her face, and she moaned a bit before her eyes fluttered open.

I couldn't stop the smile that took over my mouth—she looked too perfect. "Hi."

"Hi," she replied with a stretch. Then her hand came up to caress my cheek. "You're even more handsome without the mask."

"And you're even more beautiful without yours," I kissed her cheek. "Did you sleep well?" Before she could answer, I pulled her into my arms, holding her in a way I rarely did with anyone, especially not anyone I'd done this sort of thing with.

She cuddled into my chest. "You wore me out completely. I slept like a baby. Not even a dream made it through."

With a chuckle, I agreed, "We did seem to give it our all, didn't we?"

"I should think so. It'll tide me over for quite some time," she said then rolled off me and got out of bed, heading to the bathroom.

I watched her round ass, admiring the dimple at the top of each cheek as she left the room. And I caught myself sighing. "What have you done to me, you little vixen?"

The sex had been better than any I could recall. She felt better in my arms and underneath me than anyone ever had. But this was a one-time thing.

Sure, I could probably call her up now and then and see if she'd like to have another one-nighter, but that wasn't really how I liked to do things. I preferred to hit it and quit it. It kept things uncomplicated, and that was my goal.

I heard the shower running and decided now was the time to call the front desk and have something sent up for her to wear home. "Rhoda speaking. How may I help you, Mr. Slaughter?"

"I need some clothes sent up in size two." I'd checked the tag on her naughty nighty to get her size. She had red heels so I ordered something that would match them. "Can you send up a black dress? Something nice and expensive. Matching bra and panties too." I had to guess on the size of that. "The bra is a thirty-two D. And if you find a nice necklace that would accent it, please add that on; money isn't a concern. I want the best of everything. And please have it delivered to my room as quickly as you can."

"Yes, sir. Give me half an hour, and I'll have it sent right up."

I hung up the hotel phone and went to the closet to retrieve my clothes for the trip back home. My cell rang, and I went back to get it, seeing it wasn't a number I had in my contacts. "Hello?"

"Hey, is this Nixon?" a man asked me.

"Yes. And this is?" I looked in the mirror at my stubbled cheeks. *Maybe I'll grow my beard out,* I thought to myself. *A little something to remind me of last night.*

"This is Owen Cantrell. You gave me your card last night. I was just calling to check on you. I lost track of you last night and wanted to be sure you made it out safely."

"Um, yeah, I made it out all right." I had no idea why he'd be worried about something like that.

He soon told me why. "That was some scene, huh? I don't think I've ever been more afraid in my entire life."

"Of what?" I asked, as I was clearly in the dark.

"The explosions, of course," he enlightened me.

"Explosions?"

"Yeah," he went on. "Wait, did you leave before that happened?"

"I did." I walked back to the bed and sat down, feeling a little lightheaded. "So there were explosions? Was anyone hurt, or worse?"

"Thankfully no one was hurt. We all managed to make it out of there somehow." He stopped, and I heard him make a smacking sound. "I'm sorry. I just had to give my wife a kiss. It was like we almost lost each other last night. It was awful. The Dungeon of Decorum seems like it's probably at an end. It was completely destroyed."

"I can't believe it," I mumbled. "What time did this happen?"

"Hell, I can't even begin to tell you that. I couldn't think straight until a little while ago. I was definitely suffering from a bit of shock. I just keep thinking how close my wife and I came to meeting our maker."

"Wow. Looks like I dodged a bullet. Glad I found someone and we left early." And I was glad of that for a couple other reasons too.

"Well, you and I need to hang out a bit when we get back to Los Angeles. I'd like to see you some time before New Year's Eve. Catch you later, Nixon," he said, then hung up.

My eyes flew to the bathroom door, where Katana was coming out. She'd wrapped her perfect body in a fluffy pink towel. "Did I hear you talking to someone?"

"Yeah," I said as I put my cell down on the nightstand. "Seems we'll never be going back to that club again."

Her dark brows rose. "And why might that be?"

"It's destroyed. Some explosions occurred. I don't know the full story. One of my buddies from the club just called to ask if I had made it out okay." I got up and walked straight to her, gathering her into my arms, still naked as the day I was born. "I'm so glad I got you out of there before anything happened, Katana."

"My God, Nix. How lucky are we?" she asked, and I felt a chill run through her as her body shook a bit.

She'd called me Nix. My mother called me that. No one else ever had. I had a reputation that usually stopped anything like that. But I loved the way it sounded coming out of her mouth.

Pulling back, I didn't let her go as I looked at her with a smile on my face. "Nix, huh? Okay, I'll give you that one. But does that mean I get to call you Kat?"

With a sigh, she gave me a weak smile. "I don't know if we'll be doing anymore calling each other anything. When we leave here, this is over. No strings. I recall how this all works. We had one hot night, and there'll be nothing more. I know the rules. I'm not going to bother you."

I'd kind of like her to bother me.

I nodded, knowing she had had to sign something at the club that held her to that promise. But it didn't stop me from feeling a bit bad about it.

I genuinely liked the woman. "You do have my number if you really need me. Not that I think you would—but if you do, you have it."

"I won't use it." She turned her head. "That's not what either of us went to that club for, right? One hot night of crazy sex is what we went there for, and we got that." She looked back at me, and I saw something shimmer in the backs of her blue eyes. Her hands moved up my arms, reaching up to cradle my face. "I'll keep the memory of last night locked away in my mind forever, Nixon Slaughter. It's my most cherished one so far." She kissed my lips softly.

Now it was my turn to feel the chill, and my body quaked for a moment. I tightened my hold on her, pulling her closer to me and kissing her back in a way I'd never done with another one-night stand sub.

A knock on the door interrupted what was sure to turn into another sexual escapade. My brain was thankful; my cock was not. "That would be your clothes. Put them on while I shower. Don't you dare leave. I'll have the driver I hired take you home after he takes me to the airport. I'd get you home first but I've got to go in to the office once I get back home. Most days are work days for me."

"Okay," she said with a smile. "That's very sweet of you."

Sweet? Was I being sweet?

I let her go and walked away, knowing I wasn't being myself with her. I was anything but sweet. Back in L.A I was known for my aloofness and for never dating anyone for more than a couple weeks. Most of the time, business occupied my mind. I'd been accused of being neglectful by my dates, answering calls at dinner, getting up and walking away, leaving my dates alone with no explanation as to why.

As I showered, I tried to think about business to get my head back in working order, but Katana kept popping into my mind with memories of her sweet smile or her hot kiss.

I had to hurry up and get sexy little Katana home and away from me. Her hooks seemed to be sinking into me, and I couldn't have that at all.

41

CHAPTER 6

Katana

Sitting down at my computer to get to work on a new book cover, I still wore the gorgeous dress Nix bought me. We'd parted ways only a couple of hours before, and his goodbye kiss still tingled on my lips.

I stared blankly at the computer screen. My mind couldn't focus on anything other than the events of last night. When my cell rang, I jumped and looked at it, hoping it might be him.

But it couldn't be him. He didn't have my number. I had his, though I'd never call it. It wasn't a sub's place to call her Master, even if their pact was only for one night.

Blyss's name lit up my phone, and I answered the call. "Hi, Blyss. How's it going?"

"You sound way too calm, Katana. Didn't you go to the club last night?" she asked.

"I did, and I left it only a short time after I arrived, as the most handsome Dom picked me before I had a chance to see much of the club you've told me so much about." I got up and walked to the window to look outside as I conjured up the memory of the first time I'd laid eyes on Nix.

Blyss's voice pulled me out of my reverie before I could really start daydreaming about the man. "So you weren't in the club when all the chaos ensued then?"

Oh, that! "No. No, he and I left very early, thank God. Someone from the club called him and told him about it. Seems we dodged a bullet there."

"That you did." She seemed to be a lot calmer than before. "Okay, so this Dom, tell me all about him and what you guys did."

I leaned my shoulder against the window pane and sighed. "He was the best lover I've ever had. Not that I've had that many. Okay, I've had two, and it's been over a year since I've had sex of any kind."

"You haven't even masturbated?" she interrupted me.

"That's personal!" I laughed. "But no, not even that. Maybe it seemed so intense and hugely satisfying because of that, I don't know. But it was electric, and I can't stop thinking about it. Is it possible to have a sex hangover, Blyss?"

She laughed. "I've had more than one of those. But then when you have a man as intense as mine, you get a thorough fucking at least once a month, with major fucks most days."

"So that's what it would be like if I had a long-term thing with a Dom?" I asked as the idea did things to my insides that made me quiver.

"Does last night have you thinking about finding your-self a full-time Dom, Katana?" she asked with a hint of humor in her voice.

"Well, not just any Dom would do. But my guy wasn't into anything that lasts longer than one night. He doesn't even live in this city." I moved away from the window and went to sit back down.

"So was he able to get all that pent-up stress out of you? I know you had one hell of a crazy schedule last week—you were going insane." She laughed again. "I hope he got that off your back."

All the stress had melted away, and it had to be because of him. "Oh, yeah, he got rid of all that. Much better than the masseuse my friend recommended."

She giggled knowingly. "I bet."

Running my hand through my hair, I released the scent of the hotel shampoo and an image of Nixon flashed in my head. I had to think about something else. "So, how's the hubby, Blyss? Is Troy doing okay?"

"He's doing well. We're about to take the kids out to window shop for Christmas presents," she told me. "We do that every year so they can let us know all the things they want, and then we surprise them with a few of them on Christmas. It's a fun tradition we've had for a few years."

"Christmas already?" I had to ask. "It's barely the day after Halloween."

"Yeah, I know. This is the traditional day that we do this thing. That way we have lots of time to make sure we get them what they really want. I always have my Christmas shopping done before Thanksgiving. Because the day after Thanksgiving we set up the Christmas tree and I have presents ready to go right away. We're big on the holidays in this family."

"I'm glad you've found yourself a big family to live and love with. You deserve it all, Blyss," I gushed. She'd been the best person I'd ever met while in the foster care system.

"Aw, thanks, Katana. You know you deserve happiness too." She paused, and I could tell her wheels were spinning.

"I worry about you sometimes. You stay alone too much, holed up in your little apartment in Portland, making those book covers. I know you're making good money and all, but it takes away from your social life. You really need to get out more. Make a habit of it. Stop working at five or six, get yourself dolled up and go out instead of working all night."

"I don't know." The thought of going out and maybe ending up in bed with another guy just hit me the wrong way all of a sudden. I knew I didn't belong to Nixon, but there was something that told me I'd be disappointed if I went to bed with another man. Plus, I couldn't think about anyone else at that moment, still overwhelmed by our amazing night together. "I'm not into clubbing. The only reason I registered with The Dungeon of Decorum is because of the safety net it provided me. No abuse is tolerated, and I had a number to call if that occurred."

"Yeah, I know that bastard did a number on you back then. Do you know if he's still in jail or not?" she asked with concern etching her voice.

I didn't know a thing about the man who'd left permanent scars on my body, brain, and heart. "I don't know anything about him. It's been four years since I left Flagstaff. As far as I know, he doesn't have a clue where I moved. Lyle Strickland is a man I try hard not to think about." I paused for a moment, reflecting on the relationship I'd had two years after I left Lyle, after I'd moved to Portland. "I know he's the main reason it didn't work out with Jimmy, too. I just never trusted him the entire six months we were together."

"I know how hard it is to find that trust again. I've had my fair share of torture in the past. Not that I want to get into any of that. That's all better off left alone. Well, I better get going. I can hear the kids putting up a fuss already. Love you, Katana."

"I love you too, Blyss. I'll call you again soon. Have fun. Bye." I ended the call and leaned my head back, thinking about my past.

When Lyle had come onto me just after I turned nineteen, I'd thought I had hit the jackpot. He was older, twenty-five, and so dominant. I suppose I liked that sort of thing because I'd never had anyone care that much about me. I took it as a sign that he really loved me.

Turned out, he really loved controlling my every move, and then he really loved beating the shit out of me. My bruises and broken bones healed, but my heart and soul were left in rough shape.

Even if Nixon Slaughter were knocking down my door trying to date me, I wasn't in any shape to be the woman for him. Still having my moments of being an emotional wreck at times proved I wasn't ready to be anyone's girl.

Poor Jimmy had got the shit end of the stick when he got with me. As a couple of years had passed since the horror show with Lyle, I'd thought I was over everything. Jimmy was anything but dominating. Poor guy was a pushover. I suppose that's why things ended so fast between us. I pushed him to lord over me, but that wasn't for him. He couldn't do it.

I knew I'd had a rough life. I knew I had mental issues with that. Was it so wrong of me to need a man who would take control and treat me like I was his?

It didn't seem that modern women wanted what I wanted. Not most of them anyway. I wanted that firm hand. I wanted that rough touch. Craved it. And I thought I'd found that with Lyle. But what I found instead was that you couldn't trust every dominant man.

And I couldn't be happy with a man who wasn't at least somewhat dominating, either.

I felt stuck in a terribly deep rut. The thing I wanted the most was the thing that had hurt me so much in the past and made me wary of relationships. And I had no idea what I'd ever do to remedy that. Being alone wasn't the answer either.

Getting up, I went back to my desk and tapped on the computer to bring up pictures of hot, muscular men so I could pick one for the next book cover I'd be making.

One by one, I blew them all off as none compared to Nixon. His tight abs, his broad chest with massive pecs, his hulking biceps—no one compared to him.

How in the hell would I ever get him out of my mind?

Would time eventually rid me of that perfect memory? Would I even want it to?

It had one perfect night. The best night of my entire life. Why would I want to forget about it?

Maybe because it already haunted me. Maybe because I already knew no other man could come close to comparing to Nixon Slaughter.

I was doomed.

42

CHAPTER 7

Nixon

F all weather made the drive to work a pleasure. I didn't even mind the hour I had to sit in traffic at the airport. It gave me time to think about my night with Katana, after all.

It'd only been a little while since I'd left her, but I had to admit I found myself missing her a little too often. She had my number, and I kept wishing she'd call. Maybe she'd ask me to come down and play for the weekend or something. But the phone never rang.

When traffic began rolling again, I made it all the way to my office building. Champlain Services, located inside the Century Plaza Towers on Century Park East, was my home away from home. With six offices on the top floor, we had a great view of the city.

When I came into the reception area, I saw my admin assistant, Blake, busy on the phone. I gave him a wave and headed to my office. He paused in the middle of his conversation to call out to me, "Don't forget you have the Skype meeting this morning, boss."

"Thanks." I had forgotten about the meeting, but I wasn't behind schedule even with the hour lost in traffic.

Getting into my office, I turned on the computer monitor on the wall and got ready for the meeting with my partners in the nightclub endeavor. The call came in from Gannon Forester's office, and I clicked the accept button and found his adorable little secretary looking at me from the conference room in his office. "Good morning, Mr. Slaughter. It's nice to see you."

"You too, Janine. Is Gannon there?" I pulled up my most comfortable chair and settled in for the meeting.

"Yes, sir. And I'll be adding Mr. Harlow to this meeting in just one moment. Sit tight," she said with a smile, then pushed her thick-framed glasses up her nose a bit.

After a minute, August Harlow's face filled half the screen. "Hey, ugly," I joked with him.

"Hey, precious," he said with a chuckle. "How's life treating ya? You weren't in town yesterday. Where might you have been?"

"Oh, nowhere special. Did you miss me?" I winked at him.

"Of course, my little buttercup. Halloween was nothing without your sweet little ass there," he kidded with me. "But seriously, you missed one hell of a good time. Gannon and I had some fun with some nurses. At least they were dressed as nurses. There were three of them and only two of us, and one nearly got left out until I decided I could take on two at a time."

"What a hero," I said as I clapped. "Always helping out the citizens of our fair country, August." Retired from the

Marines at only thirty, August had seen some pretty grim shit that he didn't like to talk about.

"I do what I can. Being retired, I can only help stateside. I like to keep up the morale over here." He laughed again, then Gannon's face filled the other side of my screen.

Gannon's smile was bright as always as he greeted us, "Morning, gentlemen. And I do use that term lightly."

August took the lead, as usual. "So the time has come for us to put our bickering behind us and agree on a name for this nightclub."

We'd argued over this one thing for far too long. Seemed it was time to shit or get off the pot. So I gave them my idea one more time. "Let the record show, I like the name Club X."

I knew it would be Gannon who had something to say about that. "And I've told you before, that name is much too common."

August pointed out one major problem to Gannon. "Yes, but Gannon, you have yet to come up with a single name. You've had no problem shooting down all the ones we've come up with, though. So I am throwing you into the middle of this debate and challenging you to come up with a name on the fly. You have one minute."

Giving Gannon one minute to do anything was a stretch. He was a thinker, not a shoot from the hip kind of guy. "What?" He looked back and forth at August and me with a look of panic on his face. "I'm not that creative. You guys are."

I looked at my watch then back at Gannon. "You're wasting time, Gannon."

August looked at his watch too. "The time is ticking away. Thirty seconds, Gannon, or we're sticking with Club X."

"No! Wait—give me one more minute. I'm terrible under pressure." Gannon pinched the bridge of his nose, looking as if he had to use all of his concentration to get a name to come to his business brain.

August wasn't messing around and wasn't going to give him any more time. "Nope, no extra time. And we're coming in on ten, nine ..."

I sat back, pretty sure the club would get the moniker I'd come up with.

Gannon's eyes popped open wide, and he looked as if a lightbulb had just gone off inside his head. "Swank!"

I had to smile; I liked the name immediately.

August nodded, and he also wore a broad smile. "Swank. I like it."

I chuckled. "Me too. Swank it is, then." I looked at August. "Seems we've had a productive meeting, August. Time to get back to our real jobs. Catch you guys later in the week. Nixon, out." I clicked off the screen and got up to get to my real job.

There were a couple of things I needed to get to that day, and one of them looked to be lunch with my best friend, Shanna. Not business, but a necessary meeting nonetheless as it had been over a week since we'd talked.

Shanna and I had met in kindergarten at our school in the tiny South Texas town of Pettus. She and I used to walk to school together, as her family lived a few houses down from mine. Our relationship had always been like a brother-sister type thing, with no romance involved.

When I'd come out to California to go to Berkeley, she'd stayed home and gone to the community college there, the only thing she and her parents could afford. Shanna gained an associate's degree but never got past that. Instead, she got her grandmother to teach her how to sew—and she became quite good at it. She begged me to let her stay with me in L.A., and soon after her arrival she secured herself an interview at Paramount Studios, landing a job as a costume designer.

Her stay with me was short-lived, as she was able to save enough money to move into her own apartment within a month. But she and I made a pact that we'd never brush each other off or put the other to the side. She was the only family I had out here, and vice versa, even if we weren't exactly family. So whenever I saw a lunch or dinner with Shanna in my schedule, I made sure I didn't miss any of them.

When lunchtime came, I met her at Providence to enjoy some seafood. She met me at the door, and I hugged her. "There he is."

"I made it. Today has been one hell of a day." I took her hand, leading her inside.

In no time at all they had us seated, and our appetizer of oysters on the half-shell was brought to us along with some white wine. She rocked back in her seat as she swallowed one of the oysters then looked at me. "So, you disappeared on me. I thought you and I might go trick-or-treating last night, just like we did in the old days. I'd dress up as a witch and you'd throw a sheet over your head and cut out a couple of holes for your eyes."

"Yeah, I did do a little dressing up. I wore a mask, anyway." I sipped my wine then ate an oyster as she looked at me with narrowed eyes.

"A mask, huh?" She kept on eyeing me. "In Portland, no doubt."

Shanna was one of the few who knew about my dabbling in the darker side of sex. And she absolutely hated it. So I was always a little leery of admitting to her when I'd gone. "Um, maybe." I took another sip of wine.

"And you hooked up with a random sub?" she asked, but quickly raised her palm up to stop me from answering. "No, I'm not going to make you lie about it. I know you did pick up a little tramp and screw her mercilessly while spanking her until her ass ..."

"Shanna, stop," I hissed at her as I gestured around to the other patrons of the fine dining establishment. All conversations around us had gone silent as they honed in on what she was saying.

She looked around before lowering her voice as she leaned across our small table. "But you did find a girl. You can't lie to me, Nixon Slaughter. I've known you for too damn long."

"Okay, so I did find someone, and we had some fun. But my trips to Portland are a thing of the past." I ate another oyster as she pondered what I'd said.

"Good. But what happened to make you decide not to go there anymore?" She eyed me again, scrutinizing my every word.

"The club I belong to has been destroyed," I told her, then shrugged. "So I have nowhere to go now to get my fix."

"Good," she proclaimed as she picked up her glass and held it, as if to toast me. "The sinful place is no more, and you can stop that little bit of evil you've been doing and get to finding the right woman for you."

"I'm not looking," I said as our main courses—king salmon for her and vermillion rockfish for me—came to the table on a large round tray, carried by our helpful waiter.

"You're not getting any younger, Nixon. Twenty-nine is barking at your door," she reminded me.

So I reminded her of the same thing. "Neither are you, Shanna. And you're only three months younger than me."

The waiter left us, and she smiled at me. "Maybe it's time we both started looking for people we can settle down with. Maybe then you'd stop yearning for a submissive on occasion."

I looked down at my delicious meal, but the image wavered in front of me as Katana's face filled my head. I didn't think I'd ever stop yearning for at least one sub.

43

CHAPTER 8

Katana

The weeks after the best night of my life passed by quickly, and soon enough Thanksgiving was just a week away. Many people looked forward to Thanksgiving and the celebrations they'd have with their families, but not me. I hadn't had a real Thanksgiving since I was eighteen. I'd had to leave the foster home after that, and I wasn't gone a year before both the people who'd taken care of me had passed away.

The holidays always got me down. But this particular season was hitting me a lot harder than usual. I just didn't feel well most of the time. I had a hard time waking up in the mornings, and I couldn't make it through a day without taking a nap—a thing I'd never done.

I was just off. And my mind drifted to Nixon and that night way too often. It was like he was haunting me, and I didn't have a clue as to how to stop it from happening.

One night, when I woke up after a three-hour nap that started at seven in the evening, I flipped on the TV as I knew there was no way I'd be falling back to sleep anytime soon.

After clicking through the channels, I found a romantic movie and sighed as I lay back on the sofa to watch it. It was all well and good until a steamy scene came on and I felt a surge in my lower regions. And whose handsome face had to pop into my mind once again? That's right, Nix's.

A moan escaped me as I closed my eyes and relived the feeling of his hands moving over my body. I stretched out and arched my back as I pretended his mouth was on my skin again.

My hand moved on its own to the soft hairs that topped my pussy. I left a bit on top but kept the rest cleanly shaven. I didn't want to look like a little girl, but I also didn't want to look like a Sasquatch down there, either.

Dipping my finger into my wetness, I pulled it up my slit then tapped my clit. In my mind, Nix's mouth had found mine, and he gifted me with a gentle kiss. Our warm breaths mingled as he eased his mouth off mine and looked into my eyes. "Good little slave. Now your Master will satisfy your cravings for him."

"Yes," I moaned. "I'm yours, Master. Only yours."

I imagined him taking my tit into his mouth, sucking on it softly. He was teasing me, not letting me have the harder sucking I craved. Light licks and gentle pulls were all he did. I grew antsy for more.

Pushing my hand under my T-shirt, my finger traced a circle around my nipple, pretending it was his tongue. "Oh, Master, it feels so good."

I could hear his deep voice in my mind. "You make me feel so good, slave. My sexy little slave girl."

In my mind I belonged to him. I had no desire to be with anyone else. And that thought made me inexplicably sad. I knew what I'd gotten myself into. I'd been told the rules of membership at that BDSM club. Essentially, I was nothing more than a body for some rich man to use for a while.

I stopped touching myself and sat up, sick to my stomach. Even as I hurried to the bathroom, afraid I would puke on the light tan carpet, I thought about what I'd eaten last. That morning I'd had two bites of a bagel with cream cheese. My stomach just didn't agree with it, and I never found my appetite for the rest of the day.

When I got into the bathroom, I stepped on the scale as a series of burps popped out of my mouth. I'd lost five pounds in the last week.

I barely ate and slept all the damn time. Did I have mono?

After a couple of dry heaves, I left the bathroom to get my laptop to search the symptoms of mononucleosis. Fatigue was at the very top, but everything that followed that—high fever, body aches, headache, muscle weakness, sore throat, swollen glands in the neck and underarms, rash —I didn't have.

Well, at least it wasn't mono. At least it wasn't something I could've contracted from my one beautiful night with Nix. I wouldn't have wanted the memory of that night to be tarnished by anything negative, like me getting sick.

And I'd also really hate to have to call Nixon to let him know that he should get checked for the virus because of our night together. That would be uber-embarrassing.

I turned off the television and headed to my bedroom to finish watching the movie in there. Grabbing a bottle of water and a sleeve of saltines out of the cabinet, I brought the crackers with me to eat in bed. Not a thing that a person with a partner would get to do. I guess I was lucky.

I could eat in bed, sleep at odd hours, work when I felt

like it. Many had it far worse than me. I wondered if depression had caused my problems. I knew a lot of people only got depressed during the holidays—maybe I'd become one of those people. The good Lord knew I didn't have anything to be happy about this season. Nothing to look forward to.

As a matter of fact, one of my clients had asked me why in the world I had given her December 25th as the date I'd deliver her cover to her. I'd told her that it was just another day for me. She'd told me that was sad, and I supposed it was.

With no family, days like Thanksgiving, Christmas, and even New Year's meant little to me. Hell, even Halloween hardly registered on my radar—I hadn't participated in that since I was a kid in foster care. My mother had never taken me out on Halloween from what I could remember. I also didn't remember ever having a Christmas tree or anything else special when I lived with her. My birthday must've come and gone without me knowing it, up until I was put into the system.

My heart felt heavy as I lay in my bed, the television off. I didn't feel like watching any romantic shit anymore. It settled in that I had to be depressed. Who the hell wouldn't be, considering my past?

While my night with Nixon Slaughter had made something inside of me light, there was no one there to keep that flame going. It had started to dwindle into nothingness the moment we parted ways.

I'd been a damn fool to go to that club. Up until that night, I'd been just fine with how things were in my life. Yes, I did work myself too hard at times. Yes, sometimes I drank a bottle of wine all alone as I sat in bed and watched scary movies until I'd end up looking around my room, paranoid about what might sneak out to get me. But I'd been okay with that life.

Right?

I moaned as I got into bed, pulled the blanket up to my chin, and closed my eyes. They burned, and I felt dehydrated.

Sitting up, I chugged the water, praying I could just rehydrate and make everything okay again. I would put Nixon out of my head—refuse to let that memory enter my brain. I'd whack at it with everything I had each and every time he tried to come back to visit me in my imagination.

No more Nixon Slaughter!

Even though I'd slept some ten hours that day with all my naps, I found myself tired still. As I drifted closer to sleep, I began to think about one of the ideas my client had run by me.

Baily Sever routinely ordered book covers from me. She wrote young adult romance under a pen name, specializing in BDSM. When I'd told her about my little encounter with that world, she'd begged me to let her interview me. She'd pay me for my time, and better yet, she'd give me part of the royalties and tag me as a co-author.

I hadn't taken her up on the offer yet but as I lay there and thought about what I'd been doing, falling down the rabbit hole, I decided I would take her up on that offer.

Getting back out of bed, I headed to the living room and my desk. Right then and there, I got on my laptop and sent her an email, telling her I wanted to take her up on her offer. She could call me as soon as she wanted to do the interview. Hell, I'd even make the cover of the book free of charge since she'd said she'd give me credit as the co-author.

The prospect of this new work had me feeling pretty peppy, and I headed to the kitchen to make me some eggs and bacon. Crazy how getting a new project started can get you up and going again.

I had to move on from that night. As spectacular as it had been, it was over. I had to get that through my head; I'd never have another night like that one. Not ever.

44

CHAPTER 9

Nixon

The month after Halloween both dragged on and flew by somehow. It was the day before Thanksgiving and Shanna and I were on my private jet, heading back to Texas to spend the holiday with our families.

Like every day before that one, my mind was on Katana, wondering what she'd be doing for Thanksgiving. Shana sat across the narrow aisle from me, filing her nails as we sped through the sky. "Why do you seem so zoned out, Nixon?"

I'd been laying my head on the headrest, eyes closed, picturing Katana in that hotel room. I turned my head to look at her. "I'm just wondering what Katana is doing tomorrow. And wishing like hell I'd gotten her number or at least her address so I could send her flowers or something."

One blonde brow arched as she looked at me with an incredulous expression. "Why? Why would you still be thinking about that little brainless twit?"

I sat up, taking offense at what she'd said. "Hey, no reason to call her names, Shanna. And need I remind you that you don't even know her? What grounds do you have for calling her anything at all?"

"I know all I need to know about the girl. She's into some sick shit and can't have a brain in her head if she's into that stuff. Now, I can see a man being into that lifestyle. Of course, who wouldn't get off at least a little bit, ruling over someone? But being the one who's ruled over—well, that only means one thing in my book: no brains." She put the nail file down and picked up a magazine, thumbing through the pages. "Put her out of your head, Nixon."

Closing my eyes again, I tried not to think about Katana —but did anyway. Shanna was wrong about her. She wasn't brainless. Sure, I didn't know her that well—or at all really —but I knew she wasn't dumb.

"You know who I bet will be in town, too, Nixon?" Shanna asked with a lilt to her voice.

"Nope," I said without even opening my eyes.

"Bianca."

My cock twitched. Bianca had been a couple of years older than me and often taunted me when we were kids. By the time we were in high school though, I'd caught her giving me sideways glances, admiring how I'd grown up.

I'd always had a crush on her—she was the hottest girl in school. Long legs, tanned skin, dark hair that hung to her waist. And then it hit me—Katana and Bianca had a lot of similarities. Maybe that was why I had felt so instantly attracted to Katana.

I sat up and looked at Shanna. "You really think she might be visiting her parents?" I had to admit I was a little excited about seeing her.

"Why wouldn't she be there?" Shanna asked. "Everyone comes home for the holidays."

I nodded and lay my head back again. I tried to picture Bianca. It'd been two years since I'd seen her last. That was at Christmas. She'd been with some guy then, but gave me a sexy little smile that told me she would've given me a bit of her time if she'd been alone. It was a smile she'd never given me before.

But as hard as I tried to bring Bianca's face into my mind, I couldn't. The only face I saw was Katana's, and it was beautiful. So beautiful it made my heart ache.

I should've gotten her damn number!

When the jet stopped at the San Antonio International Airport, we hopped into a rental car and headed for Pettus. It took us a little over an hour to get home, and when we did, we were greeted with open arms by our families.

Just like we always did during the holidays, everyone ended up at the only café in town, the Dairy Queen. Shanna and I were sitting in a booth, catching up with a couple of guys I played football with in high school. They'd never left the tiny town, both working as guards at the nearby prison.

I hadn't even noticed anyone coming into the place, but when a hand moved across my shoulders, I looked back to find Bianca. "Hey!"

"Hi," she purred. Wearing a maroon jacket, her dark hair pulled up into a long ponytail, she looked just like she had back in high school. "When did you get here and how long are you staying, Nixon?"

"Today, and leaving the day after tomorrow," I answered as she came around to stand at the end of the table.

The conversation at our table ceased as she ran her finger along my jaw. "I like the beard. It makes you look distinguished."

I chuckled. "I was going for dangerous, but thanks."

Her dark brown eyes cut to the side, looking out at the parking lot. "I was thinking about going to Charlie's for a beer or two. Wanna take me?"

I sat perfectly still, unsure if I truly did want to take her. It was pretty easy to see she wanted me. And after all these years, that was a pleasant surprise.

Shanna jabbed me in the ribs as she whispered, "Are you crazy? Get the hell up and take her. I can walk home from here."

There went my only excuse not to take Bianca to the bar.

The guys looked at me like I was insane for not jumping at the chance to be with one of the hottest chicks ever to grace our little hick town. But the fact was, I wasn't jumping. And there was only one reason why.

Katana.

Before I could say a word, the bell on the door jingled, and this time I noticed it. When I looked to see who it was, a tall, decently built dude was heading our way. "Shit," Bianca hissed. She walked toward him. "There you are. I was looking for you."

He gave me a look before he looked back at her. "Come on."

She glanced back at me and shrugged. "See you guys around."

I'd missed my chance with her and knew it. I couldn't say I actually cared, but Shanna seemed invested, as she waited until Bianca and her guy walked out before lighting into my ass. "Are you crazy, Nixon? You mooned over that girl all through junior high and high school. You said if she gave you half a chance you'd make her see God. Well, she just gave you a hell of lot more than half a damn chance. She was throwing herself at you, Bianca style."

With a shake of my head, I said, "Did you not notice that she has a man, Shanna? Damn. I'm not about to get some redneck pissed off at me over a piece of ass."

Plus, even before he walked in, I couldn't seem to make myself get up and do it. Katana just kept flashing through my mind like a strobe light. I had to do something to get myself over the girl who obviously wanted nothing more to do with me. She had my number, and she had never called.

The fact was Katana had signed a paper that had had her promise not to contact any man she encountered at the club. But after Halloween, the Dungeon of Decorum was destroyed, destroying all that with it. Nothing could stop her from calling me if she wanted to. She wouldn't be in trouble or get fined by the club.

So why didn't she ever call?

The answer was simple. She didn't want to.

Maybe I'd been too rough. Maybe I'd gone too far. Or maybe I hadn't gone far enough or been rough enough. Who knew what the reason was.

Why should I care? I kept asking myself that question over and over again.

There wasn't any reason for me to care why she hadn't called.

As I sat there, sipping on my chocolate shake, a thought I'd never had before popped into my head. What if she had lost my card?

If I went back to Portland, I might be able to find her apartment building again. I had no idea what her address was, but I wasn't opposed to knocking on every door until I found hers.

Suddenly I had a plan, a real plan to find her.

I got up, and Shanna looked at me in surprise. "Where're you going now, Nixon?"

"Back to Mom and Dad's. I know it's noisy there and chaotic with all the nieces and nephews running around, but I need to visit them. You want a ride to your parents' place?"

She got up to come with me. After shaking hands with my old friends and wishing them well, we left, and I dropped Shanna off. I couldn't help but feel excited about what I'd be doing as soon as we got back to L.A., and my plan began to get more and more detailed as the night went on.

THANKSGIVING DAY

The next afternoon Dad and I sat in the backyard, watching all the kids play. He opened the Yeti ice chest I'd bought him just that morning when we went shopping. He'd filled it up with beer and took a couple out, tossing one to me.

I popped the top on it and took a nice long drink. The cold brew felt good going down my parched throat. Although it was the end of November, the temperature hovered around ninety that day—pretty hot for Thanksgiving. I didn't miss the South Texas heat one tiny bit.

"So, how's it going out west, son?" Dad asked me, then took a drink of his beer.

"Great." I put the bottle of beer between my legs to hold it steady as a football sailed in my direction. Catching it, I tossed it back to my oldest nephew.

"Any girls you like out there?" Dad asked me.

"One," I found myself saying. "But she's playing hard to get."

"You're not used to that, are you, son?" He winked at me.

"Not at all. But I've got a plan now." I smiled then took another drink.

Tomorrow I'd start that little plan, and soon I'd have that sexy vixen right where I wanted her.

45

CHAPTER 10

Katana

Thanksgiving Day

I had never felt worse than I did on Thanksgiving as I waited for my turkey pot pie to cook in the oven. Normally I'd just nuke the thing, but it being a holiday that was celebrated with turkey, I gave it a bit more love and put it in the oven.

An acrid taste had plagued my mouth for over an hour, so I gave up trying to use water to get rid of it and went to brush my teeth again. While in the restroom, I noticed the unopened box of birth control pills that were sitting on the vanity. I hadn't taken any in weeks, since my stomach had been giving me fits. But something compelled me to pick up the box and look at it.

When I opened it, I began to count how many I'd taken out of it. There'd been fourteen pills I knew I hadn't taken. And those were there. There were three missing, but before those three there was a week's worth that I hadn't taken.

My heart stopped. I'd forgotten to take my pills during that crazy week. The week right before I was with Nix.

I dropped to my knees, which had suddenly gone weak, and looked up. "Lord, please don't let this be what I think it is."

Shaking, I got up and went into my bedroom to grab my purse and car keys. The smell of the turkey pot pie had me going to turn the oven off before leaving the pie behind and going to go to the store.

As I drove around town, I found most places were closed for the holiday, but I did manage to find a convenience store and was lucky enough to find a pregnancy test.

When I took it to the checkout, the clerk scanned it then asked, "Congratulations?"

A shake of my head told her that was not the case. Not at all. I couldn't speak—I thought I might just burst into tears if I tried. I quickly grabbed my purchase and went back home.

There were two sticks in the package, and I took one and headed to the bathroom. Once all set and ready to go, I found I couldn't. I was dry as a bone.

Back I went to the kitchen to drink copious amounts of water. My stomach felt like it was floating in deep water, yet I still couldn't pee. I guess my nerves had shut things down.

Digging through my purse, I found the business card Nixon had given me. I just stared at it for the longest time. "I'm so sorry, Nix. I didn't do this on purpose."

If I am pregnant, should I tell him about it?

Did he have to know? He'd made sure to ask me about birth control before we ever did a thing and I had told him I'd taken care of it. I hadn't meant to lie about it—I thought I had been telling the truth.

That damn busy as hell week was to blame for this!

I sat at the kitchen table, my head in my hands as I stared at the card on the table, his name staring a hole in me. Nixon Slaughter, my baby's father's name.

I shook my head back and forth—I had to stop thinking like that. I couldn't hold him accountable for this. I couldn't do that to the man. He didn't deserve that.

What did he deserve?

Did he deserve to know if he was going to be a father? Did he deserve the right to make his own decision about what part he wanted or didn't want to play in his child's life?

I knew the answer to those questions. I wasn't without morals. I had never known my father. My mother had often said she had no idea who it was. Being a bastard child wasn't a thing I'd want for my son or daughter.

But I was getting ahead of myself. I had to take the test before I could totally freak out—though I was pretty sure I already knew what the result would be.

I would tell Nix if the test came back positive. I wasn't heartless. But I wouldn't ask him for a thing. He could do for the child whatever he wanted. He could see it or not. Whatever he wanted.

All of this was my fault, and I'd carry the burden alone if I had to.

My phone rang, jerking me back to reality. Blyss's name popped up on my screen, and I answered it, my voice shaky. "Hello, Blyss. Happy Thanksgiving."

"You sound bad. What's wrong, Katana?" She knew me better than most people did.

"Oh, nothing," I lied. "How are the kids enjoying their yummy Thanksgiving dinner?"

"They hate it. No kid likes a meal that's half vegetable-based sides. Troy made a homemade pepperoni pizza for them. He's the best dad ever," she gushed. "But enough about us, how about you? What are you doing to celebrate this day?"

God, I couldn't tell her I was going to maybe eat a pot pie that came out of a box—and that was the best I could expect of my night at this point. I couldn't tell her that it all depended on the results of the pregnancy test, because I knew I wouldn't have an appetite if it was positive.

"Oh, not much," I finally said. "Just working."

"Please tell me you and a couple of friends went to eat somewhere. Please tell me you're just coming in from a fun time and are now chilling because you're so full," she begged me.

Oh, how I wish I could tell her those things. "I wanted to stay in. I haven't felt well in a couple of weeks. I think I have a bug or something," I told her. That was the truth after all. I had thought that up until a short time ago.

"No one gets a bug for a few weeks," she griped at me. "You need to go to the doctor as soon as possible. Is there a non-emergency care facility open near you today? You should go today if possible. That's much too long to be sick, Katana."

She might be right. I certainly would go see someone if the test came back negative—and I guess I'd be going to the doctor if it came back positive, too. "I'm not sure if there is anything open other than the emergency room at the hospital. I don't think this constitutes an emergency. I don't always feel bad. I'm tired all the time and have no appetite. I've made myself eat little bits here and there, but sometimes it comes back up."

"Are you drinking water?" she asked. "Because you need to drink lots of it. Even if it just comes back up, you need to keep drinking it. And you said this has been going on for a couple of weeks?"

"Yes." I didn't want to tell her about it, but I'd lost five pounds in the week following Halloween, and I'd lost five more in last five days. My ribs were beginning to show, as were my hipbones.

Then she gave me some helpful advice. "You need to get those drinks that elderly people drink to keep their nutrients up."

"Oh, I forgot about those things. My foster parents, Mr. and Mrs. Baker, used to drink those. I recall liking them when I tasted them once. I got in trouble for doing that, but at least I know I like them." Sitting back, I put my hand on my stomach, as if I would even be able to feel a tiny little embryo at that point if I was preggo.

I wasn't a kid. At twenty-four, I felt mature enough to have a child. Things would work great with my job, so I could stay home to raise him or her. There wasn't much to fear. Except having to do it all alone.

Would Nix want to be there for the baby? Would he want to be there for me?

"You should go out and buy some of those right away. If you've been sick that long I bet you're losing weight, aren't you?" Blyss asked with a knowing tone in her voice.

"A little. I promise I'll pick some up. And I'll go to the doctor." I would do that, one way or the other. If I was knocked up, then I'd have to, and if not, then I'd have to see what the hell was wrong with me. It couldn't just be depression.

I wasn't sure if I even had depression. The only thing I was kind of sad about was Nix. I missed him every single day. But I knew time would take care of that. I couldn't be feeling this bad over missing him. Could I?

And if it was that, then what could I do about it? Call him?

I'd told him I wouldn't be doing that. I'd signed a contract stating that I'd never try to contact anyone I encountered at the club.

But the club was no more, as were all the contracts in their system, right? And did the contract really matter if he wanted to hear from me too? He hadn't seemed opposed to the idea when we'd parted ways.

I made a pact with myself—if I wasn't pregnant, I'd go to the doctor. If they couldn't find a thing wrong with me, I'd give Nix a call and see if he wanted to come for a visit. Maybe I'd test the relationship waters with him if I found out he missed me the way I had missed him.

There were so many variables though.

The urge to pee hit me suddenly, and I hurried to the bathroom. "Okay, Blyss, I'll do everything you told me. I've gotta get off here now. Love you. Happy Thanksgiving. Bye." I ended the call before she said a word as I was about to bust.

The three bottles of water all seemed to be ready to come out at the same time. The stream I let loose easily covered the little stick and I placed it on a washcloth next to the sink.

The next three minutes went by like three whole days. I covered my eyes the whole time until the timer on my cell went off, telling me I could look now.

Moving my fingers apart, I snuck a peek at the stick.

"Oh, shit!"

46

CHAPTER 11

Nixon

The day after Thanksgiving Shanna and I left early to get back to the L.A. grind. Only I wasn't going to be staying in L.A long, or going home at all. No, I was going to Portland to search for Katana Reeves.

Shanna and I lived miles apart, so she took a cab back to her place, and I acted as if I was waiting for my driver to come pick me up. I wasn't; I'd already told the pilot to take an hour off, then I'd be ready to head to Portland.

Chilling in one of the lounges at LAX, I was sipping on some Scotch. At only a bit past noon, I knew it was a bit on the early side to be drinking alcohol, but my nerves had been stirred up. I had to do something to soothe them.

My cell beeped, letting me know a text had come in. I didn't recognize the number but opened the message anyway.

Nix, it's Katana Reeves, from Portland. I don't know if you remember me at all, but I need to talk to you. Can you call me when you get a chance?

Why would she think I wouldn't remember her? Shit, it hadn't been a month since we'd been together. I wasted no time calling her. Her voice was soft as she answered. "Nix?"

"Yeah, it's me. How've you been?" I ran my finger around the top of my glass, picturing her lovely face in my mind.

"Okay. And you?"

"Same. It's funny you sent me that message. I grew tired of waiting for you to call, so I'm sitting at the airport right now, waiting for my pilot to finish his break so he can take me your way," I told her and hoped she was going to be cool with that.

"Really?" she asked, sounding as if she didn't quite believe that.

I held up the phone and asked the bartender. "Hey, buddy, can you verify where I am right now?"

"LAX," he said without hesitation.

"See," I said. "I just got back from visiting my family in Texas, and all I could think about was getting to Portland to find you."

She let out a heavy sigh, as if she were holding her breath. "That's good to know. I've got a lot to talk to you about. When do you think you'll get here?" she asked and I heard her voice crack a little.

"A couple of hours. I'll be at the Heathman. I can send someone to get you and bring you over." I took another drink and waited to see what she'd say.

"I can't do what we did before," she mumbled.

My heart fell. I definitely wanted to do what we'd done before. But I didn't ask why. "Okay. That's fine. I just want to see you." I also wanted to find out what had taken her so damn long to contact me. "If I'd had the forethought to get your number, I'd have called you a long time ago. That was my mistake." I hesitated then went for it, "I've missed you, Katana."

"I've missed you, too," she said, and it made me sigh. She'd missed me! "To be honest, I've thought about calling you often. The contract had me holding back. But then I finally realized only yesterday that the contract probably doesn't matter now that the club is closed It's nice to hear that you missed me."

I saw my pilot walking past the lounge toward the gate he'd parked the jet at. "Hey, I see my pilot. I'm going to see if we can take off now. I'll call you as soon as I get there."

"K, bye," she said, then hung up.

I hurried to catch up to Bernie, the pilot. "Hey, Bernie, wait up."

He stopped and turned to look at me. "Yes, sir."

I caught up with him. "Are you doing anything? I mean, I'm ready to take off if you don't have anything else to do."

"No, we can go. The plane's been fueled up. Can I ask how long we'll be in Portland, sir? My wife is wondering how long I'll be gone this time."

"You can come right back if you want. I can just call you when I'm ready to come back. It's not like it's that far." I clapped him on the back, and we started walking to the jet. "How long have you been married?"

"Ten years," he said. "We've got three kids."

"Kids, wow." I shook my head. "I've never even thought about having kids. My sisters and brothers all do. I come from an enormous family. Mom and Dad had six of us. I'm the oldest and I've just never found anyone I've wanted to settle down with. Tell me how you knew your wife was the one for you, Bernie."

"She and I clicked right from the beginning. I mean, we had a small stretch of time there where it was a little awkward, but we fell into step with each other pretty quickly. And I'd never felt about anyone else the way I felt about her. For me, it was a no-brainer. Married that girl as fast as I could."

We stepped onto the plane, and I went to my seat while he went to the cockpit. "Thanks, Bernie."

"You sweet on someone, sir?" he asked me then winked at me. "Maybe someone in Portland?"

"Maybe," I said with a chuckle. "And Bernie, do me a huge favor and stop calling me sir. Hell, you're older than I am. It's Nixon, okay?"

"Copy that, Nixon. Buckle up now."

I napped all the way to Portland. Just knowing I'd get to see Katana allowed me to have one of the calmest sleeps I'd had in a month. It wasn't until I relaxed back in that seat that I realized how pent up I'd actually been.

When I got off the plane, I called Katana to let her know that I'd landed and was hiring a car to pick her up. But she told me she'd drive her own car over to meet me. I just needed to let her know when I had a room, and she'd come.

The fact that she didn't want to be without her car had me a little on edge. But then again, I couldn't expect her to be at my beck and call just because I was in town.

Once I'd gotten all checked in and up to my room, I called her, and she said she was heading my way. As I waited, I began to get nervous and thoughts crept into my head that I hadn't considered in my excitement. What in the hell could she possibly want to talk about?

I mean, I knew what I wanted, and that was another go at her. But I didn't necessarily have anything I wanted to discuss with her. She had said we couldn't do what we did last time, and that we needed to talk. So what could it be about?

Had she caught an STD and wanted to blame me?

I knew I was clean. Or maybe now I wasn't.

Shit!

A knock came at the door, and I walked over to open it, unsure how I'd react to seeing her with my current thoughts clouding my mind.

But when I saw her again, my mind went quiet, and my heart sped up.

Wearing some jeans and a light sweater with a pair of black flats, Katana stood there, looking at me. Her blue eyes ran up and down me. I'd worn jeans and a T-shirt and had kicked off my shoes as soon as had I gotten into the room.

We just stood there, our eyes feasting on each other, until a flurry of movement broke the stillness. I grabbed her, pulling her inside and straight into my arms. Pinning her to the door, my mouth crashed down on hers, and I couldn't get enough of her.

Clothes ripped as we pulled them off each other, and before either of us knew what the hell was happening, we were both naked. She wrapped her legs around my waist, and I plowed into her soft, hot cunt as we groaned with relief.

I fucked her hard, using the wall to hold her up for me just where I needed her. We both came in a heated rush, and then I carried her like that, with her legs still wrapped around me, to the bed.

Laying her down, I let our bodies part for only a moment before I was on top of her, my cock growing hard already. I pushed myself back into her, thrusting with a force that seemed inhuman. We looked into each other's eyes as I stabbed my dick into her still pussy, which was still pulsing from the orgasm I'd just given her.

Her hands moved through my hair and then over my beard. "That looks good on you, Nix."

I kissed her sweet lips then moved my mouth over to kiss her neck, my thrusts finally slowing to a less urgent pace. Her body arched to meet mine, and we moved as one until both of us were shaking with another orgasm. We'd come together once more. Seemed we had a connection that not even our bodies could deny.

There wouldn't be any more walking away from her and expecting nothing more. I had to have more of her. And it sure did seem like she had to have more of me, too.

She'd told me there'd be none of this. So I wondered what made her change her mind. But I'd ask that later. For now, I wanted to flip her over and spank her sweet ass while I took her from behind. But when I grabbed her by the waist, it became clear she wasn't going to let me do that.

It also became clear that she'd lost some weight. I felt the bones of her hips, and when I ran my hands up her sides, I felt her ribs. I hadn't taken time to notice anything; I'd wanted her too badly.

Her hands caught my wrists. "I have to tell you something, Nix."

The way her lips began to quiver told me it wasn't anything good. Was she sick? Dying?

"Tell me," I whispered as I stayed right where I was, my dick still inside of her. I didn't want to lose the connection. I couldn't lose it.

"Nix, I'm pregnant with your baby."

Shit!

47

CHAPTER 12

Katana

Silence filled the room. Nix stared at me for a long time then rolled off me and hurried to the bathroom without saying a word. Without a clue as to what he thought about the baby, I lay there and started crying, pulling the blanket up to cover my body.

I'd had no idea how he would take the news. I didn't know if there was any right way he could have reacted that would've made me happy. But this reaction definitely didn't make me happy.

A few minutes later he came out of the bathroom, a wet washcloth in his hand. He didn't look at me as he ran it over his face and came to sit on the edge of the bed. "Are you positive it's mine? I know you told me that it had been over a year since you'd had sex, but people lie. So I need to know the truth." He looked directly into my eyes. "It's okay if you lied to me. What's important now is that you and I both know the truth about everything. If there's the slightest chance it's not mine, I need to know. Did you sleep with anyone after me?"

I shook my head and wiped my tears away. "I told you the truth before about not having sex for over a year. And I haven't had sex with anyone else. I've been sick. I thought I had a bug. But yesterday I took a look at my birth control pills. I hadn't taken them in a couple of weeks, since I first started feeling sick to my stomach. I saw that I'd skipped the week before I met you. I didn't do it on purpose; I swear that to you."

He nodded. "I believe you. I recall you telling me you'd had a rough week. It must've been one hell of a week."

"It was. But I can't believe I forgot to take so many pills. I'm so sorry." I began to sob and covered my face with my hands so he couldn't see me ugly crying.

I felt his hands move over mine and he pulled them away, grabbing me up and hugging me, swaying back and forth. "Don't cry. We'll handle this. I'm so glad you told me right away. I'm so glad you didn't leave me out of this."

He was glad I hadn't left him out. That was so good to hear. The truth was I'd been worried he'd be mad at me and tell me the problem was all mine since I had caused it.

But he hadn't said that. He was holding me and telling me we'd handle things. Things were turning out better than I'd thought they would. But I knew I had to pull myself together so I could let him know a bit more.

Sniffling, I pulled back and looked at him. He took the damp cloth and wiped my tears away. "Nix, I just want you to know that I'm not going to hold you to anything. You can have as much or as little to do with this baby as you want. I can take care of him all on my own if you want nothing to do with it. I'm not trying to trap you into a relationship with me either."

"I'm sure you're not," he whispered. "You've only known about the baby for a day. You're sure you want to keep it?"

I nodded. "It may seem like I haven't thought it all out. But I can't kill a baby. No matter how small it is. No matter if it hasn't developed its tiny little heart yet. I can't do it." I looked him right in the eyes. "I won't do it."

He smiled. "Good. I'm glad to hear that. We got pregnant for a reason. God doesn't make mistakes."

He'd used the word *we*. We'd gotten pregnant. I wasn't in this alone. He was right here with me. For the first time in my life, I had someone who was going to stick with me.

I sighed. "You don't know how good it is to hear that, Nix. I promise you I won't bother you about anything. We'll figure it all out, and things will be okay."

"Sure they will," he said then kissed the top of my head. "Now I understand why you said we couldn't do what we did before. I have to tell you I was pretty disappointed when you told me that. But now I get it. And I want to tell you that makes me feel very good about the kind of mother you'll be. A pretty damn great one, I expect."

I laughed a little. "I guess you should know some things about me, Nix. My mother never knew who my father was. She left me alone a lot and one day she just didn't come home at all. I was taken to an orphanage, and later an elderly couple took me into their home and fostered me until I turned eighteen."

"Damn," he muttered. "That's rough."

"I think I should take some parenting classes. It's not like I know how to care for a baby, or a child for that matter." I looked down, feeling pretty pathetic.

His hand on my chin brought my face up, and he kissed my lips before he said, "My mother had six kids. I think she'd love to teach you about babies and raising kids."

His mother?

"You'd take me to meet your family?" I asked with surprise.

"Of course. You're having my baby. You have to meet the people who'll love him almost as much as we will." He kissed me again.

This was all going too perfectly. It didn't make sense. Things never went perfectly in my world. Something would eventually happen to fuck it all up. But for now, things were going well, and I could enjoy the moment.

When our lips parted, he had more great things to tell me. "I know this is sudden. I mean, we've been hit with a lot. But you're not in this alone. And I want to be there for you just as much as the baby. Come to Malibu. Live in my home. I'm not rushing a relationship or anything like that, so don't get scared off by what I'm saying here."

"You aren't?" I asked. "I mean, I don't want to force anything either. Do you have enough room for me to have my own bedroom, so we're not moving things too fast?"

"I've got four bedrooms. You'll have one, and the baby will have one, and we'll still have one for guests. All of the bedrooms have their own bathrooms so we won't be getting in each other's way." He kissed my cheek. "I mean it. I want to be a part of this whole thing, the pregnancy too. I don't want to miss a single thing where this child is concerned."

I was grateful to hear how optimistic he was about this whole thing. But I didn't want to become a burden to him. "I'll pay half the rent and all the other bills."

"Like hell, you will." He got underneath the blanket with me and put his arm around me. "What is it you do for a living, anyway?"

"I design book covers. I'm a freelancer. I can work from home. I'll never have to leave the baby with a sitter to do my job." I smiled. The flexibility of my job made me happy. With all the worries I had about having this child, knowing that I wouldn't have to find a babysitter was a great relief.

"Cool. Not that you'll have to work. I've got more than enough money. But if you want to do it to keep yourself busy, go right ahead." He gave my shoulders a little squeeze.

"I won't be able to be your little slave for quite some time. Are you going to be okay with that, Nix?" I asked, as I had no idea what he'd want.

He chuckled. "Yeah, I know. It's okay. I only get that urge a couple of times a year anyway. It's not my full-time thing."

Glad to have heard that, I laid my head on his chest and felt safe in his arms. I'd never felt as safe as I did when he held me. I had a father for my child. A man who wanted to be there for me and our baby.

I couldn't believe that a chance meeting at a BDSM club had ended up like this.

With me pregnant with a wealthy man's child, being swept off to Malibu, California, to live for who knew how long. The future looked a hell of a lot brighter than it ever had before.

But that niggling thing inside of me that hated to get my hopes up about anything came to pester me. *Things never go right for you, Katana Reeves, you know that. Something will rear its ugly head and make this thing go south. Just you watch.*

I pressed my lips against Nix's chest and tried to silence the nagging voice in my head. For now, everything was going right. For now, I had a man who was going to stand up and do the right thing. This hadn't been planned, but it had happened, and he'd had the level-headedness to deal with that.

For now, I would be okay.

48
_____

CHAPTER 13

Nixon

Katana slept like a baby in my arms the rest of the
night. I suppose finally having someone there
for her might have had something to do with
that. I had no idea what it felt like to be all alone in the
world. It must feel terrible. That's not a thing I would wish
on anyone.

I found it hard to believe a woman as beautiful as she
could be so alone in this world. Whatever her past held, her
future was bright. She'd never be alone again now that she
carried our child. And no matter what, I'd never turn my
back on her. But I had no idea how much of my heart I'd be
able to give her.

It wouldn't be fair to her to ask her to marry me after
knowing each other such a short amount of time. I didn't
believe in divorce—that's just the way I was raised. My
parents had been married a long time and taught us all that
when you married someone, you stuck with them through
thick and thin.

Mom and Dad didn't let any of us in on their bad times, but we knew they had them. Things would get a bit tense in our household and words were barely spoken between them at times, but before we knew it, they'd managed to work things out behind closed doors. Mom always told us it was important for a mother and father to put their marriage above everything else. Treat it the same way you'd treat a business partnership at a highly profitable company.

I didn't really understand why she'd say such a thing when I was younger. I mean, shouldn't a couple always put their kids first?

But I'd overheard Mom explaining her ideology to my sister just before she got married. Mom had told her that the marriage was the foundation for the family that would soon follow. Without a firm foundation, everything would crumble. Each and every part of the family was important, and everyone had their part in it. But without a solid marriage, things could fall apart.

I couldn't make a solid marriage with Katana at this point. It wouldn't be fair to either of us or the baby. But I could be kind, and I could be there for her. I knew she blamed herself for the pregnancy; she'd told me as much. But I wanted desperately to take that burden off her narrow shoulders.

Then and there, I made a pact with myself to always let Katana know I was over the moon about having a baby. Because that was the truth. I'd never contemplated having a child. Not even once. But I believed that was only because I hadn't found the right woman for me—that was another strong belief that my parents had instilled in me.

With Katana already pregnant, accident or not, I had no choice. I was going to be a father, end of subject. Why fight it? Why not enjoy it?

My parents wouldn't be too thrilled with me at first, but they'd come around. They adored every one of their grand-children, and they'd adore mine too, even if they didn't agree with Katana and me not being married.

As I held her in my arms and breathed in the sweet scent of her lavender shampoo, I wondered how we'd end up getting along. Would she be okay with us being more like friends and co-parents rather than a couple? Because that's how I imagined this turning out.

Even as that thought went through my mind, I felt her snuggling into me, letting out a sigh as she did. My heart pumped a bit harder—it made me feel good to make her feel good. She felt safe, I could tell. I could keep her safe. I could keep her mind free from worry about most things. With my money, resources, and family, there was a lot I could make happen for her, and I could do that for the rest of her life.

What I couldn't do was tell her I loved her. I didn't, and I wouldn't lie to her about that. And I hoped she'd never lie to me about that either.

Katana was no gold digger—at least she didn't seem to be. But that was neither here nor there. She carried my child; I'd always make sure she had more than enough to take care of the child for the rest of her life. She'd kind of hit the lottery when my seed took hold inside of her.

Another thought hit me, and this one knocked me back a bit. What if I fell in love with her, but she never fell in love with me? What if she met some man someday that she did fall in love with and wanted to marry? Where would that leave me?

A deep sigh came out of me, realizing how rough things could get in the future. The future was uncertain. All I could do was my best. Suddenly I felt the tremendous weight of responsibility resting on my shoulders.

A father to a child, a co-parent with a woman who had no one else in the world, and the responsibility to make sure no one got lost or left out of our little family.

I was going to have a family of my own!

It might not have happened in the way I'd imagined it happening someday, but I was about to have my own family. My father had taught us all that the man of the house had more responsibility to the family than anyone else did.

I kind of hoped that wasn't true. I liked to think both parents carried that responsibility together. And for the most part, from what I had seen in other's marriages, that proved to be true. But then, I'd had few up close and personal experiences with marriages.

When my sister had had her first baby with her husband a couple of years after they married, I was there. Things were going fine. She and her husband were working together to keep her calm and breathing through the painful contractions. A real team.

Everyone had come up to the hospital to welcome the first of our expanding family. Taking turns visiting the expecting couple, some of us had waited in the waiting room while others spent some time in the room with them. I happened to be in the room with them when the shit hit the fan.

Some alarm went off while she was having a contraction and suddenly two nurses were coming through the door in a rush. My sister held her husband's hand, and both looked nervous. I had no idea what was happening.

"We have to get her to the OR right now," one of the nurses said.

"Wait, why?" my brother-in-law asked. *"What's going on?"*

The nurse, who was busily taking IV bags off the stand and placing them on the bed, answered him. "That alarm is letting us know the baby's heart has stopped beating. We'll have to do an emergency C-section." She pressed the call button on the bed, and another nurse asked what she needed. "Get the OR ready and get the doctor and everyone else in there now," she told her.

My sister began to cry. "What's going to happen?" she asked the room in general.

The nurse nearest to her patted her on the arm. "You'll be put under, and we'll get the baby out and see what we can do about getting its heart going again." She looked at my brother-in-law. "Daddy, can you help keep Mommy calm until we put her under? And you'll need to throw on some scrubs—they're in the room just before we get to the operating room. You'll need to hurry. You'll have decisions to make once the baby is delivered. Decisions your wife won't be able to make, as she'll be asleep."

His face paled, and he nodded. But the color quickly rushed back to his face, and he looked at his wife with a strength he hadn't had before. "I love you. I've got this. I've got you, and I've got our son. You have nothing to worry about. You can count on me." He looked at me, frozen in my place with shock and worry. "Nixon, I need you to go out and inform the family about what's happening. Tell them I will come out and let you all know how things are going as soon as we have everything under control."

"I love you, sis," I managed to say, and then I hurried out of the room.

In that moment, I'd seen the transfer of energy. I'd seen what a wife looked like when put into a situation where she was completely helpless, and I'd seen the weight of responsibility come to rest on the husband's shoulders.

Later, after the baby was born, and after they'd discovered that the umbilical cord had prolapsed and been pinched by the baby's head, causing the heart to stop beating, my brother-in-law had come out.

"He's fine. And so is she. It was scary, but I don't want any of you to worry. I'll take good care of my wife and son," he said.

My mother went to hug him, and she started to cry. "You're a great man. Our daughter is lucky to have you."

We'd all nodded, and everyone had gained a lot of respect for the man our sister had married. And after witnessing similar scenes with the rest of my family, I knew the possible obstacles that could come my way with a baby and a woman to take care of. A heaping load of responsibility.

Daunting, yes, but completely doable.

I kissed the top of Katana's head, closing my eyes and trying to stop thinking about everything so I could fall asleep.

My future had been changed forever, and I could rest well knowing that I'd been brought up right and could handle all I'd just been given.

49

CHAPTER 14

Katana

After finally getting a good night's sleep, I woke up feeling refreshed and better than I had in a very long time. I heard noise coming from the bathroom and knew Nixon had gotten up before me. When I sat up and stretched, I saw something hanging on the hook on the closet door, and saw a brand-new pair of black flats sitting at the bottom of a garment bag.

A smile curled my lips, realizing Nix had already had something sent up for me to wear since my clothes had been pretty much destroyed. He really knew how to take care of a girl. I had to count myself lucky that I'd gotten myself knocked up by him and not some low-life.

The bathroom door opened and steam poured out of it, shrouding a hulking figure. Nixon stood there with a towel wrapped around his waist as he used another one to dry his hair, rubbing his head. "Hey, pretty lady. Glad to see you up. Wanna go grab some breakfast?" He jerked his head toward the garment bag. "I got you something to wear."

Climbing out of bed, I took the sheet with me to wrap around myself. The weight loss had me feeling self-conscious about my thin body. "I'll get showered and dressed so we can head out."

He stepped out of my way but reached out to me, grabbing the top of the sheet. "Why are you hiding behind that?"

Ducking my head, I mumbled, "I'm not hiding."

He let the sheet go and took me by the chin. "You're not happy with your weight, are you?"

I shook my head. "Not really."

"Don't worry. I'll make sure you're well taken care of now. We'll find a doctor in Los Angeles to help you feel better." He kissed my forehead. "I've got you. Don't worry about a thing."

"I already feel a lot better," I admitted, looking into his green eyes. "Your support means the world to me. I know this wasn't planned ..."

He put his finger to my lips. "Hush. I want you to know something. It doesn't matter that this wasn't planned. I'm over the moon about this baby, and I can't thank you enough for making this all so easy."

I couldn't believe what I heard coming out of his mouth. He was over the moon? "You're a surprising man, Nixon Slaughter. It's been less than a day since you found out about this baby, and already you're stepping up to the plate much faster than I'd ever thought possible."

"Yeah, well, what's done is done. Why fight it? Might as well enjoy this as much as a real couple would, right?" he asked, then walked away from me.

"That's a great attitude to have," I said as I went into the bathroom.

As great as his attitude was, what he'd said hit me harder than it should have. Maybe it was the hormones, I couldn't tell, but I felt tears welling up in my eyes, and they fell down my cheeks.

We weren't a couple. We were hardly more than strangers. And we had been pushed together by this pregnancy. How'd I ever gotten myself into such an awkward situation?

How would a child fare with parents who didn't even love one another?

I stepped into the shower, letting the water wash my tears away. My hands trembled as I moved them over my flat stomach. There was something growing inside of me, a tiny human that would grow bigger and bigger with each passing day. And the father and I barely knew one another.

Trying my best to pull myself together, I tried to stop thinking such thoughts and concentrate on the fact that I had someone who'd be by my side through all of this. Granted, I had no real idea how helpful Nixon would prove to be, but what he'd said told me he'd be great. Having him would be a hell of a lot better than doing this all on my own.

A knock on the door jolted me out of my internal thoughts. "Hey, if you don't feel up to going out, I can order room service. It's all up to you."

"If you want to order in then you can do that," I called out, and then finished rinsing my hair.

He opened the door and stepped inside. "I want you to decide, Katana."

"It doesn't matter to me." I moved back a bit, hoping the water hitting the clear glass shower door would distort my image somewhat. My hipbones jutted out, and I hated the way they looked.

"Pick," he said, undeterred by my lack of an answer. "There's a breakfast buffet going on in one of the cafés downstairs. Doesn't that sound good?"

I could see he wasn't going to make the decision so I made one. "Yeah, let's do that. I'm getting out now."

"K." He walked back out, leaving the door wide open.

As I dried off, I thought about how nice Nix was. Things might really work out with us. Not that I expected him to fall in love with me or anything like that, but it would be nice to get along well with him. I might be living with the guy for the next eighteen years or so, and getting along would make that easier.

Wrapping the towel around myself, I went to grab the garment bag and saw him watching television. "How are you feeling?"

"Pretty good," I said, taking the bag of clothes and heading back to the bathroom to get dressed. I found another very expensive dress in the bag and pulled on the dark blue knee-length dress. It zipped up the back, and I couldn't seem to get it all the way up.

Doing the best I could, I headed out and asked him to zip me the rest of the way up. I slipped on the flats and we headed out. His hand on the small of my back felt nice. The way people looked at us as we came into the breakfast area had me smiling as they gave us polite nods and morning greetings.

It was very unlike the way people had looked at us when we'd come to the same place nearly a month ago. Now we were seen differently than we'd been before—something closer to a couple than a dirty one-night stand. And it made me feel even better.

A hostess told us to sit anywhere we liked after letting us know that the cost of the buffet would be added to the hotel room bill. The food was decadent, and everything looked and smelled terrific.

Nixon led me to a table near the window. "Like this? Or want to sit somewhere else?"

"This is fine, Nix." I placed my purse on the chair, and we headed to the buffet.

He stood close to me as we filled our plates, pointing out healthy things like the fresh fruits and telling me they'd be great for the baby and me. A smile stayed on my face as he doted on me and our little unborn baby already.

When we sat down to eat, he reached across the table, taking my hand. "Thanks again for letting me know about this so early on. I doubt most women would be as nice as you are about this. Would you like me to set up a moving service to get your things to my place today?"

"Today?" I asked, just before I put a piece of delicious hickory smoked bacon into my mouth.

"Sure, why not today?" he asked and then cut his stack of pancakes, taking a bite.

"Well, I have to let my landlord know I'm moving. I have a lease. He might not let me out of it." I took a drink of apple juice and waited to see what he thought about that.

"I'll pay to get you out of the lease. Should we go see him today and get that taken care of?" he asked, putting his fork down and looking at me. "I want to take you home with me."

Flattered, I had no idea what to say. There were things I had to take care of. Not a ton of things, but there were some. I had laundry I had to get done, and I'd need to pack my things. I'd have to get boxes to do that. "Nix, I'll need about a week to get things done."

"A week?" He looked stunned as he shook his head. "That's too long. I want to get you to a doctor."

"I don't think this is an emergency," I said with a laugh. "And I don't think we'll get an appointment that quickly anyway. A week's not that long."

He looked at his plate then picked up a piece of bacon, munching on it as he thought about what I'd said. His brow furrowed, probably thinking about what he could say to speed me up. "I can stay with you then; help you get everything done."

My apartment was a complete wreck. Being sick—or pregnant, I guess—had left me too tired to do much of anything. In no way did I want him to see the mess the place had become. "Nix, can I be honest with you?"

"Please do," he said then reached out and took my hand. "You can always be honest with me, Katana."

"Great," I sighed as I readied myself to come clean with him. "My place is a wreck right now. I don't want you to see it. Since I've been so sick..."

He gave my hand a squeeze as he interrupted me. "Stop right there. If you think I'm going to judge you about the state of your apartment, you're dead wrong. As a matter of fact, let me hire a maid service to get things cleaned up for you. Let me take care of you." He shook his head before changing his mind about what he'd said. "No—scratch that. I am going to take care of you. I'm hiring a maid service to clean your place. I'm hiring movers to pack your things and bring them to Malibu. And I'm going to go with you to talk to your landlord to settle any money owed for breaking the lease. No discussion."

I didn't know what to think or say to all that. But then my mouth opened and out came the words I'd had no idea would come. "No, I'll take care of those things myself, Nix. I'll be at your place in a week. And I'll take care of any money my landlord says I owe. Thank you, but I can do this part on my own."

Now where did that come from?

50

CHAPTER 15

Nixon

I had to admit that Katana had stupefied me when she flat-out turned down my help. But it did let me know the woman was no gold digger, not that I'd truly suspected that anyways. It'd been a week since I'd left her to take care of things on her end, and I expected her to show up at any time. The movers had already brought her things to my place the day before, and everything had already been put away. She'd come home to find she had nothing to do. I hoped she'd be pleased about that.

Before I left her in Portland, I gave her a house key and wrote down the code to the security system for her, just in case I wasn't home when she arrived for some reason. But I couldn't wait for her to come home, so I took off early to be there.

When the front door opened around noon, I hopped up, feeling excited about our new beginning. "Hey!"

My face dropped, and I stopped right where I was as I

saw it wasn't Katana, but Shanna who'd come in. "Hey, yourself. What in the hell are you doing home so early on a workday?"

I hadn't said one word about my news to anyone. And out of everyone in my life, I knew Shanna would be the one to think what I was doing was stupid.

Sitting back on the sofa, I said, "I've got something going on. And just what are you doing here? And why aren't you at work?"

"It's Friday. I always get off early on Friday's. And I often come over here to lie out on your deck and chill from the weekly grind for a few hours." She took the seat across from me. "You did give me your key, and you did tell me to come over anytime I wanted."

I had done that. And now I kind of regretted doing so. How would Shanna take Katana, and vice versa?

Leaning forward, I rested my elbows on my thighs and steepled my fingers, trying to think of how I should tell Shanna my news. There really was no right way to tell her about this, so I just went for it. "Okay, you need to know something. Things are about to change. And I mean a whole hell of a lot."

I saw her eyes move across the room to the brand-new rocking chair I'd bought for us for when the baby was here. She jerked her chin at it. "Why the new rocker, Grandpa?"

She'd left me a perfect opening, and I went for it. "I'm going to be a father, Shanna."

Her blue eyes came back to me, and her jaw hung open. "No!"

I nodded and sat back. "The woman I told you about, the one who'd been on my mind so much ..."

"The mindless whore?" she gasped.

"Hey!" I narrowed my eyes at her. "Shanna, you've been my best friend for a very long time, but I'm not about to let you talk that way about the mother of my child. She's not what you think she is. She's actually a freelance book cover designer, and a sweet woman. She'd thought we'd be fine, but she'd forgotten to take her birth control pills before we met that night at the club."

"Sure she did," Shanna said as she narrowed her eyes right back at me. "This whore might not be mindless after all. She might be very devious. Going to a club like that, filled with rich men—she knew exactly what she was doing. You're a fool, Nixon. Lucky for you, I can take care of this gold digging bitch."

"You won't be taking care of a thing, Shanna. Katana isn't at all what you think she is. She'd had a hell of a rough week and forgot to take the pills. I believe her." I got up and paced, trying to calm myself down. She'd gotten me pretty damn mad, which didn't happen very often, especially with her.

"Nixon, you need to face the facts. She used you to get her broke ass pregnant so she'd have a meal ticket she could use the rest of her pitiful life." Shanna got up too and walked toward me, grabbing me by the shoulders to stop my pacing. "You'll need to get a DNA test done once the kid's born. If it is yours, you should get custody of it and leave her ass out in the cold. I'll help you raise the kid, and you know your parents would drop everything to come help you too. Don't let this tramp screw you any further than she already has."

As I stood there looking into the eyes of this woman who I'd always trusted, I didn't know what to think. What if she was right?

I didn't know Katana Reeves at all. I knew so little about her, and yet I'd already made a huge commitment to her. Shanna might be right about everything. But what could I do now?

"She'll be here today. I asked her to come live with me," I blurted out.

Shanna let me go and turned around, slapping her forehead. "Shit! Are you fucking serious right now? Why in the hell would you do something that damn drastic, Nixon?"

"I want to do what's right. Look, you really don't know her. She's not what you think. If she were a gold digger, then she'd have let me do all I wanted to do for her. She wouldn't let me spend a dime to get her out here. She offered to pay half the bills here, which I said no to, of course."

Shanna spun around with a terrible frown on her face. "Nixon, please tell me you can see through all of that. Sure, why not take on the little expenses of moving all her things and whatever else she had to do? In the end, she'll be rich— because you're being a fool."

I just couldn't see Katana being that type of person. "She'd never even been to that club before. She's a foster kid with no family she knows of. I couldn't leave her to fend for herself while carrying my baby. She's been sick with the pregnancy ..."

"Is that what she told you?" Shanna asked as her hands went to her narrow hips. "Because people can lie, you know."

"She's lost weight—at least a good ten pounds, and in a very short amount of time. She's not lying. I want to be a part of this whole thing. I want to share this with her. Understand or not, it doesn't matter. I'm moving her in with me, and we're going to raise this child together."

"Are you saying you're going to marry her?" she asked, then blew her blonde bangs out of her eyes.

"I didn't say that. We're not in love. We've only been together twice. It would be insane to ask her to marry me, right?" I asked, as it kind of had been on my mind, the idea to make things real between us. The last week had me thinking about her even more than I had been before she'd told me her news. I kept picturing her beautiful face, hearing her delicate voice, and I missed her even more than I had in the first place.

"This entire thing is insane, so yes," she answered. "Asking her to marry you would be such a giant mistake."

I sat down and put my head in my hands. Shanna's reaction was the exact reason I hadn't told a soul about what I was doing with Katana. Without other people's input, I'd made every decision quite easily. But now I was second guessing everything I'd decided.

"I miss her, Shanna. You know I already missed her before." I decided to do some confessing to my best friend. Maybe I'd been wrong to hide so much from her. Maybe that was why she'd taken this firm position, because she didn't understand everything. "When we got back from Texas, I had already decided I was getting back on the jet and going to Portland to find her. But she called me before I even started heading her way. When we met at my hotel, we couldn't keep our hands off one another and ended up in bed before she could even tell me a thing."

She looked stunned. "You hid that from me? Why?"

"I knew you would've tried to stop me." I looked at her and hoped she could see how I really felt about Katana. "I didn't want to take Bianca to the bar that night because I had Katana on my mind. I've had her on my mind since I left her that first day. I have no idea if she'll ever fall in love with me, but I can tell you this—I'm on the fast track to falling in love with her. But I won't push her about that. I don't want her to feel she has to love me for me to be in the baby's life."

"Well, fuck, dude." She shook her head.

And her words just about summed it all up.

51

CHAPTER 16

Katana

As I drove up the hill toward the address Nix had given me, my GPS told me the next house was my destination. Someone was coming out the front door, a tall, lithe, pretty blonde—and she didn't look too happy as she got into her car and sped off in the opposite direction.

Pulling into the driveway she'd just left, I found a bit of jealousy piercing my heart. *Maybe she's just the maid.*

Shrugging off the bit of negative emotion, I readied myself to go into what would be my home for the next little while. I didn't have high hopes of staying forever in Nixon's home. While his intentions were good, I assumed that sometime in the future he'd find a woman who was good for him—someone clearly in his league, a thing I wasn't.

Getting out of the car, I grabbed my purse and the overnight bag I'd packed for my brief stay at a motel in Portland, which I'd gone to after making sure the movers got everything from my old place. They'd taken off right away, aiming to get my things to Nixon's ahead of my arrival. Now I'd have to get inside and try to get things put away so my crap wouldn't be looming in boxes, taking up space.

When I got to the door, I went to punch in the code to disarm the security system before I used the key to open the door, just as Nix had told me to. But I thought it might be best to ring the bell instead, just in case he was home, which I couldn't tell from out here as his garage was closed.

When the door opened, I saw Nix's handsome face. "Hey, why'd you ring the bell? I told you to come on in." He wasted no time pulling me inside and hugging me. "I've missed you."

His arms around me did what they always seemed to do—made me wet and aching for him. When he closed the door and pinned me to it, I got the feeling his body reacted much as mine did.

He looked at me with hungry eyes, and I ran my hands over his bearded face. "It's grown even more. You look so dangerous."

Leaning down, he kissed me softly. "Good, that's exactly what I was going for. Did you miss me at all?"

Only every waking moment.

I didn't want to go that far. It was never my intention to make him feel like I wanted more than he was willing to give me. "I might've."

His hands moved down my arms as he pressed his bulge against me. "You have this crazy effect on me."

I laughed but stopped short when I heard someone in the kitchen. "Someone's here?"

"Yeah, the maid." He kissed me again. "Damn, I guess I should introduce you to her."

So the woman I saw wasn't the maid ... then who was she?

I kept my thoughts to myself. "Yes, you should introduce

us. After that, I really need to get to work putting my things away."

"No need, I had that all taken care of," he said, moving to one side and draping his arm across my shoulders.

"You had everything unpacked and put away? Already?" I was shocked and amazed and thankful.

"Yeah, I had the movers do some, and my maid and her son did the rest. I hope you don't mind." He stopped and pointed at a rocking chair that sat near the glass doors, which led outside to a gorgeous wooden deck. "I bought that yesterday for us to rock our baby in. Do you like it?"

The wooden rocker had been whitewashed, making it look rustic. "It's nice. I do like it. How thoughtful you are."

He shrugged and moved on, pulling me with him. "I don't know what's getting into me." When we stepped into the kitchen, my eyes landed on a middle-aged woman who was a little red in the face from cleaning the inside of a cabinet. "Mona Black, I'd like you to meet the lady of the house, Katana Reeves."

Wiping her hands on her white apron, she made her way to me. "It's a pleasure to meet you, ma'am." I shook her hand and took in her friendly smile. "Mr. Slaughter has told me your good news. Congratulations."

I looked at Nix and wondered why on earth he'd have this woman, who was clearly older than him, calling him such a formal name. Whatever his preference was, I wasn't about to be called ma'am or Miss Reeves. "Thank you. It's nice to meet you. And please call me Katana."

"I'll do that." She went back to what she was doing before, still talking. "I've planned roasted chicken with asparagus and wild rice for dinner this evening. Will that be okay with you, Katana?"

I looked at Nix, who smiled at me then winked. "She works for you too, Katana."

Not sure I liked that at all, I answered, "Anything you make will be fine with me. Just keep on doing what you've been doing for Nix. I don't need any special treatment."

"You don't hesitate to let me know if you want anything special, Katana. That is what I'm paid to do, after all—look after you guys." She got back to work as Nixon pulled me away from the kitchen.

"Let me show you around." He pointed out the glass doors. "That's the deck. There's a set of stairs that lead down to the beach." He had my hand in his and led me across the large living room. "On the other side of the kitchen is a formal dining room that I rarely use." He pointed to a door under the stairs. "That's a closet where things are stored. Next to this is the room we'll leave as the guestroom." Then up the stairs we went, and he pointed to the room at the end of the long hallway. "That's my bedroom back there. The door on the left is the baby's, and the one on the right is yours. You have access to a balcony through a set of French doors. You and I share that balcony; my room has another set of French doors that lead out to it as well."

"This place is gorgeous, Nix. I can't believe I get to call it home for a while," I gushed. Then I thought about the maid we'd left back in the kitchen, and looked at him as I put my hand on his chest. "Since I'm here, I can help with the daily chores. I can wash our clothes and keep things clean up here in our rooms and bathrooms. If you won't let me pay you anything, then I want to help out around the house."

He chuckled. "No way. I'm paying the maid to do that work. You wouldn't want to put Mona out of a paying job, now would you?" He pulled me along with him and opened the door to my new bedroom. "What do you think? We can change it up any way you want."

"It's perfect just the way that it is," I said as I looked at the gorgeous furnishings. The bed, a small desk, and the bedside tables were all made of cherry wood. A very large flat screen television hung on the wall, making it easy to lie in bed and watch it—which I might do whenever I wasn't gazing out the windows or doors at the perfect view of the blue waters of the Pacific Ocean. "This is more than I ever expected."

Nix's hand went into his pocket and came back with what looked to be a credit card. "This is for you. I want you to buy whatever you want or need."

I shook my head as I held up my hands in protest. "Nix, I can't take that. I have my own money."

He took my right hand and placed the card in my palm. "You will take this. I know you have your own money, but I want you to have access to more than just that. Just take it and don't fight me on it. Please."

I'd take it, but I wasn't planning to ever use it.

I laid it and my bag and purse on the bed. "Thank you, Nix. Thank you for everything."

He took both my hands in his and kissed them. "Thank you, Katana Reeves. I can honestly say that I've never felt more at home than I feel with you here. You and I will make a happy home for our child, I can tell that already."

"What kid wouldn't be happy here?" I asked as I glanced around the room again.

"I mean happy with us. You and me," he clarified, then kissed me and pulled me in close. His hands moved over my back then down to my ass, pulling me to him.

I moaned and melted into him. This wasn't what I'd expected, but I was happy he wanted me sexually. I wanted him that way too. But with the sex, we ran the risk that feelings might get in our way of making this work for our baby.

When he released my lips, I asked, "Nix, is what we're doing really smart? I mean, I love having sex with you—you know I do. No one could fake that. But should we be doing this?"

His sigh was long, and his eyes drooped a bit. "You don't want to anymore?"

I did want to. I wanted to very badly. But I didn't know how smart it was to keep doing the things that other couples would do. I bit my lip then finally said, "I don't want to force a relationship on you. Having sex will have some effects—on me at least. I can't stop my feelings for you from developing if we continue as we have been."

He let me go and turned away from me, rubbing his head. "I want you, Katana." He turned back around. "Do you want me?"

I nodded. "But I don't think it's smart."

"Then sex is off the table?"

Is it?

52

CHAPTER 17

Nixon

Katana's eyes stared a hole in the floor. She looked as if she was contemplating actually take sex off the table. So I had to step in. I took her chin in my hand and made her look at me. "Hey, I don't want to stop anything from happening with us, either. If that's what you're thinking, just stop doing that. We have some pretty amazing chemistry. Why try to act like we don't?"

The fear in her blue eyes became evident. "I'm just afraid ..."

I kissed her plump red lips with one feather-soft kiss. "I can see that. Don't be afraid of anything, Katana. Let's just ride this wave, doing whatever we want. Let's not let the fear of what might happen stand in our way of being happy with what we have right now."

"Which is what exactly?" she asked before running her hands up my arms and resting them on my shoulders. "I mean what are we, Nix?"

"Two people who happen to be extremely attracted to

each other, but are doing things backward. We're having a baby while also getting to know one another and seeing what the future might hold for us." I kissed her again, softly and sweetly.

When our lips parted, I loved the smile that moved over her face. "Okay. I think I can handle that." Her long dark lashes fluttered as a blush covered her cheeks. "I've got one more thing to ask you."

"Shoot," I said, then kissed the tip of her adorable nose. "If we have a girl, I hope she has this precious little turned up nose, just like you do."

She giggled, and the blush went a shade deeper. "You're so sweet, Nix. Being pregnant with your child, I—I don't have any intentions of being with other men." She looked at me, and I saw concern in her eyes. "What about you?"

"Me neither, but then again I've never been with any men." I chuckled, and she smacked my chest lightly.

"You know what I mean," she said with a scowl on her pretty face. "Are you going to stop seeing other women?"

Oh boy, things just got real, didn't they?

Was I going to take myself off the market? Was I ready to do that? I didn't even know Katana that well at all. What if there were things about her that just didn't sit well with me?

She could have some nasty habits I just couldn't cotton to. I mean, who knew if we'd actually get along or not?

But looking into her eyes I told myself that I should forgo seeing other women until I knew for certain that she and I weren't compatible. "I think I can be satisfied with just little ol' you. We don't have to put this agreement in stone. We have a lot to get to know about one another before we decide whether we're interested in pursuing more later on if we want. But for now, yeah, I'll stay away from other women, and you stay away from other men."

She let out a big breath. "Good."

Then she kissed me, and we fell into that blissful state of just being together. It seemed the most natural thing to me, being with her. But as we continued kissing and my cock grew, I heard her tummy growling and stopped the kiss—if I didn't stop now I knew this would lead all the way to the bed. "You're hungry."

"Not so hungry that we need to stop where we were headed," she protested.

I wasn't having any of that. I took her hand in mine, leading her out the bedroom door. "I'm getting you something to eat. I'll have Mona make you a sandwich to tide you over until dinner's ready."

She lagged behind, whining, "Really Nix, I can wait for dinner. I'm not that hungry. My tummy has just started growling a lot—I have no idea why that is."

I had to laugh. Was she really so clueless? "Baby, you have a little human you're growing inside of you. You need to eat a lot more so our kid will be healthy."

Taking her straight into the kitchen, I didn't see Mona anywhere and figured she was doing something elsewhere. So I sat Katana down and went to the fridge to make her a sandwich myself. "Ham?" I asked.

"I kind of hate ham. Do you have turkey?" she asked then tried to get up. "I can make my own sandwich, Nix."

I turned around and placed my hands on her shoulders. "I've got this. So turkey and Swiss?" I asked as I found some sliced Swiss cheese in the lunch meat drawer.

"Sounds great. And thank you," she said, then pulled out her cell and looked at her social media while I got to work.

A beep from the alarm system alerted me that it was being deactivated again and my stomach went tight. I knew there were only four people who had the code to my system, and three of them were already in the house.

"That would be Shanna," I told Katana, watching her eyes go big.

"Shanna? Who's that?" she asked.

Shanna came into the kitchen before I could answer her. And she didn't wait one second for me to introduce the two. "I'm Shanna, Nixon's best friend. You must be the woman who says she's pregnant by him."

Katana got up and extended her hand in a polite gesture, but Shanna didn't shake it. "I'm Katana Reeves. It's a pleasure to meet you, Shanna." When Shanna just looked at Katana's hand for several moments, Katana pulled it back and took a seat.

Shanna did the same, sitting across the small table from her. I hated the way she was eyeing Katana and stepped in, placing the plate with the sandwich and chips in front of Katana. "I think milk would be best for you to drink." I turned to grab a glass and then wondered if she had any allergies. I turned back, placing my hand on her shoulder. "Wait, are you lactose intolerant, or do you have any allergies I should know about?"

"No, I'm allergy-free as far as I know, and I can have dairy. Thank you, Nix," Katana said then bit into her sandwich as Shanna stared at her. I had to hand it to Katana—she didn't seem to be intimidated by Shanna in the least.

But then I remembered that Katana had been in an orphanage and then in foster care. She'd probably had to learn at a very early age how to deal with assholes—which my best friend was definitely being.

After placing the glass of milk on the table, I took a seat, pulling my chair closer to Katana's than Shanna's. "So what brought you back here, Shanna?"

"I wanted to meet her, of course," she answered me. "So what's the deal with you two?"

"What do you mean?" Katana asked, wiping her mouth with the napkin I'd given her.

"I mean, do you think you're going to come in here and take over my best friend's life?" Shanna tapped her foot as she stared Katana down.

I'd had enough. "Shanna, stop."

Shanna's light brows rose and she looked appalled. "Nixon, someone has to look out for you. I'm not about to let some money-grubbing bitch ..."

I stood up and took her by the arm. "I will not have you speaking that way in my house, Shanna." I jerked her up and pulled her toward the door.

But Katana stopped me. "It's okay, Nix. She can ask me anything she wants to. She just cares about you. That's why she's upset right now—I understand that. Please, let her sit back down, and she and I can get to know one another. If she's your best friend, then she's pretty important to you, and will be to our baby as well."

I let Shanna's arm go and wagged my finger in her face. "You chill on the name calling. You're lucky she's nice, Shanna, or you'd have been out on your ass. Be nice. She's the mother of my child. My blood. And you know how I am about blood. It takes priority over everyone else. Don't make me cut you out of my life."

Shanna went pale. I suppose she'd never imagined I'd actually do such a thing to her. "Nixon?"

I nodded and took my seat again. "I am dead serious. Now play nice."

Shanna took her seat and looked apologetic. "Well, seems he's got a protective instinct for you, Katana. I'm sorry. I've known this man since we were little kids. He and I were in the same classes all through our school years. I lived three houses down from his, and we walked to school together every day for thirteen years. He's beaten up my jackass boyfriends when they hurt me, and he's let me cry on his shoulder about them too. He's a rare man, and I count myself lucky to be able to call him a friend, let alone my best friend."

Katana finished up her sandwich and then took a long drink of her milk before saying anything else. "Sorry, I didn't realize just how hungry I was until I took that first bite." She patted my leg underneath the table. "Thanks, sweetie." Then she turned her attention to Shanna. "I think it's admirable of you to want to watch out for Nix. He's lucky to have a friend like you who cares so much. I'd like to set the record straight, though. I am not a money-grubbing bitch."

"She isn't," I agreed. "I have told you that before."

Katana smiled at me and ran her hand over my bearded cheek. "Aw, you stood up for me before? That's so sweet of you."

"Yeah, he's a real sweetheart," Shanna said then shook her head. "Not. At least, not usually." She narrowed her eyes at me, looking like she was trying to solve a puzzle. "I don't think I've ever seen you make anything for anybody in my entire life, Nixon. And I've never seen him look at anyone the way he looks at you, Katana. But I want to warn you both: you don't know one another. Try your best not to rush into things more than you already have."

But it felt like life was rushing ahead for us—and at a staggering pace.

53

CHAPTER 18

Katana

After several days had passed, I began to feel more settled. Nix and I had chosen an obstetrician and had an appointment set up for the late afternoon. Nerves were getting the best of me, and I ended up puking three times before he arrived at three to pick me up.

Holding my hand on the console between the seats, his thumb ran back and forth over the top of my hand. "You look pretty in that pink dress." He pulled my hand up and kissed it. "Can I assume that means you're hoping for a girl?"

I shook my head. "I'm hoping for a healthy baby—the sex doesn't matter to me." I looked out the window. "I don't know how to take care of either, anyway."

Nix told me he wanted to wait to be sure I stayed pregnant before he told his family about our situation, but once we were past the critical three-month mark, he'd tell them about everything.

"You know I told you my mother would help you with all that. I don't want you to worry even a little bit about that—

you'll be a great mother. I know you will." He kissed my hand again, and I couldn't help but smile.

I don't know how he made me feel so much better just by being with me, but he did. "I know you'll be a great father."

"I'm going to try." He chuckled. "I had to lie to my mother a while ago."

"Why?" I asked, surprised he'd have to lie about anything.

"She wanted me to come for Christmas, and I told her I'd made plans with my business partners for that day so I couldn't come this year." He shook his head. "I don't lie often. It felt pretty unnatural doing it, but I don't want to jump the gun with our news."

Thinking about losing the baby made my stomach roll, and I swallowed as saliva suddenly began to produce rapidly. I saw a stoplight ahead and prayed he'd make it to that before I had to open the door and hurl. I couldn't even say a word as I felt sure I'd projectile vomit all over his expensive car.

When Nix stopped at the light, I opened the door and let it all out. "Baby?" he called out.

It took no time to expel the little that was left in my stomach, and I closed the door and leaned my head back on the headrest when I was done. "God, I hate that."

He handed me a tissue as he shook his head. "Damn, I hate that for you."

By the time we got to the doctor's office, the butterflies in my tummy had turned into pterodactyls, and I had to cling to Nix for support. I'd never really leaned on anyone in my life. It felt odd—and even a little dangerous—but I couldn't help it.

The waiting room was full of expecting mothers in

various stages of pregnancy. A few small kids were playing with some toys in one corner, and I noticed only a handful of fathers there with the women. I squeezed Nix's arm, which I had wrapped mine around. "Thank you, Nix."

"For?" he asked as he grinned at me.

"Being here with me. For me." I kissed his cheek. "You're my rock."

He kissed mine right back. "I am that. And I wouldn't miss this for anything."

When my name was called, we got up. He wrapped his arm around me, supporting me, and I knew he could feel my body shaking. "I'm so scared."

"No reason to be. Nothing bad will happen to you. Come on, be brave. For our baby, be brave." He kissed my cheek once more and in we went.

The doctor was a man in his late fifties. He passed us in the hallway and stopped to introduce himself. "You're new." He extended his hand, and we took turns shaking it. "I'm Doctor Sheffield."

Nix took the lead. "I'm Nixon Slaughter, and this is Katana Reeves."

"Nice to meet you both. Do the deal with the nurses, and I'll come see you soon." He walked away, leaving us to follow the nurse once more.

"He seemed nice," I said, and felt a tiny bit better about this whole thing.

"I'm sure he's very nice. And he had many high recommendations. I think we picked the right man for the job, baby." He gave me a confident smile, and I had to smile back.

After an hour of being weighed and measured, and giving urine and blood samples, I was handed a paper robe and Nix and I were sent to a room to wait for the doctor.

I undressed behind a little curtain while Nix looked at the posters on the walls, which depicted the stages of a developing fetus. "Let's see here," he said as I changed. "It's now the twelfth of December, and that means we're six weeks. That means we should be able to hear the baby's heartbeat, according to this chart."

I came out wearing the unflattering paper robe and looked at the table I had to climb up on. Then I felt hands on my waist, turning me around. Nix lifted me up, putting me on the table. "Thank you." I couldn't help the smile that took over my face. The man was just too damn good.

"You look adorable. Can I take a picture of you? I swear I won't post it on anything; I just want to chronicle everything." He pulled his cell out of his jacket pocket and cocked his head as he waited for my approval.

"Swear to make me look good in this silly thing?" I asked.

He nodded. "You'll look like a pinup girl, I swear."

With a nod, I gave him approval and found him snapping a ton of pictures and taking selfies with me in the pictures too. He had me laughing and feeling a lot less nervous in no time at all.

When Doctor Sheffield came in, he wore a wide grin on his face. He pushed one hand through his salt and pepper hair as he came to us. "Glad to see you two having a good time. It's nice to see people celebrating bringing a new life into the world." He opened up the folder with all my information and looked it over. "Says here you two are certain about the date of conception and that some people must've had a fun time on Halloween." He grinned knowingly at us.

"That we did," Nixon confirmed. "So when are we going to be seeing our little baby's face, doc?"

"If everything goes right, you'll see your baby on the

twenty-fourth of July. How does that sound?" The doctor walked over to the counter to put on a pair of gloves.

My heart began to pound then. I knew what the gloves meant and wasn't real keen on Nix being there while the doctor poked and prodded me. But I guessed that would be something I'd have to get used to. Nix did seem set on being a part of every little bit of the pregnancy—as much as he could be, at least.

I must've had a wild-eyed look on my face as the doctor came and pushed me gently back. Nix took the place on my right, holding my hand and smiling at me reassuringly. "You'll be just fine, baby."

I nodded but didn't feel just fine as the doctor placed my feet in the stirrups. Then he pushed something cold inside of me as he said, "We'll just get this Pap smear out of the way, then I'll do a transvaginal ultrasound and see if we can hear a heartbeat."

My entire body tensed as he cranked the mechanism, opening me up so he could do the test. "Ow," I whined when it pinched me.

"Almost done, Katana," the doctor assured me.

When I looked at Nix, I saw he wasn't even breathing as he stared at the top of the doctor's head. He was nervous too. He never said one word about it, but I could read his body language. All the while, his only mission seemed to be trying his best to keep me calm.

I had lucked into getting the best baby-daddy in the whole world. I had no idea what I'd done to deserve all of this. But I was thankful for it all. I squeezed his hand, and he looked at me. "Thanks again for being here for me."

He nodded. "Thanks again for including me." He leaned over and kissed my forehead.

The doctor finished with the uncomfortable procedure

then pushed something else inside me before flipping a switch on a small screen on his left. We could see the screen too, but I had no idea what we were looking at.

He moved the device inside of me as he searched for our baby. "Here we go." He smiled at us as he pointed to a small orb on the screen. The orb pulsed as the doctor turned up the sound, and there was the tiny heartbeat.

A tear fell, and I gasped. Nix squeezed my hand and looked at me. "So there it is. Our baby, Katana."

My heart filled with love. Love for the little orb, and love for Nixon Slaughter.

God help me, how can anyone fall in love this quickly?

54

CHAPTER 19

Nixon

A few days had passed since we'd gone to the doctor. I was having lunch with August as our other partner, Gannon, was busy with other things that day. I guessed a two-year-old could take up a lot of time, but my bet was that it was actually the hot young babysitter that had Gannon Forester so busy these days.

I'd made this vow to myself about telling as few people as possible about the pregnancy, but I couldn't stop myself. "So, I'm going to be a little busy myself come the end of July." I put a piece of pepper steak into my mouth as I waited for August to ask me why that was.

"That's some time off, Nixon. You have another deal going on or something?" he asked me, then took a long drink of his iced tea.

"You remember when I left town for Halloween?" I ran my hand over my beard, remembering how that night had marked the beginning of me growing it out. I'd soon have a much more permanent reminder of that fateful night.

"Yeah, I remember you ditching us that night. So, what about it?" He stopped eating to give me his full attention. "You look different, Nixon."

"Yeah?" I asked. "How so?"

He shrugged. "Not exactly sure about that. You just look a little different. A little happier or something. You must be getting more sleep than you usually do. You have a healthy look going on."

I'd had less sleep than usual lately, as Katana and I had spent at least two hours of every night since she moved in engaged in some mind-blowing sex. Her bedroom was merely a place for her clothes to be kept. But I had been eating better—spending more time at home with Katana eating the healthy foods Mona made us instead of eating out so much.

"So, the thing that will have me so busy by late July is actually a baby." I stopped, waiting for his reaction—dropping the mic, so to speak.

August blinked a few times. "Have you been seeing someone seriously that you've left out of our conversations?"

"Well, now I am." I chuckled. "The woman I met on Halloween is pregnant—and it's mine. When she called me and told me she took a test that came back positive, I moved her into my place."

Being a wealthy man himself, August was cautious where women were concerned. "Hold on. This woman, have you had her checked out? You can't be sure that baby is yours, not until after it's born and you can have a paternity test done. Don't you think that moving her in with you is jumping the gun by a whole hell of a lot?" He shook his head. "It's not like you to do something stupid like this."

"No, it's not." I fidgeted in my seat, as it never sat right with me when anyone thought I was making a mistake.

"And I will have a test done after the baby's born. But I don't want to miss out on a thing if the kid is mine. Which I do think it is. This woman has given me no reason to believe she's a liar."

"And what does this woman do for a living?" August asked as he put his hands behind his head and leaned back, as if he was my therapist getting ready for one long session.

"She's a book cover designer. She freelances and works from home." I winked at him. "Pretty cool, right?"

He finally smiled and sat upright. "Thank God. I was pretty sure you were going to tell me she's a stripper."

"Damn, August!" I laughed, and so did he.

"I'll have to introduce you to her soon. You'll see, she's genuine. And I must admit, I'm starting to fall pretty hard for her." I shoved my hand into my pocket and looked down. "She sure is making me think a lot."

"Uh oh." August shook his head at me.

Now, why would that be considered an uh oh?

"Care to add to that, August?" I asked him as I picked up my iced tea and took a sip.

"You wouldn't do anything stupid, right?" he asked, then tapped the tabletop with his finger. "Like marry her on a spur of the moment kind of thing, without having a prenup, right?"

"A prenup?" I asked then shook my head. "Why would I need one of those things? I don't believe in divorce. My parents raised me right, August."

"But did hers?" he winked at me and wagged his finger at me. "You aren't the only one who can file for a thing like a divorce, Nixon. She could too. And she could take you for half of everything you've got."

His question about her upbringing did send a red flag floating through my brain. "She was raised in foster care.

She didn't know her father and her mother abandoned her."

"Damn," he murmured. "That sounds like one hell of a rough life. My heart goes out to the poor thing. That said, now you really need a prenup. She's what I like to call a wildcard. You have no clue what she might turn into. When you know a person's family, you can get a rough idea of what the person is like and will be like later on in life. You've heard the saying, look at her mother to see how she'll be in twenty years, right?"

"And her mother is a low-life," I mumbled. The thought wasn't pretty, nor was the vision that appeared in my head of Katana turning into her absentee mother. "Damn."

"Look, don't rush into anything. Just because she's pregnant, that's no reason to go faster than you would with anyone else." He waved the waiter over. "Can you bring the bill?"

The waiter gave him a nod and headed off.

August's words hit me like a punch to the gut. How could I have forgotten about Katana's horrible past?

Something like that had to really screw with a person's head. And Katana did have a certain vulnerability about her. Sometimes vulnerability could lead to weakness, and that could lead to self-destructive tendencies. Those were the kinds of things that can end relationships.

Maybe I was moving too fast. Thinking too much about making things permanent much too quickly.

But even as I thought about that, my heart beat harder, as if it were trying to pump more blood to my brain. It reminded of how my pulse had kicked when I looked into her pretty eyes as we listened to the first sounds we'd ever heard of our baby. That was real.

All the "what ifs" were not.

There could be a billion "what ifs." What if she did turn out like her mother? What if she did turn into some self-destructive person, bent on ruining me? There was just no end to them.

But then I began to think about my own "what ifs." What if I never made a commitment to her? What if I lost her to another man who would give her the stability I knew she'd craved her whole life? What if I lost her only because I was too worried about "what ifs?"

My thoughts were consuming me as August paid the bill. He interrupted my internal battle as he asked, "How about Friday? You still going out?"

I shook my head. "No. There's no point—I promised Katana I wouldn't see anyone else."

His eyes went wide with what looked like shock. "Fuck! Are you kidding me, man? You've already made a promise like that to her? You barely know this chick, Nixon. Damn, does she have some voodoo shit on you or something? This is so unlike you."

"She's pregnant with my child," I said, wanting him to understand what I was doing. "She told me she wouldn't see anyone and I told her the same. I also told her that it wasn't a thing that was set in stone."

"Again, you're making some pretty big decisions based on the assumption that this baby is yours," he pointed out as we got up and started heading for the door. "And what about me?"

The doorman opened the door, letting us out, and we walked into the cool afternoon. A slight breeze stirred my hair, and I ran my hand through it. "What about you?" I had to ask.

"I don't want to hit the town all alone. Gannon already called, and he's backed out on us. And now you too?" He shook his head as we headed for our cars. "We have a night-club to put together. That is one of the main reasons we hit the town on Friday nights, if you'll recall. To get ideas about what people like, what they flock to."

We stopped at his BMW, and I had to tell him something I'd been thinking about for a while anyway. "We're not making a club for everyday people. We're making one for the super-rich. And that means our clientele won't have the same desires as the people who go to the clubs that are already here. Our clients will be looking for sophistication, style, and ways to rub elbows with other people with money who can help them further expand their businesses."

All he could do was nod. But he still wore a frown. "I guess you're right."

"When we came up with that grand plan, we were all single and free. And we were all looking for a good time. Well, my good time is waiting for me at home. And although Gannon has yet to come clean with us, his good time is also at home. Those clubbing days are most likely a thing of the past for the two of us." I watched August's expression grow grim. "I hope that doesn't upset you, man."

With a shake of his head, he opened the driver's side door and looked at me. "You guys are growing up on me."

I guess we were. And it was long overdue.

55

CHAPTER 20

Katana

The afternoon had a cool, gentle breeze blowing in off the ocean water, bringing with it a wonderful scent. I sat on the deck getting some vitamin D from the sun and enjoying the gorgeous day.

Nix had had lunch with one of his business partners, then he said he'd be home after that. I loved the fact that I had someone coming home to me every day. It was so different from my life before.

A man cleared his throat, taking my attention away from my thoughts, and I pulled my shades down to see who it was. A tall man stood on the stairs looking at me. "Hi there. You're a new addition to this neighborhood." He gestured to the deck. "May I?"

"Of course," I said, sitting up and making sure my dress was straight. I'd been lounging and had no idea what kind of state I was in. "I'm Katana Reeves."

He came to me and shook my hand. "John Simmons. I live next door. You related to Nixon?"

"No—no, I'm not." I didn't know how much to tell the man.

"Oh, okay." He pointed to the other chair. "You mind?"

"No, please sit down." I pointed to the unopened bottle of water on the small table between us. "Thirsty?"

He shook his head. "Nah. So, where are you from, Katana Reeves?"

"Portland," I told him. "But now I live here."

He nodded and ran his hand through his thick, dark wavy hair. "And why's that?"

I found him quite nosy, but I supposed neighbors liked to know who was living next to them. "Well, if you must know, I'm pregnant with Nixon's baby."

"Oh!" he said with raised brows. "Now that's some news."

"Are you a reporter?" I joked with him.

"No," he said with a chuckle. "Just a nosy old man with little to do."

"You're not old," I said as I looked him over. He wasn't super young, but he wasn't old either.

"How old do you think I am?" he asked with a smile. "And don't sugarcoat it. I really want to know how old I look to you."

"Forty," I said without thinking too much about it.

He nodded. "Forty-two. But I feel much older than that. I guess going through a divorce does that to people."

"I'm sorry to hear that. How long ago was it?" A little stab in my heart had me asking.

"It's nearly been a year since it became finalized. But it took two years to get the whole ugly thing done." He ran his hand over his brow. "I waited too long to leave my wife. I stayed for our two kids. I spent twenty years with the woman I thought loved me. Some six years back I caught her cheating, and only then did I find out she'd been doing it all along. I even had to get my kids tested to make sure they were mine. They were, so I stayed. I stayed and stayed until our youngest graduated from high school and moved off to college. Then I left, and that woman who'd done me so wrong tried to do even more to me. She wanted half of everything. So it took a long time to get the divorce finalized —my lawyer had to fight hers just so I could come out losing only a quarter of what I had, instead of half."

"That sounds awful," I said as I shook my head.

"It was." He nodded. Then he pulled his shades down and looked at me over the top of them. "So you and Nixon, had you known each other long before this happened?"

I felt embarrassment heat my cheeks. "No. Not at all."

He clucked his tongue and shook his head. "Damn."

"Yeah, well, it is what it is." I didn't know what else to say.

"And your plan is what, exactly?" he asked as he slid his sunglasses back up his nose.

"To live together and have the baby and let life take us wherever it takes us." I sighed, knowing that sounded like a flighty plan.

"Oh, one of those kinds of plans. Got ya." He laughed and slapped his denim-covered leg. "I don't envy you guys, I can tell you that."

Although I was slightly offended by the blunt man, I found myself asking, "And why is that, exactly, John?"

"Well, my wife and I had a plan, and even that didn't make things work out for us." He sighed, and I could feel his sadness about how his marriage had turned out. "We started our marriage out of love, not merely because she was pregnant. The odds are stacked against you two."

"I'm not worried about any relationship between Nix and me. What worries me the most is how our child will be affected by both of us. That's all that really matters. I believe Nix and I have the baby's best interest as our focus." I leaned back, feeling great about what I'd said.

John just laughed again. "Oh, honey!"

Oh, honey?

I shook my head. "What does that mean?"

"It means you're living in a fantasy world. That's what it means." He smiled at me as if what he was saying should make me feel better, which it didn't. And I had been feeling pretty damn sure about everything before he'd arrived. Especially since the doctor's appointment and that special moment Nix and I had shared, where I had felt my heart open up to him.

Sure, I hadn't gone so far as to let Nix know about that little miracle, but I would. One day. Time had to pass, or he'd think I was telling him I loved him much too soon. I couldn't have that. So I'd keep it to myself, for now.

But this guy, this virtual stranger had just told me I was living in a fantasy world, and he didn't even know the half of it. So I enlightened him. "I don't think I am living in a fantasy world. Well, that's not entirely true. You see this place, this home, the man who comes home to me each day —now that is just like a fantasy. And not one I'd ever had before. I hadn't meant for any of this to happen, and for things to have fallen into place so easily is a gift. Nix is a gift."

John smiled. "Now that's a pretty sweet sentiment. So, you like this guy a lot then?"

I nodded. "I love him." I couldn't believe I had just admitted something so huge to this man, a man I didn't know from Adam. "And I think he'll grow to love me. I think he and I can make a fantastic family together."

John's brows shot up. "Oh? I don't suppose—since you're from Portland—that you know much about the man you're living with."

"Not a lot about his past. But I'm getting to know him more and more with each passing day—and he's a good man. A man I respect immensely." I picked up the bottle of water and took a drink of it, as my impassioned bits of speech had made my mouth dry.

A cluck of his tongue told me John wanted to fill me in on something. "Well, you should know the man has quite the eye for beautiful women. And he's never kept any of them around for long periods of time. Being his neighbor, I can tell you why that is. Would you like to know?"

I did, and I didn't. What did it matter how he'd been with other women in the past? But that damn curiosity raised her ugly head and used my mouth to say, "Yes, I would love to know why. I'm assuming it's because you think he's quite the player."

When John shook his head, I had to admit I was surprised. "Nope. I mean he's been with a boatload of women, but I don't think it was by choice necessarily. You see, Nixon Slaughter is easily distracted, and not by other women, but by business. His downfall is that he's neglectful of people. I've seen him out on this very deck with beautiful woman after beautiful woman, and I've watched him get phone call after phone call and end up leaving them all alone on his deck with the perfect view. And I watched as he forgot he had a woman waiting for his return at all, sometimes even leaving her to go somewhere else without giving so much as a goodbye."

It didn't seem that he could possibly be talking about the man I knew. "Are you sure you're talking about the man who lives here? Because the man I know isn't neglectful in the least."

"Maybe the baby has something to do with that right now," John offered. "But I do believe his natural ways will kick in sooner or later. And where will that leave you, Katana? Here, home alone with a baby and no one to help you with it?"

"I don't think ..." I tried to say.

John shook his head. "I know you don't think he'll be that way with you or with this child," he said. "I've been around the block a time or two. I've lived next door to this man for nearly three years. I've seen him. I know him. You don't. He's high on the fact he's about to be a father for the first time. The man is almost thirty and probably didn't even know himself how ready he was to be a father. Even men yearn to have children at a certain age."

"Maybe it's the baby that's changing him. Maybe that is true. But I think it's a change that will stick. I have faith in that," I said, then looked over my shoulder when I heard the familiar beep of the security system that signaled someone's arrival. "I'll have to say goodbye and nice meeting you, John. He seems to be home now."

John got up and waved as he headed down the stairs. "See you around, Katana."

When I got inside, I found Nix coming in through the kitchen, having come through the garage after parking his car. His smile was the first thing I noticed and then his arms were around me, holding me close as our mouths met in the sweet kiss we always shared when he came home.

I loved the little ritual. But I couldn't help feeling a little uncertain after the conversation I'd just had. John's words about Nix's past had me a little worried about admitting my love for the man too quickly. I couldn't stay in a neglectful situation again. No child deserved that—and neither did I. It was a total deal breaker in my book.

56

CHAPTER 21

Nixon

Each day that passed had us growing closer. Katana and I talked more than I'd ever talked to anyone about anything, even in my business life. With only a few days until Christmas, I found myself doing things without thinking about them at all, having settled into our own little routine.

After watching a movie downstairs, I turned off the television and got off the sofa. "Time for bed, baby."

A sexy little smile curved her lips as she took my hand and let me pull her up, and she moved right into my arms. "I'm feeling a little feisty tonight, Master." She pulled my hand down to cup her ass. "Maybe a little punishment will calm me down."

"I can see the healthy diet I've been making you eat has gotten you back in good shape. Maybe we can play a little." I scooped her up and took her up the stairs to my bedroom—which had quickly become our bedroom, in my mind. "You know, you should just let me move your things into this bedroom." I sat her on my bed and loved how she lit up at the idea.

"Like make this thing a bit more real?" she asked.

"Is that something you'd like?" I asked her as I unbuttoned her shirt.

Her breasts spilled over the top of her bra. Her Ds would soon become double Ds and my mouth watered for them already. Pushing her shirt off her, I took her bra off next, pausing a moment to admire the works of art I'd revealed.

Katana's voice broke the spell her tits had put me under. "I'd love nothing more than to make things more real between us. I'll move my things tomorrow if you'd like."

"Nothing would make me happier." While there was at least one thing that would make me happier, I wasn't about to mess up my Christmas surprise.

Pushing her to lie back, I pulled her jeans off and made her gasp when I ripped her panties off, tossing them on the floor. She bit her lip as she watched me.

I took my shirt off, stepping out of my jeans as well, but leaving my tight black underwear on. Wiggling my finger at her, I had her turn over to get on her hands and knees. She moved over the bed like a tigress, appearing more than ready to play.

Her dark hair hung down, covering her tits. "How do you want me, Master?"

Without saying a word, I moved my finger in a circle, indicating that I wanted her to turn around. She did, presenting her round ass to me. I moved one hand over her soft flesh while moving the other over my growing erection.

Just the sight of her tight little ass did things to me that seemed impossible. I had no idea how she did this to me. The woman consumed my thoughts. I found myself stopping everything I was doing throughout my busy workdays just to call her and hear her voice.

Without even trying, the woman had me in the palm of her hand. And what was even crazier was that she had no clue as to how much she had me. But even if she did come to realize it someday, I didn't see her ever using her hold over me in any kind of bad way.

Her moan took me out of my inner thoughts, and I came back to reality. Her smooth flesh flowed under my hand, and I pulled back and popped her one. She moaned even louder. "Yes, Master."

A smile moved across my face that I thought might never go away. I gave her three more smacks, and she wiggled her ass at me, wanting more. After another three smacks, I leaned over and kissed her sweet ass, nibbling away at her tender skin.

She made a magnificent sound when I pushed my tongue into her asshole. Then she whispered, "Oh, Master, would you please fuck me in the ass?"

Hell yeah, I will!

Her request spurred me on as I tongue fucked her ass first, getting it wet and ready to be spread wide for my cock, which was growing by leaps and bounds.

Reaching around her, I pushed a finger into her soaking pussy and knew she was ready to go. I pulled my face away from her delicious ass and dropped my underwear. Pressing the tip of my cock to her asshole, I was surprised when she pushed back with a sudden jerk, forcing my cock to sink into her as she groaned.

I smacked her ass. "You're supposed to let your Master do that, you little minx."

"Sorry, I just wanted it so bad, Master." She turned her head and looked at me over her shoulder. "My bad."

I gave another smack. "You're forgiven, slave."

She kissed the air then turned around, moving her hands up the bed and lowering her head to get her ass up higher in the air. My cock sank further into her and I could feel her spreading even more to accommodate me.

Being in such a tight area, my cock was in heaven. I moved back and forth, using her ass to stroke my engorged cock. "Faster," she begged.

I moved faster and thrust into her harder. My balls bounced off her pussy with each hard thrust, and soon her legs began to quiver. Her moans grew and grew until she made one shrill screaming sound as her body gave in and climaxed.

Not wanting to miss a thing, I pulled out of her ass and took her by the waist, turning her over. I hungered to lap up the juices I'd made her release. Pushing her legs up to bend her knees, I leaned over and planted my face in her pulsing pussy.

Sticking my tongue into her, I drank up as much of her as I could before the orgasm waned and the juices stopped flowing at such a high rate. Her hands tangled in my hair as she made the hottest sounds I'd ever heard.

"God, Nix! Baby, you fuck me so well," she moaned.

I put a halt to my delicious meal to push her up the bed a bit, and then I climbed on top of her. My cock pushed into her, feeling the last aftershocks of the orgasm.

Moving fast and hard, I pulled one of her tits into my mouth and sucked her as I fucked her. Her nails ran over my back, leaving hot streaks in their wake. Harder and harder I went until she came hard, taking me with her on that journey.

I heard a terrible groan coming out of me as I shot my load into her hot pussy. Her legs wrapped around me, holding me to her as if she never wanted me to take my cock out of her throbbing cunt.

Not that I was in a hurry to leave her warm embrace. I held my weight off her as we both caught our breath. As the heat ebbed, her legs fell away from me, and I collapsed to one side of her, my hand resting on her still-flat stomach.

She ran her hand over mine as she whispered, "Our little orb is okay. Not to worry, Daddy."

"Daddy," I echoed her. "And how's Mommy? Did she like what Daddy did to her?"

She giggled. "Now you're skirting on the edge of creepy, baby. But I very much liked what you did to me. That ass kissing was a pleasant surprise. Never thought I'd get to feel that."

"Yeah, I was waiting for a client to show up at my office earlier today and was looking for something to read. I found this smutty novel on my Kindle and scanned it for the sex scenes. That's where I got the idea. Glad you liked it." I was pretty proud of myself for taking the time to research new ways to please my lady.

"How thoughtful of you, Nix." She turned on her side to face me. Her lips touched my nose. "You know, I think you're just about the most thoughtful man I've ever met."

"I haven't always been that, Katana. It's funny how you affect me. You've changed me without even trying to." I kissed her on the forehead. "I mean, I never knew I could be like this. The truth is my business has consumed me for years. Before that, it was sports. I've never been the kind of guy who thought much at all about the woman I was with at any given time. But you—somehow you've taken over everything. It's you who consumes my thoughts now."

"I hope it stays that way. You consume my thoughts as well, you know." She ran her hand over my chest, tracing my tribal tattoo. "My life has gone from one of mere content-ment to one I'd never have even dared to dream about. Thank you, Nixon Slaughter."

"No, thank you, Katana Reeves." I pulled her closer to me, holding her tight. "I thank God every single day for taking me to you that Halloween night. I'll never forget that night."

Even if we hadn't had a permanent reminder on the way, I would never forget the night I'd found Katana and changed into the person I was meant to be.

CHAPTER 22

Katana

Christmas Eve arrived, and Nix came home with a real Christmas tree. I met him at the door as he told me he had a surprise. "Wow, a real one, huh?" I asked as he pulled it through the door, pine needles leaving a trail in its wake.

"Always a real one, baby." He leaned it against the wall and came to me, pulling me into his arms and giving me his usual hello kiss. "This is a tradition in my family. We don't put up a tree until Christmas Eve, and we take it down the day after New Year's."

"Why wait so late before you put it up, Nix?" I asked as I ran my hand over the tree, finding it somewhat sticky and prickly.

Nix went to the closet under the stairs and pulled out a box that had Christmas written on it. He came to the tree and sat it on the floor. "Well, my family is big, I told you about that. And with a lot of kids, Mom and Dad found out a lot of begging and pleading to open *just one present* got to be annoying."

"I can imagine," I said as I helped him take the things out of the box and laid them on the coffee table to sort them out.

"So they came up with the idea of only putting the tree up on Christmas Eve, and we each got to open one present that night. The next morning we'd open the rest, giving Santa a chance to bring us more presents and fill our stockings with candy and little toys." His eyes lit up as he pulled out the tree topper, an old star with hardly any silver glitter remaining. "This came from my gram-gram's Christmas ornament collection. I got this out of a box full of them after she passed away."

With a nod, I understood why he had the ugly old thing. "I see. What a sweet sentiment." I began to notice that all the ornaments looked old and worn out. "Did you inherit all of these?"

"I did." He stopped pulling things out of the box to pull something out of his jacket pocket. "But I'll be adding something new this year. It's the first ornament I've actually purchased."

A small brown bag was in his hand, and he handed it to me. "What is it?" I asked. The bag was flat, almost as if nothing was inside of it.

"Open it." His smile went wide as he watched me.

I opened the flap that closed the bag and found clear plastic inside. Pulling it out, I found a brass baby bootie inside and pulled it out too. He'd had it engraved with the words, *"Daddy and Mommy's first Christmas with their little orb.'*

Tears clouded my vision as I thought that it had to be the sweetest thing he'd ever done in his entire life. I threw myself into his arms for a hug and tried to hold back the tears, but just couldn't. "Nix, you're the sweetest man on the planet."

"Aw, it's just a little something to help us remember our first Christmas together." He looked down at the ornament I held and took it from me, placing it on the table with the rest of the things. "So, first we have to put this thing in a tree stand, and that's no easy task."

I'd never had a real tree before. My foster parents had had this little plastic tree they'd put up each year. It went up right after Thanksgiving and didn't come down until sometime after the New Year. And we never got to decorate it. Mrs. Davis did that alone.

All I'd ever gotten was one present each year. I was thankful for that. And it was always something useful, never a toy. I didn't ever have any toys that I could recall. But I'd make damn sure my kid had a ton of them.

"I nearly forgot," Nix said. As he snapped his head up, he wore a grin. "Can you go out to my car? It's parked in the front. Somebody left something for you inside. It's sitting on the passenger seat."

"For me?" I asked, surprised. I made my way to his car and opened the passenger door to find a small box and a red envelope. "Hmm, who's this from, I wonder."

I thought it had to be a small early present from Nix but when I opened the card I found it was from Shanna. The envelope housed a Christmas card with a lighted tree on front that wished me a Merry X-mas.

When I opened it, I found she'd written me a note inside. The first line hooked me.

To the woman who's stolen my best friend's heart.

I had to read it all now. How could I not?

Nixon Slaughter has been like a big brother to me since I can remember. So I might come off kind of overprotective of the man now and then.

That said, I can see that he looks at you with love-glazed eyes. And that makes me happy.

I'm sorry for my prejudice about what you two enjoy sexually speaking. (I know—not your typical Christmas card material!) Anyway, please forgive me for jumping to conclusions about you. I don't know you well yet, but you're my best friend's girl so that means we will become great friends too.

I hope you can give this old friend of the man you love a chance to prove I'm not always a bitch. Maybe that could be your Christmas gift to me, forgiveness for being an overbearing, prejudice, buttinsky.

Now open the present I gave Nixon to give to you and we will consider this hatchet buried.

My heart felt full of emotion as I put the card away, making sure to put it up nice and neat as I'd keep it forever. I felt it was such a sweet sentiment and would treasure the card.

When I opened the small black box, I found a bracelet inside. It had a sterling silver charm bracelet and there were a few charms on it already. One of the charms stood out amongst them all. One in the shape of a heart that said *friends for life* on one side and on the other she'd had our names engraved.

I took my present and card inside and found one tear had fallen. Nix looked as me as I came inside and his smile beamed at me. "Do I see a tear?"

I wiped my eye with the back of my hand. "I'm afraid so. I think I've made a new friend."

He nodded and went back to pulling decorations out of the boxes. "Good. That girl's like a sister to me. She's a little on the tomboy side and doesn't like to hang with girls much.

She's kind of rough and tumble. That's how come she and I ended up becoming such good friends. I never want you to be jealous of her. There's no reason to. I hope you can look at her like you'll look at any of my family, because she's as close to me as they are."

I came up behind him, hugging him. "I think she made a great gesture and I will accept her for who she is. I'm just so happy we can all get along. I don't want to spoil one thing in our life. I only want to enhance it."

He turned around, wrapping his arms around me. A sweet kiss told me he was happy with things and that always seemed to make me happy.

I knew the odds were stacked against us. I knew most people thought we'd never make it. But with that against us, I still wanted to see if we could beat those odds.

I wondered if Nix thought that way too.

Mona was in the kitchen, making us something for a special Christmas Eve dinner. I'd told her in secret that I wanted her to take the entire day of Christmas off. I'd been gathering recipes from the Internet and watching cooking videos all week long. I'd even made a trip to the store to buy all the ingredients I'd need to make Nix a proper Christmas dinner of ham, sweet potatoes, green bean casserole, and homemade rolls.

Nix and I managed to get the tree into its stand and were taking our time placing the ornaments on the tree. Nix told me where each and every one of them came from. His family was huge, and I had to admit that I was intimidated about meeting them all.

"How am I going to remember all of their names, babe?" I asked as I placed a pale blue satin ball on the tree. It had a large yellow stain on it and he told me that was from when it had fallen in a glass of his Aunt Rose's iced tea as she took the ornaments down on her very last Christmas.

"You shouldn't worry about that." He kissed the tip of my nose. "Half the time my mother can't even remember her own kids' names. She'll go through the gambit of family names then end up shouting, *You know who you are and why I'm calling you, dammit!*"

I laughed as he tickled my ribs. "Nix!" I wiggled to get away from him. "You're gonna make me pee!"

He stopped and pulled me in for a kiss. As our tongues twirled, I thought I'd never had such a memorable Christmas. He'd brought things to my life I'd had no idea I'd been missing.

Mona popped out of the kitchen. "The formal dining room awaits your arrival, you two. And I'll be on my way. You can just toss the dishes in the dishwasher when you're done. I'll tend to them when I come back."

Nix took my hand as I called out, "Thank you, Mona. You have a Merry Christmas."

"You too. Bye now," Mona called back just before she slipped out the garage door.

A small squeeze to my hand had me looking at Nix to find his green eyes sparkling at me. "Have I told you that you look beautiful tonight?"

A blush stained my cheeks. He made me feel so out of sorts when he looked at me that way and said things like that to me. "No, you haven't said a thing about that." I ducked my head shyly.

He lifted it with one finger and kissed me softly. "You're very beautiful all the time, but tonight even more so, somehow."

"You're very handsome tonight too." I ran my hand over

his light green sweater. "This brings out the color of your eyes."

I'd put on a red dress in honor of the occasion. He ran his fingers over my shoulder. "Red always looks good on you."

We made our way to the formal dining room, and there we found candles lighting up a gorgeous table that looked like something out of a magazine.

Two gold domes covered our plates, and sparkling water glistened in wine glasses next to them. "Mona is amazing," I whispered.

How can I ever top this when I make the meal for Christmas?

But all that worry went out of my head as Nix helped me into a chair and took the one at the head of the table. We sat there, looking at everything, and then he took my hand. "You know, back home my daddy says a prayer before we eat on special occasions. I suppose as we'll be parents from now on, we should start doing that too."

I shook my head. "I don't know any prayers. You go for it."

He bowed his head and so did I as he said, "Our father in Heaven, please bless this food that we're so thankful for. And please bless our little baby that we're also thankful for." He stopped and cleared his throat. "And bless this woman at my side as she's made this all possible. Without her, I'd be lost. Amen."

When I looked up at him, I saw unshed tears shimmering in his eyes. I ran my hand over his beard. "You'd be lost?"

He nodded and leaned over to kiss me. "You're my hero."

I gulped and tried not to start bawling. "You're mine."

He kissed me again, and I felt like I was floating on air. Would this be the right time to admit my love for him?

But when his lips left mine, he pulled the dome off his plate and smiled. "Wow, she really outdid herself. Roasted game hens, mashed potatoes and brown gravy, peas with pearl onions. Yum."

I pulled the dome off mine and enjoyed the aromas that drifted up to me. "It smells wonderful, doesn't it?"

"It does." He dug right in, and I followed suit.

The moment had passed, and now it would be awkward to say the words to him. How did one say something like that—especially for the first time—when the recipient of the sentiment was feasting on delicious food and savoring every bite?

Maybe I'd tell him on Christmas. Maybe that would be the perfect time to let him know that I loved him.

58

CHAPTER 23

Nixon

After the delicious dinner on Christmas Eve, Katana refused to just leave the dirty dishes in the dishwasher. She cleaned up the dining room and did all the dishes, and even went so far as to put them all away.

While she did that, I took a glass of wine out to the deck to look at the stars. The sound of footsteps coming up the stairs had me turning my eyes from the sky to find my neighbor, John, trotting up to visit me. "Hey, John. Merry Christmas."

"Merry Christmas to you too, Nixon." He took a seat on one of the deck chairs and pulled a bottle of beer out of his jacket pocket. "I saw you out here and thought I'd join you for a little drink."

I raised my glass of wine in a toast to him, and he did the same with his beer. "To new beginnings," I said.

"Here, here," he said then Nixon popped the bottle's top and took a drink. "Did Katana tell you I met her the other day?"

"She did," I told him then set my glass down.

His expression turned sheepish. "Did she rat me out?"

I froze for a second as I wondered what the hell he meant. What had he done? She hadn't said a word about him saying anything that would have him asking me a question like that. "No. But I'd love it if you told on yourself."

"Yeah, well," he seemed hesitant. "After I got back home, I thought about what I'd said and it sunk in that I might have said things that might've put her off about you."

"Well, if Katana's put off about me, she's not showing it." I laughed and picked up my glass, taking a drink. At least whatever he'd said hadn't affected her.

"Good. I can be a motormouth sometimes and talking to her proved to be one of those times." He took a long drink of his beer before he went on. "You see, I pointed out how you are, or were, anyway. I told her that you could be very neglectful of people. Especially women."

"Oh, that." I was well aware of that major downfall. "Well, I'm not that person when I'm with her. She makes me a better person. I don't know how she does it. She doesn't ask me to be any certain way. I just want to be around her—with her—or at least talking to her throughout the day when I can't be with her. She's what I think about most of the time."

"And there's the baby now too. She told me about that. And how that's why she's here with you, so you guys can raise it together." He took another drink. "You know about my divorce and how I'd never get married again. Plus, if I could have a do-over, I'd leave the kids out of it."

"Now, come on, John. You've whined a lot about the divorce and how your wife cheated, but how can you second guess your children? That's just going too far. There are no mistakes in bringing a child into this world. I believe that with everything in me." I knew I'd gotten up on my soapbox a bit as I was talking a little louder than normal, but he had to stop beating himself up over this thing.

"They have some issues because of what they went through, Nixon. I don't always let that be known. Sandy has trouble trusting people. And Brady is a womanizer. Both drink too much." John shook his head. "If I would've known they would end up with problems, then I might've left sooner and just taken them with me."

"As if you could've done that," I said as I ran my hand through my hair. The wind had kicked up and mussed it up a bit. "In this day and age, you could've never gotten complete custody of them."

"I didn't mean like legitimately take them. I meant run off with them. Escape from the woman who ruined all of our lives. Rescue them." He took another drink, looking like a man who had too many regrets.

"I doubt your kids are that messed up—I've seen them. As a matter of fact, are they going to be stopping by to visit you tomorrow for Christmas?" I asked to try to get him off his pity party and on to something better.

"Yeah," he said then finished his beer. "After they stop by their mother's place. She's got a new man—poor son of a bitch. They're having a real old-fashioned Christmas with his three kids as well. I guess she's pretending she has a big happy family with love just flowing in the air now that she's rid of me."

It was wrong of me to do, and I knew it even as the chuckle left my mouth. "Sorry. I really am. I know you've had it rough, but listen to yourself. She didn't get rid of you. You left her. And you did what you thought you needed to do for your kids—and that's admirable. You did the best you could with what you ended up with. Now don't you think it's time to move on?"

John looked at me with a frown. "No. I don't want to move on. And I didn't come over to talk about me, anyways. I wanted to come over here to talk to you about your upcoming bundle of joy. Don't make Katana think you'll be there for her through the raising of this child. We both know you'll get busy with some new and exciting project and she and this kid will be left alone, waiting for your attention to return to them. Which it won't. It won't because men like you are driven."

I was slightly incensed that the man thought he knew me better than I knew myself. "Driven isn't a bad thing to be —look at where it's gotten me," I said, gesturing around my deck. "And as far as how I was, that doesn't matter. I want Katana and this baby. I've already put her and this baby ahead of everything else. And I happen to have a project on the table right now. We're going to open the nightclub, Swank, on New Year's Eve. And I haven't lost sight of her as I've been moving forward with that project."

"Maybe that's because she and this baby have become your new project. You were already working on that night-club when you met her." His words sent my heart into a spiral.

He was absolutely right. I had already been working on the nightclub for months. John did know me well. I always had a project in mind before finishing the one I was on at the time. My mind just worked that way.

Even when I'd been a kid playing sports, I'd be near the end of football season, and already I'd be messing around, playing basketball and getting ready for that season.

I was the kind of person who always looked for the next thing.

Would I do that to Katana? Would I do that to my own kid?

"I can see your wheels turning, Nixon. I hope you're not mad at me. But having a kid is a big deal." He stopped as I waved my hand at him to get him to quit talking.

"I'm not mad. I know you think a lot about kids and what happens to them if their family life is sucky. And I know you don't mean any harm." I gulped down the rest of my wine as I tried to wrap my head around everything.

"I don't mean any harm to anyone. But you need to be realistic about the girl and that kid you've got coming." He got up and tossed his beer bottle into the small trash bin at the top of the stairs. "You're a great guy, Nixon. I don't want you to think I think anything else. But you're a driven man, and men like you make lousy husbands and fathers. People get left behind by men like you. Just don't lead this girl into thinking you can be something you're not. Let her do what she needs to with this baby." And with that, he left me.

Alone now, I sat there thinking about who I really was.

I knew I'd never turn my back on Katana or our child. She'd always have everything she'd ever need to take care of our kid. *Always.*

But was I putting Katana in a position where she'd be hurt and alone when I moved on to my next project?

When I looked up, the stars seemed to blur and spin. My life had just started to resemble the world I'd always dreamed of having. I'd never been home so much and been so happy to leave the office behind. But it wasn't just about coming home to my Malibu beach house—it was Katana.

I'd always been a bit more than merely content with my life. But I'd never been as happy as I'd been since Katana came into my life.

Since the night we met, I'd had a thing for her that

wouldn't quit. So there was only one real question. Was this real?

Were my feelings real or just the typical excitement I always got when starting a new project?

Katana didn't feel like a project to me. I wasn't trying to mold her or shape her into what I wanted her to be. That's what I did with projects. I built things, changed things, rearranged things. I didn't stop until I was completely satisfied with what I'd done.

I didn't look at her and think she'd look better with blonde hair. I didn't think she should change the style of her clothes. I didn't think she needed to have a different job.

I didn't want to change a thing about the woman. Well, there was one thing I wanted to change about her. So I guess I was only lying to myself.

59

CHAPTER 24

Katana

Christmas Day

    On Christmas morning, I woke up alone in bed. After stretching, yawning, and trying to wake my sleepy self up, I sat up and called out, "Nix?"

No one answered, and I got up to take a shower and get myself all prettied up for the day. *Our first Christmas!*

I'd put the presents I'd bought him under the tree last night, and he'd put some for me under there too. And I thought it was pretty sweet that we'd each bought something for our baby too and put those under there.

There was a bigger stack of presents under my very first tree than I'd ever had growing up. Everything was better with Nix.

As I showered, I noticed there was some expensive new shampoo and conditioner in there, and Nix had drawn hearts on the bottles and written, "*just for you,*" on them.

I lathered up my hair with the minty shampoo that had my head tingling, and I thought about what a treasure the man was. I'd take that man even if he didn't have a dime. I'd live in a treehouse with the man. I didn't care. I knew I'd been lucky he'd found me in that club that night.

After getting myself as pretty as I could, I pulled on the red dress I'd bought just for this day. It fit tight at the top and all the way to my still narrow waist—which I knew I'd lose soon enough. The dress flared out at the waist, making it look like I had a petticoat underneath it. The fabric came to just below my knees and when I added the flats—as Nix told me he never wanted to see me in heels while I was pregnant or he'd give me a real spanking—my legs looked long and slender.

I felt pretty, and I couldn't wait to find Nix. I wasn't going to let this day pass without telling him how I really felt about him.

When I walked out the bedroom door, I found something littering the floor. The white rose petals stood out, contrasting against the dark stone tiles. It looked as if he'd placed each one just the way he wanted it.

What's this about?

I had to wonder what the man had up his sleeve. With him, I just didn't know what he was up to.

A thought hit me, and I stopped. *What if he's bought me an expensive car?*

Trying to steady myself for the shock of that, I thought about how scared I'd be to drive something so expensive. I'd only ever had old pieces of barely held together crap. Could I pull off being excited instead of afraid?

Moving on, I shook off the nerves and got to the top of the stairs. The rose petals went all the way down the stairs and on the floor at the very bottom, the entire floor was covered in a circular pattern.

It looked as if something was missing from that circle,

and I had to wonder what that could be. Okay, maybe he hadn't bought me a car. Maybe it was a really large gift, and he hadn't gotten it inside yet to put it there.

Should I go back and wait a few more minutes?

As I stood there, thinking about what I should do, I noticed something else. Two suitcases were sitting by the door.

Now why in the world would those be there?

Was he surprising me with a trip of some kind?

I had absolutely no clue what he was up to and had no idea if I should turn back to wait or not. I didn't want to screw up his big surprise when he'd gone to so much trouble.

No one had ever done anything nearly as grand as all this. I looked over my shoulder, wondering if I should go back to the bedroom to grab my cell so I could take a picture. I wanted to remember this scene forever.

Just as I turned around, I heard a noise—the sound of rustling met my ears and I turned to see what it was.

Down on one knee and wearing a black tuxedo, Nix held out a box. The stone in the ring was so big, I could see it all the way from the top of the stairs.

His green eyes met mine as he gazed up at me. I took each step one at a time, slowly, so I could take him all in. The way he smiled up at me. The way his eyes sparkled. His clean-shaven face, bare of the beard I'd gotten so used to. The cute dimple that I could now see he only had in his left cheek.

I could barely breathe. He was about to propose to me, and I knew damn good and well what my answer would be. Some people might think it was too fast, but I knew I loved the man and was positive there was no other one out there in the world for me. Nixon Slaughter was it.

He waited so patiently for me to get to him. When I did, he finally spoke. "You look beyond beautiful, baby."

I was close to crying, but I managed to say, "You too." I ran my hands over my own cheeks. "You shaved."

He nodded. "Yeah, I wanted the pictures to be nice."

So he planned on taking some more pictures. The man would make sure we had something to remember all of our pivotal moments. He was perfect that way.

Today would be the day we got engaged and celebrated our first Christmas. One day there would be a wedding. One day there would be the birth of our child.

"I'm sure they will be nice, Nix." I smiled at him and loved the way his dark hair was so nicely combed, parted on one side, making him even more handsome.

"I'd like to ask you a question," he said. "Is that okay with you?"

I nodded. "Yes."

"Good, I've gotten my first yes, now I'll shoot for more." He chuckled, and his eyes shone with amusement. "Katana Grace Reeves." He stopped and winked at me. "I snooped in your purse last night and found your driver's license, that's how I know your middle name."

"I see." I laughed lightly. "Please, go on."

He cleared his throat before he moved on. "Katana Grace Reeves, I love you." My heart pounded, and I felt the first tear break free. "I've been a fool for you since the night we met. A night I know neither of us will ever forget. I'm not asking you this just because you're carrying our baby. I'm asking you this because I don't want to think of a life that doesn't have you in it—right by my side—until death do us part. And I mean that. So, I'm asking you if you love me too, and if you'll become my wife. Today. In Las Vegas."

Today?

I swayed a bit, feeling like I'd been knocked back. Not only did he want to marry me, but he wanted to do it right now. My mouth went dry. My head spun. And my heart lurched in my chest.

Tears poured down like rain as my lips parted. "I love you, Nixon Slaughter. Nothing would make me happier than marrying you today."

His smile got even wider as he stood up and slipped that huge diamond engagement ring onto my finger. "Thank you, baby. I promise you'll never regret your answer."

When his arms slid around me, bringing me to him so our lips could touch, I knew I'd made the right decision.

Where Nixon was concerned, every decision I'd made had been the right one. From taking him up on his offer to leave that club with him on Halloween night, to telling him as soon as I could about the baby, to accepting the invitation to move in with him—everything had been right.

This had to be the right thing too.

When our mouths parted, we were both panting. "I'd take you upstairs and make sweet love to you, Katana, but we have these presents to open and a private jet to get to. I took the liberty of booking us a bridal suite already. I didn't want to take any chances."

We slowed down a bit and opened the presents we'd given each other. He gave me more expensive jewelry, and then there was one more small box. When I opened it, I found a set of keys with the Mercedes emblem on them. "Nix!"

"You look a little shocked, baby," he said with a laugh. "You know my wife can't be driving around in a clunker. I do have standards to keep, you know."

I shook my head as I put the keys down. I picked up the special present I'd gotten him and handed it to him. "Thank you for the car and all the jewelry, among the other things you've given me. Open this one next."

He smiled the entire time he opened that package, and when he found the simple paperweight I'd given him, he laughed. "An "I Love You" paperweight?"

"Well, I had no idea you were going to do all this. And I wanted to tell you that I loved you today. You kind of stole my thunder there with the marriage proposal, but I wanted you to know that I was going to declare my love for you today anyway. I knew it the day we heard our baby's heart beating." I wrapped my arms around his neck and kissed him.

We just kept on having one perfect day after another. I was no fool—I knew some days wouldn't be all wine and roses, but I had a feeling there'd be more good days than bad ones.

A few hours later, he and I stood in front of a preacher who looked a hell of a lot like Elvis as soft music played in a tiny chapel in Vegas. I'd never dreamt about having a wedding, but this surpassed anything I could've ever come up with.

When our lips met as husband and wife for the first time, I knew we'd beat all the odds and make a marriage and family we both could be proud of. Nix and I had found our happily ever after; I had no doubts about that.

The End

NIGHTCLUB SURPRISE BOOK 3

A Bad Boy Billionaire Romance (Nightclub Sins 3)

By Michelle Love

Billionaire and nightclub entrepreneur, August Harlow, runs into a girl who was his neighbor from their small hometown. They're both shocked to see one another, but he's even more shocked to find she has a son. A son who's 6 years old. And he knows he and she had a little secret sex just before he left to join the Marines a little less than 7 years ago.

Could the kid be his?

He looks a hell of a lot like him. Has a crooked smile just like he does. Same shade of dark hair and green eyes too. Should he ask her if the kid is his or dodge the same bullet he may have dodged for 6 years?

60

CHAPTER 1

August

Smoke loomed over the distant hills. The fires had been burning in Big Bear for three days. My office in downtown Los Angeles would be safe, or that's what the authorities preferred us to believe. My home in Hidden Hills, a suburb of L.A., was okay, too, for the time being anyway.

Moving away from the window and trying to get the scene of wildfires out of my mind, I headed toward my desk when my cell rang. My sister's name flashed across the screen of my iPhone. "And how can I help you today, big sister?" Leila had six children, a husband who worked out of town most of the time, and a career as a hairdresser to the stars that kept her more than busy. So, she turned to me more often than not for help with the herd of kids she and her husband had.

"Now what makes you think I need your help, August?" sarcasm laced her voice. "Maybe I'm just calling to say hello and ask how your day is going."

"Sure, you are." A light chuckle punctuated the sentence. "And my day has been relatively uneventful. Thankfully. Thanks so much for asking. And I assume your day is going about the way it usually does. Hectic."

"Right you are. I don't suppose you'd like to go to the California Science Center to pick up your nephew for me? Gino's grounded from using the car you so generously gave him for his sixteenth birthday last week."

"Already?" Plopping into my office chair, I brushed my hand through my hair. The kid had promised me he'd be cool with the brand-spanking-new Chevy Camaro. "What did he do?"

"He took it out after curfew. Snuck out sometime in the wee hours of the morning and came back around seven in the morning, pretending to have gone out to get us all some donuts. Except the fool forgot to actually buy any donuts, letting me and his father know he'd been out and up to no good." She sighed heavily. "He's only the third oldest, August. I've got three more to get through the troublesome teens. My future is looking dimmer and dimmer with each passing day."

"Come on, you're Mother of the Year every year, and you know it." Getting up, I headed to the door to leave. If I knew anything, it was that my sister had left this to the last minute, and the kid was most likely already waiting to be picked up. "I'll head out now."

"Thank you, dear brother. I've got to do a dye job on Miss Perfect today and I'm not looking forward to it." She sighed again, a thing she did far too much.

"You don't even have to work, Leila. Your husband's job would keep you guys more than comfortable. So why push yourself so hard? You've got six—count them—six kids to worry about." The key fob in hand, I pushed the button to let myself into my BMW.

"August, I've told you this a million times, but here it goes, one million and one. I work to get away from the mother and wife role for a few hours each day. I know you don't get it. But that's because you're single and kid-free." She paused for a moment, the phone clearly leaving her ear. "I've got to go. Her entourage has arrived, and the queen bee will soon be following—after the spritzing of the air with lilac oils and the spreading of rose petals occurs, of course."

"Of course," I echoed. "I'll talk with Gino while I take him home. Give him the wise old uncle lecture."

"Good. Give that boy hell, little brother. Bye now. And thanks."

"Bye." I ended the call and started up the car.

Traffic was light at one in the afternoon as I made my way to the Science Center. When I got there and headed inside, I found Gino still working. "Hey, Uncle August! Cool, Mom sent you to get me."

"Yeah, she did, you rebel without applause." My fist connected with his scrawny bicep, making him wince. "That wasn't even hard, wimpy. So, what has you working on a school day, and when do you get off?"

"I'm on a four-day school week, did you forget that, Unc? No school on Fridays for me. And I get off in a half hour." He shrugged. "Can you wait around for me?"

"I guess so." Looking around, I saw all kinds of things that might interest me. "I'll check the place out. I've never been here before. It looks cool."

"Yeah, it is. Lots of tour groups come through the place. Lots of field trips come through here with kids of all ages." He grabbed his broom and got back to work as I walked away.

The space shuttle Endeavor hung from the rafters nearby, capturing my attention. It seemed to be taking lots of people's attention as several groups surrounded it, leaving minimal room to see it, even with its giant stature.

Standing behind a group of little kids, I spotted one little boy who seemed familiar. Not sure why, since I didn't even know any little kids, but something about him drew my attention more than the giant airship above us.

He giggled along with a couple of other boys. Then he turned toward me, and I saw that his eyes were hazel, just like mine. And his hair was the same shade of brown, too.

That's freaky...

"Mom!" his excited little voice shouted as someone moved past me. Our arms brushed for just a split second, but the electric current that came along with that touch pulsed all the way through my body.

"Calum!" the curvy redhead who'd just shocked my system with a simple touch called out to the kid. She picked him up, hugging him, and all I could do was look at her spectacular ass.

Hubba, hubba!

"I didn't think you was comin', Momma," the boy said as he clung to her.

"I wouldn't miss your first-ever field trip." She put him down, taking his hand then turning to the side to look up at the space shuttle.

Her profile was pretty; her nose turned up a bit at the end. Her pink lips were on the plump side. The way the blue jeans hugged her curvy hips and the light beige sweater clung to her double D's enchanted me—and my cock, which thumped inside my slacks. She turned all the way around, taking in everything that surrounded us, and I finally saw her entire face.

Tawny Matthews!

My pulse raced, my body heated. The feeling was familiar—it was the same way she'd always affected me from the moment she went from a gangly little girl to a curvy teen dream. But there was more than mere attraction with this one. Tawny had a place in my heart she'd stolen long ago.

Like a time warp had opened up, my mind left where I was to head back to where I'd been seven years earlier...

A full moon hung low in the night sky as I looked out the backdoor window of my parents' home—a home I'd be leaving in the morning. Destination San Diego. Marine boot camp. After graduating early from college with a degree in engineering, I'd enlisted with the marines to do my part in the ongoing war. At twenty-one, I was heading into danger for the first time in my life.

The midnight hour was at hand, but sleep was not. I'd headed to the kitchen in search of a glass of milk, hoping that would help me relax and get some sleep before I had to leave for San Diego at six a.m. The moon captured my attention first though, drawing me to the window. And out that window, I spied another thing that would keep me from the glass of milk. The girl next door was outside, lying back in a lounge chair.

We didn't have privacy fences in our neighborhood, just short chain-link ones. The small town of Sebastopol, California wasn't the kind of place where you hid from your neighbors. And one of my neighbors was Tawny Matthews, a recent high school graduate who'd turned eighteen only a few weeks ago, if I recalled correctly. And she had her eyes on the sky, doing a little moon gazing.

Music floated on the breeze as I opened the back door.

The sounds were light, airy, and romantic. Something inside of me stirred.

Tawny was pretty; I'd always thought so. We'd lived next door to each other forever. When we were really young, we'd played together in our backyards. When we were both little kids, we used to love tossing a beach ball back and forth over that chain link fence that separated our yards.

But once I left grade school for junior high, she and I lost that friendship we'd had. Puberty had started having its way with me while Tawny was still a kid with pigtails who played with dolls. My attention went to the girls my age and older, the more mature ones. Tawny got left behind, a thing I hadn't really noticed until she started sprouting up and growing the female parts that took my interest.

But we were four years apart, and she was too young for me then. A senior in high school definitely couldn't be with a girl in the eighth grade, after all. But that didn't stop me noticing how attractive she'd become. So, I'd kept my distance from her on purpose.

But now that she'd turned eighteen, she wasn't so young anymore.

Like a moth to a flame, I was drawn to her. I stepped out into the night. "Hey."

She smiled at me. "Hey."

Shoving my hands into the pockets of my jeans, I rocked back and forth on my bare feet. "You're up late."

She chewed her lower lip as she looked me up and down with her pretty green eyes. My t-shirt was black and tight, hugging my pecs and biceps. I'd worked hard to get my body into excellent shape, so boot camp wouldn't completely kick my ass. "So are you."

The way she eyed me made me think that she might be

more interested in me than I'd ever known. "You want some company?"

Plump pink lips pulled up to one side. "Why, you want some?"

Everything about her told me she was into me, so I headed through the gate that separated our yards, taking the lounge chair next to hers. "I do want some. I'm heading out to boot camp in the morning, and my mind's a mess about it."

Her lips formed a straight line as she looked into my eyes. "So, you're really going then?"

With a nod I went on, "I'm not afraid to fight in this war. But I am afraid I'll never see home again."

With my words, she glanced up at the rising moon. "If it helps at all, I think you're a hero, August."

"I'm no hero. Not yet anyway. But thanks." Thinking about what lay ahead of me put me in a mood for some midnight confessions, so I told her, "And I should tell you since I might never see you again, that I think you're beautiful. I've thought so ever since you turned fifteen. You and I were too far apart in age to ever do anything about that though."

She sat up, looking me right in the eyes as she smiled. "Okay, if we're being honest then I can tell you that I've always thought you were smoking hot."

A tantalizing idea popped into my head as my cock sprang to attention. "Well, I may never make it back, Tawny."

She already seemed to be on board. "My parents aren't home. I'm here alone, August."

Something compelled me to make sure she knew how things had to be with us before we took this step. "It would be a one-night thing. You understand that, don't you?"

With a knowing expression, she nodded. "It would be an honor to lose my virginity to a real hero."

Whoa, what?

"You're a virgin?" Heat coursed through me—I'd never had a virgin before. To think that after I'd lusted after Tawny for years, I would get to pop that cherry had me on fire.

All she did was nod as she got up, taking my hand in hers before leading me into her empty house.

61

CHAPTER 2

Tawny

Not in a zillion years did I expect to look around the California Science Center in Los Angeles and find the man that I'd given my virginity to looking right at me. His hazel eyes clung to mine, much the same way the expensive-looking black suit clung to his body, which was even more muscular than it had been seven years earlier. Those chiseled features, the sharp nose, and those high cheekbones offset by lips that looked soft and inviting took my complete attention as my heart raced. My hands fisted at my sides, yearning to run them through his thick, wavy, chestnut brown hair once again.

My feet moved without me telling them to, carrying me to the man who'd given me so much. I'd always been drawn to him, even when we were just two neighborhood kids hanging out after school. I guess some things never change.

"August Harlow!" Our bodies slammed together as I threw my arms around him. He hugged me tightly, picking me up so my feet left the ground. "I thought I might never get to see you again."

His hold on me loosened as he placed my feet back on the floor. His hazel eyes sparkled, just the way I remembered them doing all those years ago when he'd first kissed me. "I have to say the same thing about you, Tawny Matthews." He let me go entirely, and I felt the loss right away. Being in his arms felt like being home again. "Let me get a look at you." His eyes roamed over my body, making me heat up inside. "You've grown up, haven't you? And filled out perfectly."

Just as my core began to pulse—August's compliment had me wanting to jump his bones right then and there—a tug on the bottom of my sweater had me looking down. Hazel eyes shone up at me, and I ran my hand through my son's silky chestnut hair. "Momma, who's that?"

"This man used to be my next-door neighbor, Calum." I looked back at August. "I'd like you to meet August Harlow."

August extended his hand, which I found to be a funny thing to do to a six-year-old. "Hi, Calum. It's nice to meet you."

Calum let him shake his hand but ran his other arm around my leg, clinging to me. Then he buried his face in the side of my leg, and I rested my hand on his little shoulder. "He tends to be on the shy side until he gets to know someone."

August's eyes met mine again. "So, you got married?"

"No," I said quickly, and didn't offer any more information about that. "Do you live in L.A. now?"

"Yeah. And you?" August asked as he shoved his hands into the pockets of his slacks, rocking back and forth on his feet the same way he did the night he changed my life.

"We've just moved here." I watched August as he eyed my son but didn't ask a thing about who his father was. "I left Sebastopol a few months ago, just before school started. Calum's in first grade now. I didn't want to make him change schools in the middle of the year once the new job I came here for starts."

August pulled his eyes off Calum to look at me. "And what job would that be?"

"I'm a nurse. I got on with Cedars-Sinai in the maternity ward. But the job doesn't start for a few more months." Calum's class was moving on, and he looked back at them, then at me. "Go ahead, baby. Go with your class. I'll catch up, don't worry."

"'Kay, Momma," he said, then took off like a flash to catch up with his friends. Kyle and Jasper were a couple of little boys that he talked about nonstop each day when I picked him up from school.

"You're a nurse?" August asked as his dark brows rose.

"Yeah. I worked in San Francisco after I graduated and got my RN. The drive was a real killer, an hour there and an hour back home. Mom watched Calum for me as I had to work the night shift. At Cedars, I'll get the day shift and weekends off. Calum will be in school all day while I work, and he'll only have to stay at daycare for a couple of hours before I get off. Things will be a lot better with the new job."

"Color me impressed." He looked me over without an ounce of shame in his game. "You and I should have dinner some time. You know, catch up."

I agreed wholeheartedly and reached out my hand. "Give me your cell and I'll put my number in your contacts. I'd love to catch up with you, August Harlow."

As I typed in my number, my mind skipped back seven years to that fateful night...

Alone at home with my parents in Napa Valley for the weekend, I found myself looking out my bedroom window at the full moon that night. It called me to sit outside and do a bit of moon bathing.

Sitting outside in one of the lounge chairs in the back-yard, I had no idea the hot guy next door would be joining me soon. "Just the Way You Are" by Bruno Mars played on my cell, keeping me company until the sound of the back door opening at the house next to ours took my attention.

I turned the volume down as my hunky neighbor stepped outside, his eyes on the moon before landing on me. August Harlow and I had a four-year age difference that separated us, but that'd never stopped me from having a huge crush on him. As he started making small talk, I got the feeling that he knew I'd turned eighteen a few weeks back—and that it mattered to him.

We'd played together when we were kids. But junior high had taken him away from being my friend anymore. He was always going after he left our grade school to go to what I had called The Big Kids' School. I felt like he'd left me behind.

But after puberty changed my body, I had caught him looking at me from time to time, on the school bus, and in my backyard from his upstairs bedroom window. I'd fanta-size about him coming over, asking me out on a date. But fantasy was all I thought I'd ever have.

In no time at all, my insides were on fire for him. Hell, they'd been smoldering for years. Equipped with the knowl-edge that he'd be leaving the next day to go to boot camp before heading to war, I lost every inhibition I'd ever had.

A part of me I never knew existed came alive inside of me, and suddenly I was taking the guy's hand and leading him into my parents' home. Once inside, he kicked the door closed and pulled me to him, turning us around before pushing me up against the door.

My heart was beating so hard we both felt it. "Seems I've excited you, Tawny."

My name coming out of his mouth with him so close to me compelled me to trail my fingers over his lips. "They are as soft as I thought they'd be."

Those luscious lips curled into a sexy smile as he moved them closer and closer to mine, until they touched, sending fire rushing through my veins. "Oh..." I moaned, making my lips part. He took advantage, and his tongue moved into my mouth to twirl around with mine.

My body, pressed as it was between the door and his strength, felt like it belonged to him. Every little touch he made had me aching deep inside. I'd never wanted anything more than I wanted him.

When one of his hands made its way under my t-shirt, cupping my naked breast, I gasped with desire, not understanding how the heat I'd already felt could continue to intensify. His mouth left mine, moving down to join his hand at the tit he played with as his tongue danced over my skin. "God!"

He bit my nipple playfully then held it between his lips as he licked it over and over before sucking on it. "You like that?" he asked, and all I could do was moan in response.

My hands flew to run through his wavy, dark hair, relishing how it felt. "Damn, your hair's so soft," my voice but a whisper.

"And you taste like heaven," he growled before picking me up, bridal-style, and carrying me to the living room. He laid me on the sofa and put his body on top of mine.

The weight of his body on mine gave me a sense of

ownership—like he was mine now. Like I'd hold part of him forever—at least in my head and my heart.

He kissed me hard as he pushed the top of my pajama pants down and moved his hand into my panties. Another gasp escaped me as his finger slid into my virgin hole. "Fuck, you're tight as hell, baby." He grinned at me. "I cannot wait to feel your tight pussy clamped around my hard cock."

My head went light with his naughty words.

Holy hell, he's fucking hot!

I grabbed the hem of his t-shirt, pulling it up and running my hands all over his muscular back. His finger pumping inside me only made me more eager to feel his cock within me.

He moved off me and began undressing right in front of me. When he reached down to pull my pajama bottoms off, I stopped him. "Let's go to my bed, August. I'm a virgin, and I'm going to bleed a little when you break my hymen. If I get blood on Mom's sofa, she'll kill me."

Gathering me in his arms, he kissed me once more, soft and sweet. "Point me to your room then."

Pointing the way for him, he took me into the room I'd grown up in and put me down on my twin-sized bed. As he pulled my nightclothes off, his lips moved over every inch of flesh that he exposed. The panties were the last things to go, and then his lips grazed my sex. The moan that escaped me was deep and throaty. "August..."

Warm air moved over my pussy as he blew on me. I had no idea sex could be so great—no idea sex with August could be this good. And it hurt like hell that I'd only get the one night with the man...

"Mom!" the sound of my son's voice tore me from my memory. Back to the reality that stood in front of me.

August's hazel eyes peered into mine. He was real and right in front of me. The man I thought I'd never get to feel again stood two feet away from me.

By some miracle, I had another chance with him.

62

CHAPTER 3

August

My nephew Gino left work starving to death, so we stopped to eat before I took him home. I spotted my sister's car in the drive, so I got out and headed inside to have a little chat with her about the day's activities and my chance meeting with Tawny.

Seeing Tawny and her son had raised a lot of questions in my mind, and I needed to talk it out with someone. Leila and I have always been close, and she's been my sounding board for most of my life.

We walked into the kitchen and were met by the rest of her brood of children. "Mom, I don't like spaghetti the way you cook it," her oldest, Jeanna, griped.

"Then cook it yourself, Jeanna. Damn!" Leila bitched as she slammed a monster-sized package of pasta on the granite countertop.

"Hi," I called out to get my sister to look at me.

Her eyes ran over the kids who filled the kitchen before landing on me. "Hey, you." She looked at her oldest daughter as she went to the wine chiller, grabbing a bottle and two glasses. "You're on dinner tonight, my darling daughter."

"I'll help," the youngest of the bunch, ten-year-old Jacob, shouted as he raised his hand as if he was in school.

"Great," came Jeanna's sarcastic reply.

Leila walked past me, jerking her head as a gesture for me to follow her. "Come on, little brother."

Leaving the noisy kitchen, I followed my sister to the patio out back. She popped the cork on the bottle and filled her glass to the very top before only filling mine halfway.

"Feeling stingy, sis?" I asked as I took a seat on the other side of the small table that sat between two chairs. My sister purposely put only two chairs and the little table on this particular patio to discourage the children from bothering her out there.

"No, you're driving so you only get half a glass." She sat down with a long sigh then took a dainty sip of her wine. "Oh, this is delicious." A hearty gulp followed and then she sat back and looked relaxed. "So, what's up?"

"You remember the Matthews from next door back home, right?" I asked then took a drink of the wine, finding it a bit on the bitter side. It seemed my sister could find any wine delicious.

"Sure, there were the parents and that one kid. A girl. Um, Tawny." Another long drink took her to half a glass already. "What about them?"

"Well, I saw Tawny today when I went to the Science Center to pick up Gino." I stopped as I contemplated Leila's role in my chance meeting with the young lady I'd thought of often since our one night together. "Thanks for asking me to go pick him up, by the way. If I hadn't been there at that exact time, I'd never have seen her. And man, did I enjoy seeing her."

"She's too young for you, Romeo," Leila informed me with a snippy attitude. Always the older, wiser sister.

"No, she wasn't." The wine, although bitter, called to me and I took another sip.

Nope, still bitter.

Leila's dark brows raised. "Wasn't? Don't you mean to say, isn't?"

"She wasn't, and she isn't now either," I clarified. "You see, the night before I left for boot camp there was a full moon. I went outside to look at it when I couldn't sleep, and there I found Tawny. One thing led to another, and bada-bing bada-boom, I ended up having sex with her and ridding her of her pesky virginity."

The wine glass nearly fell out of her hand. But my sister wasn't one to commit party fouls and quickly regained her grip on it before so much as a drop could spill out of the deeply welled glass. "No! She was just a kid, August!"

"No, she was eighteen, and I was only twenty-one," I corrected her.

"The day you left for boot camp you were twenty-one, but three days after that you turned twenty-two. You're almost four full years older than that girl. August, you should be ashamed of yourself." She stopped long enough to take a drink before going on, "And the fact that you took this girl's virginity then left her is...well, it's a shitty-ass thing to do is what that is."

"Yeah, I know." I looked up at the sky at the low-hanging sun—evening was setting in. "She's got a son. He's in first grade. How old is a kid when they're in that grade, Leila?"

"Six," she said without missing a beat. She had so many kids she didn't even have to stop to think about that.

"Six?" I asked, as I thought about the kid's age. "Are you sure they're not, like, four or something? The boy was pretty small. I thought he had to be about four."

"Kids are little, August. But if he's in first grade, then he's six or seven." She drained her glass then promptly refilled it.

If the kid was six, and Tawny and I had been together approximately seven years ago, then could he be...? "It was seven years ago that she and I were together. Do you think he could be mine?"

"I dunno." Leila looked at the red wine as she swirled it in her glass. She had a special affection for the fermented grape. "Does he look like you?"

"He's got brown hair and hazel eyes." I pushed my hand through my own brown locks as I thought about the little boy. "And he's adorable, just like me." I grinned at her.

Her brows raised. "Wow. You didn't just ask Tawny if he's yours?"

Was she crazy? "Hell no! That would've been rude. And the boy was standing right there most of the time."

My response to her absurd question had earned me a nod. "You're right...especially with the kid standing right there. Is she married though?"

With a shake of my head, I answered, "Nope."

Leila's eyes went wide as a thought must've popped into her head. "Is she aware of your billionaire status?"

"Nope." I winked at her. "That's not a thing I throw around, sis. Can you imagine what she'd think of me if I just blurted that out? Like, 'Oh, nice to see you again, and by the way, I'm filthy rich now, so there's that.'"

Still, my sister's wheels turned. "Hmm, if she were to discover that information, do you think she'd go after you for child support if the kid's yours?"

As if I'd merely give the fruit of my loins child support

and nothing else! "If that boy is mine, I'll gladly support him. Do you think I should call her up and ask her to join me for dinner tonight?"

"Why are you asking me?" She looked off to one side as the sound of a door opening took her attention. "If it's not important, it can wait. Go back inside, Jenna," she hadn't even looked to see who it was, but somehow she sensed it. Leila shook her head as the door closed. "She's my little tattletale. At fourteen, I thought she'd be done with that crap. But nope, still tattling. And Jeanna is the one she likes to tell on the most."

"She's probably out to get Jeanna because you named them almost the same damn thing, and it pisses her off," I offered as an explanation. "Who does that, Leila? Jeanna and Jenna—were you stoned when you named your fourth child? Or had you simply run out of name ideas by then?"

"The latter." She took a sip. "And some of the former, if I'm to be perfectly honest. So back to our conversation before the interruption—I'm way older than Tawny, since I'm three years older than you. I never really knew her at all. I have no idea if you should ask her out for dinner tonight or not. Maybe she's holding on to some resentment towards you—I know I would. Whether you're that boy's dad or not, you screwed her, took her virginity, and then left her all alone. Man, that would've fucked me up."

"She didn't act mad at all—not seven years ago and not when I saw her today. I think taking her for dinner is a good idea, but she might need a babysitter. I thought you might volunteer. It'd give you a chance to see the kid who just might be your nephew," I enticed my sister.

The fact was, I wasn't sure if the kid was mine or not. Part of me wanted to jump up and down and shout it to the world that I was a father. But the rational part of me told me to stay calm, that the kid might not be mine. It was easier to make light of it all than to think too hard on that conundrum.

Putting the glass down, a smile filled her face. "I'm in! You know how I am about kids."

She was a nut over kids. "You know, one of my business partners has recently become a father. Wouldn't that be crazy if I became one, too?"

Leaning back in her chair, she looked up at the sky. "Crazier things have happened, August. But you should really think about this before you ask her out. Say the kid isn't yours—do you really want to get involved with a single mom? It'd be cruel to Tawny for you to get involved with her and her son when all you're looking for is a quick second round with her. And say he is yours—she's been fine without you for six years; do you really want to take on such a huge responsibility right now? It's hard enough becoming a parent when you've planned for it, never mind becoming a dad overnight—and you've got a lot going on right now with the nightclub opening soon."

"Maybe you're right." The club had kind of faded to the far reaches of my mind for once, what with Tawny showing up in my life out of the blue. My business partners and I were all busy planning the grand opening of our club, Swank. We had set the opening night for New Year's Eve, which was just a couple of months away. "Maybe I should hold off. But man, Tawny was pretty enough seven years ago when I last saw her, but now, she's absolutely gorgeous. I can't stop thinking about her."

"My advice," my sister said as she got up. "Put this off for a bit. See if you're still thinking about her in...let's say a week. Even if he's not your kid, you should think about how it might be, dating a woman with one. It's not always easy.

We moms are weird about bringing men around our kids. It's not always the easiest relationship when you have to share your woman with someone right from the get-go, either."

What she said settled in my brain. "Yeah, I think you're right. I'll hold off for a week and see how I feel then. If that boy is mine, I think she'd tell me anyway, even if I didn't ask her out. I mean, why wouldn't she?"

Thinking Tawny would've told me if he was mine, or at the very least told me we should talk, made me think Calum couldn't be mine. No matter how much he looked like me.

Maybe Tawny just had a type. Or maybe she was just pining away for me after our night together. She could've gone out and found a guy with the same color hair and eyes I had so she could pretend it was me again. And the poor girl found out that not just any man could fulfill her like I could, so she broke up with the dude.

I chuckled at my arrogance, but a part of me hoped that was the case. It was better than thinking of the alternative.

63

CHAPTER 4

Tawny

The day had faded into night, and still August hadn't called me. I supposed it was stupid for me to think he would call me right away. He looked to be a busy man—that suit told me he had to be some bigwig somewhere. Probably just very busy, is what I told myself.

After putting Calum to bed, I poured myself a glass of red wine and settled into my bed. Sipping on the wine, I tried in vain to read an e-book I'd downloaded, but the romantic scenes didn't do a thing for me. What August and I had done that night so long ago was hotter than anything the writer had written in her book.

Putting my Kindle down on the nightstand, I laid back, closing my eyes and picking up the memory of that night, right where I'd left off when Calum distracted me at the Science Center...

August had undressed me, and he was gloriously naked as well. He'd taken me to my bed, and his mouth was on my mound—kissing, nipping, and licking me into a state of bliss I hadn't known existed.

I'd given myself a handful of orgasms before, and they'd felt pretty good, but what August did felt out of this world. His tongue pushed into me, making me gasp with the odd pressure it gave me. "August!"

He didn't let up; he kept pushing his tongue into me, fucking me with it. The way his hands gripped my hips, holding me still for him as he did what he pleased, had me screaming with ecstasy when his oral stimulation took me over the edge.

My entire body pulsed with the climax. I'd never felt anything like that before. And then August was kissing his way up my body, stopping to run his tongue around my belly button a few times. He caught each tit, nipping and sucking them back and forth, before coming up to my face and kissing me with a hard kiss. "Ready?" he asked when he pulled his mouth away from mine.

I searched his eyes as I bit my lower lip. "Do it. Take my virginity, August Harlow."

He eased down onto me, no longer hovering over my body, but letting his weight bear me down into the mattress. His mouth took mine again as he hooked his hands behind each of my knees, bringing them up so my feet were on the mattress. The next thing I knew a burning sensation hit me hard and heavy as he thrust his cock into me.

"August!" I screamed with the pain.

"Hush, baby. It's going to be okay." He stayed perfectly still, letting the pain ebb. When my desperate pants eased, he pulled his cock nearly all the way out then pushed it in again. And this time, it didn't hurt as much.

Although the pain was there, so was something else. Pleasure.

His hands moved up and down my arms as he started his smooth, even thrusts into me. Soft lips grazed up and down my neck and then went further, stopping at the spot just behind my right ear. He bit, licked and sucked that same spot until my body quaked with an orgasm.

"August!" I screamed again and again as the orgasm shook me to my core.

If anyone had told me that sex could feel that amazing, then I'd have told them they were lying. Nothing seemed real in that moment. The feelings coursing through my body were too great, too fantastic. It had to all be a dream. It had to be!

The hot guy from next door hadn't really come to me as I sat outside in the middle of the night. He'd never paid any real attention to me before, so why now?

"Baby, you've given me the best going away present." His lips were back on mine, his tongue forcing its way in, taking me over.

Oh, yeah. He'd be leaving me soon. The dream-like state faded as reality set in. I'd just given my virginity to a man who couldn't be with me. A marine who had dangerous missions to get to. A marine who might never come back home.

And with those thoughts, I turned into one sexy, insatiable girl—I needed more. "Oh, baby. I had no idea how good this would be. You've given me one hell of a going away present, too." I arched my body up, letting him know I wanted more.

The smile he gave me sent my heart into triple time. "Oh, Tawny Matthews, you are something else, aren't you?"

"I want you to do things to me that you've only dreamt about. Show me things I've never even thought about before. Fuck me all night long. Leave me burning with memories I'll carry with me for the rest of my life—memories of the one night I had August Harlow between my legs." My hand ran around to the back of his neck, and I pulled him in to kiss me again.

Moving his cock inside me again, he thrust harder than ever as he pulled my legs to wrap around him. He came with a loud groan, and the wet heat of his cum filling me spurred my body into another orgasm.

Panting like wild animals on the hunt, we fought to regain our breath. His cock still lay inside of me; I'd never felt more connected to another person than I did just then with him inside of me like that. His dick, not nearly as hard as it had been, felt good inside my walls, which had been burning with the stretching they'd done to fit his girth and length.

Our breathing grew softer, and he pulled his head off my shoulder to look at me. "Hey, beautiful." His lips pressed against my forehead. "At least you'll never have to go through that again. From here on out, you'll only feel pleasure when you do this." He began to move his cock inside of me, and I could feel it pulsing back to a hard state. "It would be selfish of me to ask you not to let another man touch you, with where I'm heading, wouldn't it?"

Blinking, I couldn't quite figure out what he was saying. Did he want me? Like, long term?

"August, if you didn't have to go, would you and I..." I didn't know how to say the words and closed my eyes in frustration.

"I'd want to be with you if I didn't have to go." He kissed my cheek. "You'd be my girl if I could stay. I'd take you out on dates and take you to cheap motels where we'd screw like rabbits—if I didn't have to go. Hell, one day we might even have gotten married and had a houseful of babies."

"If you didn't have to go," I finished his thought.

"But I do have to go." He began peppering my face with soft kisses as his cock got even harder and he started moving back and forth within me.

He was right about the pain being a thing of the past, as now his girth only served to excite me. The way he moved on top of me had me moaning and making odd little mewling sounds that I'd never made before. "I'll never give what I'm giving you to another man. Not ever. I'm yours, August Harlow. Only yours. Take that promise with you, August."

The smile that spread over his handsome face left me nearly breathless. "And I'm yours, Tawny Matthews. Always and forever." His lips pressed against mine, sealing our little fake pact.

We both knew that it wasn't real. Well, I knew he'd have sex with other women. But my words were real—I meant them at the time. I was his. Only his. There was no way I could imagine having sex with another man in that moment, or having it be this good with anyone else.

That night, August took me so many ways it boggled my mind. He'd left me with so many memories that I had enough to last me a lifetime. We made love in the shower, on the floor in the hallway—he couldn't seem to keep his cock out of me...

With all the memories flooding my mind, I opened my eyes, feeling the need for a little self-love. Pulling the drawer on the nightstand open, I'd just reached inside to get my vibrator when a knock came at my door.

For the briefest of moments, I thought it might be August. But then a little voice called out, "Momma, I'm scared. Can I sleep with you?"

Ah, reality hit me once more. *No self-love tonight, Tawny.*

64

CHAPTER 5

August

After a video conference with my partners about the nightclub, I headed out of the conference room and into my office.

I'd gotten myself a suite of offices to work out of for the charities I gave to regularly. With myself and one other member to staff the place, I only needed three rooms: my office, Tammy's, and the conference room. Tammy's served as the lobby too.

"Tammy, you can leave after lunch today since it's Friday," I called out to her as I walked past her office.

"Thanks, sir," she shouted back at me. The poor old thing was hard of hearing, but she was a wiz with research and helped me pick the best charities to give to.

As I took the seat at my desk, I spotted the date on the large calendar. It had been a solid week, seven whole days since I'd seen Tawny. She had taken up permanent space in my mind, and I couldn't stop thinking about her all the time.

So, I called my sister up. "Happy Friday, August."

"To you, too." I tapped a pencil on the desktop. "So, it's been a week, and Tawny Matthews is still on my mind. That said, are you free to babysit tonight?"

"I am," she said, then paused. "I've been thinking, though."

"About what?" I swiveled my chair around and looked out the window. The sky was a clear blue, telling me they had finally gotten the Big Bear fires put out.

"About your, um, uh...I guess you'd call it a condition." She stopped, and I gritted my teeth.

"What about it?" My hand went right to my head, massaging my temples as tension filled it.

"Well, have you talked to your therapist about this? You know you haven't dated since you were discharged. You might not do well with that kind of pressure." She meant well, I knew that. But she didn't understand.

"I've been with women since I've been back, Leila," I corrected her.

"But you haven't dated," she attempted to correct me. "You've met women at bars and hooked up, but you haven't tried to have a relationship with anyone. And you've probably already done a number on Tawny before, loving her, then leaving her."

"Like I had a choice, Leila," aggravation filled my voice. Tawny knew I'd had to go.

"Back then you didn't. But now that you do, she'll want more from you if you guys go out. She'd expect more this time around. You have to admit that to yourself. And you're not exactly in a condition to be there for anyone yet," my sister said gently, reminding me of my problems.

"I've only had three episodes in the last four months.

That's progress, considering I had one almost every day when I first came back." Getting up, I headed to the window to look outside as I tried to hold onto my temper.

"You've only been in therapy for one year, August. Give yourself more time, man. Don't push yourself to do too much too soon. A relationship takes work."

I had to butt in, "Leila, a relationship, really? I'm talking about taking the girl to dinner, not asking her to marry me."

She laughed a little. "Okay, maybe I'm getting ahead of myself. I live in the future, you know that. Always thinking ahead. Dating isn't like meeting a girl in a club, August. It's not like fucking girls while you're in the marines either. One date leads to another and another and more after that, then there's just hanging out together, doing nothing at all. And then there's her kid to think about."

"And what about him?" I asked. She wasn't making sense to me.

"Kids make sudden noises. Sudden noises have been known to set you off," she said. "Just call your therapist before you ask her out. See what he thinks."

"Fuck!" She was right. I had to think ahead. "I'll call him now. Bye."

"I love you, baby brother." She hung up, and I pounded the wall with my fist.

Why can't I just be normal?

Taking a seat at my desk again, I made the call to my therapist. His secretary patched me through to his personal cell since he wasn't in the office. "Doctor Schmidt here."

"Hey, Doc, it's August." My head began to pound; my mouth went dry.

"August, how are you doing?" his voice cracked. Age had taken a toll on the old therapist, who specialized in helping ex-military people deal with PTSD. The good doctor had served in Vietnam and knew all too well the perils of war and what goes along with them.

But even Dr. Schmidt hadn't seen the kinds of things that people serving in this war had seen. But I had. Everything I'd been through during my deployment continued to clutter up my head, making me see things that weren't there, people who were no longer here, but showed up in my brain anyway.

"I'm doing okay. I'm calling because a woman from my past has moved into town. I saw her last week and would like to take her out. She was my neighbor in the little town we grew up in. She's got a young son, too. I think he might be mine," I said, as I smiled at the thought.

I might have a son.

"Is the young lady unsure of who the father is?" he asked with concern.

"I don't think so. I mean, I don't know. We didn't get to talk much. I ran into her at the Science Center; she was there for her son's field trip. She had to get going, but I told her I'd like to take her out sometime and she agreed."

"Oh, I don't think you're ready for a relationship, August," he interrupted me. "You're doing well, but that might put too much stress on you. I know I've cautioned you about your business dealings being too much for you, and for the most part they haven't been. But a woman and a child, too? I'm afraid of what might happen. A grown woman might be able to handle one of your episodes, but a child...well, you'd scare a child if you had one in front of the poor thing."

Even he thought I wasn't ready. But why did everyone keep saying shit about a relationship? It was one damn date!

"Okay, so a relationship is out for me right now. But how about one date, Doc?"

"You knew this girl from back home. You think you might be the father of her child, and you think this is about one date?" he asked me with a hard tone. "This isn't about one date and you know it, or else you wouldn't have called me. This is about getting involved with two people, her and her son. And that's a thing you're not ready for. Perhaps if you'd stayed on either of the medications I've prescribed for you, then you'd be ready for something like this. You're the one who refuses to take medication to help your condition."

"I didn't like the way they made me feel. I don't like to go through life feeling numb, Doc. And therapy is working for me. If you'll recall, I've only had three episodes in the last four months. I'm getting a hell of a lot better." Someone besides me had to see the fact that I was whipping this PTSD shit's ass without the use of pills.

"Wait until after our usual appointment to ask this young woman out. That's my opinion—the thing you called me to get, I'll remind you. Goodbye, August, see you next Thursday."

The call over, my doctor's orders given, I put my phone down and dropped my head.

If I could do anything over again, it would be to make sure I didn't lose my Glock on that raid that night. If I had never lost it, then I would've never been issued a new one. A faulty one. It wouldn't have misfired, and it wouldn't have left one of my good friends and fellow marines dead. Then I wouldn't have this PTSD shit—or not quite as bad as I had it, anyway.

John Black, a good man and a friend, is the reason I received the millions of dollars that I then turned into billions. I'd won a lawsuit against the manufacturer of the gun that killed John, and walked the payout into an investment firm owned by my now partner, Gannon Forester. Gannon took the money and invested it in the same things he'd invested in.

All I wanted the money for in the first place was to keep John Black's name alive. I might've accidentally killed the man, but by the Grace of God, I was able to make generous donations to charities around the world, helping people in his name.

I'd achieved my goal in that regard, but I had yet to reach my goal of being able to live a normal life as a civilian—to reach my goal of not being tortured by what happened that awful day. The attacks would always start out of nowhere; I'd be living my life as usual, and then I'd see John, clear as day. My heart would pound, thinking the same damn thing every time: he's alive!

I'd smile at the man who looked healthy as a horse, the way he always had. I'd call out his name then something would flash, and the sound of a bullet ripping through the air would sizzle in my head. John's face would become distorted, and then he'd get hit in the side of the head with the bullet that had exited my Glock all on its own.

Blood would pool around him as he lay on the floor, his blue eyes open still, looking at me, silently asking what I had done to him. And that's when I'd begin screaming. Over and over, I'd scream his name and then I'd just scream until someone managed to drag me back to reality.

I wouldn't wish that life on anyone. But I sure as hell wish it would just go the fuck away and leave me alone.

John Black couldn't come back. The money I'd made went to helping others. I'd made sure that some positives would come out of that terrible moment. But my brain refused to let it go. My mind held that horrible memory in a steel cage. And when I least expected it, the cage would open, replaying the scene for me to experience in its entirety once more.

When would the pain end?

65

CHAPTER 6

Tawny

A week and a half passed with no call from August. Maybe he'd been too busy, or too involved with someone else to make the call. I had no idea, but I knew one thing for sure—I didn't ever want to be a burden to the man, especially not after he'd served our country.

If he didn't want to see me, then so be it. I'd dealt with worse scenarios before—I'd already handled the idea that I'd never get to lay eyes on him again, or that he'd never come back alive. I could learn to handle the fact that we lived in the same town, and that he knew that, but just didn't want me.

That night we'd shared, the things we'd said to each other, it was all just a fantasy. Our emotions were heightened, and we were both living a dream, afraid of the future. None of it was real. Well, none of it on his part anyway.

The fact remained that I'd felt as if I belonged to August Harlow for a long time. A big piece of my heart had become his with our first touch. I wouldn't say I'd pined for him after he left—not exactly—but a part of me had changed that night. He'd filled my dreams for years, and even in the more recent years, he'd sneak into them every now and then.

Lately, ever since I'd seen him again, he'd become all I could think about: about the scent of his hair and how it'd feel if I could run my hands through it again; about how his body would look now with nothing covering it.

I bet he's got tats now.

What kinds of tattoos would I find covering his tanned flesh? What new and interesting things did he have to talk about or show me? Would that old chemistry still ignite the passion it had seven years ago?

I wanted nothing more than to get answers to all those questions and the many others that filled my mind. But I wasn't going to get any answers because, for whatever reason, August chose not to call me. He chose not to take me out the way he'd said he wanted to at the Science Center. He chose to ignore me.

And I was going to let him. Because he didn't owe me a thing.

After dropping Calum off at school, I headed to do a little shopping—window shopping, that is. I couldn't afford a thing on Rodeo Drive, but it didn't stop me from walking up and down the sidewalks to look at all the hip and trendy things displayed in the many windows.

A pretty red dress caught my eye. Being a redhead, whose favorite color also happened to be red, has proved to be difficult. The wrong shade of red looked terrible on me, but there were a handful of red items in my wardrobe that worked. The dress that had caught my eye was a design I loved, but the shade wouldn't work on me.

The price tag peeked out from under the sleeve, and I saw a four-digit number there. Whistling, I walked away, knowing there was absolutely no reason to waste any thought on that expensive dress. I couldn't afford that in my wildest dreams.

But I looked back longingly for a second anyway, and that's when I ran into someone. "Shit! Sorry."

"Hey!" came a surprised male voice that I instantly recognized.

"August!" This time I fought the urge to jump into his arms, but was happy to find him pulling me in for a hug. Once again, my feet left the ground as he picked me up, hugging me tightly.

My arms wrapped around his neck, and when his lips met my cheek, an inferno erupted inside of me.

Damn, I'm easy!

Putting me down, he looked into my eyes. "Tawny, I'm sorry I haven't called."

Even though I wanted to ask him why he hadn't called, I just waved my hand in the air, as if waving the words away. "No, that's okay. I mean, I'm sure you've been busy. Or maybe you just didn't want to call. It's not like you owe me anything. I understand."

"No, it's not like that." He looked around then took me by the hand, pulling me along with him. "Let's get some coffee and talk."

We went into a café, the trendy 208 Rodeo Beverly Hills, where he ordered us a couple of cappuccinos, and then we took seats at an outside table.

"August, you don't have to feel bad or try to explain anything to me," I said before blowing across the top of my steaming cup.

"I want to, though." He took my cup, setting it down before taking my hand and holding it on the tabletop. "I've only held off because of my condition."

"Condition?" That threw me off. I couldn't see a damn thing wrong with the man.

His eyes clouded, and his demeanor changed. "I have PTSD. I don't talk about this with many people, but I want you to understand. When I was serving, a gun misfired, and I accidentally shot and killed one of my fellow marines. He was also my good friend. It's done a number on my brain—that and the other things I've seen during my missions."

My heart stopped. He'd gone through so much more than I ever would have guessed while serving our country. "Oh, God! I'm so sorry, August."

He squeezed my hand. "Thanks, Tawny. It happened a few years ago, and I'm in therapy. I don't get violent or anything like that, but sometimes I go into this state where... it can be pretty scary for the people around me."

"I am a nurse, August. I'm accustomed to helping people deal with things like that."

He laughed as he let my hand go, only to run his fingers over the back of it, making butterflies swirl around in my stomach. "I hadn't thought about that, Tawny. I really hadn't. I suppose you could handle me if an episode came on."

I nodded, knowing I'd handled a lot of tough situations. I could definitely handle anything he had going on. "So, anything else stopping you from taking me out? My son perhaps?"

"No, just my condition. I don't have an aversion to kids if that's what you're thinking." One wink told me that was true.

An aversion to kids or not, I wasn't the kind of mother who brought strange men around her kid. But there was one man I'd let Calum be around—if that man wanted and when the time was right. "That's good to hear. That said, I'm picky about the men I bring around my son. I don't think it's healthy for a child."

He didn't seem put off by my words and even smiled. "I think that's the sign of a pretty good mom. So, I can take you out, but the kid's going to be left out of it?"

I nodded. "So, it'll just be you and me on any date you'd care to take me on, August."

He looked away and then back at me as he contemplated what I'd said. "I can handle that. For now." He took my hand in his again and squeezed a bit. "I thought about you a lot while I was away. Your going away present was a thing I cherished. I still do. It was the best present I've ever gotten."

A yearning filled me, a desire to tell him more, but I managed to stuff it away. "Oh, yeah?" With so little, the man set my senses on fire. It amazed me, how much he could affect me. No one else had ever come close to bringing out this side of me—and August could do it without even trying.

He nodded. "And that night is just about all I've thought about since I saw you ten days ago."

"You've been counting the days?" I asked with surprise, and a little smile. I thought he hadn't been thinking of me at all.

"I have. I was going to call you and take you out that very night we met, but my sister put me off the idea. She told me to wait a week and see if you were still on my mind, and you were. Then I called my therapist, and he told me I should wait a while longer before inserting myself into anyone's life."

I laughed. "One date doesn't mean you'd be inserting yourself into my life."

"I know." He smiled sexily and pulled my hand up, kissing it. With just that kiss, wet heat pooled inside of me.

"But I can think of at least one place that I would like to insert myself."

My cheeks were hot, and my entire body flushed. "August!"

"I've missed you, Tawny. You've always held a place in my mind, and even my heart." His words only served to affect me even more. I'd always thought he probably didn't think much about me at all. I assumed he'd have other things on his mind, with what he was doing and all.

"We hardly knew each other. It doesn't seem possible that one night of having sex..."

"Making love," he corrected me, and then began kissing each one of my fingertips.

God help me, this man is going to make me have an orgasm right here by doing hardly a thing to me!

"Okay. Anyway, it doesn't seem possible that we could form a bond so quickly. Not that we have a real bond, but you know what I mean. I've missed you, too. I've thought a lot about you, too. Even more so once we ran into each other after so many years." I sucked in my breath as he leveled his eyes on mine.

Those hazel eyes took on an intensity that made me squirm in my seat. "Seven very long years. And now that I've gotten to sit and talk to you, I know I want more. Screw what my therapist said. I forgot to tell him that you're a highly trained nurse, and that you're more than capable of dealing with me if an episode occurs. So how about tonight? Wanna go out with me?"

"I'd love to." But then reality hit me, and I groaned, "Ugh. I've got to find a sitter. Crap."

"My sister would love to watch Calum for you," came his quick response.

"You think she would?" My heart skipped a beat at the knowledge that he'd remembered my son's name.

With a nod, he answered, "I know she would. She's got six kids. They're all older now, and she misses having little kids around."

I remembered his sister. She was a down-to-earth young woman; I bet she'd be even more settled now. And with six kids of her own, she had to know what she was doing in that department. "Well, if she doesn't mind, then I guess we have a date."

"Looks like we do."

Well, I wonder just how long this date will last before he and I topple into bed together. I'm thinking a half hour, tops.

66

CHAPTER 7

August

I'd sent my driver to pick up Tawny and her son to take them to my sister's, understanding Tawny's desire to keep the men she dates away from Calum. My driver then returned Tawny back to her place so that she could get ready for our date, which I was getting increasingly excited for as time ticked by.

I'd gotten us a table at a restaurant that usually took reservations three months in advance. Money talks in this city, and when I offered to make a very generous donation to the chef's favorite charity, he was quick to give me two seats in his limited-seating establishment.

I had every intention of showing Tawny a very good time —a better time than anyone else could give her.

What my sister had said to me earlier curled around my brain. I had taken the girl's virginity and given her nothing in return. Sure, we'd both had an amazing time, and our night had left her with some great memories, but I hadn't given her anything else.

We'd exchanged a few promises that night, promises that veered dangerously close to faithfulness. Of course, I was just talking, the way men sometimes do. I remember telling her that if I hadn't had to leave her that she'd be my girl. I'd meant that, yet when I came back I didn't even try to find her.

My parents had moved shortly after I took off for the military. I had no idea if Tawny or her family still lived in the house next to my parents' old place. But I could've made some calls or even taken a drive through our old neighborhood to find out. The fact was, I hadn't even tried. And that seemed odd to me, because Tawny had been a part of so many of my dreams and fantasies through the years—before and after we'd had sex. But life just hadn't seemed to send me her way—until the day at the Science Center. And then again on Rodeo Drive.

Forces seemed to be throwing us in each other's paths now. Who was I to fight unseen forces?

I'd told my sister about the date, of course, as she had to babysit. She seemed to understand why I'd gone against the advice of my therapist but cautioned me, telling me to let Tawny in on my tells, the things that I did before the onslaught of an episode. And she told me to call my therapist to let him know what I was doing as well.

That conversation was a bit tenser than I cared for. Doctor Schmidt had major concerns about Calum. Even though I'd assured him that the boy wasn't going to be around me, he said that he might be eventually, and that worried him.

His concern for the welfare of Calum was unfounded in my opinion. Tawny hadn't told me the boy was mine, so there was absolutely no reason for me to get to know him. I could have a thing with Tawny without the boy being involved at all.

It might sound callous to some, but Tawny and I had some unfinished business to attend to. One night with her had never been enough for me. I'd fucked many a woman in the last seven years, thinking of Tawny on more than one occasion. I needed to feel her body underneath mine again. Craved it at times. Especially since seeing her again.

My driver stopped in front of her apartment, and I walked up to her door to get her. After only one knock, she was opening the door and there stood a vision of perfection. I felt my jaw drop.

"You..." I looked her up and down, and my breathing stopped as I took her all in. Her long red waves had been tamed into one silky-straight sheet of shiny hair. Tawny's hair wasn't copper red, but more on the auburn side, with copper strands throughout that made it shine. Her green eyes popped, her makeup perfectly applied to accentuate them. It was a toss-up as to whether I found her hair or her eyes more attractive. "You look amazing."

Her green dress hit her just above her knees, hugging her curves. It had a deep plunging neckline that exposed her generous breasts in such a way that was daring, sexy, and absolutely fascinating. I could look at those babies all night. Or rather, I could suck those babies all night.

Sweet Jesus, I hope she lets me fuck her!

Images of taking her sweet ass in the back of my town car had already begun to flitter through my mind. Tawny on her knees, that emerald green dress pushed up to expose her ass—an ass that had become even rounder and plumper than when I'd last touched it. My cock had gone stiff just thinking about it.

Tawny's hand moved over my shoulder. "These suits you wear make you look so handsome, August. You don't look much like the young man I knew back then. You're much more sophisticated. And you have your own driver, too. Thank you for sending him to take Calum and me to your sister's by the way. That was very nice of you."

My eyes were glued to hers. "It was nothing, really. Was Calum okay with you leaving him with Leila and her brood of children?"

She shook her head, making me frown for a moment before she smiled. "No need to frown. He loved her and all the children. She does have a houseful, doesn't she?"

"Yeah, she does." I took her hand, leading her to the waiting car. "I'm glad he liked them all."

"He told me I could leave, and that he'd be fine with Aunt Leila. Your sister introduced herself to him as that. I hope you don't mind." She looked back at me as I opened the car door for her.

All I could do was smile. "Of course, I don't mind that." It was a little shocking how much I didn't mind—how much I was hoping that might be the case in truth.

She breathed a sigh of relief. "Good. It just occurred to me that you might think that was a bit forward."

"Nah." I slid in after her, making sure to stay close. Any bit of contact I could get with her did things to me that I'd never experienced with anyone else—whether it was her hand on my shoulder or my thigh pressed tightly to hers as we sat side by side. "So, I've scored us a couple of seats at Maude this evening."

"Maude?" She looked enthused. "August, that's like impossible to get into. How'd you manage that? Oh, wait. You must've had reservations already, didn't you? I heard you have to make them three months in advance."

"No, I didn't have reservations. I just did a little wheeling and dealing is all." I took her hand, kissing the top of it before trailing my lips up her arm until they met hers.

My heart beat like a base drum as I kissed her softly, not wanting to rush, only wanting to take my time, tasting her in the way I'd dreamt about doing for years.

Our chests were heaving when our mouths parted. The kiss hadn't gone beyond just lips touching lips, yet it had affected us in a way that neither of us had expected, judging by the dazed look in her eyes.

"I'll take it slow tonight, Tawny. I won't rush a thing. There's no reason to now. I'm not going anywhere." Her hand felt so good in mine as I ran my hand down her arm to grasp it.

She blinked a few times. "I think I'd like that. Nice and slow. We haven't done nice and slow, have we?"

"No, we did it hard and fast, if I recall that night correctly." My fingertip ran over her bronze-tinted lips. "Hard and fast was good, but I think long and slow will be even better."

"I agree wholeheartedly." She leaned her head on my shoulder. The smell of her hair captivated me.

"Lemons and honey," I commented as I took a long sniff.

She looked up with a questioning gaze. "What?"

"Your hair. It smells like lemons and honey. That night, it smelled like strawberries." The smile she gave me hit me like a fist to my heart.

"You remember that?" She blushed, and I loved how I'd already made her do that. I was yearning to see her entire body flush with that same color. Plans for later that night were already beginning to form in my head.

Dinner, a bit of dancing, then back to her place to get horizontal once again. The way my cock pulsed had me wondering if we'd be able to get through all the courses that night before giving the chemistry between us what it demanded.

67

CHAPTER 8

Tawny

The date went far past any expectations I'd had. Dinner at a restaurant that defied imagination: small, quiet, and phenomenal food. Later, August held me in his arms as we swayed to soft music. Soft kisses placed on random areas of my head then down my neck, leaving my legs feeling like jelly.

The man had me, and he knew it. What he'd do with me was still a question that needed to be answered. We'd gotten back into the backseat of his car, the driver taking us to his place. A surge of disappointment traveled through me when I found out he'd be getting out there, leaving me alone so his driver could take me to pick up Calum before dropping me home.

My thighs clenched as he told me the plan.

No sex?

I bit my lower lip, unsure of how to tell him that I wanted more. "Um, August, you don't have to go to all that trouble. I can take my car and run by your sister's to pick

Calum up. It's not a problem at all. And you could maybe come in for a little...um, what do they call those things?" I searched my memory and found an old Love Boat episode locked away. "Oh, yeah. Nightcap."

"A drink?" he asked, his fingertip moving along my jawline.

"Sure, a drink." My body sizzled at his soft touch. I'd been on fire for hours, and I needed the flame doused. Only August had the magic elixir to do that.

"I don't want you to have to do any driving after even one drink." He leaned in close, trailing kisses along my collarbone.

So, I had to come up with another idea, and I did so quite quickly. "Ride with me then. Stay with me while we go get Calum."

"But you said you don't like to introduce men to your son, Tawny." His lips moved up my neck. When his hands took my wrists, holding my arms to my sides, I almost begged him to take me right then and there.

"I don't. I haven't." My breathing became sporadic as he nibbled my earlobe then blew warm breath into my ear. It reminded me of the way he'd given me oral sex that night so many years ago, how he blew on my sex before eating me until I came, screaming his name over and over.

God, I want to feel that again!

"I don't want to make you do anything that would make you uncomfortable," he whispered as he moved those soft lips all around my ear, then licked the spot just behind it.

I'd already been wet for him, but with that sensation, I gushed. "Oh, August!" I gasped. "Please, just ride with me to get him. I don't care about my old rules. I won't feel uncomfortable."

"Well, if you're really sure, then your wish is my

command, Princess." He pulled his mouth off me then pressed a button. "Max, change of plans. Go to my sister's first, please."

"Yes, sir," came the driver's answer.

Then hazel eyes sparkling with desire leveled on my breasts before moving up to meet my eyes. "Hmm, since your son will be here when I drop you off at your place, we'll miss our goodnight kiss."

I couldn't breathe or even think straight. So, a nod was all I could muster as I saw that look in his eyes. The one that told me without a doubt that he wanted me.

His lips quirked up to one side. "So, we should probably do the goodnight kiss now, before we pick him up. I don't want to miss out on the best part of the night. Do you?"

All I could do was shake my head. He'd rendered me speechless.

When he got off the seat to get on his knees in front of me, I began to shake with anticipation. His hands moved up my legs, bunching the bottom of my dress as he pushed it up until my panties were exposed. One warm hand moved over my pulsating pussy then he looked up at me, licking his lips.

With a nod, I gave him the go-ahead then leaned my head back on the seat and closed my eyes. Pushing the silky fabric of the panties to one side, he blew hot breath over my sex before kissing it with more soft kisses.

My hands fisted at my sides as he ran his tongue through my folds then tapped my clit with it. Over and over, he tormented me. I wanted that tongue thrusting into my cunt, hard and fast.

As if reading my mind, August flattened his tongue, licking the opening that craved feeling any part of him inside of it. When he pushed his tongue into me, he made a deep guttural groan that sent shivers through my body, only adding to the sensations that came from the actual penetration.

The way his hands gripped my hips reminded me of that night, and I moaned with the new memories I'd now have of this man. "August," I growled as I couldn't stop myself from running my hands through his hair, messing it up.

He ate me as if he were a starving man. But he'd eaten plenty that night—his hunger now was only for me. Within minutes, a wave built inside of me, crashing and taking me to new heights. I bit my bottom lip to stop a scream of pure pleasure from erupting, letting the driver know exactly what we were doing behind the dark glass that separated us from him.

August panted as he raised his head. "Fuck, you still taste like heaven, baby."

I hadn't even caught my breath before his mouth was on mine. His tongue pushed through my lips, and I tasted my juices on him. With a swift movement, he sat on the bench seat and pulled me to sit on his lap, facing him. My crotch to his, his cock as hard as a rock between us.

My body ached for him as we kissed, and I moved over his fabric-covered cock, yearning to set it free. But as I moved my hands to do just that, he grabbed my wrists, stopping me. His mouth left mine, moving up my neck until his lips were on my ear. "Not this way."

"August, please," I begged quietly.

"No, not this way." He pulled his head back to look at me, fire in his eyes, telling me he wanted it just as bad as I did. "No, Tawny. I want you to feel special. I owe you that."

"You don't owe me a thing, August." I moved my body seductively over his swollen appendage, which I needed to be inside of me.

The fire in his eyes flickered before going out, quickly replaced by concern. He let my wrists go to run his hands up my arms, and then took my face in them. "I owe you more than you know. Your face filled my head almost nonstop those first years. And every single time things got hard for me, you were there, Tawny Matthews. I made love to you, then left you. I took your innocence, then walked away. I could've called, wrote, or gotten in touch with you somehow. I didn't do any of those things. I thought you deserved to move on with your life—find a real man to love you. A man who'd be there for you in a way I couldn't."

"Stop," I whispered. My hands moved up his muscled back. "I never wanted more from you than what you gave me."

"You didn't want me to be yours, Tawny?" He smiled that crooked smile that I'd always adored.

"I did. But I knew what you were doing was far more important than staying around Sebastopol to be with me. So, I took the memory of that night and kept it close, knowing that I'd given you something you could take with you too. And that's been enough for me throughout these last seven years." I kissed his cheek. "But I have to be honest with you."

"Please, always be honest with me, baby." His lips touched mine again. Then he pulled them away, looking at me.

"I think it's sweet that you feel that way, and frankly, it surprises me. You're quite the romantic now, August. I like that."

He moved me off his lap, fixing my dress as I ran my hands through his hair, putting it back in the style he'd had it in, slicked to one side, looking handsome as hell. The way he kept his beard meticulously groomed pleased me to no end, too.

My pussy still tingled from the way he had pleasured me. I figured it might tingle all night long. It would've been great to have August in my bed that night; there could be no denying that. But somehow, waiting made more sense this time.

Before there had been no chance of a relationship between us, and now there was. Rushing things wasn't necessary. But I wanted some things to be rushed. I wanted to feel that powerful man between my legs.

August had been a young man when we'd first had sex. His body had been great back then. Now, he was all grown up, and his body was ripped beyond my wildest imagination: his thighs, thick as tree trunks; his biceps larger than before—and they'd been big before.

I'd matured, too. My breasts and hips had become round with my pregnancy, and they never went back to their previous state. My body wanted to know what his body felt like. But I'd let August take the lead. I'd let him go as slow as he wanted to.

Pleasing him made me happy—happier than I'd been in a long time.

August Harlow was back in my life, and my goal was to keep him there.

68

CHAPTER 9

August

The date had gone even better than I'd imagined—and I'd had high hopes to begin with—although it'd been hard as hell not to have sex with Tawny. But I wanted things to progress nice and slow. Sex right off the bat would feel too similar to the first time—like we were rushing out of desperation. I wanted things to be different this time around.

Sitting at home, I wasn't doing a thing but looking out my bedroom window. The wildfires that burned around Southern California were always a concern to me. Thankfully, there was no threat to Hidden Hills, and the smoke steered clear of us.

My thoughts went to Tawny and Calum. The garage apartment she rented was in West Hollywood. She'd told me that a woman who worked in the human resources department at Cedars owned the home there. She'd offered Tawny the small two-bedroom, one bath for the low rate of fifteen hundred a month, and that included the utility bills, too. In West Hollywood, rent that low was unheard of. That told me Tawny was in high demand.

I had no right to feel pride in her accomplishments, but I did just the same. Tawny had made something of herself, despite having Calum at the young age of nineteen.

Thinking about Calum made me remember the ride from Leila's to their place the night before. He'd been very talkative, chattering away about how much fun he'd had that night.

"I had so much fun, Momma," he'd said as soon as he climbed into the car. "Aunt Leila is the funnest person ever!"

My sister could be pretty fun. Especially with little kids. She'd play chase with them, hide and seek—you name it, she'd play it.

"Tell me what you guys did, Calum," Tawny told him, her face glowing with delight that he'd had such a good time.

"I played a game called hopscotch. It was real fun. And um, his name's, um..."

"Gino," I offered. Leila had a lot of kids; chances are Calum couldn't remember every one of their names.

"No, not that man." Calum tapped his finger to his chin as he thought.

The fact that he'd called Gino, a sixteen-year-old, a man had me laughing. "Raphael or Jacob," I added to the list he could choose from.

"Yes!" he shouted as if he'd made a wonderful discovery. "Jacob! He taught me how to play that game. Then we went inside when it got dark, and I played checkers with Aunt Leila." His hazel eyes went huge as he gasped. "And I won!"

"Great job, Calum," Tawny congratulated him with a high five.

"I know, I'm very good at that game." His grin made me chuckle again. He was adorable.

The way Calum had gone on and on reminded me of my nieces and nephews when they were little kids. They all had endless amounts of things to say.

An idea crept into my head. If Tawny had let me be around him last night, letting him know we'd gone out on a date, would she let him come along on a date?

I'd sent her flowers that morning, having them delivered along with a box of candy and a stuffed tiger for Calum. She'd yet to call or text me that she'd gotten them. I was sure she'd do that once she received them.

When she contacted me, I wanted to ask her out again and include Calum if she'd let me. The boy interested me— I couldn't shake the feeling that he might be mine. I did know for certain that I wanted to spend more time with him, to try and find out—regardless of how long this thing between Tawny and I lasted.

If Calum was mine, why hadn't Tawny told me as much? Why would she keep that a secret from me?

I shook my head. She'd never do that. He had to be some other man's. Tawny would've told me by now if he was mine.

Wouldn't she have?

More than once she'd said that I didn't owe her anything. Tawny acted as if my being in the marines was all I ever needed to do for her. Like that act alone was enough to give me a free pass for anything.

I didn't want her to sell herself short or, God forbid, a child that might be mine, just because I'd served our country for a while. Would she do that to her own son? Would she deny him his father only to keep that burden off my shoulders? And had my telling her that I had PTSD affected things?

Maybe she'd been planning to tell me about Calum, but then I'd told her about my condition, and she decided not to. Maybe she felt she needed to protect the boy from me. At least for a while, until she could see how my episodes went.

There were so many questions I wanted to ask her, but I didn't know how to do so without being presumptuous. This thing between us was so new still, and I didn't want to scare her off by prying or asking too much of her before she was ready to share. In my experience, women didn't like it when men asked too many questions about the men they'd been with in the past, at least not so early on.

My phone dinged, telling me a text had come in. Tawny had gotten the flowers and wanted to know if I was too busy for her to call me. I called her right away, and her sweet voice answered, "Hello, August. What a sweet thing to do. The flowers are gorgeous. Peonies are my favorite. And the chocolates are to die for. Calum will love the stuffed tiger, too. Thank you so much."

"It was nothing. I just wanted you to know that I had a good time." I drummed my fingers on the dresser as I leaned against it, still looking out the window. "How's West Hollywood looking today? Fires smoking you guys out yet?"

"No, it's clear today. There's a little breeze—I suppose it's keeping the smoke away for now anyway." I heard her walking around, her shoes clicking as she did.

The way I missed her didn't make sense to me. She and I didn't know each other well at all. I had no idea what kinds of things she liked or disliked, no idea what her favorite color was or what food she liked the best. "Wanna get some lunch?"

"I'd love to, but I've got to go to the hospital to fill out insurance papers today. They called me a little while ago and asked me to stop by around one."

The real question I wanted to ask her kind of hung in my throat. But then I went for it. "What do you think about taking a trip to the San Diego Zoo tomorrow, since it's Saturday and Calum won't have school?"

"He'd love that!" she sounded excited.

But all I could think about was that she'd said she didn't take him around men. So why was it okay for him to be around me?

"You sure about that, Tawny? I know he was with us last night for a little, but I don't want you to change all your rules if you don't want to." I crossed my bedroom to take a seat on the bed. Running my hand over the chocolate brown comforter, I made a mental note to get my housekeeper to put the emerald green one on. Tawny's auburn hair would look fantastic splayed out against it. And I did mean to get the woman into my bed in the near future. I just wanted to lay the groundwork first.

"Well, you're different," she said, making me think she might be on the verge of a confession.

"How's that?" I asked as I leaned back on the pillows, wondering how I'd respond if she told me I was his father. It was one thing to speculate about it, but the reality would be much different.

"Well, he likes you. And he adores your sister. All the way to school today he talked about her and her kids. He can hardly remember their names, but he definitely knows your name and your sister's."

"I'd like to get to know him, if that's okay with you, baby. I want to get to know you, too. I mean, I know the basics, and I know the intimates, but the real you—well, I don't know that woman yet. I'd like to get to that if that's okay with you." The soft blanket brought to mind how soft her hair was when I ran my hands through it.

"Let's see...my favorite color is red like my hair. I know that sounds like I'm a little too into my own looks, but I just love the color. I'd wear it every day if I could, but it has to be the right shade to look good on me or else it clashes. I don't even decorate with that color. I have to simply be satisfied to like it, but not use too much of it."

"Mine's green. Like the color or your eyes." I closed mine to picture her eyes, how they'd shine for no reason at all. She was just that happy person who always had a sparkle in her eye—the kind of person that people liked to be around.

"Hmm, really? Or is that a line?" she asked with a knowing tone in her voice.

"No, it's not a line. Green really is my favorite color. And I love Mexican food, how about you?" Taking about these small things was so much easier over the phone—when she was around all I wanted to do was kiss her and touch her. It'd take forever for us to get to these details about each other if we were face-to-face.

"Chinese is my favorite, but I like Mexican. But only authentic Mexican, not like Taco Hell," she laughed lightly, and the sound captivated me.

"What made you become a nurse, Tawny?" I asked, as that seemed like a thing a boyfriend should know about his girlfriend.

Hold up! You've got to take things slow.

Between this thing with Tawny and me and my compulsive desire to spend more time with Calum, I knew I was getting wrapped up in this woman too quickly. Despite that, I knew one thing for sure—my therapist was right about me needing to take things slowly.

"I became a nurse after having my son. And I wanted to specialize in pediatrics. You see, Calum was born with a small hernia. It had to be operated on right away, it was that bad. The nurses helped me when I started crying and freaking out that my newborn had to go straight into surgery."

My heart sped up. "God, Tawny. Were your parents there?" I felt terrible for her.

"No, they'd gone out of town. Calum came two weeks early. It wasn't anyone's fault that I had to go through that alone. It's just the way it happened. Anyway, the nurses stepped up and helped me through everything. I had to stay a week in the hospital, and they taught me how to take care of Calum. So, it was a godsend that my parents weren't around, because Calum and I bonded right away, thanks to the nurses who helped me." Though the story was a sad and scary one, Tawny told it with an upbeat attitude.

The girl was amazing.

Despite her perseverance and easy reflection, I felt like a complete dick while listening to her story. Because I knew one person whose fault it was that she'd had to go through all that alone—the father's.

Whoever that might be.

69

CHAPTER 10

Tawny

The sun warmed the cool early December air as we strolled through the zoo. Well, August and I strolled while Calum mostly ran, beating us to each exhibit.

Calum was about to careen around a corner out of our line of sight. August quickly called out, "Hey, buddy, stay where we can see ya'."

To my surprise, Calum slammed on the brakes. "Yes, sir." He was all smiles as he waited for us to catch up before turning the corner.

"Wow. If I'd said that, he'd have ignored me, and I'd be running after him." I looped my arm through his, leaning my head on his shoulder. "And I've never heard him say 'yes, sir,' to anyone before."

"He asked me a question earlier, and I said 'yes, sir' to him. I guess he picked it up." August kissed the top of my head. "I can be a good influence when I try hard enough."

"I like it when you're a bad influence, too. Only on me,

though." August had been a perfect gentleman with me since the moment he'd picked us up. He drove himself in a new Mercedes, saying we might just stay the night in San Diego if it got too late.

I'd been about to run back inside to pack us an overnight bag just in case when he told me not to bother. He'd casually said that if we did end up staying, he'd buy us whatever we'd need—as if that was normal.

I hadn't mustered up the courage to ask him just how much he was worth. I knew it had to be a lot. I didn't know how he made his money either. There shouldn't be anything wrong with wanting to know what he did to make a living. "Would it be rude of me to ask you what it is you do to earn this vast amount of money you seem to have, August?"

He stopped walking, looking into my eyes. "Can I tell you about that another time, Tawny? I will tell you, but now's not a good time to do that."

Clueless as to why he couldn't talk about it at that moment, I wondered what the hell he did for a living that made him say such a thing. Was he a spy? Did he work for the CIA or the FBI? Did those people make as much money as it seemed he had? "'Kay." My eyes turned away from his as my mind went crazy with all the questions.

August pointed out ahead of us, directing Calum's attention to something he was sure to love. "Is that an arcade, Calum?"

My son shot toward the open area, which was covered by a red and white circus-like tent. "Oh, yeah!"

"He's going to beggar us in there, August," I warned him. "And getting him out of there won't be easy either."

"I can take it," he said with a chuckle.

But as we entered the area, with games making loud sounds everywhere—including the sounds of gunfire and explosions—I grew worried. "August, are you sure you're okay with this?"

He knew I referred to his PTSD and nodded. "It's okay. I've conquered the loud noises triggering an episode."

So, if those no longer set him off, what did?

Standing back, I watched as August and Calum climbed onto a couple of motorcycles to have a virtual race, August obviously letting Calum win. "Aw, man. You beat me," August whined to Calum. Then he pointed to some fishing game across the room. "Hey, wanna see who can catch the biggest fish, Calum?"

"Yes, sir!" Calum was off the bike, running top speed, or as fast as one little boy can go through a crowd of kids. And August was hot on his heels, having just as much fun as my little boy.

As I watched them go from one game to another, my heart pounded in my chest. August and his sister were great with Calum. Maybe it was time I was more honest with all three of them.

Maybe I would be, but not at this moment. This wasn't the time or the place, but soon. Maybe even later, after we left the zoo.

My mind grew more and more determined as the day went on. When August grabbed Calum up, putting him on his shoulders so he could see an elusive bear who'd hidden itself in its cave, I nearly cried.

They'd barely known each other from Adam when the day started, having only spent a spot of time together in the car on the way home the other night. But there they were, acting as if they'd always known one another.

When we went to find something to eat, both of them ordered a cheeseburger, plain and dry with a side of onion rings and an orange soda. The way they laughed after saying the same thing had me tearing up.

"Jinx, you owe me a Coke," August said after they'd said the same words at the same time.

"What does that mean?" Calum asked him with a crooked smile.

August wore a very similar smile as he explained the little saying, and then they both laughed. The sounds of August's deep tones mixed with the high tones of my son sent chills through me.

The day hadn't gotten away from us, and we left with plenty of time to get back home to Los Angeles. The car ride was quiet as Calum had fallen asleep, completely worn out.

August took hold of my hand, pulling it up to kiss as he drove along the highway. "Thanks for today. I've never had that much fun in my entire life."

Raising one eyebrow, I gave him a questioning look. "Oh, really?"

"I mean, in that kind of way. Of course, I've had a few great times with you, baby." He took my hand, resting it on top of his thigh.

"Thanks," I said with sarcasm. "And thank you for taking us on this little outing. It did wonders for me as well," I told him, referring in secret to my new thoughts on what I should do. I thought about when the time would be right for what I'd planned. "You should stay for dinner at my place tonight. I can whip up some pasta."

"Or you two could come to my place, and I could have Tara whip us up something," he said as his lips grazed the back of my hand, sending chills all through me.

His place?

It was very tempting to be able to see how the man lived —to learn that much more about him. "And Tara is your..."

"Chef." He smiled at me with that crooked grin. "And Denise is the head housekeeper. Max is my driver, and Joel is the groundskeeper. There are a couple of younger girls who come in with Denise twice a week to do the deep cleaning. To be honest, I don't know their names."

"And you live where, exactly?" I had to ask. With a staff that size, it had to be somewhere glamorous.

"Hidden Hills," he said as he glanced at me, catching my mouth hanging open.

"No! Did you know that Kim Kardashian lives there?" I was flabbergasted.

"Well, yeah, she and Kanye only live two houses from mine." He shrugged to accent how typical that was.

"Get out! No way!" My mind could only form two words at a time. Then I had to ask again, "So, what is it that you do, August?"

"Well, at the moment, I'm working with a couple of other men to open an incredibly exclusive nightclub, catering to only the wealthiest of people. We've named it Swank—it's due to open on New Year's Eve. I haven't asked you yet, but I can now. Will you please be my date for that, Tawny?"

"So, you're some kind of a nightclub mogul? And my answer is yes, I'd love to be your date for that." I wondered how the hell a former marine had gotten into that.

"Yeah, on top of other things. My fingers are in a lot of pies, so to speak." Traffic slowed to a stop, and I found August looking out the window at the passengers in the car next to him.

"You'll have to fill me in on all the pies eventually," I said as I watched him.

I realized that he hadn't heard a word I said, transfixed as he was by the people in the car beside us. Too many seconds ticked by with him motionless, then I finally heard him whisper, "John?"

Everything seemed to happen in slow motion, like the calm before an explosion. One second August was fine, and the next, the name 'John' pealed out of his mouth in short bursts that changed to high pitched screams.

To make matters worse, his screaming woke up Calum, who began to cry, "What's wrong with him, Momma?"

Taking off my seatbelt, I got on my knees in my seat and reached over, jerking on August's shoulders to draw him out of the episode. "It's okay, honey," I said calmly, trying to get things under control. "August, it's okay, babe. It's not real."

"Momma!" Calum shouted as he cried hysterically. "Momma, make him stop!"

Looking at my son, I said firmly, "I need you to stop crying, Calum. August is having a hard time. You have to be quiet now. Right now." Being so strict with my frightened son wasn't an easy thing to do, but it was done, and thankfully, Calum's loud cries became soft whimpers.

Turning my attention back to August, I climbed over the console that separated us, landing sideways on his lap and putting the car into park. "August, it's okay. It's me, Tawny. Everything is okay. What you're seeing isn't really happening right now. You're fine. Everyone is fine."

With a loud gasp, August's eyes finally blinked, and his screaming stopped. "Oh, God!" he grabbed my wrists as I held his face between my hands. "God..." He took deep, heaving breaths as he slowly came back to reality. "Tawny, I'm so sorry!"

"It's okay now." I stroked his face and his hair for a few moments as he continued to calm down. "I'll drive."

He nodded, and we both got out of the car as the people in the traffic all around us watched with gaping jaws. I saw my son's red-rimmed eyes as he watched August walk around the front of the car, getting in the passenger side— the side Calum had been sitting behind.

My son took off his seat belt with frightened eyes, sliding to the seat behind the driver's side. My heart broke at the sight. All of the trust that August had built with Calum had just been destroyed in a matter of minutes.

Who knew how long it would take to get that back?

70

CHAPTER 11

August

M y episode had spoiled the rest of that night. After stopping at Tawny's place to drop them off, I drove myself home. A smell of smoke hung in the air even though no flames were in sight. It troubled me as I headed into my home.

Joel, the groundskeeper, was inside talking to Tara, my chef. I was pretty sure the two liked one another, but they seemed to be taking things slow—maybe due to the fact they were both approaching sixty. But their progress was really slow, like hurry-up-before-one-of-you-guys-dies slow. But I kept that to myself. It wasn't my business, after all.

I did ask them about the smoke though, "Did you guys smell that smoke out there? Is there a fire near here that I don't know about?"

"No, boss. I guess the winds have picked up around the current fires out in Angeles National Forest. They're calling them the Creek Fires. Nothing to worry about here, sir," Joel answered.

"Cool," I said with relief. "I'm heading to bed. It's been a long day."

Sleep proved hard to achieve that night. After an hour of trying, I called Tawny. "Hi, August. You get home okay?"

"I did. Are you and Calum okay?" I put my hand over my eyes, wishing that the incident had never happened.

"I'm fine. I told you I could handle that," she said, then paused.

"Calum's not, is he?" I asked, but I didn't have to—I knew I'd upset the boy.

"Well, he's young, August. You've got to understand." She sighed, and I hated to hear that.

"I do understand. Believe me, I do. I just keep wishing I could go back in time and figure out what the hell triggered that episode." As hard as I could, I tried to figure out what had caused it, but like many times before, I couldn't.

It was crazy; I had determined that loud noises could trigger one type of episode, one where I saw myself in battle with my fellow marines and where people I'd worked with for years were killed. Once I realized that specific catalyst, those kinds of episodes came less frequently until they finally stopped. But I still hadn't been able to figure out what the trigger was for the episodes reliving those moments with John Black.

"I think it might've been because I was asking you about your job and how you got your money," Tawny offered. "When I asked you about that at the zoo, you told me that you'd tell me later, that that wasn't the place. Since you're home now and safe, why don't you tell me about it now? It might help."

She might've been on the right track. So, I began my tale, "I told you about the accident with John Black, but I didn't tell you that I sued the manufacturer of that gun and won millions. The first thing I did was look for an investment firm to help me grow that money. All I wanted to do was keep John's name alive. I wanted to make as much money as I could from the settlement money so that I could make donations to charities in his name."

"So, you found a firm that helped you reach that goal?" she asked.

"I did. I met Gannon Forester at the first firm I went to. He's one of my business partners now. He put the whole settlement into the same investments and ventures he'd had a ton of his money in. He made me a billionaire and helped me see my dream come true. And now I live off part of that money and invest other parts of it, all the while giving chunks to different charities each month." I felt better about telling Tawny about this. A weight lifted off my shoulders once I realized that it must have been the line of conversation that triggered that particular episode.

For a while Tawny was quiet, and then she said, "What a weight you must carry around, August. My God."

Did I carry a lot of weight around? I hadn't realized that. "I don't feel burdened by it, Tawny."

"You may not feel it, but you hold yourself solely responsible for making sure that man's name is kept alive. And you've gone to such lengths to do that, too. Going to court, suing a huge weapons-manufacturing company, winning, and then turning that money into an even bigger fortune—that's not nothing. And you're still not done—finding the right charities every month, that's got to be difficult. That's a lot to do for someone who isn't even walking the earth anymore."

"But he's not here because of me," I reminded her.

"No, he's not here because of the malfunction of the weapon, not because of you, August." She tapped her nails on something, and I could hear it through the phone. "If it had been your fault, then you would've never won that case against the manufacturer. You are not to blame for what happened to John Black, and you need to let go of that guilt. You've devoted your entire life to him since the accident—how do you expect to move on from that horror when it's always lurking there at the edge of everything you do? I'm not saying stop what you're doing—giving money to charities is a wonderful thing to do. But let the guilt go."

Her words were making my heart do flips inside my chest. Tears welled up in my eyes. In the year that I'd been seeing Dr. Schmidt, he'd told me a number of times that I needed to reconcile my guilt with the event, but he'd never hit on that as a trigger for my episodes. And he'd never quite gotten to the core of the issue as Tawny had—never gotten me to realize the immensity of the burden I carried, however subconsciously.

Tawny had done that in record time. "You're an amazing woman, Tawny Matthews."

"And you're an amazing man, August Harlow. I think we make a pretty great couple, don't you?" she asked with a sexy lilt to her voice.

Pushing my hand through my hair, I had another thought. If I'd frightened her son, then why would she want anything else to do with me? Tawny wasn't acting like the mother my sister said she'd be. She wasn't taking her son and running in the opposite direction.

"A couple, huh?" I had to ask. "You're not going to stop seeing me now that Calum's afraid of me?"

"He'll come around, eventually. I can talk to him, get

him to understand things better," she told me. "I don't want to stop seeing you just because this happened. As a matter of fact, if I did stop seeing you over this, then that might adversely affect your PTSD, making it worse. I'd never want to do that to you."

But what about her son? What about him and how he felt about me?

"Tawny, I want you to know that I'd never fault you for ending things with me. I know that your son is the most important thing to you, as he should be. And he's afraid of me now. I would never say one harsh word against you if you ended this." I waited to see what she'd say to that. I'd given her a pass to end it all and walk away without a fight.

"Listen to me, August," she began. "Calum is my life. He has been for six years now, and he always will be. But you have a place in my heart that no one else has been able to take. I know we weren't close in any real way back then, but what we did that night made us close, closer than a lot of couples are after years together. I've told you this before—I feel a bond with you. I don't know if you feel it, too."

I jumped in. "I do feel it. But why do you think two people who barely know one another have such an important bond, Tawny?"

Please, tell me Calum is mine!

My fingers crossed and I waited for her next words, which I prayed would be the ones I wanted to hear.

"That night, you took more than just my virginity. You took a piece of my heart," she said, her voice but a whisper. "I fell a little bit in love with you that night, and spending time with you these last few days has made me realize that it was more than just some girlish infatuation."

"You love me?" I asked, as that hadn't even entered my

mind. But I had to admit, this girl had a hold on me that no one else had ever managed.

"I have since that night, August. And I think I always will," she said softly.

Her words echoed in my mind, and I couldn't hold back my own confession. "I thought about you over and over these past years. I replayed that night in my head so many damn times I've lost count. And when you brushed my arm as you walked past me at the Science Center, I felt an electric charge. Is that love, Tawny? Because I've never felt that with anyone else—not before our night together, and certainly not after."

"I can't tell you if that's love, August, but I'd like to explore the idea with you." She paused for a moment, as if thinking if there was anything else to say on the matter. "We had a long day, and it's late—I should get some sleep."

The phone seemed glued to my hand; I couldn't put it down. "Wait."

"Yes?" she asked.

"Tell me, Tawny. Say the words to me."

"I love you, August Harlow," she said sweetly. "Now you have a good night, babe. Call me in the morning."

My head started spinning at those words, and I was overtly aware that I hadn't said any words of love back to her. But I couldn't make the words come out of my mouth. "'Night, Tawny."

Lying in my bed, alone, I ran my hand over the empty space beside me. Had Tawny's feelings about me grown into love because she'd had a constant reminder of me?

Had all those fantasies and thoughts I'd had through the years made me fall in love with her?

God knew I never gave any female half a chance to win my heart. Hell, I hadn't slept with any woman more than a handful of times, and each and every time was purely fucking—no emotions involved. Not the way I'd been with Tawny that night. Not the way I'd been with her on our dinner date, either.

Shit, do I love the woman?

71

CHAPTER 12

Tawny

My feelings for August were out in the open now, to him at least. But my son was unaware of them. Any time I brought up the man's name, Calum made a face. He'd cross his arms in front of his chest, puffing it out and telling me he didn't like August so much anymore, and he didn't think he wanted to see him again.

August and I had let a few days pass, talking on the phone each day, making suggestions to each other about what the best way to handle this situation would be. All the while, August never confessed any love for me, but asked, each and every time our calls came to an end, to hear the words I'd told him. So, each conversation ended with an 'I love you' from me, and a goodbye from him.

Lopsided, I knew.

I also knew it was early to be throwing around the L-word, but I'd pushed those feelings deep inside myself for so many years already. It was hard saying goodbye to August all those years ago, having to let go of the incredible spark between us, no matter how important I knew his leaving to be. But seeing him again and us spending time together had only made me realize that I'd been holding onto those feelings for seven long years—it was no wonder they came blooming to the surface so quickly.

I chalked my ease with expressing my love to August up to the fact that I'd been telling my son that I loved him at least once a day since the day he was born. Being honest about my feelings helped me accept the fact that August just wasn't ready yet.

He might not have been ready to tell me that he loved me, but he sure as hell was ready to see me again. So ready, in fact, that he'd devised a plan. He'd decided he would show up at my apartment for dinner and talk to Calum directly about why he'd had the attack.

When a knock came to the door, I casually asked Calum to see who was there. "'Kay, Momma." I watched him look out the window beside the door as I stirred the pot of beef stew I'd prepared for dinner.

When he turned around, heading out of the living room at top speed, the slam of his bedroom door punctuating the moment, I knew he wasn't about to listen to a word August had to say.

So, I opened the door for August, a frown on my face. "He saw you and took off. He's in his bedroom."

Arms came around my body, pulling me close. Our bodies were flush against the other, and heat filled mine. "I'll fix this. Just watch." His lips touched mine. "I've missed seeing you, baby."

I couldn't even respond as his mouth took mine in a hungry kiss. His hands went to my ass, picking me up. Knowing Calum wouldn't be coming out of his room without assistance any time soon, I wrapped my legs around

August. I kissed him back, wishing like hell we could just drop to the floor right there and make love, which we'd yet to do since our reunion.

But August had another agenda in coming here, so he let me down and smacked my ass, sending me back to the kitchen. "I've got bigger fish to fry right now, Momma. I'll get back to you soon, don't worry. But first, I want to hear you say those words to my face."

A blush heated my cheeks as I smiled shyly. "August!"

One finger traced my lips as he gazed at me. "Please. For courage, if nothing else."

Though almost inaudible, the words came out, "I love you, August Harlow."

A slow smile spread across his handsome face. "Oh, yeah. That's what I thought would happen when you said those words to my face." Suddenly I was pulled back into his strong arms, his mouth on mine again. The bulge in his pants pressed against my core, and he didn't have to say a word—I knew what my words had done to him. When our mouths parted, he whispered in my ear, "I love you too, Tawny Matthews."

"August?" I asked, surprised. "You don't have to..."

His mouth came back to mine, making me shut up as he kissed me in a way he hadn't before.

He loved me, and he'd finally told me so!

When he ended the kiss, he nuzzled his nose to mine. "It felt good telling you that, baby. Better than having you tell me those three little words that have such an effect on me."

"They have a pretty amazing effect on me as well," I admitted.

With a groan, he let me go. "Okay, off to fix things."

He headed down the short hallway and stood just outside the closed door my son had slammed. "Hi, Calum.

It's me, August. I know I scared you the other day, but I wanted to tell you a little story about why I zone out sometimes and end up screaming like that."

Listening to him try to make peace with my son, I went on cooking dinner and wondering how Calum would take August's little story. All the while, I wondered how August would clean it up, so he didn't scare Calum any further.

August went on, "You see, I was in the war." He paused for a moment, giving Calum time to try to understand what he meant. "You remember that game we played in the arcade, the one where we were soldiers, and we had to shoot all the bad guys? Well, I did that in real life. When you do that in real life, it can make you have bad dreams, even while you're awake. That's what happened that day in the car." He stopped again for a few seconds, likely knowing that this next part would be the hardest to tell. "You probably heard me say the name John the other day in the car. John was a very good friend of mine, and something bad happened to him by accident, and I was there for the whole thing. Sometimes my brain plays tricks on me—like a very bad and mean prank—and the memory of what happened to John comes back to me, even though I know it's not real. It's like I have a nightmare even though I'm awake, and sometimes I scream until someone helps me and tells me it's not real—like your momma did that day in the car. You probably have bad dreams, too, sometimes, right? Mine don't happen very often, but I know they can be scary. I'm sorry I scared you that day, Calum, and I hope we can be friends again like we were before that happened."

The squeak of the door opening had me looking around the corner.

Calum had come out, and August got down on his

knees, so he was closer to my little boy's height. "So, you were a soldier, like on TV?"

"I was," August answered him. "And it's a lot scarier than it is on TV, too."

Calum nodded. "I bet it is." He blinked a few times. "And your friend John, the one who had something bad happen to him? Did he die?"

August nodded, his expression solemn. "Yes, he did, and I was there when that happened. It was very sad, and it's made me see things that aren't there. I know it sounds crazy."

Calum nodded in agreement. "Yeah. It is crazy. But one time, I saw a monkey in a tree at Granny's. It was a real monkey, but no one believed me."

"How'd that make you feel, Calum?" August asked him as he ran his hand through Calum's dark hair. Hair that matched his perfectly.

"Crazy and mad," he said with a huff as he threw his hands in the air. "Why would I make that up?"

August shook his head. "I don't see why you'd do a thing like that."

"I wouldn't. I ain't no liar!" Calum huffed again.

August nodded in agreement. "I bet you're not."

Then Calum looked at August, and he reached out to put his hand on his cheek. "I bet it made you sad when you saw that happen to your friend."

"Sadder than I've ever been. I'm trying like crazy to stop these nightmares, because I don't want you to be scared of me. Your momma is trying to help me, too, so I'd like to stick around if that's okay with you, Calum. I like your momma a lot, and I like you, too." August placed his hand on my son's shoulder. "So, what do you say, Calum? Can I hang around with you guys? I'd sure appreciate it if you'd let me."

"Momma did help you. And I think she likes you, too" Calum said, then took two steps forward, wrapping his arms around August's neck. "I'm sorry. I'm sorry I was afraid of you. You can hang around with us."

August got up, carrying Calum as he did. "Thank you. You have no idea how much this means to me, Calum. You sure do have a big heart."

They walked over to me, catching me wiping tears away from that scene, which had touched my heart in a way I couldn't describe. "So, I see you two have worked things out then." A sniffle would've confirmed to them that I'd been crying a little, if they hadn't noticed already.

"Yep," Calum said. "We're friends again."

Friends. No, they were more than just friends. But when would the time be right to tell them that?

72

CHAPTER 13

August

Although Calum had seen fit to forgive me for the episode he'd witnessed, I wasn't ready to forgive myself. I'd been warned by my sister and my therapist, but I'd still made the unfortunate decision to ignore their sage advice. It didn't sit well with me that I'd scared the poor kid.

Although a part of me, the rational part, told me to leave Tawny and her son alone and be on my merry way, my selfish side simply wouldn't allow me to do that. No, that side of me wanted Tawny—and Calum—in my life more than it had ever wanted anything.

So, after eating the delicious beef stew she'd made, I told her what I wanted after we'd retreated to the living room while Calum filled the dishwasher with our dirty dishes. Slipping one arm around her as we sat on the sofa, I whispered, "So, what are the chances of you letting me sleep over?"

Her pretty green eyes went wide as she shook her head.

"No way, August. You know I'd love that, but this place is tiny, and Calum's a light sleeper."

My cock wasn't going to give up so easily. "Okay, then how about we figure out a way to get him out of the house for a little while?"

Her expression turned from stern to intrigued. "Like how?"

I only had one go-to for that answer, so I took my cell out of my pocket to call my sister. The sound of a group of people all talking over each other hit my ears immediately as Leila answered my call, "August, what's up?"

"I was wondering what you were doing this evening," I said as I played with a strand of Tawny's red hair.

"Actually, Jacob wants to go see some new cartoon movie tonight. He and I are about to head out now. Why do you ask?"

"Well, I'm at Tawny's and..."

She stopped me. "I see. Yeah, I know what you want now. I can take Calum with us if he wants to go."

"I'll ask him." With a kiss to Tawny's cheek, I got up to go ask Calum if he'd like to watch a cartoon movie with his Aunt Leila and Jacob.

"Yes, sir!" he shrieked then slammed the dishwasher shut before making a beeline for his bedroom.

"He's in," I told my sister. "When can we expect you?"

"About a half hour. At least, that's what Tawny said it took for your driver to bring them over that one time. Text me her address."

And with that, I'd managed to get Tawny all alone for at least a couple hours. Sure, I'd rather have an entire night, but I'd take anything I could get.

Going back to the sofa, I sat down next to her, running one fingertip over her shoulder. She bit her lower lip.

"Maybe I should jump in the shower and do myself up a bit. I've been dreaming about this, and I'd like to look my best."

"Whatever you want. I'll be right here." Before she could get up, I left a kiss on her lips that told her what she was in for.

She left the room with a flushed face that made my cock thump in my jeans. Things were turning around for us, I could feel it in the air. It felt heavy and light at the same time. Heavy with what was to come, and light with happiness.

By the time Leila arrived, Calum was chomping at the bit to get going and ran out the door as soon as she knocked. Slowing only to give her a brief hug and thank her for taking him, Calum was quickly on his way.

Leila leveled her eyes on me as she stood at the door. "Don't do anything I wouldn't do, little brother."

"Never," I said with a laugh then closed the door, locking it before I turned to head toward Tawny's bedroom.

Tawny was still in the bathroom, so I stripped down, wanting to surprise her in her bed. My cock was ready for her already, but I'd be taking my time with her tonight.

"August?" she called out from the hallway.

"In here," I called back to her.

I'd turned off the overhead light and turned on a small lamp beside the bed.

"I thought you said you'd wait in the—" she paused, mouth agape as she saw me in her bed, sitting up with my head resting on the pillows.

I patted the empty side of the bed as she stood in the doorway, giving her an eager grin.

Tawny had a towel wrapped around her, her damp hair hanging in loose waves around her shoulders. She clamped her mouth shut, taking in my bare chest and arms. "Oh, you're naked, huh?"

Tossing the blanket back, I let her see just how naked I was. "Drop the towel, baby."

She took a deep breath then let the white towel fall to the floor. One of her feet flew back, kicking the door closed before she came to me.

Each step she took made her large breasts jiggle. My cock pulsed, and my mouth watered, wanting to taste every bit of her juicy body.

She sat on the edge of the bed, her breath already coming in quick gasps. It reminded me of our one night together, and I laughed as I grabbed her, pulling her on top of me.

She straddled my stomach as I played with her tits, first with my hands then with my mouth. Her hands fisted in my hair as she made quiet moans. The last moan was filled with words that did something to me I'd never experienced while in bed, "I love you, August Harlow."

My cock couldn't wait any longer. I threw all my plans for a slow seduction out of my mind, and with one swift movement I had her on her back, my body hovering over hers as she spread her legs for me. "I love you, Tawny Matthews. Are you ready for me?"

With a nod, she confessed, "I'm soaked for you."

"Good, because I'm about to slam this cock into that wet pussy and fuck you the way I've been dreaming about for far too long now." And with that, I slammed into her tight pussy.

She let out a scream as my cock stretched her, as her body worked to fit me, "August!" Her nails curled into my shoulders, making them burn.

A groan escaped me—she was unbelievably tight. "Oh,

baby!"

Moving in and out of her, I felt every part of her again. Her soft skin rubbed against my chest with each thrust, her hips jutted up, hitting my stomach as she arched her back—everything was sensation, every move she made took me back to seven years ago.

But now she was mine for real, not just the girl I'd found sitting outside at midnight, looking at the same moon I was.

Auburn hair fanned out over the white pillowcase, green eyes looked up at me and pink lips trembled, and I had to take them with my own. Passion made the kiss hard and demanding, and our tongues moved in circles as I made her mine once more.

The sound of her moans mixed with my harsh breathing, and our flesh slapped together over and over in a rhythm that took us to our first climax of the night—and it took us at the same time, just as it had seven years ago.

I'd never had an orgasm at the same time with any other woman. What Tawny and I shared was special, and I knew that without any doubt.

Resting my body on top of hers, but being careful not to put my full weight on her, I panted until I regained my breath. When I looked down at her glowing face, with her eyes closed, lips parted, still panting a bit, I knew without a doubt that this was what love felt like.

It took root inside my heart. Pure love, a love I'd never felt before. I'd do anything for this woman. She felt like a part of me I'd always been missing.

Her eyes opened, and she caught my face between her hands. "My God, August." One tear rolled down her cheek.

Kissing it away, I echoed, "My God."

Words were hard to come by to explain how I felt. And it seemed to be the same for Tawny, too. I hadn't always been the best with words anyway, but I sure could show her what she meant to me.

Rolling onto my back, I kept her close, not allowing our bodies to separate for even a moment. She lay on top of me, and then I gently pushed her to sit up. Those big boobs called to my hands and I played with them again.

One eyebrow cocked as she asked in a husky voice, "You do like the tits, don't you, August?"

"Nope, I love 'em." I sat up, taking one into my mouth and licking the nipple as I rolled it between my lips. Her moans had my cock growing stiff again, and soon she was riding my cock to another simultaneous orgasm.

I didn't want to let her out of that bed. Like, not ever. Keeping her in bed with me would've been a dream come true, and that thought had me remembering the way I'd felt that first night. It had seemed like I couldn't get enough of her back then, and that feeling was still there.

Cupping the back of her head, I kissed her softly. "Leaving you after all we'd done was one of the hardest things I've ever had to do. And now that I've got you, I don't think I can ever leave you again."

She giggled as she pushed her hands through my hair. "I hope you don't leave me again. I never told you this, but I cried every night for a month after you left. And my prayers for your safe return never stopped. I suppose they were answered, huh?"

Her kiss-swollen lower lip begged me to take it between my teeth. I bit it gently, tugging it as I said, "Thank you for praying for this."

And then I felt my cock pulsing back to life again, and she did, too, moaning as she started to move again. "Yes, babe. Take me again, you insatiable man."

With her, I was insatiable—only with her.

73

CHAPTER 14

Tawny

August seemed content with the way things had to be. He came over during the day while Calum was at school, and we'd make love the whole time, stopping only to eat and drink a bit to replenish our strength. He'd stay for dinner and would leave when the time came to put Calum to bed. That went on for a week.

But then one day, that wasn't enough for August. Sweeping into my little apartment moments after I'd gotten back from dropping Calum off at school, I found a serious expression clouding his handsome face. "Tawny, this isn't working for me."

Wrapping my arms around him, kissing his sweet lips, I felt the tension leave his body as he and I melded into each other. Once everything felt settled, our mouths parted. "Now, what's not working for you?"

He took my hands in his, pulling them up and kissing each knuckle as he eyed me carefully. "Not having you in my bed at night."

"But you have me all day long," I reminded him.

"Yes, but I won't always have this. You'll start work, and then we won't get to do this anymore." His lips pressed against my palm, making my insides turn into melted butter.

"August Harlow, have you become addicted to me?" I laughed as he nodded without an ounce of shame. "Well, that can't be good for you."

"But it is good for me." He pulled me along with him to place me on his lap after he'd taken a seat on the sofa. "You see, you're very good for me, and I just want you around all the time. I know you'll have to go to work soon, and then I'll have to give you up during the daytime hours. Then what will I get?"

To be honest, I hadn't even thought about it. What would he get? What would I get?

I needed my time with August just as much as he needed his time with me. But there was one thing that stopped me from wanting to change our routine—Calum.

The hard thing about keeping a secret is knowing when the right time might be to confess. At first, I didn't want to burden August with anything. And then, after witnessing his PTSD episode, I knew he wasn't up for any surprises just yet. But when would he be ready?

Living with PTSD was no easy thing for any veteran, and when you added in the fact that he'd accidentally killed a fellow marine and one of his good friends...well, you had a recipe for disaster.

And then there was the fact that August was now a billionaire. To some women that would be the best news ever. To me, it wasn't.

Although he and I came from similar backgrounds, he'd become phenomenally wealthy. Wealth like his came with a lot of responsibilities and problems that I was unfamiliar with. Like living in the public eye or needing to have bodyguards for protection on occasion, not to mention the women who threw themselves at wealthy men.

If I told him my secret, which I'd kept from every person in my life, then things would change drastically. And maybe not all for the better. August, and my parents too, would probably see me as a liar.

I didn't want that.

Sure, with time they'd likely forgive me, but how could they not have a little niggling feeling inside of them, knowing that I'd kept the truth from them for years? Especially when it was about something as important as the identity of my son's father.

No, I couldn't do it. Not yet.

"So, what would you suggest we do, August?" I asked him as I ran my hands through his silky dark hair.

"Why don't you two move in with me?" His eyes danced and glittered as he smiled at me.

Now, I knew most women would fall all over themselves over such a request. But again, I wasn't most women. So, when my answer came out, the frown I got wasn't unexpected. "No."

One solid huff forced a burst of air out of him as he stared at me with a questioning expression. "Well, you won't let me stay the night here with you. You've said it's too small, and Calum would hear everything. I think my idea is great, if you ask me."

"Look, Calum is a large part of why I can't move in with you. He gets up almost every night and climbs into bed with me. That would be a problem if you and I slept together each night."

With a roll of his eyes, his reply was blunt, "You're grasping at straws, Tawny."

"I am not," I said as I got off his lap. "I'm getting a cup of coffee. You want one?"

He nodded and followed me to the kitchen. What I really needed was a glass of wine to soothe my nerves, which had grown jagged.

"I don't see why he can't learn not to get out of his bed at night, is all I'm saying. Maybe Leila can give you some tips on that. That shouldn't be something that keeps us apart, Tawny, surely you can see that." Coming up behind me, August ran his arms around my waist, leaning his chin on top of my shoulder.

Turning in his arms, I wrapped my arms around him and told him a bit more of the truth. "Another reason is for our safety and privacy. I know you live in a high-profile neighborhood—not to mention that your lifestyle must be wildly different from what we're used to. If we were to move in with you, I think we'd need to be protected—by a body-guard or security, at least. I get that you don't need anyone to protect you, but your philanthropy and the opening of your club are turning you into a household name in this city. People will be curious about us, and Calum and I would have to have protection. I don't think I'd like living that way."

Sadness filtered into his hazel eyes. "Baby, what are you saying? Are you telling me that we can't ever move forward? Are you saying this is all we'll ever have?"

"I don't know what I'm saying, August. This has all happened very quickly, and I'm just a little confused." I kissed him. "The only thing I'm not confused about is the fact that I love you. But everything else needs a little sorting out still."

His chest swelled with a deep sigh. He was not a happy man at that moment. But I knew I could take his mind off things, at least for a little while.

Running my hands down his arms, I took his hands. "Let's skip the coffee and go to bed."

"No," his word came out sternly. His eyes moved up to meet mine. "If this is all we can ever have... I don't think I can take that."

"August, we haven't even been seeing each other that long," I argued.

"We've known each other forever, Tawny. I want to share my life with you. So what if I have to hire a couple of body-guards to watch over you and Calum when I can't? I don't care about that. Shit, more than half the kids in Los Angeles have them, and most of the wives and girlfriends do, too." The pad of his thumb ran over my lower lip as he looked at me with adoring eyes.

How could I say no to him when he looked at me that way? His hold on me had my body vibrating with more than just lust—love shook me, and I wanted so badly to make him happy.

But I just couldn't move in with him—not with my secret still hanging between us.

It wouldn't be right.

My cell rang. It was in the living room, so August let me out of his embrace, and I went to answer it. "It's Calum's school," I told August, who loomed just behind me. "Hello."

"Miss Matthews?" a woman asked me.

"Yes, this is she."

"You were aware of the field trip your son's class took today, right?" she asked me, her tone tense.

Chills ran through me, my gut telling me something was

wrong. "Yes, the trip to Big Bear. I packed him a special lunch for it. Is everything okay?"

"Um, have you watched any news today, Miss Matthews?"

August's arms encircled me, as I must've begun looking a bit pale. "I haven't watched any news. Please just tell me what's going on."

August let go of me to grab the television remote, and he turned it on, changing the channel to one of the local stations.

And there it was. A yellow school bus, along with some other cars, trapped between two lines of wildfire.

I collapsed onto the sofa as the lady finally filled me in, "There are fifteen people in total on the bus with your son—three adults and twelve children. Evacuations are underway, but with the fires moving and the winds picking up...well, it's a very dangerous situation."

August took the phone from my hand, as I couldn't find the strength to say a word or move a muscle. He spoke to the woman on the other end, "We'll handle it, thank you."

Putting my phone down, he picked his up and made a call—to whom, I hadn't a clue. All I knew was that my little boy was in danger. Horrible danger. "August, what if he's burned alive?"

"Hush, don't think like that, baby." He came to sit next to me. I heard a man answer his call and he put it on speakerphone. "Gannon, I need your help," he said, all business. "There's a school bus full of little kids—one of them is especially important to me—they're trapped up in Big Bear by some wildfires. I need some choppers up there to help evacuate them, and my boy is the first to be helped, you got me?"

"I've got you. I'll call my pilot and set things up. Meet us at the Beverly Center Heliport."

"Got it," August hung up without as much as a goodbye. "Come on, baby. Let's go bring Calum home." He pulled me up with him, and I followed.

My body and mind were numb with shock.

But August had a plan, and that was more than I had.

74

CHAPTER 15

August

The thick smoke filling the sky made it impossible to see the ground below us for a few tension-filled moments. I'd left Tawny at the heliport, as she'd demanded to be left behind so there'd be more room for evacuees in Gannon's chopper.

His pilot and I headed out in the first one, with Gannon and another pilot taking off just after we did. My other partner, Nixon, headed out just after him. Three helicopters that could fit three more riders were on the way to save as many people as we could.

The conditions weren't great. High winds caused by the blazing infernos made traveling through the air difficult. The birds swung from side to side as the winds pushed us, but the engines were strong and we all made forward progress.

One Coast Guard chopper flew past us as we neared our destination. It felt good to know that their large helicopter could carry a lot more people to safety. Maybe we could get all of them out, and no one would die or get hurt.

The yellow school bus shone through the smoke, and I pointed at it. The pilot looked for a good place to land and found one not too far away. The Coast Guard's chopper had already landed, but they had to land further away due to the size of the craft.

My feet hit the ground running as fast as I could to reach Calum. The kids were being kept on the school bus, and I banged on the glass door to be let inside.

Only then did it occur to me that I had no legal right to take Calum anywhere, just as a lady who I assumed was his teacher stood up. "Unless you're with the Coast Guard, we can't let you take any child who isn't yours, sir. I am truly sorry."

Calum stood up, shouting, "August! You're here!" He ran to me, throwing his arms around my legs, hugging me.

I picked him up and handed my cell to the teacher. I'd hit the button to call Tawny, putting it on speaker in case I could help with her argument. "Hello?" came her frightened voice.

"Um, this is Mrs. Copperfield, Calum's..."

Tawny wasted no time. "Yes, I know. Let my son go with the man who came for him."

"I'm sorry, I can't," the teacher replied grimly.

"Are you kidding me? You can, and you will," Tawny informed her. "I also have Kyle's and Jasper's mothers right here, and they want their sons to go with August Harlow as well. He'll take them all, with your permission or not, Mrs. Copperfield. We'll deal with the school ourselves, no need for you to worry about your job."

"I, uh...hell, I don't know what to do," the lady said with despair.

"Let us get these kids to safety. Between the three helicopters we brought, we have room for nine," I told her before looking at Calum. "Where are your friends? Let's get them and go."

"Come on, guys!" Calum shouted, and two little boys jumped out of their seats, running to me.

Just as I left the bus with my prize in hand, one of the Coast Guard men came up to me. "How much room do you have, sir?"

"Mine is filled," I told him. "Two more are behind me. There's room for three in each one."

"The children are small," the man said. "I think you can get two in each seat. Would you try that?"

"Sure will. Grab me three more from the bus, and I'll see if they fit." I knew that with that man's help, the teacher would get over her fear of being fired and let the kids go with us.

In no time at all, we had six kids loaded into our helicopter and were heading back to the heliport. Calum was all smiles as we flew through the smoke, even though the wind pitched us around a bit. The kid was fearless.

When we touched down, I helped them out one by one, and they all ran to their parents—the parents must've gotten the memo somehow that the kids would be arriving at the heliport. Calum jumped into his mother's waiting arms as she cried with relief.

Letting them have a moment, I hung back, making sure each kid had found someone before joining Tawny and Calum.

Calum was talking a mile a minute, telling her about the fire and the helicopter ride and how I was like a hero, coming in and saving everyone.

Tawny looked at me over her son's shoulder. "You are a hero, August. You always have been."

What I'd just done was nothing compared to the things I'd done in the war. But I took the compliment. "Thanks, baby. You ready to head home?"

She nodded, still clinging to her son. "I am. I just want to get my baby boy home and hug him for a very long time."

"I bet you do." Wrapping my arm around her and Calum, I led them to the car as the second helicopter arrived, reuniting six more children with their relieved parents.

Although Tawny seemed to still be in a state of shock, Calum was anything but. He rattled on and on about the events, saying how he'd never forget any of it.

Tawny ran her fingers over my arm as tears fell from her pretty green eyes. "How are you, August? Are you okay?"

"I'm fine. You don't need to worry about either of us, we're good, baby. You look like you need a stiff drink and a hot bath though." Turning the corner, I headed to my place. Tawny was in no condition to complain, and she needed some tender loving care.

She looked around, then at me. "Where are you going?"

"To my place," I said with a grin.

"Yes!" Calum shouted. "Finally, we get to see your place!"

"No," Tawny said. "Go to my apartment."

"Baby, you need..."

I didn't get to finish as she said, "No, August. Take us home. I want to go home."

"Well, I'm already on the freeway, and I'll have to find an exit, and that'll take a while," I tried to stall her.

"Momma, I wanna go to his place," Calum demanded.

"No," came her stern reply.

"Tawny, it would be quicker and better if we go to my

house." I took the next exit, turning around to go to her little apartment anyways, but hoping she'd change her mind. "I've got a jacuzzi tub where you can relax. And there's an indoor pool where Calum can play too."

"I don't want to go there, August. Please," she said, and then broke down, crying hard.

"Okay, baby. Okay, you don't have to cry," I tried to soothe her. "I'm taking you home, baby."

My words should've eased her cries, but they didn't. She went on and on, her face in her hands as her sobs continued. I supposed it was because it was the first time she'd come close to losing her son. Leila had been right, there were definitely some differences between a single mom and women who didn't have children.

"Mamma, it's okay. You don't gotta cry," Calum made his own attempt at soothing his mother.

"You don't understand. Neither of you understands at all," Tawny wailed.

"You're right," I admitted. "We don't understand. But I'm taking you home the way you wanted. You can calm down now. I had no idea taking you to my place to pamper you would do this to you." My response had come out sterner than I had intended, and I took a deep breath to calm myself. "I'm sorry. I didn't mean to upset you—you don't know how sorry I am."

That only made her cries go an octave higher, and I had no idea why. Calum was out of danger, and we were getting closer to her home by the second, so I didn't understand why she was carrying on the way she was.

She cried all the way to her place, and once we got inside, she went to her bedroom and closed the door behind her, shutting Calum and me out. I could still hear her crying, and every now and then she would shout something, but it was always a grief-stricken question like 'how?' and 'why did I do this?'

Did she mean me? Why did she get involved with me?

Calum and I sat in the living room after I'd fetched us both bowls of ice cream. Finding a cartoon on TV that I could stomach, we sat and ate our snack, trying to ignore the sounds coming out of his mother's bedroom.

"Man, I'm never goin' on a field trip again," Calum mumbled then took another bite.

"Don't let one little disaster stop you from having fun, Calum. Life's full of them, but we can't stop living just because bad things happen. If we did, we'd never have fun at all. And I like to have fun." Running my hand over his head, I nudged him with my shoulder. "And she'll be okay. Moms, huh?"

"You're tellin' me," Calum agreed, rolling his eyes and sighing, trying to act like an adult.

Lucky for me, Calum liked the same kinds of cartoons I did—having watched my six nieces and nephews grow up, I was no stranger to kids' shows. Before I knew it, we'd talked over the whole last season of Ninja Buddies. Ninja Steve proved to be both of our favorite.

When an hour had passed, we finally heard silence coming from Tawny's bedroom. "Maybe I should go check to make sure she's okay," I told Calum before getting up to go see if she'd passed out, or what had her being so quiet all of a sudden.

But just as I got up, the squeaking of the door stopped me, and I stood right where I was. Calum got on his knees on the sofa, peering at the hallway. "Momma?"

Her auburn waves were a mess. I could tell she'd been running her hands through it incessantly. Her red-rimmed eyes were smudged black with makeup underneath as they looked at me and then at Calum. Her mouth opened, but then snapped shut.

"Baby, are you okay?" I had to ask. I'd never seen anything close to this side of her before, and I didn't know what to do for her.

Shaking her head slowly, her lips parted once more. "I'm not okay at all. I've done something that I wish I hadn't."

"What could possibly be so bad, Tawny?" having asked that, my mind went on a spree through ideas of what she might've done to make her look so guilty. Cheating on me was the only thing that sprang to my mind.

My gut twisted at the thought.

Her eyes darted from me to Calum and back again. "You're both going to be mad at me."

"No way, Momma," Calum quickly said, shaking his head.

All she did was nod in response. Seconds ticked by like hours as she stood there on the other side of the room, barely out of the hallway. "I've been keeping a secret."

She had?

75

CHAPTER 16

Tawny

I was frozen to my spot as both of their eyes were glued on me. In my complete and utter distress, I'd assumed the words would flow out me, unable to stay inside a moment longer. Instead, nothing came to mind as to how to tell the two people in front of me to the information I knew they deserved.

In hindsight, if I'd have been in my right mind, I probably would have done things differently. But the terror of having my baby boy so close to death, and with August almost stopped from doing anything about it...

Well, something inside of me had snapped, and I couldn't keep it to myself any longer.

"A secret?" August asked, his face full of fear.

He'd begun to assume the worst, and that alone had me speeding up my confession. "August, you're the only man..." I paused, looking at my six-year-old son, knowing I had to phrase this the right way for his innocent ears.

"I'm the only man, what, baby?" August asked with

narrowed eyes. He knew something was up, and that he had something to do with it.

"There's never been anyone but you, August Harlow. From the night before you left for boot camp until we met again at the Science Center, there's only been you. I've never been with..." I couldn't say it. Not with my son looking at me.

"Oh..." August murmured. "I see what you're saying." He looked at Calum, and then at me. "So, tell us what you have to say, Tawny," he demanded, a serious yet unreadable expression on his face.

My eyes came to rest on Calum. "Calum, August is your father."

My son looked at me with so much confusion before he asked, "How do you know that?"

August laughed and picked him up, and I let out the breath I hadn't realized I'd been holding. "Because mommies and daddies just know, that's why. I've been wondering about you, Calum. We've got the same hair."

Calum looked up at August's hair, a contemplative gleam in his eyes as his gaze traveled to his father's eyes. "And you have my color eyes, too," Calum said as they looked one another over.

"I think your mom had a good reason for keeping this a secret, because she was worried. But she shouldn't have been worried. I would've been there for you guys. But we shouldn't be mad at her, okay, buddy? She was young and did what she thought best," August told Calum. Then he looked at me. "Come over here and get in on this, baby. No one's mad at you."

My heart began to beat again, so much relief passing through me that for a moment I couldn't move. I'd prepared myself for August to yell at me for a while before storming out. And I'd figured Calum would be mad at me and not understand anything. Seems I'd been wrong.

"I'm sorry for not telling you guys earlier. I was waiting for the right time to tell you, but it's a hard thing to figure out."

August pulled me to his side, his arm wrapping around me as he kissed the side of my head. "You're forgiven. I had a very strong idea Calum was my son, just so you know. I was waiting for you to bring it up—I didn't want to seem rude, if I'd been wrong."

Relief flooded me with his touch and his words. "Thank you."

"I forgive you, too, Momma," Calum said, leaning in to kiss my cheek. "And thanks for telling me. Now when I go back to school, I get to tell all my friends that it was my dad who saved us all. Man, I'm gonna be popler."

August put Calum down and went to the kitchen to grab a bottle of water, bringing it back and handing it to me. "Here, you need to replenish your water. I think you cried just about all of it out."

Taking the bottle from his hand, I said, "Thank you. By the way you guys are taking this news, I can see all that crying was for nothing."

"Yeah," August agreed. He took a seat next to Calum, and I took the one on the other side of our son. "You know, I've had a nagging worry over those fires since the day I ran into you two. I thought it was weird, as there've been wild-fires in California before, and I've never worried this much about them. Maybe the worry will go away now. Maybe I knew one day I'd have to save my little boy from one." He shrugged. "Stranger things have happened."

"Wow," I said as I looked at him. "A little psychic ability

to add to your other superpowers." Giving him a wink, I blew him a kiss.

"And I'm all yours, baby." He ran his hand over Calum's head. "I'd like to sign his birth certificate and give him my last name. And I'll start up a trust fund for him right away."

"What's a trust fund?" Calum asked.

"Oh, just this little thing that'll help you out for the rest of your life. A bonus you get for being my son." August laughed. "Man, that sounds so crazy coming out of my mouth. I have a son!"

"And I have a dad!" Calum added. "I always wanted a dad real bad. Everybody else has one. Well, 'cept for Kaylanna, who has two moms instead of a mom and dad."

As we laughed, I saw the look August had in his hazel eyes. He had a family now. A real family. And it was then that I realized that I'd lost a lot of the control I'd had up to this point. Calum was his son, too, and I knew August well enough to know he was going to do right by the boy, no matter what.

Again, most women would probably be over the moon to finally be able to share this responsibility. But I'd been a single mother for years. I was the one who'd made every decision there'd ever been made concerning Calum. Now August would get to do that, too.

How would we be as co-parents? Would we see eye to eye on everything, or butt heads on everything? And what would that mean for our relationship?

When August got up again, he wiggled his finger at me. "Can I talk to you, Momma, in private?"

Calum went back to watching his cartoon as August took my hand, leading me to my bedroom. When he saw the state of my bed, he chuckled. The blankets were everywhere as I'd fisted them and tossed them around in my little fit of self-pity.

He didn't say a word about the state of the room though. He just closed the door behind us, keeping me between him and the door. His hands moved gently over my cheeks, and then his lips found mine. My chest swelled with love and relief. Everything was going to be okay.

When his mouth left mine, he looked into my eyes. "I want you both to come home with me. I want you both to be with me as much as humanly possible."

And there it was—his first demand. And who was I to turn him down now? Now that he knew Calum was his, I had no right to deny him access to his son. I'd already done so for far too long.

But I was anything but an irresponsible parent. "August, what happens if you and I don't work out? What about Calum?"

Shaking his head as his finger traced a line across my jaw then down to my collarbone, he answered my question. "Tawny, not even married couples know what the future holds for them or their children. We shouldn't worry about all the 'what-ifs'—there are way too many of those. And I can assure you that no matter what happens between us, that boy is mine, and I'll never turn my back on him, or you for that matter. You're both a part of me now."

Knowing he was right, I turned my attention away from the negative to focus on the positive. And the positive was standing right in front of me. I wasn't about to let any 'what-ifs' take away from what we had.

"I'll come, but I should have my own bedroom. Just until I get Calum to stop getting in bed with me," I agreed. "He seems excited and fine now, but this might get a little confusing to him."

"It's not everything that I want, but it's a start," August said, then kissed me again. "At the very least, I'll get to make love to you before you leave my room for the night. And I'll get to wake up and see you every morning. You have no idea how much that excites me."

The way I felt his cock pulse inside his jeans let me know he wasn't lying.

Then his lips trailed up my neck, and his words tickled my ear, "So, you kept your promise to me after all. No one has ever touched you but me. Baby, you have no idea how that makes me feel."

"I think it makes you feel pretty damn good," I said as I jutted my hips out, letting his erection press against my cunt. If there wasn't a little boy sitting in the next room, I would've already been halfway undressed by now.

I didn't even bother to ask if he'd kept his promise, knowing he'd been with other women. It didn't matter. Not really. I knew he loved me, and doubted he'd ever loved anyone else.

"Let's get Calum's and your things packed up and get you home, where you belong." August took my hand, leading me back out to our son. "Hey, Calum, you want to come see your new home, son?"

"Yes, sir!" he jumped up, nearly knocking the empty ice cream bowls off the coffee table. "Oops!" He grabbed them up, taking them to the kitchen then ran to August, grabbing his pants leg. "Hey, can I call you Dad now?"

"You better," August said then messed up his hair. "Son."

My heart was on overdrive. I'd done it. I'd managed to tell the truth, and now we were going to be a happy family. I still had to tell my parents, which I was not looking forward to, but they'd be easy now that the two who really mattered knew the truth.

My world was shaping up rather well. No matter what happened between me and August, my son would always be taken care of. I knew August would see to that—he was a hero right down to his core.

As we left the apartment, August asked, "So, what in that apartment is yours, and what belongs to the owners?"

"Well, we've got all of our clothes and personal things. That's really all that's ours. The place was furnished, all the way down to the dishes and the towels. Except for a few cleaning supplies, everything else belongs to the owner. There's really nothing left for us to do," I told him. "But it's going to feel weird not to have my own place. I mean, I lived with Mom and Dad up until I moved to Los Angeles. This was the first place I'd had on my own, and I was really enjoying it."

"I think you'll like your new place in Hidden Hills," he said with a chuckle before taking my hand. "And for the record, I love the idea of having a family to fill what's been an empty home for way too long."

So that was it. My life had officially been turned upside down—by the father of my child—and in record time, too.

76

CHAPTER 17

August

Bringing Tawny and Calum home had me on cloud nine. I couldn't recall a time I'd been so happy. It was like I was on love overload, and I couldn't quit thinking about our future. "So, that little death trap of a car you drive can be sold, Tawny. I've got plenty of cars for you to choose from. Not to mention the town car with my driver."

"August, you're doing too much for me already. And my car's not a death trap—I'll have you know that the '05 Nissan Sentra is exceptionally designed to withstand a head-on collision or being rear-ended. There are two crumple zones in the frame that..."

I gave her a sideways glance before interrupting her. "Tawny, forget about it. The thing's an ancient piece of crap. And what's mine is yours now anyway."

The laugh that came out of her didn't make sense. "August, we're not married. What's yours isn't mine at all."

"Well, you're the mother of my son—that makes you

something to me. And if I say what's mine is yours, then it is, Tawny Matthews. Fight it all you want, but you're my baby's momma, and I'm going to take care of you both."

"Jesus, I hate being called that," she mumbled. "That makes me sound like some woman from the Jerry Springer show."

"Okay, I'll come up with something better then. But you're important to me, and I'm going to treat you that way. Like it or not, I love you. And now that I know you carried my child inside of you and raised him all on your own for six long years, I owe *you*." The entrance to my place was just ahead, and when I turned into the area in front of the twin gates, Tawny and Calum gasped.

"August, you live behind gates?" Tawny asked me then shook her head. "That sounded so hickish. Ignore me, please. I've never been around any wealthy people before. I don't know how to act."

"Act like yourself," I told her.

Calum took off his seatbelt to get a better look at the house, leaning up on the back of my seat. "Wow!"

"I know, right?" The grandeur of my home wasn't lost on me. I'd grown up in a modest three-bedroom house back in Sebastopol; I knew the home I'd bought was a thing of beauty.

The driveway wasn't as long as some, but it was surrounded by lush vegetation, making it appear jungle-like. "August, I had no idea," Tawny gushed.

"You knew I lived in Hidden Hills; what do you mean you had no idea?" I asked her as I pulled to a stop at the front entrance.

"I mean I had no idea how huge this place would be, or how wonderful," she replied with a smile.

"Yeah, it sure is," Calum chimed in as he got out of the

car. Tawny and I followed his lead, getting out, too. "I can't wait to see the inside."

Standing in front of the house, I pointed to the right side. "Okay, this home is divided into three sections. Right in the middle is the entrance room, also called a foyer. The staircase is located there. Behind that room is the main living area—it's huge. Off to the right, you'll find the indoor pool, the bar, the game room, a media room, and another sitting area."

"All that's just on the right side?" Tawny asked with curiosity.

"All of that is just on the ground floor. Upstairs are three bedrooms, all with their own private baths, enormous walk-in closets, and sitting areas," I informed her.

"And on the left?" she asked as she turned to look at the other side of the home.

"On the left, you have the kitchen, the breakfast nook, the informal dining room, and the formal dining room, the theater room, plus a sitting area. And above them on the second floor are four more bedrooms with all the same amenities of the rooms in the other wing. My bedroom is located in the left wing, so I'd love it if you two chose rooms in that wing, too. I'd like to be close to you guys." Wrapping my arm around Tawny's waist, I pulled her close to me, whispering, "Especially you, baby."

A sexy smile curled her pink lips as she looked down, batting her lashes. "August, you're so bad."

Give her one soft kiss to the side of her neck. "Only with you, baby."

Heading inside, I prepared myself for their reactions—and was pleased with them as Calum gasped after I opened the door. "Gosh!"

"Lord, August, you've lived here all alone?" Tawny asked.

"This place is enormous." Her eyes moved over the redwood staircase. Two sets of curved stairs ran up to the next floor, the ceiling open all the way to the top, where a skylight bathed the room with light. The grey marble glistened in the rays, shining brightly.

"I've lived here all alone," I answered as I gave her a little squeeze. "And now I have you two to share this place with. Tawny, I've never been this happy in my entire life. I want you guys to make this place your home."

"That'll take some doing, August." Her eyes were wide as she looked all over the place. "This place is like a five-star hotel or something."

"It took me a minute to get used to it, too." I kissed her cheek. "You guys will get used to it before you know it."

The door at the back of the room opened, and there stood my head housekeeper. "Ah, Denise, how nice to see you. I've got a couple of people who'll be joining me here from now on. I'd like to introduce you to Tawny Matthews, my girlfriend."

Tawny reached out to shake Denise's hand. "It's a pleasure to meet you, Denise."

"And you too," Denise said with raised brows. "And who's this little guy?"

"I'm Calum," my son said as he stepped up to shake her hand, too. "I just found out that August is my daddy."

Denise's eyebrows rose even higher as she looked at me and opened her arms up wide. "Well, congratulations, August!"

Denise was incredibly maternal, with three children of her own, and she always treated me as if I were her fourth. "Thank you, Denise." She let me go as she looked at Calum. "And he looks just like his strapping daddy, too."

"Tawny and Calum will be living with me from now on,

so please help them settle in the same way you did with me. They're from my hometown, so this is an adjustment for them, the same as it was for me when I bought the place and hired you on." Running my arm back around Tawny, I went on, "After hiring Denise, I thought I didn't need anyone else to help with the upkeep of this place. She helped me hire the rest of the staff—she has a lot of experience working for people with large homes."

"Good to know," Tawny said as she looked at Denise, "because I already feel overwhelmed, and we're just in the foyer."

"I'll draw you a map, so you don't get lost," Denise said as she clapped her hands. "I'll be in the kitchen, come there last, and I'll give you the map."

The skip in my housekeeper's step told me she was just as excited as I was to have more people in the home she took pride in caring for. As she headed toward the kitchen, I moved my little family into the next room.

Windows ran along the back wall of the main living area, the mountains offering a gorgeous view. "This is one of my favorite places to sit and watch the sunrise." I nuzzled my nose against Tawny's. "And now you guys can join me to watch it, too."

"This view is to die for," she murmured. "God, August, this is just too good to be true."

"No, it's not. I thought the same when I first bought the place. But it is true, and now you're a part of this as well." Taking her by the chin, I placed a soft kiss on her lips while Calum was distracted with his own exploration of the room. "How about we see the rest of the downstairs, and then I'll take you up, and you two can pick out your new bedrooms."

The rest of the tour had them nearly speechless, which was a rare thing for Calum. When I took them up to the left wing, I pointed at my door, which was at the end of the hall-way. "That's my room down there. If you'll notice, there are rooms very close to mine and right across the hall from each other. Should we check those out first?"

Calum ran to the door on the right and stopped, frozen in place as Tawny and I caught up. "Momma, look," he muttered.

Tawny's eyes looked like they were about to fall out of their sockets—and I couldn't blame her. The room was bigger than the apartment they'd been staying in. "Oh, Lord!"

I walked in, explaining as I went. "This is the sitting area with a television," I gestured to the flat screen that hung on the wall in front of a couple of tan leather sofas. I opened the door at the back of that room, going into the bedroom. "There's tons of room in here to fill this place with toys of all kinds. What do you think, Calum?"

"I think I'm in heaven," he said with a giggle as he ran all over the room. A queen-sized bed caught his attention, and he hopped up on it and spread his little body out as wide as he could. "I can't believe this! Is this whole bed for me?"

"It is." Tawny went to sit on it too, moaning at how comfortable it was. "Oh, August, this bed's so comfy." She pulled Calum up and put him on her lap. "I bet you'll sleep like a baby in this bed, don't you?"

"Prolly," he agreed.

After showing them the attached bathroom with a stand-up tiled shower and a bathtub, I took them to the closet at the back. Neither Calum nor Tawny knew what it was. "And what kinda room's this?" he asked.

"This is your closet." I opened the doors, which were built to look like they were only walls. "See, your things will go in here. And the bench is for you to sit on to put your shoes on." I went to the other side of the room, opening those hidden doors. "Your shoes will go in here on these shelves."

"That's a whole lotta shelves, Dad," Calum told me as his eyes grew wide.

"It is." I opened the last two doors, showing him the drawers that were inside of them. "And here are the drawers for your other things."

Neither quite knew how to act; they were clearly overwhelmed. And when I took Tawny to a room that was very similar to Calum's, she began to cry. I held her in my arms to soothe her. "This is too much, August."

"No, this is what your life is now, Tawny. You belong here with me. Our son deserves this. And so do you." I kissed her on top of her head as I swayed with her.

Resting her head on my chest, we watched our son as he ran around the room, marveling at everything. The puzzle of my life felt as if it was finally being solved. Hope filled me for our future.

Nothing could stop me now.

77

CHAPTER 18

August

"I started out this day nearly catching on fire, and now I'm swimmin' in a pool that's inside a house that I get to live in!" Calum said just before he jumped off the diving board, creating a splash that echoed inside the glass room.

Tawny and I sat on the edge of the pool, our feet dangling in the water. She didn't have a bathing suit, so she couldn't get in. I opted to sit out with her, and Calum was happy to swim in a pair of shorts.

Our fingers entwined, our shoulders touching as we leaned against each other, we watched our son playing away in front of us. I don't think I'd ever been in a better mood. The sound of the door opening had us turning to see who it was. "Good evening, sir," my chef, Tara, greeted us. "I've come to see what you all want for dinner. With the new additions, I'd like to prepare a meal they'll enjoy, too."

Calum dog-paddled his way to us, the red life jacket he

wore keeping him afloat. "I love chili dogs. Oh, and I love French fries."

Tawny cleared her throat. "But little boys who want to grow up to be strong men like their fathers have to eat more than junk food to get that way." She directed her attention to Tara. "So, anything healthy is good with us. I don't like to eat fried foods and don't like Calum to, either. I've always stayed away from sugary foods and drinks as well. I'm a nurse, so nutrition is more important to me than taste."

"Ah, I see. So, let me see if this is a typical meal you'd enjoy," Tara said, getting a bead on Tawny. "Roasted chicken in an almond sauce, organic fresh green beans with wild mushrooms, and baked sweet potatoes with a touch of cinnamon and brown sugar butter. How's that sound?"

"That sounds nutritious and delicious," Tawny said with a wide smile. "And I usually give Calum an eight-ounce glass of almond or coconut milk, or a mixture of the two, unsweetened, of course. And a glass of water, too."

With a nod, Tara had one more question, "I usually serve fowl with white wine. Is that okay with you, ma'am?"

"Yes, of course. And water though, please make sure there's water on the table," Tawny said with a smile. "I'm an avid water drinker. It's like a little miracle, health-wise."

"I will remember that then. I'll have the minifridge in your bedroom stocked with some bottled water, and I'll stock Calum's with some healthy choices, too." And with that, Tara left us alone once more.

Tawny shook her head. "That was weird, huh?"

"What, telling our chef how you want to eat?" I asked with a chuckle. "No, it's what you're supposed to do. Tara's a great chef and eager to please, so feel free to let her know whatever you want." Her lips were just too close not to kiss, so I stole one kiss from her as Calum paddled around the pool. "He's wearing himself out rather well, don't you think?"

She nodded and gave me a sexy little grin. "After this, a filling meal, a warm bath, and a bedtime story, he should be out like a light."

"Then Mommy and Daddy can play." I kissed her again. "Thank you for coming here with me."

Leaning her head on my shoulder, she ran her hand over my chest. "Thank you for asking us to come. My pride gets in my way sometimes."

"That's okay." One look at Calum as he climbed out of the pool to go down the slide reminded me of something that had been on my mind. "Tawny, I thought you told me you were on the pill that night."

She ducked her head, suddenly shy—and maybe feeling a little guilty. "Yeah, you remember that right."

"So, how did you manage to get pregnant?" I took her by the chin to get her to look at me again.

"Well," she said, then her eyes cut to the left before coming back to meet mine. "I lied about that."

"Why on Earth would you lie about that?" I asked her.

"Because I wanted you. And I didn't have any condoms and doubted you did. And I wanted to feel you and only you. I know that was immature of me—and very wrong and unfair to you. And I knew the risk I was taking. But I didn't care. I wanted you so damn badly, nothing else mattered to me." Her cheeks heated with embarrassment. "I'm sorry, August. I never meant to get pregnant. I never meant to hurt you in any way. That's why I kept it to myself. I felt it to be my responsibility, not yours."

"But he's my blood, baby. I'm not trying to make you feel bad, but you should know that if you had told me you were pregnant, then I wouldn't have stayed in the marines past my initial two-year commitment." My thoughts turned to what had happened after the first two years had gone by. I'd been on some very dangerous missions, missions I would never have taken if I'd known I had a kid.

"I'm sorry. I really am," she whispered. "You and I were nothing to each other at the time. That was my biggest reason behind keeping things to myself."

I nodded, understanding her much better then. "I'm sorry, too. I shouldn't have just loved you and left you like that. There were plenty of ways we could've stayed in touch. My reason for not staying in touch was because I wanted you to feel free to be with other guys, maybe even fall in love. Not in a million years did I think you'd actually keep the promise you made to me that night."

Blinking a few times, Tawny sighed. "Yeah, well, having a kid makes dating pretty difficult. Hell, I've had doctors ask me out, and I've turned every one of them down. Bringing anyone around Calum just seemed wrong to me. Being with anyone else just didn't excite me the way being with you did."

Stroking her hair, I had something to admit to her, too. "I can't lie and tell you that I kept my promise I made to you that night. But I can tell you this—no one compared to you. No one ever filled my mind and heart the way the memory of you did—the way you do now."

Her green eyes looked at me, filled with love and hope. "I hate what happened today with Calum and the wildfire scare, but I love the fact that it drew the truth out of me. I knew it the moment you took over, and I couldn't think of anything else other than that you both needed to know what you truly are to each other."

"It's crazy how things in this world work." My fingers played with the collar of her dress, touching her skin lightly, loving how each touch sent sparks of electricity traveling up my fingers, through my hand, and up my arm. Our connection was real. Our love was real.

One little voice nagged at my brain, though. *If she'd told you that you were a father, you would've been out of the marines long before that gun misfired.*

Closing my eyes, I tried to rid my mind of that thought. What happened had happened. I couldn't allow my inner demons to get in the way of my happiness.

So, I opened my eyes to look at the woman I loved. "I love you, Tawny. No matter what's happened, I love you."

The smile she gave me made my heart melt as her hand moved over my cheek. "And I love you, too. I'll spend the rest of my life proving that to you and making up for the years you lost with our son."

Sure, she will, the nagging voice in my head said. *She can't change the past though, can she?*

78

CHAPTER 19

Tawny

The day had taken its toll on Calum, and when he laid his head on the soft pillow, his eyes closed almost immediately. August read him a story, but only got a quarter of the way through it before Calum made light snoring sounds.

"He's out," I said, taking the book out of August's hands to put it on the nightstand.

August gazed at me as he sat on the edge of the bed. "Now what should we do?"

My body ached for his; it had for hours. Taking his hand, I pulled him up, and then linked my arm around his. "I'm thinking I'll just turn in and see you in the morning."

He'd waited until we'd gotten out of Calum's room and closed the door behind us before he lifted me and threw me effortlessly over his shoulder. "I'm thinking something very different from that." His hand connected with my ass, making me yelp with excitement.

I had yet to see his bedroom. A dark green comforter

spread over his huge bed. "Is this bigger than a king-sized bed, August?" I asked as he threw me down on it.

"It is. But as big as this Texas king is, you still won't be able to get away from me on it." He shucked off his jeans, then his shirt, leaving him in his tight black boxer briefs.

Grabbing me by the legs, he pulled me to the edge of the bed, my dress riding up as he pulled me to him to splay one hand over the front of my panties. He fisted the silky material before ripping them off. "Oh, how sweet it is to know I've got you right where I've wanted you for so long now."

"Do you always get what you're after, August Harlow?" I asked with a wicked grin.

He nodded before stepped back. The bulge in his underwear told me he'd been thinking about taking me to his bedroom for some time. Extending one finger, he wiggled it in a come-hither gesture.

My dress and bra still on, I got on my hands and knees, making my way to the edge of the bed where he stood waiting for me. His cock was at the right level, and I stopped crawling to pull the waistband down, releasing his massive erection. "Oh, my, my, my." I licked my lips as I looked up at him. "Now this looks delicious. Do you mind if I sample this tasty treat?"

He shook his head and I went to work, licking the tip while moving my hands up and down his long shaft. After teasing him for a while, I opened my mouth, sliding it over the soft skin. The groan he made had me feeling pretty great about my skills.

I'd been doing a little research on the subject and had seen a few videos on how to please your man. And my man was sounding pretty pleased at that moment.

Moving my mouth up and down while playing with his balls, he made the sexiest sounds, pulling my hair as he hissed some choice curse words. "Oh, baby, damn you're good at this."

I'd just gotten the slightest taste of salty pre-cum on my tongue when he pulled my hair, yanking my head back with a solid jerk. When my eyes met his, I saw fire in them and knew he didn't want to shoot his load down my throat the way I thought he'd like to. "No?" I asked as I wiped my mouth with the back of my hand.

"No, I want to be inside of you when I do that." He lifted my dress off over my head then took off my bra. "On your knees, but face the other way this time."

I complied, ready to do whatever he said. My trust in the man knew no bounds. His hands moved over my ass, caressing it. One hard slap made me yelp, but I wiggled it for him to do it again. He gave me another and another, leaving it stinging before he kissed it all over.

Soft kisses peppered my ass then one long lick down my crack had me tingling inside. He'd flattened his tongue, pulling my cheeks apart to lick me over and over, all the way up then all the way down the crack of my ass.

Wetness dripped down the insides of my thighs as I grew more desperate for him with every passing moment. He reached around me as he licked me, taking my nub between his thumb and forefinger and twisting it. A continuous moan came from me as he played with my body until I was on the brink of an orgasm.

He stopped licking, taking me by the waist and turning me over to finish me off. The man loved to drink me up and did so as often as he could. His tongue ran through my folds, pointed and sharp. Then he flattened his tongue again to lick up my mound, tapping my clit with each stroke.

My hands fisted in his hair as I watched him eat me. Inside, I was one hot mess, my stomach tight as it readied for an intense climax. When his lips pressed against my vagina and he blew warm air into me, I cried out with pleasure, "Yes!"

In went his tongue as he fucked me with it. I arched my body up to help him go deeper into me, and he took my ass in his hands, holding my hips off the bed as he feasted on me.

The damn broke inside of me, and I cried out as the orgasm took over, "August! Yes!"

His hungry mouth took everything I'd released for him. When he was satisfied, he moved up my body, kissing me all the way up until his mouth landed on mine, and his body pressed me to the bed.

Our tongues dueled with each other, taking everything they could as we shared our combined tastes. I pulled my legs up, bending my knees, and his cock thrust into me. The orgasm was still rolling through me, and he groaned as I spasmed around him. Wrenching his mouth from mine as I held tightly to his head in protest, he moaned, "Fuck, baby, you feel so damn good."

"Your cock fills me up perfectly," I moaned right back as I moved my body with his, creating waves of sensation.

His hazel eyes glistened down at me. "You like it when this fat cock fucks your sweet pussy, baby?"

His dirty talk never failed to turn me on even more. "Yeah, I do." I pulled my head up to bite his lower lip, tugging it.

He growled, flipped us over so that I was on top, then put his hands on my waist, lifting me up to stroke his hard dick. My tits jiggled, and he watched them with a hungry expression on his handsome face. "God, those tits are so full and bouncy. I bet they were even bigger when you were pregnant."

I ran my hands over my tits as I rode him. "They were nearly twice this size. I had to have a special bra back then."

The way he bit his lip as he looked at my tits thrilled me. Then he leaned up, taking one in his mouth and sucking on it hard while licking the nipple.

His dark, silky hair called to me, and I ran my hands through it as he sucked me, making my stomach pull with each tug. It took me no time at all to come again, writhing on top of him as he continued to suck.

Gasping with the intensity of the climax, I screamed, "August! August!"

But he kept sucking me while moving me up and down his cock. When his mouth left that tit, I moaned—half in protest and half in relief—and he took the other one, sucking it hard as he rolled the nipple between his teeth. Moving me faster, he took me to another climax.

I could barely breathe as the orgasms took everything out of me. He turned, putting me on my back and plunging his cock into me as he held the top part of his body off me, making sure I could breathe.

Hanging onto his neck, I looked right back into his eyes as he moved in and out of me. There was something in those hazel eyes. Then his lips parted as he said, "I want you to have another baby."

He kept moving as I lay there, barely able to think. The way he moved, the way he filled me, the way he looked at me all compelled me to say one word, "Yes."

With a loud growl, he moved faster and much harder as he plunged into me with a fierceness I'd never seen in him before. Over and over, he thrust into me until he bellowed with his release, a release that took my body along for the ride as an orgasm flushed through my body, all the way to the ends of my toes.

Loudly, we panted as we tried to catch our breath. He stayed right where he was until the last jerk of his cock, then he fell to one side of me. We laid there, side by side, looking up the ceiling.

As the high I'd been on slowly came down, I realized what I'd told him. He rolled to lie on his side, his palm flattening on my stomach. "Soon that'll be filled with my child once again. And this time I'll get to experience every bit of it."

This kind of talk was new to me. He wanted me to have his baby. His body glowed with the desire to see me pregnant with his child. And that's when it hit me. The guilt that I'd hidden from myself for too long.

Tears came in waves, falling down the sides of my face. "I am so sorry, August. So damn sorry for what I did."

He watched me cry, just looking at me as I cried. Then his hand moved over my eyes, covering them. "Okay, that's all the tears you get to shed over that, Tawny. I don't want to see any more come out of you over that. What's done is done. We can't change it. We can only move forward from here. You and I will build a family. You and I will be here for our children. Forever and always. Do you understand me?"

Gasping to try to control myself, I choked out, "I do."

"You do," he echoed me. "And when the preacher asks you his questions in that little white church back in Sebastopol, I want you to say those exact two words to everything he says. And I promise to do the same."

Gulping back the tears, I tried to comprehend what he was saying. The smile he wore made my heart flip. "Are you asking me to marry you, August Harlow?"

He nodded. "So, what do you say? Wanna get hitched and have lots of my babies?"

I had to laugh. "Lots of babies? I only remember agreeing to one."

"Yep. I want a dozen or so," he laughed, and then kissed me. "Keeping you barefoot and pregnant sounds good to me."

"Neanderthal," I hissed playfully as I batted his chest.

I'd never given any thought to having more kids. But then again, I'd never given any thought to being married. So, what did I want?

I wanted August in my life forever, that was a given. I wanted Calum to have a great life, and it would be better if he had brothers and sisters. And August and I had already made one great little boy.

His fingers trailed over my stomach. "I promise to make you happy, Tawny."

"You already do," I said then pulled my head up to kiss him.

He gripped the back of my neck, holding me tight and kissing me deeply. The way my heart pounded, and my body shook told me I had to do it. I had to just give in and give myself entirely to the man I loved.

When he released my lips, he rested his forehead against mine. "So, what do you say? Want to become Mrs. Harlow?"

"I do."

79

CHAPTER 20

August

Waking up alone wasn't how I'd envisioned spending my first morning with my brand spanking-new fiancé. But that's exactly how I woke up. No soft skin next to me to caress, no vanilla-scented silky auburn hair to smell, no warm body to hold for a while before I had to get up.

There were meetings to get to. Swank's grand opening was getting closer and closer, and so much had to be done. We'd suffered a setback when the mother of Gannon's son had arranged to have a small explosive device go off inside the unfinished club, so we were doubling up on projects, trying to meet our opening night. More construction workers had to be hired, and we were all meeting with the crew foreman to plan out the strategy to make sure things got done on time.

New Year's Eve would bring our joint endeavor to life. I couldn't wait to see how the club would turn out with my own eyes. And knowing I'd have Tawny, my fiancé, on my arm was the icing on that magnificent cake.

Groaning as I rolled out of bed, I went to shower and dress before heading to Tawny's bedroom to see if Calum had indeed ventured to her bed in the middle of the night.

When I opened the door, I saw her sitting up on the side of the bed, yawning and stretching. Her hair a wild mess; she wore one of my t-shirts. It hit her near her knees, it was so much bigger than she.

Smack dab in the middle of the king-sized bed lay Calum. "So, he did come to find you then," I said, drawing her attention to me.

"August, what the heck are you doing?" She ran her hands through her hair, knowing it was a wreck.

Making strides across the room, I got to her and picked her up, kissing her on the mouth. She pushed at my chest to make me let her go. "You look cute when you wake up, Tawny."

"No, I don't. Let me go. I need to pee." She pushed at my chest a little harder, and I let her go. Dashing away to the bathroom, I watched her ass jiggle under the white t-shirt, my cock twitching to life.

Looking down, I whispered, "Not right now. Just chill."

I had a plan to put into action after my meeting, and I looked around the room, finding her rings on the night-stand. She must've taken them off to sleep. I noticed the little sapphire ring she wore on her ring finger and scooped it up, putting it in the breast pocket of my Armani suit.

I knew she'd miss it, but figured I'd be replacing it with a sparkling, enormous engagement ring later on anyway. Calum wasn't stirring at all but was still snoring lightly, his dark hair standing straight up on one side.

Leaning over, I kissed his forehead, and then heard the

bathroom door open. Out stepped a fresh-faced Tawny, her hair combed, face washed, and teeth brushed.

I went straight for her, gathering her in my arms and rocking back and forth with her. I went in for a proper good morning kiss, and our mouths collided softly and tenderly. She tasted like the mint toothpaste she'd used, and she smelled like apricots—I assumed from whatever she'd used to wash her face with.

I rested my forehead against hers when our kiss ended. "Hi there, fiancé."

"Hi to you, too, fiancé." She giggled softly. "I've got to get Calum up and get him ready for school."

"Have Max drive you two. I've got a meeting this morning and a few things to do after that." Taking out the credit card I'd taken from my wallet for her, I slipped it into her hand. "And have Max take you to Rodeo Drive. I want you to do a bit of shopping today. That enormous closet looks a little empty right now."

"Oh, no, August. I can't..." she tried to protest.

But I kissed her again, putting an end to her protests. "You can, and you will. And buy Calum a bunch of new clothes, too. And don't skimp at all. I want my family looking sharp. When I come home, I'm going to inspect the closets, and I better see them close to bursting. I do realize you can only do so much shopping in a day, but I want to see a lot more in there, including shoes and underclothes, too. Buy yourself some sexy underwear and bras, too—don't forget about those."

She shook her head as she looked at me. "August, that's just not me."

"Fine, I'll have a personal shopper do that then if you're going to refuse." I would get my way, one way or another.

"Fine," she admitted with a sigh of defeat. "I'll do it."

"You know, Tawny, most women would be over the moon if a billionaire handed them a credit card—one that has no limit by the way—and told them to go crazy." I kissed the tip of her little turned up nose, ending my lecture.

"I know. Thank you," she conceded. "I'll try to get used to being spoiled rotten."

"Yes, you will, because I aim to spoil both of you rotten, and when our next one comes along, they'll get the same treatment." Moving one hand down between us, I ran it over her flat stomach. "You can ditch the birth control pills now."

She blinked at me. "Are you sure, August? I mean, you want to get married, and that's going to be a lot on its own. You sure about bringing a baby into this so quickly?"

"We already have one kid, so why wait?" I couldn't say I liked her line of questioning. Why should we wait? What did it matter?

"Well, okay then. I'll stop taking my pills. But it'll take a little while for them to get completely out of my system, months actually." She ran her hands up and down my arms as she looked at me. "So, don't get upset when it doesn't happen right away, okay?"

"Okay," I said, then pecked her cheek. "I've got to run. I'll be back by dinner time tonight. You have a great day shopping, and don't you dare forget to eat some lunch. Hell, call a girlfriend to go with you—treat her to a day out, too."

"August, I don't have any friends here yet. I haven't started working, so I haven't had many opportunities to make friends since I moved here." She looked down but then looked back at me. "Hey, do you think Leila would like to join me?"

"I know she would. Give her a call after you drop Calum off at school, and see if she's free." With one more kiss, I left her and headed off to my meeting.

Gannon and Nixon were already at the King's Road Café when I got there, though our foreman had yet to show. Scones and coffee had already been served, so I took a seat and helped myself. "How are you gentlemen doing this fine morning?"

Gannon's eyes were bright. "I'm doing pretty damn good, considering all the shit that's come my way lately."

Nixon chuckled as he sipped his steaming hot coffee. "Would that little blonde babysitter have anything to do with that?"

"She might," Gannon said as he winked at our other business partner. Then his eyes fell on me. "And you look like you've got extra pep in your step as well, August. Any particular reason for that?"

"Well, I found out yesterday that I'm a father to a six-year-old boy. His mother and I had one night of mind-blowing sex the night before I left for boot camp, producing a child that she's just confessed is mine." The waiter came up, interrupting my news. He stood, poised for my drink order without saying a thing. "Espresso macchiato, please." He hurried off to get my drink, and I turned my attention back to my friends.

"And you're happy about it, so that means it's with a woman you like," Nixon said. "So, both you guys are fathers. Well, now I feel left out—not that I wish some random woman would show up and tell me I've fathered a child."

I nodded. "The mother of my child isn't some random woman. She and I were neighbors back home—I've known her as long as I can remember. I've already asked Tawny to marry me. That's her name, by the way, and my son's name is Calum."

Nixon smiled. "Way to go. I'm glad you've found some-one. I'm actually a little jealous—to tell you the truth, I can't get this one girl off my mind. We had one crazy Halloween night, and she's been stuck in my head ever since. But that wasn't that long ago, so maybe this feeling will fade, who knows?"

Gannon laughed. "I'm asking Brooke to marry me on Thanksgiving at her family's get-together. Wish me luck, guys. Her brother Brad is my best friend, and I've been told to keep my hands off his baby sister. As if I could help that. She's the most lovable woman I've ever met. So, I'll face Brad and the rest of her family's wrath if I must to make her mine in every way possible."

I didn't envy Gannon with that mess. "At least I don't have to worry about Tawny's family. She's an only child, so there're no siblings to deal with there. And her parents don't seem to interfere too much in her life. I think Tawny and I have found what everyone looks for. True love." I looked at the waiter as he brought the drink to me, placing it in front of me on the table.

"Are you three ready to order?" he asked us.

"Not yet," Gannon informed him. "We have one more coming."

With a nod the waiter left us, and we got back to our conversation. Nixon mused, "So, this grand opening we're having won't be at all like we initially envisioned. For you guys, anyway. I'm still a free man. Hey, maybe Katana will call me, and I can invite her to be my date for that night!"

Gannon looked at Nixon with wide eyes. "You don't have her number?"

"Nah, it was a one-night thing, but I gave her mine just in case." Nixon looked hopeful. "Maybe she'll call. I hope she calls."

I laughed. "You sound like you really like this girl, Nixon."

He nodded, and then took a sip of his coffee. "When we came up with this grand idea to open a nightclub for the uber-wealthy, part of the plan was for us to score hot chicks. Now that's not even on the agenda for any of us, really."

"Who knew?" Gannon added.

There we sat, three friends who'd gone into a business venture together with the grand fantasies of single men. Only now we all seemed to be preoccupied with special women. It seemed we'd never get to have even one night of unadulterated philandering.

But they'd both had years of living that kind of life, and I'd had my fair share as well. How funny that things change so quickly.

Things were going much better than I had ever expected, and my life was changing for the better with each passing moment. Things could only get better from here.

80

CHAPTER 21

Tawny

When I realized my sapphire ring was missing, I had a pretty good idea where it had gone. August had to have taken it to use it to buy me an engagement ring. That didn't surprise me one bit.

I'd spent the day shopping with Leila, and we had a very nice time. With her help, I actually made a lot of purchases and was waiting patiently for August to come home so I could show him just how much I'd added to Calum's closet as well as mine.

But the hours ticked by and finally, at seven in the evening, he graced us with his presence. We'd been waiting in the main living area which was right behind the foyer. I thought that would be the best place if we wanted to see him when he first arrived home.

Calum ran to August as he came through the doorway. "Dad!"

"Calum!" August shouted right back at him. Picking him up, I noticed him whispering something to our son, and

Calum's little head nodded in a fast motion. "Good, glad you agree."

August was up to something, and I sidled up to him, my arms open wide. "Good evening."

"Ah, did you miss me?" he asked as he put Calum down, so I could hug him.

"A little," I said as he moved into my arms. The way his body wrapped around me made my heart skip a beat. I loved being in his arms.

When our hug ended, August got down on one knee and looked up at me, still holding my left hand. "Tawny Susan Matthews, would you do me the great honor of becoming my lawfully wedded wife?"

"Um, yeah," I said as I rolled my eyes. "I told you yes last night."

Narrowing his eyes at me, he whispered, "I'm doing this for him."

Oh! For Calum!

"Oh, then my answer is yes. Yes, my one and only true love, I will marry you."

He pulled something out of his pocket and flipped the lid of a small black box. Inside was a sparkling solitaire that looked like it cost a small fortune. Now I was surprised, and my free hand flew to cover my gaping jaw. "August!"

"Ah, now that's the reaction I was looking for." He slipped the ring on my finger, and Calum came to look at it.

"Man, that's big, Momma." Calum took my hand to get a closer look at the ring. "So, my dad will be your husband, just like in real families. This is great!"

Rising from his position on the floor, August placed his hands on my hips then kissed my lips. "Thank you, baby."

I looked at the ring then back at him. "Thank you, too."

August turned away, picking up Calum and then taking my hand. He took us to sit on one of the sofas, placing Calum on his knee. "We'd like to talk to you about something, Calum."

I looked at August with a questioning expression. "Oh, we would?"

August nodded then pointed at my tummy. "Yeah, we would."

Now I understood, but I wasn't sure I wanted to talk to my six-year-old about a thing like that. "August, maybe it's a bit too soon. And he's already had one big shot of news today with the marriage."

"Well, I think he should know," August argued.

Huffing with resolve, I nodded. I knew August's tenacity would win out in the end anyway. "Proceed."

Calum looked back and forth at us. "What's up?"

August took the lead. "Calum, what do you think about becoming a big brother?"

Calum looked at me. "Are you gonna have a baby, Momma?"

"No, there's not one in my tummy yet. But your daddy and I would like to have one. Is that something you'd be okay with?" I asked my son.

Calum looked at August with a thoughtful expression. "But I just got you, and if you have a baby then I'll have to share you."

"Calum, you're my oldest son. My very first child. You'll always have a place in my heart that no one else will ever have." August ran his hand over Calum's head. "I promise that you and I will spend tons of time together, no matter who or what comes along. And you'd get to help a lot with the baby too, you know. You'd get to be a big brother—the oldest of the family your mom and I would like to have."

"That might be fun," Calum said as he looked up at the ceiling, thinking.

"I'd like to have a big family, Calum. That would mean you'd have lots of kids—brothers and sisters—to play with. You'd never be lonely." August took him by the chin. "You'll never be alone."

"Well, I think it'll be okay then," Calum said. "So, go ahead, have a baby if you want to."

"Glad to have your blessing, son," August said then kissed him on the forehead. "Now, I've got one more thing I want to talk to you about."

"What else could there possibly be, August?" I asked him, as I thought Calum already had too much on his plate as it was.

"The sleeping situation," he informed me. "I want you to sleep in my room with me."

Sucking in air, I couldn't believe what he'd blurted out. "August!"

Calum was the one to say something first. "Don't mommies and daddies sleep in the same room, Momma?"

August answered him, "Yes, they do, Calum. But you seem to have a little habit of getting into your momma's bed in the middle of the night, and that might be a problem."

"Why?" Calum asked as he looked at August. "I can just come to your bed and climb in."

My brows rose as I looked at my fiancé, who seemed to think he knew more than I did where Calum was concerned. "Now, how do you plan to explain that, August Harlow?"

"Easy," he said with a wink. "Well, you could do that, Calum. But I was thinking you could get used to sleeping the whole night in your own bed. You see, that way you'll be a good influence on your younger brothers and sisters when they come along and face the same problem you're having."

"Oh, I don't think it's a problem," Calum said as he shook his head. "I just like snuggling with Momma is all."

"Me, too," August said, making me blush.

Calum nodded. "She's very cozy."

"I agree," August added. "Maybe we can come up with a deal, so she doesn't get sick of us snuggling her all the time. I get her at night, and you get her all day."

Calum chewed his lower lip as he thought about that. "Well, maybe that might be okay. But how 'bout this idea. If I wake up, and I'm feeling scared, can Momma come sleep with me then?"

August smiled, and he reached out to shake our son's little hand. "That's a deal, son."

As they shook hands, I sighed, knowing my life really was changing—and fast.

After we ate dinner and gave Calum a bath, we tucked him in, August reading him a book while I sat on the other side of our son, stroking his hair. The way Calum looked at us both made my heart swell with joy.

My little boy was finally getting to feel what his friends had felt their whole lives, the love of a mother and father who adored him.

We stayed with him until he'd fallen asleep. True to what his father had told him just after dinner, there was a baby monitor placed on the nightstand next to his bed. All he had to do if he woke up and was afraid was call out to me, and I'd come running. August had placed the receiving monitor on the nightstand on the right side of his bed, which he told me was mine now.

August was trying hard to make things work perfectly.

And so far, everything was going the way he wanted—and I loved it all, too.

Somehow August made Calum do things I couldn't. And he did so without hurting our son. More love built up in my heart for the man with each passing day.

When we climbed into bed that first night, I felt a sense of relief. No longer did I have to carry all the responsibility of raising our son on my shoulders alone. Now there was a father to share that with. And soon he'd be my husband, and we'd grow our family together.

In my wildest dreams, I had never imagined my life turning out like this.

We made love that night, soft and sweet. Our bodies moved together like they'd been built just for each other. He moved with soft thrusts, and I arched up to meet each one. Our love filled the entire room as we simultaneously climaxed.

He brushed my hair back as he looked into my eyes. "I love you more than you can even understand, baby."

"I understand perfectly because I love you that much too." I kissed his bearded cheek and ran my hand over the tattoo on his left pec. SEMPER FI was written in text, surrounded by guns, an eagle, and a chopper. Quite the work of art, and I loved the way it looked on him.

My marine was one rugged man. He would always be my hero.

Falling asleep in his arms was like heaven to me. Though I was a little annoyed when he'd brought it up, I couldn't be happier that he'd made our son feel comfortable with us being able to do this.

Life would be fantastic with August by my side.

Hours had passed when my eyes suddenly flew open, my sleep disturbed by August as he tossed and turned beside me. Some mumbled words came from him, and I reached over to shake him awake. "August, wake up, you're having a bad dream."

His left arm flew back, smacking me in the face. I tasted blood right away, my lip busted from the blow. "August!" I shouted and moved back.

Blood was rolling down my arm as my hand covered my mouth. I rolled over and over until I got to the edge of the huge bed. Grabbing some tissue off the nightstand, I held it to my lip and went to the bathroom as August continued to move around, mumbling indiscernible things in his sleep.

The bathroom light turned on remotely as I entered the room, the way all the lights in the house did. I found my lower lip had been split pretty good, but it wouldn't need stitches. Wetting a cloth, I held it to my lip until the bleeding stopped, then headed back into the bedroom to try to wake August without getting hit this time.

The blankets were a mess as he tossed back and forth before sitting up abruptly, his eyes open and scanning the room.

"August," I said in a calm voice. "Are you awake?"

"You!" he shouted as his eyes came to rest on me. Then he looked over his shoulder as if he saw someone else there. "Get her!" he shouted as he pointed at me.

"August, stop!" I shouted as he got off the bed, coming toward me. "No! Wake up, dammit!"

I was only a few steps out of the bathroom, and I quickly turned to lock myself in. When he saw I planned to retreat into the bathroom, he sped up. His hands caught me by the throat. "I've got the spy."

I couldn't say a thing as he'd cut off my wind. Then he lifted me by the throat until my feet left the ground. I struggled and hit him to make him let me go, but my efforts proved to be futile.

Once more, he looked back over his shoulder as if someone was talking to him. "Yes, sir," he said, and then placed my feet on the ground, releasing his grip on my throat. "On your knees. Don't even think about trying to get away or I'll kill you, you damn spy."

I went to my knees, gasping to get air into my lungs. Then I saw his feet walking away from me as he barked an order to some imaginary soldier, "Take her to camp."

Crawling on my hands and knees as fast as I could, I made it into the bathroom. Closing and locking the door behind me, I took a few minutes to breath and calm down before filling two cups with cold water and heading back out. I found August still in his dream-like state, glaring at me.

"How'd you get away from my men, you dirty spy?" he bellowed as he moved toward me.

Once he was close enough, I tossed both cups of water in his face, and he stopped solidly in place. Shaking his head, he wiped his face with his hands. The look in his eyes had changed, and August was back. "August!"

He blinked as he looked at me. "Your lip's busted."

My chest heaved as I tried hard not to cry, but failed miserably. Breaking down, I ended up on the floor, a puddle of emotion.

"Baby, what's happening?" he asked as he scooped me up. "Did you fall and hit your mouth on something?"

Carrying me to the bed, he laid me down then ran his hands over his face once more. "Why am I wet?"

I had to pull myself together to explain what happened. So, breathing deep, I choked back the sobs and sat up. "You had some kind of a dream. Your arm flew back and connected with my face when I tried to shake you awake. Then you..." I broke down again.

I've never considered myself to be weak. I'd stayed in control through some terrible situations since I first became a nurse, but this was different.

I wasn't safe with the man I loved. What the hell could we do when he wasn't in control of himself while he slept?

"I hit you?" he asked, as he sat down on the bed beside me.

With a nod, I answered his question. "Then you called me a spy and started choking me."

He reached out, pushing my hair back, looking at the marks his hands must've left on my neck. "My God!" Horror filled his expression. "I've hurt you."

We stared at one another for the longest time, both of us knowing this was too serious to ignore. After a while he got up, walked around the bed, grabbed the baby monitor and came back to me. We were both naked, as we'd fallen asleep that way after making love. He didn't bother to put anything on either of us as he scooped me up his arms then took me to my old bedroom, placing me in that bed. "You're safe here."

He turned to leave, and I couldn't stop myself as I called out, "Don't. Don't leave me, August."

Without looking back at me, he shook his head. "I can't put you in danger. I'll go see my therapist first thing in the morning. I love you. Try to get some sleep."

With that, he left me alone in my bedroom. And as I laid there, I couldn't shake the feeling that something terrible had intercepted all the joy we'd found. And my heart hurt because I didn't know if I could feel safe here anymore.

Going to my closet, I put on some pajamas then went to Calum's room. Locking the door behind me, I climbed into his bed, pulling him to cuddle with me. With the locked door between August and us, I felt better.

This wasn't how I thought things would go at all. In my fantasies, August and I would be this perfect couple. I'd dreamt about it many times, about August coming back into my life and us getting our fairy tale ending, especially when I was pregnant with our son. Back then, my biggest dream had been that one day he'd come back into my life and ask me to marry him, making us a real family.

That part had happened. But I'd never thought in a million years that we'd have a problem as big as this one seemed to be.

He'd shut me out. That wasn't a thing I ever saw in my fantasies. No, I saw us getting along well. But for that to happen, he'd need to listen to me about things—especially important things like this. And he wasn't doing that. He was taking everything on himself, leaving me out.

Would I be able to deal with a life with him that was so very different from the life I'd envisioned? How would I be able to handle the disappointment of another dream shattered?

81

CHAPTER 22

August

I left the house early the next morning. Facing Tawny after what I'd done to her proved too hard for me to do. My therapist's office didn't open until nine, so I waited in the park nearby.

My cell rang at eight-thirty. Tawny's name shone up at me. "Hi," I answered.

"August, where are you?" she asked, concern etching her tone.

"I told you last night I'd be seeing my therapist first thing this morning, Tawny." A car drove by, and I saw Doctor Schmidt inside of it. "Hey, he's here. I'll call you later."

"August, call me as soon as you're done there. I've been doing some research. I want to talk to you about it."

My heart ached, and my head felt as if I'd been in a boxing match with Mike Tyson. I felt hopeless.

Everything had been going so right. But I'd failed to

remember my little affliction. It would never be safe for Calum or Tawny.

Coming in just behind the doctor, I seemed to have startled him. "Oh, goodness, August. What has you here so early?" He looked at the calendar that hung on the wall. "Wait, today isn't your normal day."

"No, it's not. Something's happened. I've hurt someone." I took a seat on the sofa, the one I usually sat on for our therapy sessions. "Someone I love."

"I was afraid of this," he said as he took his usual seat. "August, I know you've made great strides, but you're not far enough along that there wouldn't be complications when seeing someone seriously. So, tell me what happened."

I told him what I knew. "I had a bad dream. I don't remember the dream at all, or even recall having one. She said she tried to wake me up and I hit her in the face, busting her lip. That was bad enough. But she said I choked her, too. My handprints were all over her neck, Doc." Tears trickled down my face as shame and horror overtook me. "How can I make this stop?"

"It takes time," he told me, handing me a box of tissue. "August, you were a working marine for six years. You've seen things, participated in things, and performed acts of war that most civilians could never imagine. That all builds up inside of a person's brain."

"I had no idea I was having these types of dreams, Doc. How could I not know that?" I asked him. It was tearing me apart that I'd brought the woman I loved to my bed not knowing I might hurt her physically.

"My advice, for now, is to let me prescribe something for you. Zoloft, I think, might be best." He pulled out a prescription pad and began to write on it.

I didn't want to take pills. I hated the way they made me feel—numb and unfocused. "No."

He looked at me with a frown on his wrinkled old face. "August, you need more than just therapy to manage this at the moment. You need medication. If you had, let's say... hypertension, then you'd take a pill for that. If you had diabetes, you'd take medication for that. Why can't you look at this like the disease it is?"

"Because this is mental. This isn't physical, and I will not turn into a damn zombie to win this battle." I got up and slammed out of his office.

Nothing he did was working for me. I needed more. I needed some real help. Maybe a whole damn team to help me get over this thing.

I could do this. I knew I could. I could do it because I had at least two reasons to, now. Before, I didn't have anyone to do it for. But now I did, and I'd beat this thing.

Getting into my car, I pounded the steering wheel in frustration. I had all the money in the world at my disposal and no idea how to get the help I really needed.

My cell dinged, and I looked at it. Tawny had sent me a text, telling me to come home and talk to her, that she had a lot to tell me.

So, I drove home, not sure what she had to say, but putting my trust in her the way she'd done me. If she and I were going to get married, then I had to learn to lean on her, too. It was time to admit to myself for once that I had weaknesses, just like anyone else. I wasn't the hero she thought I was.

I'd been a merciless killer at times. I'd been a man who shot first and asked questions later—that was what I was trained to be. I may have killed innocent people; I had no way of knowing for sure. Shooting from a moving helicopter at a shifting mass of what we thought were rebels, I could've killed innocents. That was the terrible consequence of war, the casualties of combat.

Thankfully, Calum was away at school when I got home. Facing the little guy would've made everything even harder. Tawny must've been waiting with her ears pricked because she ran to me as soon as I came into the foyer. "August!" She threw her arms around me, hugging me.

My arms moved to hold her, wishing like hell I wasn't so fucked up. "Baby, I am so sorry."

"Don't be. You didn't do anything on purpose." She pulled back to look at me, and her swollen lower lip hurt to look at. "August, I've been bitten by scared little kids, kicked by expectant mothers with low pain thresholds, and once I was smacked in the face by an old lady's purse when I came up behind her too fast and frightened her. Her purse left *both* lips busted." She tried to make light of the situation, but it didn't help me at all.

"Don't, Tawny. This is bad. This is really bad. I had no idea I did things like that when I slept." I took her hand, rubbing the back of it, loving the way her soft skin felt beneath my fingers.

"Well, that's understandable, as no one's ever actually slept a whole night with you on a regular basis." She pulled me into the main living room and we sat down. Her laptop was open on the coffee table. She swiped the screen, and a picture came up. "This is what I wanted you to see. This is in West L.A., and I think it would be the perfect place for you. The stuff they do with people who have PTSD is ground-breaking and revolutionary."

She picked up the computer, placing it on her lap and showing me everything about the place. One thing that stuck out was the fourteen-day treatment period where I'd have to stay in their facility. And the fact that they treated with drugs. And not the regular ones, either. No, they used a form of the drug known as ecstasy on the street, but they called it MDMA.

"Wow, that's not your normal PTSD drug, Tawny." I looked at her with concern. "My doctor has put me on every other drug they use for this, and I've never done well on any of them."

"Well, this one works very differently from those," she told me as she pointed out some of the testimonials. "These results can't be ignored, baby."

One of the patient testimonials said that the person who'd gone to the facility to try the treatment—which included taking the medication and receiving intense therapy—felt as if their soul had snapped back into their body.

That was a strong thing to say, I thought.

"I'd be away for two weeks." I looked at Tawny, taking her face in my hands. "That seems like a long time to not get to see your beautiful face."

"Well, I can get through half a month if it means we can have a lifetime together, sleeping together each night. You can do this, August. With the right help, you can get through this thing. And I'll be here every step of the way. I'm not going anywhere." She ran her hands over my whiskered cheeks.

"The truth is, I'm surprised you're still here. I thought I'd hurt you so bad you'd feel you had to leave me. For your protection and Calum's," I admitted to her.

"I'm not that afraid of you. If I have to keep a bottle of water with me to pull you out of an episode, or chain you to your bed so your hands can't do any damage, so be it. I'll do whatever I have to, to keep you with me. I don't give up on people in general, and those are mostly people who don't mean a thing to me. You mean everything to me, August Harlow, and I'll never give up on you. Not ever."

She should give up, and I knew that. But dammit, that selfish part of me clung to her as if she were my only lifeline. "I'll do it. I'll go to that place, and I'll try everything. I can be stubborn..."

"You don't have to tell me that," she interjected, smiling.

With a laugh, I picked up the computer, put it back on the coffee table and pulled her to sit on my lap. "Thank God for that full moon seven years ago."

"I do all the time," she added.

Our mouths met, and her sweet kiss made me believe that everything would be okay. It had to be. I had the best woman by my side. With her, I could beat anything that came my way.

In the meantime, I wasn't going to waste a single moment I had with Tawny before I had to go. Moving her to lie back on the sofa, I moved my body to cover hers. She pushed on my shoulders, making our mouths part. "What are you doing?"

"I'm going to take your sweet ass right here, baby. That's what I'm doing. And then maybe I'll take you in the swimming pool while we skinny dip. After that..."

She sighed, stopping me. "So, today is all about getting your fill of me, is that it?"

"Baby, I will never get my fill of you. But today is about getting as much of you as I can get. Because tomorrow I'll leave to go get better." Putting my mouth back on hers, I found her pushing my shoulders once more. "Now what?"

"What about the staff, August?" She looked worried. "I don't want to get caught."

Little did she know that I'd called Denise and told her to

give the entire staff the day off. I wanted to be completely alone with Tawny for the entire day. But I didn't let her in on that—a little fear of getting caught added some spice to things. "Don't worry about that." I kissed her again.

The kiss was so hard and so full of passion that she melted underneath me, letting me have my way. She knew I wasn't going to quit until I got what I wanted, and so she didn't fight me on most things—not when she wanted those things as badly as I did. I loved that about her.

I loved everything about her, and I'd do anything to make myself the man she deserved.

82

CHAPTER 23

Tawny

After one hell of a great day, where August gave me all of his attention just as he promised, we had to come up for air when Calum came home from school. Max, the driver, had picked Calum up for us and brought him home.

We managed to keep our hands mostly off one another until Calum went to sleep, then we went at it like animals again until the wee hours of the morning, when August carried me to my own bed, locking the door behind him.

I cried then. Cried for all he had gone through. For all he'd seen. For all he'd had to do. The man was my hero. He always would be.

After a shower, I put on some nightclothes and went to sleep. I'd brought the baby monitor with me to my bedroom and was shocked when I woke up the next morning alone in my bed.

No Calum.

Progress was being made there, and I prayed our little family would just keep on progressing.

Later, after getting myself and Calum dressed, I found August in the breakfast nook. Steam swirled over his coffee cup, and he jerked his head over at the carafe. "Grab a cup and join me." He looked at Calum. "There's juice in the other one for you, buddy."

I poured us something to drink then we took seats at the small round table with August. He put his cell down, looking at our son. I knew leaving him for fourteen entire days wasn't sitting well with him.

Placing my hand on top of August's, I said, "I'll explain things to him, don't worry."

"'Splain, what?" Calum asked before he gulped down some apple juice.

"I want to tell him," August said before he directed his attention to his son. "Calum, I've gotta go away for a little while."

"Why?" Calum asked with furrowed brows.

"You remember me telling you about why I had that weird screaming episode that day in the car, right?" August moved his hand through Calum's dark hair.

"Yes, sir," Calum said, then took another drink.

"Well, I think it's time I finally fixed that problem. Your momma found this place that we think can help me. But I've gotta go and stay there for two weeks. Do you think you can be a big help to me and keep your momma company while I'm gone?"

Calum looked a little worried. "You're comin' back, right?" His lower lip began to tremble. "'Cause I'm gonna miss you."

"I'm gonna miss you too, buddy. But I need my little man

to step up and keep his momma happy while I'm gone." August got up and went to pick Calum up.

Calum rested his head on his father's broad shoulder as he cried. "I'll try, Dad."

"Daddy has to get some help to get better." August patted him on the back, and I had to bite my lip to hold back the tears that welled in my eyes.

August looked at me. "Leila will be here soon to pick him up and take him for the day. I didn't think it would be a good idea to send him to school today. And I'd like you to come with me to the facility. I kind of need you with me, to hold my hand."

Nodding, I picked up a napkin to dry my tears before they fell. "'Kay."

We sat there in silence as we all picked at the breakfast Tara had made for us. Not one of us was hungry anymore.

After Leila came and picked up Calum, Max drove us to the facility, which I prayed would be able to help the man I loved. "So, here we are," he said as he got out and took my hand, helping me out, too.

Being a nurse, I was used to medical facilities. This one was something else, though. Everything was state of the art. The building was large, but it didn't have that morose hospital feel to it. Positive energy flowed invisibly through the air.

Gripping August's arm, I whispered, "I like the atmosphere here, babe."

"It does seem upbeat, doesn't it?" he asked, as we went to the reception desk. "August Harlow. I spoke with someone earlier about seeking treatment."

"Of course," the young woman said with a smile. She pointed to a frosted glass door. "Dr. Sheldon is waiting for you right through those doors. He'll go over the treatment plan, and once you agree with it, you'll sign papers, and we'll get you started on your road to success, Mr. Harlow."

With a nod, we headed the way she'd pointed and found soft music playing when we came into the doctor's office. The man we met there had a soft voice and the kind of demeanor that put one at ease right away.

I had to admit; he seemed so genuine. Much more so than any other doctor I'd ever dealt with. Confidence filled me as he told us how they went about doing things. "While we have had much success with our treatments here, it's important that you understand that therapy is something you will have to be in for the rest of your life, August. You should get used to that fact."

August didn't seem to be pleased by that and asked, "Isn't your mission to cure me?"

"There is no cure for what ails you. Can you imagine being the victim of a shooting, or a child who's been horribly abused?" the doctor asked him.

August shrugged. "I guess so."

"Well, would you expect them ever to be cured of their memories?" The way the doctor smiled made my heart sore. He was the real deal—like an angel sent here to help others.

August could only shake his head. "No, I guess you can't cure memories. So, how the hell can you help me?"

"While we can't wipe your memory bank clean, we can help you handle those memories a lot better. People who've had an overload of terrible things happen to them have it much harder than your average person. Hence, why so many military personnel in particular end up with PTSD." The doctor took out a bottle of pills. "This is what MDMA looks like."

"You should know that I don't like taking pills, Doc."

August shrugged again. "I don't like the effects they have on me, and I don't want to depend on them either."

"Let me explain this drug to you first, and let's see if I can help you understand what this can do to help you. And let me tell you this, too—this is not a drug you will take forever, the way you'll have to have therapy forever." The doctor opened the bottle, spilling all the pills out on the desk in front of him.

"That's a lot of pills," August mumbled.

"This is your personal one-month supply," the doctor let him know. "And with our help and observations, you'll learn when to take one and when you don't need to take one."

"Okay, wait. I've got to ask this," August interjected, "this is ecstasy, right? So, I'll get aroused, won't I? How am I supposed to handle that sexual frustration when you'll have me locked up in here?"

With a knowing smile, the doctor answered him, "No one says you can't masturbate, August. You'll have a room to yourself here—lots of privacy. Now, let me explain this medication to you. These pills are made up of three neuro-transmitters. Serotonin makes up most of it. Now, you can purchase serotonin in any drugstore over the counter. It's most often used as an aid to those who have trouble falling asleep. People with mild anxiety take serotonin as well. Does any of that worry you so far, August?"

"I suppose if it can be sold like that then it hasn't got any bad side effects," August said. "And it might be like taking the vitamin supplements I take every day. Right?"

With a nod, the doctor went on. "So, you're on board with the serotonin. The other two ingredients, dopamine and norepinephrine, have similar effects. They're the components that will increase alertness—they'll increase your energy level, too. And with all that positive blood flow, well, your arousal is also increased. And lastly, the relaxing effects of the serotonin act as a base that help level everything out."

"Okay, is this feel-good drug addictive?" August pointed out. "I do not want to leave this place addicted to anything."

"Tell me, do you think you have an addictive personality? Do you need alcohol or tobacco or anything like that?" the doctor asked.

Pulling up our clasped hands, August kissed mine. "She's the only thing I've ever been addicted to. Yet, I'm finding the strength to stay away from her for fourteen days, aren't I?"

A blush heated my cheeks, and I ducked my head as the doctor went on, "Well, I'm glad to hear that, August. While you're taking this medication, you will be strictly observed. It's not our intention to get anyone addicted to anything. We're not a pharmaceutical company, nor do we have any connections to any of them. We're in the business of helping people. And we do so by lightening their mood before we have deep therapy sessions. Our sessions sometimes last twelve hours, mostly eight though. This pill will help you think about things you've shoved into the deepest recesses of your mind and deal with those memories while in a calm, cool state of consciousness."

"So, what you're saying is you guys will pull out all the shit I've seen, done, and dealt with, and teach me how to interpret it in a new way? A positive way? Because let me tell you, there are things I've seen and done that no amount of spin will turn into a positive thing," August argued.

The doctor smiled at that, and I started to feel a bit confused, thinking August might not do as well here as we'd hoped. "Maybe this isn't the best place for him," I said, as I squeezed August's hand.

The doctor leaned forward, steepling his fingers then resting his chin on them. "I feel exactly the opposite, Tawny. You see, your fiancé is the perfect candidate for this. His concerns are valid, and he has conviction in his heart. It is clear he is ready to work hard to deal with this issue. My bets are on August, and I rarely lose my bets."

August looked at me, and then took a deep breath. "I'm going to stay, Tawny. I'm going to give this my all. And I'm doing it for you, Calum, and those future kids we're going to have. But I'm also doing it for me."

"Better words have never been spoken, August," the doctor complimented him.

When it came time to leave August there, I did so with hope in my heart and a smile on my face, even though tears filled my eyes. I was going to miss him so much, but this was something he had to do.

83

CHAPTER 24

August

"I have a little test I need you to take, August," a female therapist named Tasha told me as she placed a laptop computer on the desk in my room.

I'd been admitted to the PTSD treatment facility and taken to what would be my room for the next two weeks. It had only been a couple of hours, and already I missed Tawny and Calum like crazy. But I wanted to do this for us. I had to do it.

"Okay, I just check the yes or no boxes?" I asked as I looked at the list of questions. The first question asked whether I had ever been exposed to a traumatic event.

"Yes," Tasha said as she nodded. "And be truthful with this. Therapy works best if you're honest and vulnerable, especially when you're used to being a tough guy. No one is strong all the time, and it's important for you to let those weaknesses show." She headed for the door. "I'll leave you to it then."

Alone, I looked around the room. A small full-sized bed

was in one corner and a desk sat right across from it— that's where I sat. The walls were a pale blue, the door pristinely white, and the floor was done in bamboo wood flooring—giving the room a serene, calming feel. The few pictures that hung on the walls were of flowers, butterflies, and one was of a flock of birds. A small bathroom was attached to the room, giving me all the privacy I could ask for.

Turning my attention back to the test, I checked *yes* for the first question. The next question asked if I'd ever experienced the threat of injury or death, to which I again checked the *yes* box.

Although I tried not to think about that, I guess it was part of the process of fixing my fucked-up mind. The next question asked if I'd felt fear, helplessness, or horror. That one had me going back and trying to count the number of times I'd felt those emotions.

Shaking my head, I had to stop that line of thought. There were too many to count. Another *yes* box had to be checked.

Do you regularly experience intrusive thoughts about the traumatic event?

I had to ask myself what regularly meant. But then the thought of these nightmares I'd been unaware of came to mind, and I had to check *yes* again.

The next question asked if I felt at times like I was reliving the event, and another *yes* was at hand. Recurring nightmares, stress over the memory, avoiding thoughts about the event, avoiding people that reminded me of the event, all of those had to be checked with a *yes* as well.

I was on a roll. A bad one. And I wondered if all these *yes* answers would only earn me more time in the place.

Then I got to check a *no* when asked if there were things

I wasn't able to recall about the event. No, I recalled every-thing well—too well, actually.

Had I lost interest in anything I had once enjoyed doing? I was able to check another *no* on that one.

Whew, for a minute there I thought I was a goner!

More *no* boxes followed as it asked if I had difficulty trusting people, or showing emotions. Did I fear I'd never have a normal future? I was able to check the *no* boxes about having trouble falling asleep. I thought I'd been sleeping like a baby, but I'd been wrong about that. But I knew I never had trouble falling asleep.

Angry outbursts got a *no*, too, and so did difficulty concentrating. But then the question about having guilt over those who died while I survived had to get a *yes*.

Oh, well, they can't all be no.

I was there for a reason, after all. I had a mix of *yes* and *no* answers as I continued through the questionnaire. Did I startle easily; did I feel as if I had to be on guard all the time, ready to spring into action?

I could spring into action whenever I needed to, like I did with the wildfire situation and Calum—but I didn't go around tense and ready to spring.

I checked the *yes* box for the question about whether I'd been experiencing this for longer than a month. The last question made me pause, though.

Do your symptoms interfere with normal routines, such as work, school, or social engagements?

Did they?

I had to think about that one. I could go out without any trouble. Ah, but there had been the incident on the freeway, and then a couple of others in the past—one in a nightclub, one in a restaurant. Another *yes* had to be checked, and then I hit the Submit button.

The score said twelve, and I thought that was pretty good. But when I looked at the bottom portion, I read that anything over ten was considered to be evidence of symptoms of PTSD.

Well, that wasn't anything I didn't know already. I would indeed be spending the next fourteen days here with the good doctors and therapists. I supposed things could've been worse. I could've lost Tawny and Calum, which thankfully hadn't happened yet—and wouldn't, whether I had to stay here fourteen day or fourteen months to fix this.

With the test submitted, Tasha came back into the room. "August, the results showed us what areas you need to work on. Just a few more questions, so we can get you all set up." She tapped a pen on the top of her clipboard then put it to the paper. "Do you feel more at ease speaking with a male or female?"

"Hmm, I think I'd like it to be a male." I liked talking to Tawny, but mostly it felt easier talking to men about my weaknesses.

"Okay," she said, as she took note of that. "And do you like being in a group or alone when you discuss private matters?"

"Alone," came my quick answer. I wasn't one to talk freely in a group—never was, never would be.

"Okay, then just one more thing," she said, as she looked at me. "Are you a daytime person or a nighttime kind of guy?"

"I get up early each morning, so put me down as daytime." I got up out of the chair, eager to get things started. "So, when can we get started?"

"Soon. I'll input this data into my computer and have a schedule for you in about an hour. Lunch is being served, so why don't you head to the cafeteria and introduce yourself to the others?" She left the room, and I stood there, wondering if I really wanted to go meet anyone.

The idea of hobnobbing wasn't sitting well with me. But the growl of my stomach told me to go eat, so out I went to find my way to the cafeteria.

About fifteen people were seated at various tables. Just like high school, they seemed to have their cliques. When I spotted a USMC tat on one guy's arm, I headed to that table after picking up a tray of food and a bottle of water. "Hi, I'm August Harlow, formerly known as Major Harlow, First of the First."

The bulky man shook my extended hand. "Tom Moore, formerly Second Lieutenant Moore, Combat Logistics Regiment Three." He gestured to the man to his right. "This is Frank Wilson, non-military, son of a Mafia drug lord."

I shook that man's hand, too. "Nice to meet you, Frank."

"You too, August." Frank went back to eating his turkey on rye, which was the main dish for lunch.

A set of blue eyes found mine as I looked at the woman seated next to him at the round table. "Natasha Granger, formerly Captain Granger of the Tenth Regiment."

"Ah, the Arm of Decision. Too many decisions you'd rather not have made—is that was brought you here?" I asked her as I shook her hand.

"You could say that," she answered. Her blonde hair was pulled up into a high ponytail.

The first thing they'd done was give me a set of light blue scrubs to wear, and I found everyone else had them on, too. I'd been told this was because the MDMA could make some people hypersensitive to touch, so they tried to lessen this distraction with the soft, roomy material of the scrubs. The clinical staff all wore white sets of the same scrubs. The others workers in the facility all wore yellow scrubs. As I looked around, it seemed like something out of a sci-fi movie.

One empty chair remained at the table, and one remaining person had yet to introduce herself to me: a quiet young woman with dark hair and eyes. Eyes that looked like they'd seen some shit. With a nod to the empty chair, I introduced myself to her, "Hi. August Harlow. Mind if I take this seat here?"

"Do what you want to. Who am I to stop you?" she said, with a snarky tone to her deep voice.

I took the seat. "And I didn't catch your name?" I had to say.

"Tillie," she said, then took a large bite of her sandwich, chewing it as she looked at me.

Natasha nudged me with her shoulder. "She's an abuse victim," she told me quietly. "Human trafficking, sold into sex slavery at the age of ten. Rescued last year by DEA agents."

Tillie's deep voice took my attention. "My master was all I'd ever known. Now it seems I have no idea how to function in society. So, I came here to see if I can be taught."

"How old are you?" I asked with concern.

"Twenty-one," she said with her mouth full of food.

No manners to speak of, it seemed, but who could blame her? "Your family?"

She shook her head. "It was my father who sold me. Mom died when I was eight."

"Fuck me," I mumbled. "I'm sorry to hear that. I hope you find help here, Tillie."

I didn't have anything compared to that poor girl.

Tom looked across the table at me. "How long were you in for?"

"Six years," I said, then took a bite of the sandwich, finding it pretty good.

"I barely made the two-year mark I'd signed up for. I can't see how you did six." He took a drink of water from the bottle in front of him, and I noticed there were already three empty bottles of water he'd already drunk.

Natasha chimed in, "I made nearly ten years before this hit me. It was just like, bam! One day sane, the next day screaming at some poor lady in line at the grocery store for no reason other than that she moved too slowly." She shook her head. "My husband told me I'd been waking up screaming, too. I don't recall doing that."

"I've been doing things in my sleep, too," I admitted. "And last night I hit my fiancé in the mouth, busting her lip, then went so far as to choke her. I don't remember any of it. But the cut on her lip and the marks my fingers left on her throat told me all I needed to know. I had to get help and fast, or I'd lose her and our son."

Natasha nodded in agreement. "This is my second marriage. I got married when I was only twenty—he was an oil-field worker who didn't understand why I wanted to be in the military. Now, my husband and our two kids are afraid of where I'm headed. He told me to get help or get out. At thirty years old, starting all over is the last thing I want to do. So, I retired from the marines and came here afterward."

"Damn," I murmured. "My girl told me she'd be behind me every step of the way. She said she'd never turn her back on me."

"Don't believe her, buddy," Frank came into the conversation. "No one can take abuse for long, whether you do it in your sleep or not. She'll leave if you don't get control of this."

I doubted the young guy's words. "If you don't mind, Frank, how old are you anyway?"

"Twenty-two. A very old twenty-two. I've seen shit no one should see, and I didn't have to leave home to see it." He downed his water then opened a new one.

Looking around the table, I noticed everyone had at least four bottles of water, and I'd only picked up one. So, I had to ask, "I'm not trying to be rude, but what's the deal with you all drinking so much water?"

Tom chuckled. "A side effect from the MDMA. Excessive thirst."

With a nod, my jaw clenched. I didn't like that at all. But I'd promised to give this whole thing a try. "I've never taken MDMA before. What can I expect?"

Natasha answered first, "I call it truth serum. The drug lulls you, leaving you feeling good about everything. Safe, you know? Like you can say anything you've done or seen to your therapist and not worry that they'll think you're sick, crazy, or a monster. I can't quite bring myself to admit the things I've done unless I'm on the pill."

Tom added, "And then there's the arousal." He looked me up and down, as if trying to get a measure of my personality. "If you're anything like me, you're probably worried about that part of the drug."

I nodded. "A bit, yes. Especially since my fiancé isn't available to scratch that itch."

Everyone laughed then, and Tillie answered, "The therapeutic sessions go on for at least eight hours. I don't begin to get antsy until the end, and when my therapist notices me squirming, she ends the session, and I have to go masturbate for at least an hour."

Natasha added, "It's like a little inside joke around here. Don't let it bother you if you see someone walking real fast to get to their room, and they ignore you. It's just that they have to deal with some more personal matters in private."

"I've got to ask," I said as one question ate at me. "Is there a lot of hooking up in here?"

They all looked back and forth at each other, then each one of them looked at a table in the far corner where six people sat. One female and five males. "If you're into hooking up, she's really the only one into that here."

"No," I said quickly as I shook my head. "I'm not into that at all. I was just wondering."

Tom laughed then downed the last of his water, and I saw Tasha coming into the cafeteria. She waved me over, and I excused myself to go get my schedule.

Things were about to begin, and I felt ready for that.

84

CHAPTER 25

Tawny

A week had passed, and I hadn't heard a thing from August. Leila had come over to our place to do some planning. She'd called me up, explaining that the family wanted to have the holiday at August's place that year, which would work great, as August was set be released from the facility just a couple of days before Thanksgiving.

I was happy to oblige as I'd already requested that my start date at the hospital be moved to January fifth; I was free as a bird and knew the planning would help take my mind off missing August.

Leila's kids had come over, too. It was the weekend, and they helped keep Calum entertained while Leila and I chatted over a few glasses of the wine she'd brought with her. She'd handed the car keys to her oldest, Jeanna, just after coming inside. "Here, Jeanna, I'm drinking, so you're driving us home."

Her daughter took the keys and followed the others to the game room. "Got it, Mom."

Leila showed me the bag with the three bottles inside. "I've brought us some refreshments, Tawny. But I drink responsibly, never drinking and driving. My hubby's Uncle Alonzo died in a car wreck ten years ago after drinking and driving, and I vowed then and there never to do it—even after just one drink."

With a nod, I led her to the bar so that we could find some glasses and a corkscrew. Texting Tara along the way, I asked the chef if she could bring us a cheeseboard and fresh fruit tray.

Leila and I settled in, sitting on tall barstools at the gorgeous dark wood bar. Leila had found the stereo system and put on some soft rock music. "I just love visiting this place. It's like a hotel, don't you think?" she asked me.

"That's what I said when I first saw it." I chuckled, taking of sip and loving the salty undertones of the red wine. "Yummy."

"I know, right?" Leila asked. "I just love Napa Valley wine."

"A true Californian," I added, smiling.

Tara brought in the trays I requested, and Leila was quick to invite her to join us. "Tara, we're going to be discussing the Thanksgiving holiday. Would you care to grab a glass and join us? Your input would be appreciated."

Going behind the bar, Tara got a glass and poured herself some wine. She took a pad of paper and a pen out of her apron and placed it on the top of the bar. "Okay, so we're having it here then?"

With a smile, I was happy to tell her the news, "We are. Our first holiday together, and I get to be the hostess. I'm so excited."

"Mom and Dad are coming, too," Leila informed her. "The total headcount is thirteen. Even my elusive hubby will be home for once and will be there."

"So, I'll get to meet the man behind the remarkable woman," I said with a laugh.

"That you will."

Tara tapped her nails on the bar. "Okay. Turkey is a must."

"Ham, too," I added.

Then Leila looked at me. "Tawny, please tell me your parents are going to come, too." She looked at Tara. "Put down two more people. I forgot to add them."

Tara jotted that down. "Okay, fifteen people."

"Make it nineteen, Tara," I quickly pointed out. "I certainly expect you and the rest of the staff would like to enjoy the meal, too."

A little smile crept across her lips. "Sweet of you. So, our final count is nineteen then."

"Do you think August wants to invite his business partners?" Leila asked me. "He used to go out every weekend with them. They're all pretty close."

"I'll ask him if he ever calls me." And with that my cell buzzed. Pulling it out of my back pocket, I didn't recognize the number, but saw that it was a local call. "Hello?"

"Baby, have you missed me?" came August's voice.

I screamed and jumped off the barstool, too excited to stay sitting. "August! Yes! Yes, of course, I've missed you!" Glancing over at the two women who were laughing at me, I excused myself and headed to the next room, which happened to be a sitting area. "How are you, babe?"

"Doing pretty good," came his reply. "I'm feeling a little exhausted right now. A lot of memories are being dredged up. When I'm on the MDMA, I can take it all well. But afterward, when the drug wears off, then I feel drained."

That didn't seem like progress to me, so I asked, "Do you feel like this is a waste of your time, August?"

"No, they told me it would be like this at first. This is a process, and these first fourteen days are just the tip of the iceberg." He sighed heavily. "The hardest part is being without you and Calum. I'm not sure why they think it's so important to have us here without any kind of friends or family around, but they do think it's important. I've asked quite a few times if you could at least come for a visit, only to be told that's not allowed."

Biting my lower lip, I felt the same angst he did. "Well, most recovery programs want the person to know they have to handle things on their own. There can be emotional support, but the idea is to make you see that you're okay all on your own, and that you don't have to depend on anyone but yourself."

"I guess you're right. I don't know or care really. I've talked to a lot of people here this last week, about what they've gone through, too, and to say the overall atmosphere of depression is demoralizing is an understatement." I could hear his breathing, and I longed to feel his warm breath on my neck.

"Um, your sister's here. We're going to host Thanksgiving this year. Is that okay with you?" I asked him to get my mind off his breath and lips and everything else.

Ugh! I needed him so badly.

"Oh, are we?" he asked with a laugh. "So, Leila and her brood want to come trash our place, huh?"

"They're here now, the whole lot of them." I chewed on my thumbnail as memories of his body on top of mine filled my head. "Oh, and do you want to invite your business partners? Leila said you're pretty close to them."

"No, Gannon has big plans this year, and Nixon is flying home to Texas to be with his family. Thank you for asking though. That's nice of you, baby." Another long sigh came out of him. "God, I hope the next week goes by faster than this one. Once I get out, I have to come to therapy every day. The sessions last eight hours, so I'll be gone all day."

"Even Thanksgiving?" I asked, despair filling my voice.

"Yeah, even Thanksgiving. They told me it'd be from nine in the morning until five in the evening. Can we have the party during the dinner hour?" he asked.

I wasn't about to let him down. "Of course, I'll make sure to tell them all that it'll be a dinner party, with dinner being served at, say, eightish?"

"That sounds good to me. Invite your parents, baby. I can't wait to see them again. Your mom's fudge was the best ever. She came over and gave us a batch every Christmas."

"And your mother gave us her famous peanut brittle, too," I added.

We did go way back. We did have a history. Maybe we hadn't ever been a couple, but we'd spent a bit of time together as neighbors. Backyard barbeques and neighborhood block parties. Every New Year's Eve watching the fireworks, all of us in our own backyards, but sharing things over the chain-link fence—the only thing that separated us from each other.

"One more week," he said quietly. "I can hold out that long. Can you, Tawny?"

"I have to, don't I?" I laughed to lighten things up. "So, how is it besides feeling so drained? Are there people there you can relate to?"

"A couple of fellow former marines are here. We sit at

the same table for all the meals. Natasha is thirty, and she's married with kids. Her marriage is on the line because of her PTSD. Tom's a kid who barely made it two years in the service. He's seen shit that haunts him. I worry about them both. But not as much as I worry about Tillie. She's this young girl whose father sold her into sex slavery when she was only ten. Can you believe someone would do that to their own child, baby? It's too disgusting to even think about. And I'll tell you, it makes me feel like a wimp that I'm having so many problems, when what I've been through is nothing compared to what she's been through."

"You're still human, August. You've still been through bad things yourself. Don't lose sight of what you have to work on just because others have had it bad, too," I gently chided him. "But that is a very sad thing for the poor girl." My stomach knotted as I thought about what a horrible life she must've had, and how hard it would be to ever get over that.

The world could be a terrible place. It would be wonderful if things could be perfect all the time, but that's not the way of the world. And my poor man had been through awful things, too—things that would break the average person.

August was beyond average. He was a hero through and through. If he could learn how to manage his bad memories, things would get better for him and for the rest of us, too.

"When you come to pick me up, have Max drive you," he told me.

"Why is that?" I asked him as I pushed my hand through my hair, pretending it was his hand instead. My body tingled as I thought about him touching me.

"Because I'm going to devour you completely on the ride home," his voice had gone deep with lust.

My panties were soaked with his words alone. "August!"

"My doctors have been monitoring my sleep, too. They're working on an idea to help me stop this nighttime shit I've been doing. They're coming up with a plan that'll let me keep you in my bed." He groaned. "I want that so bad, baby. My arms hurt they want to hold you so damn bad. Fuck!"

"It's okay, August. One more week, and you'll be home. Just work on learning how to use the pills to help you and use the therapy, too. I know you can beat this. I read a story..." I stopped myself. "Never mind. Let's talk about something else." When I thought about what I'd been about to say, I recalled that though the success story was great, it had taken the woman about thirty years to be completely free of PTSD.

"Never mind?" he asked. "Why is that?"

With a sigh, I went ahead and told him anyway. "Well, there was this success story I read. This woman had suffered an abusive upbringing. I mean—very abusive. It was a real horror story, what her father did to her until she was eighteen, and then he kicked her out of the house. Anyway, she was one of the first people to go through the program you're going through now. It was just in its beginning stages though, so maybe that's why it took her so long to be completely free of any PTSD symptoms. But that's what I wanted you to hear about—she did become free of all the symptoms and didn't have to take MDMA anymore either. The therapy you're going through can work, and it can work to completely relieve you of all the symptoms, babe. Isn't that great news?"

"How long did it take her, Tawny?" he asked in a grim tone.

"Thirty years," I said quickly. "But that had to be because she'd been involved at the start of the whole program. They hadn't worked out all the kinks, you know?"

"Hmm," came his uncertain answer. "Well, I'm not about to let it give me false hopes. Things haven't been going that great for me. And the sexual arousal isn't comfortable. Thank God I only have to take one of those pills a day, right before my session each day."

A thought grew in my head, and I blurted it out. "What if you took that pill at night? Say, just before you go to sleep? Maybe that would stop your nighttime episodes from occurring, and I'd be here to help you with that sexual arousal." My body heated with the thought of how hot our love life would be if his doctors agreed with that.

"That's not how it works. I can't even take the pills home anyway." He stopped and then laughed. "But I get to come home after the sessions, and then you could definitely help me with that 'little problem'."

"I don't see it as a problem at all." The idea had me excited already. "God, you have to go to therapy every day for...how long did they say?"

He laughed. "You naughty little vixen. I have to go every day for two more weeks, then it goes down to every other day for a month, then every three days for the next month, and finally, it goes down to a day each month until I'm only going once a week."

"Sounds like fun to me. Why not make this into an exceptionally good thing, babe?" I asked him as I ran my hands all over my body, thinking of the evenings we were going to have.

Things were looking up!

85

CHAPTER 26

August

My body must've gotten used to the MDMA by the second week of therapy, because things started to change. My mind felt different; my thoughts became more evident. Besides the need to drink more water, there were no other side effects, other than a sense of peace—and that lingering arousal.

The last day of therapy saw me sitting on the sofa in Dr. Baker's quarters. We didn't go into an office for the sessions —the spaces were more like living rooms in someone's home instead.

"So, you say five men were coming through the small village, killing only the male children?" he asked me.

I'd been telling him about one of the missions that stood out in my memory. This was one I'd hidden from myself because it was just too hard to think about. But now, I was able to not only think about it, but talk about it without feeling that overwhelming hopelessness I usually felt when I thought about such terrible things.

"Yeah, and me and the three other marines who'd been sent to deal with those men were pretty mad. You know—because they were killing innocent children. Taking sons away from fathers and mothers who loved them." I leaned forward, putting my elbows on my knees then putting my face in my hands as powerful emotion suddenly flooded me.

"It's okay to let that sadness out. Let it escape your mind, August. Of course, you felt sorrow for the parents, the siblings of the boys, and the boys themselves. That's completely natural," Doctor Baker told me in a calm voice.

Tears streamed from my eyes. I felt sorrow, no doubt, but there was another emotion at the forefront. Love.

No sobs came from me, only tears as emotion filled me. It was the oddest thing I'd ever felt. Gulping, I sat back, grabbed some tissues from the box that sat on the sofa beside me, and dabbed my eyes. "So, these men hardly resembled humans at all. In my eyes, they looked like demons. I suppose that was what my brain did to make it okay to kill them. Dehumanize them to make it okay."

"Well, that's interesting, isn't it, August?" the doc asked me. "Turning a man into a monster would make it easier for you to do your job—which was, ultimately, to save lives."

"It did." I dried the rest of the tears as they stopped flowing. "I took two of them out as I hid behind a partial wall of someone's home, blown up in another battle sometime before. This village was war-ravaged, and I couldn't begin to fathom this happening in America."

"Why did it make you think of America?" he asked me.

I paused for a moment, working through that question as best I could before answering him. "In America, we're much more protected—by our laws, our rights. We're even able to have weapons of our own, while that country's people are just sitting ducks for terrorists. Their government doesn't seem to care about protecting them, and can't seem to comprehend what these people need to help them survive or to overcome. It's aggravating, annoying, and makes it real difficult to feel much empathy—how can we help a country that doesn't seem willing to help itself? But when you see a family who's been victimized, the empathy is there. But I have none for those who govern them."

"So, there are feelings that conflict you," Doctor Baker pointed out. "Confliction within one's self is never easy to deal with. Perhaps you should talk about this conflict, and you might figure out how to end it."

"On one hand, you have a government that makes its citizens easy targets, and that's a crime in my book. On the other hand, you have people who haven't lived freely in their entire existence." I sat there, thinking about that for a long time. The doctor sat quietly, patiently, never rushing me or giving me any words of wisdom. And as the time went by, I swear I felt a click in my head. "But maybe this isn't for me to understand. Things happen, and we aren't supposed to understand all of what happens. And that's just life. I can't solve all the world's problems—can't fight all the world's battles."

All the doctor did was nod. After a moment, he picked up his cup of tea and took a sip. I leaned back on the sofa, linking my fingers and placing my hands on my stomach. Peace filled me then, and I spent the rest of that session swimming in the peace I had found.

And the doctor allowed that. When the eighth hour had passed, he got up and stretched. "Well, it seems it's time for you to be going back home, August. I'll see you back here tomorrow morning at nine."

I sat up, and then it hit me. Tawny was waiting for me outside!

Jumping up, I hurried to my room to change into the clothes I'd come there in before hurrying out the front doors. And there was my black town car, and Max stood by the back door, waiting for me. "Max!" I shouted as I made long strides to get to the car.

"Hello, Mr. Harlow. Nice to see you again," my driver greeted me.

"Nice to see you too, Max," I said as I shook his hand.

He opened the door, and there sat Tawny. She had on a beige trench coat, her auburn hair braided and pulled over her left shoulder, and a huge, welcoming smile on her face. "Miss me?" she asked coyly.

Sliding into the backseat, I gathered her into my arms and kissed her. I didn't even notice that Max had closed the door—she'd captivated me, engulfed me, took me over completely.

The car began moving, jolting me back to reality. I pulled my mouth from hers to look at her. "God, you're real, not a dream, right?"

She nodded and pulled the belt on the coat, letting it fall open and revealing a pleasant surprise. "I thought I'd make things very easy for you, August."

"Oh, baby!" Pushing her back on the bench seat, I ran my hands all over her beautiful and very naked body. My mouth followed my hands and soon I was kissing her cunt, licking her hot folds and pecking her clit with soft kisses. She tasted like home, and my hunger only grew.

Her fingers ran through my hair as I ate her with a ferociousness that didn't abate. She came quickly, and I eagerly lapped up everything I could until my cock could take no more.

Hastily, I undid my jeans, pushing my briefs down to release my dick. Not bothering with anything else, I moved my body over hers and thrust into her. Our combined groans filled the back of the car. We weren't holding back, and Max might've even heard, but I couldn't have cared less.

Fucking her with everything I had, she was coming again in record time, but I wasn't about to end things so soon. It had been two long weeks since I'd been with her and I had every intention of making this last.

Pushing one of her legs back until her foot was next to her ear, I went at her harder, all the while kissing her neck. Her body quivered as I devoured her, her moans never ending as I took her.

"August!" she cried out, shuddering with another orgasm.

"Give it to me, baby," I growled in her ear as her cunt contracted all around my aching cock.

But I still wasn't ready to give in to my climax just yet. Lifting myself off her, I removed the coat from her shoulders, leaving her naked. I moved her still shaking body, putting her on her knees on the open expanse of the floor. Her round ass was begging for my kiss, and I leaned down, pecking the soft skin as I ran my hands over it.

My cock still ached to fill her, so I shoved back into her as I held her by the waist, slamming into her so hard you could hear my balls as they slapped her ass. With her in that position, I was buried deep. When she came this time, I had no choice but to join her. We made some terribly magnificent sounds as our bodies shuddered with our releases.

The car was slowing to a stop, and only then did I realize we were home. "Where's Calum?" I asked as I looked at the front door.

Tawny scrambled to get the coat back on as I stuffed my cock back into my jeans. "He's with your sister. I took him over there before coming for you."

A grin pulled my lips to one side. "So, we have some time then?"

"All night," she told me with a sexy grin. "If that's okay with you?"

"I miss him, don't get me wrong, but I can't do what I want to with you if he's around, can I?" I got out of the car and turned to pick her up, carrying her inside. Straight up the stairs I went, taking her to my bedroom.

As soon as I placed her feet on the floor, she dropped her coat and began undressing me. Pulling my t-shirt off, she ran her hands all over my chest. "I've missed these muscles." Her mouth moved over my pecs, grazing my flesh, leaving hot trails in her wake.

All the while her hands busily undid my jeans then pushed them along with my underwear to the floor. I stepped out of my sneakers and kicked away the rest, naked and happy to feel her skin against mine.

When she went to her knees in front of me, I stopped her. "The shower."

Standing up, she led the way to the bathroom while I followed, admiring the view. Her ass swayed with each step she took, and my mouth watered to taste her again.

She started the large tiled shower with jets everywhere. Warm water fell over us like a waterfall, and she went to her knees again, taking my hard cock into her hands and licking the tip of it until I couldn't take it any longer. "Put it in your mouth."

She smiled up at me, water dripping down her face, then put my cock into her hot mouth, sucking me off. I held her head, moving her the speed I needed. Watching her head bob as she took me all the way in, I found it hard to breathe. It was the most arousing thing I'd ever seen, and I was mesmerized by the sight. I closed my eyes as the climax began, starting up deep inside of me before rolling throughout my entire body. I shot hot cum down her throat as I groaned.

Her mouth left my cock, and she looked up and swallowed before filling her mouth with water. She rose, and I grabbed the back of her neck, kissing her. Even though she'd drunk water, cleansing her mouth, I could still taste the saltiness of my cum on her tongue.

The kiss grew in intensity, making my cock hard again. Lifting her up, I put her legs around my waist, plunging back into her. Using the tiled wall to help me hold her in place, I fucked her again.

Over and over, I pounded into her as my kiss kept her moans quiet. As soon as her body began quaking around my cock, I came, too. Moving my mouth away from hers, I kissed her neck as we caught our breaths.

Her nails had dug into the flesh of my back, and she eased her grip on me. "August, is this what I can expect every time you come home from a therapy session?"

"I don't know about that. I'm pretty sure this is just from being away from you for two weeks. But we'll see." I washed her body with strawberry scented body wash, and she washed mine with the musky body wash she liked me to use, then I took her to my bed.

I had no idea if we'd even stop long enough to eat. My body craved hers, and it seemed like hers craved mine, too. So, why not give in to what we both wanted so desperately?

There are worse ways to spend one's time.

86

CHAPTER 27

Tawny

I'd fallen asleep in August's bed as he'd completely worn me out. His hand on the back of my neck woke me up abruptly. He gripped it tightly, and then his knee was in the middle of my back. His words were slightly slurred, growled out near my ear, "How did you get in here?"

"August, it's me, Tawny," I said with a stern tone. "You need to wake up now."

But he didn't seem to hear what I'd said as he continued to hold me, calling out to someone who wasn't there. "Jones, get the zip ties. I don't know how this bastard got in here, but he's our prisoner now."

"August, please," I shouted. "It's me, Tawny. Wake up!"

There were bottles of water on both nightstands, all I had to do was reach one, and I could wake him up. But unfortunately for me, I'd fallen asleep on my stomach, and I was helpless as he pinned me to the bed.

August pulled my hands back, his fingers moving over my wrists as he pretended to use a zip tie to bind my hands together. And that's when I saw my chance. He'd think my hands were bound, but they wouldn't be.

Not struggling at all, I let him pick me up, putting me on my feet. He looked past me, as though talking to someone as his hands held my shoulders. "Get him out of here."

He removed his hands from my arms, and that's when I grabbed the bottle of water, rapidly taking the lid off and squeezing it. A stream of water hit him right in the eyes, and he moved his hands quickly to deflect it.

But it had done its job, and when he moved his hand, I saw that he'd come back to reality. "Tawny?"

"August," I put the bottle down, released my pent-up breath, and hugged him.

"What'd I do?" his voice was so quiet I barely heard him. His hold on me so tight that I could feel the uneasiness filling him.

"You didn't hurt me. You just thought I was the enemy and had snuck into your bed, I think. Everything's okay now. Come on, we can get back into bed now." His hands moved through my hair, sending a chill through me as he continued to hold me.

"Tawny, I'm taking you to your room now." In one swift movement, he had me up in his arms, carrying me away.

That was the last thing I wanted. "August, it's okay. You didn't hurt me."

"Not this time I didn't. But what happens the next time? There's no way of telling, Tawny. I'm putting you where you'll be safe." He walked to my room and opened the door, placing me on the bed. "Good night. I love you."

My heart was breaking. "August, I'll be okay. Please, let me sleep with you."

"No," came his one-word response. Then he walked out, making sure to lock my door before he closed it.

The pain and frustration I felt couldn't be tamed. I ended up getting up and taking a shower to try to ease the tension that had filled me. It wasn't fair. I had a man who I loved, and he loved me, yet we couldn't sleep together because he was afraid he'd hurt me in his sleep.

How could this be fixed?

I had no idea, and as I stood in that hot shower, I knew that wasn't the way I wanted to live. But I'd made August a promise. I'd told him I would always be there for him, that I'd never turn my back on him.

But how could I be true to myself, too?

When I climbed back into the king-sized bed, I pulled the blankets up to cover my naked body. Sadness took over and I got out of bed, leaving my room to go to his. My plan was to sneak into his bed—hopefully nothing would happen, and then I could show him that things would be okay if we slept together.

When I tried to turn his doorknob, I found he'd locked it. Turning around, I went back to my bed. My heart pounded, my head hurt, and I felt something draining away inside of myself.

I couldn't live this way, and I knew it.

Going back to my bed, I tried to decide what I should do. I had to do something.

But what?

Sometime in the night, I'd finally drifted back to sleep. When I woke up, I found it was after ten a.m., and August had already gone to his therapy session. I called my old landlady to see if that garage apartment was still available. I was glad to find she hadn't rented it out to anyone yet and would be happy to have me back.

After getting dressed, I drove over to Leila's to pick up

Calum. There was no hiding anything from her—she saw sadness written all over my face. "Tawny, what's wrong?"

"I'm moving out," I let her know.

She took my hand, pulling me inside. "We have to talk."

I let her pull me inside, and then she led me into a quiet place in her busy home. She sat me down on a chair and took the one across from me. "I know you probably don't understand why I have to leave him, Leila."

"Did something happen last night? Did he hurt you again?" she asked, knowing that was a great concern of ours.

"No, and that's why I have to leave. I'm so damn frustrated, Leila, you have no idea." I felt the tears begin to sting the backs of my eyes and looked around for something to dry them with.

Leila was already ahead of me, handing me a tissue. "Here, use this. Now tell me what's got you so frustrated that you think moving out of August's is the only answer."

"He won't let me sleep with him!" the words burst out of my mouth, and then I was crying some more.

"Because he's afraid he'll hurt you, Tawny." I could see her shaking her head through blurry, tear-filled eyes. "If you truly love my brother, you'll have to understand that things aren't going to be completely normal for a while, or possibly never. It's just what comes with the man."

"Leila, it hurts so much when he locks me out like that. He actually locked me out of his room last night—but that's not even fully what I mean. I just want to help him, but his solution seems to be to just block me out, mentally and physically. It's agonizing. You have no idea how much it hurts." Blowing my nose, I tried to get a handle on my emotions. Crying hadn't done me any good so far, so I might as well stop.

"I have some idea. My husband works out of town more

than he's home. I have more lonely nights in our bed than ones with him in it." She looked out the window as her expression turned melancholy.

"I know you're lonely, Leila. But your husband's not in the same house as you, forcing you to sleep in a different room each night. It's different. I was okay when August was at the treatment facility. But with him home, I can't take it." Getting up, I paced back and forth in front of the window. "I love him—adore him. But I can't take him pushing me away each night. It's just too hard. I don't know if we'll ever be able to live in the same house together like this, so I think I need to take some time to figure things out."

"You're right," she said, as she nodded. "Maybe you're not the right girl for him then. I don't know if there will ever be a right girl for my brother." Her legs crossed as she tapped her chin, thinking about something. "August has seen so much. Been through so much. Maybe he's broken beyond repair and will just have to deal with living his life alone."

Listening to her talk about him that way made my heart pound. "I don't believe he's broken beyond repair. I never said that. The fact is he's making progress. He didn't hurt me last night. I was able to douse him with water, and he came around very easily. I handled the situation just fine, but then he went and took me to a different room anyway. He wouldn't listen to a thing I said."

"Not my brother," she said with a smile. "Are you calling him strong-willed, tenacious, stubborn—a man who thinks he and he alone knows what's best?"

She knew the man alright. "So, what am I to do about that? Tell me, please. I want to know."

"This is just a road block, Tawny. Sure, maybe things aren't working out as perfectly as you'd hoped, but this might be the way it has to be—for now anyway. Don't let one small deviation from your dream stop you from experiencing this thing you and he have together." She got up, coming to me, then her arms were around me, hugging me. "I know it's hard. Life is hard. It's hard for August, you, me, my husband—everyone in some way or another. Don't let frustration end what you two have. Learn to accept the things that come along with loving a man who has some problems."

"I just feel like this has already hurt me so much—how will I feel after years of this? It's like I lose a little piece of my heart every time he shuts me out," I admitted. "Eventually there will be nothing left."

"You feel that way because you love him. Leaving him will only make that loss and hurt so much bigger. For both of you." Leila let me go and walked away from me, leaving me alone in the room.

Leaning against the wall near the window, I eased my body down until I was sitting on the hardwood floor. My head still ached, my stomach had an enormous knot in it, and my heart pounded.

I'd never felt so terrible in my entire life. But I knew what I had to do.

87

CHAPTER 28

August

Taking a break to eat some lunch, I found Natasha sitting at our table alone. No one else from our ragtag group had come into the cafeteria yet. Her eyes were red from crying. "So, have you had a rough morning with therapy?"

Her blue eyes glistened with unshed tears. "He left me, August. I went home last night, and my husband and our kids were gone. He left me a note, saying he couldn't handle this anymore." She burst into tears, and I quickly got up to go hug her.

"Natasha, everything's going to be okay. If he really left you, he's not worth your tears anyway," I tried to comfort her.

"What about my kids?" she wailed.

Feeling sorry for her and knowing the cafeteria was no place for her to be breaking down like this, I helped her up and took her to my doctor's quarters, vacant during the lunch hour. At least she could break down in private.

"The kids can be sorted out. I'm sure you can get custody of them. Are you okay, financially speaking?" I asked her.

"No," she cried. "I don't have anything coming in since I left the marines. He's been bringing in all the money since then. And when I went to swipe my card at the ATM, I found out my card had been canceled. He's left me without a damn thing, the fucking bastard!"

I had no idea why a person would do such a thing. But then again, I knew bad shit happened all the time.

"I'm sure things will work out," I tried to calm her down. "I'll hire a divorce lawyer for you. He'll get things straightened out before you know it. It's not legal what he's doing to you, and we can stop some of it from happening."

She threw her arms around my neck "August, thank you, thank you so much. How can I ever repay you?"

"Just by getting better, Natasha. Now come on, buck up and believe that everything will work out the way it should. I'll go grab my cell from the receptionist and call my lawyer to get his recommendation for a good divorce lawyer. With any luck, you can meet with one right after today's session. I'll do my best to set that up for you." I let her go and headed for the door. "You stay here as long as you need to. But just know that very soon things will be as right for you as they can be."

"You're my hero, August Harlow," her words stopped me. Tawny had told me those same words.

Shaking my head, I looked at her. "I'm just a guy with enough money to help out, that's all."

Natasha shook her head. "You're far more than just that. Your fiancé is lucky to have you."

I left Natasha then, feeling a bit odd about that last exchange. After I'd made the call and had good news to tell her, I went back to my doctor's quarters, finding Natasha still there, talking to my doctor.

She looked at me as I came in and rushed to hug me. "There he is, my hero!"

"Oh, come on now, I told you I'm just a guy with money, Natasha. I'm no hero." I gently pushed her to let me go, and she did so. Handing her the piece of paper I'd scribbled the name and address on, I continued, "Here you go. Meet the lawyer at her office at this address. She'll be waiting for you. I told her you're busy until five, and she understood. I've already taken care of the payment, and she said she could have things straightened out tomorrow. You have nothing to worry about. You're in very capable hands now, Natasha."

"Thank you, August." Her fingers trailed over my hand as she took the paper. "And I know this might sound kind of bad, but I'm going to say it anyway. If you and your fiancé don't work out, give me a call. I think we could make each other very happy."

And there it was. I'd thought something felt a bit off between us, but it could be just the shock of it all for her.

I didn't want to crush her spirit either way. Giving her chin a playful tap with my fist, I said, "You just get things straightened out, slugger. Things will get better, you'll see."

With a smile, she left the room, and my doctor looked at me. "I think now would be an excellent time for you to talk about your feelings for your fiancé. How are things going in that department, August?"

"I had to put her in another room last night." I took a seat on the sofa and crossed my leg, resting my hand on my ankle. "I did it again, had some dream, did something to her that might've hurt her. She woke me up by splashing me with water. I don't know how I'm going to handle this thing."

"And how did she react when you asked her to go to another room, August?" he asked me with a knowing grin.

"Not well. And I didn't ask her, I took her there and locked her door, so I couldn't get to her. Then I locked my own door, so she couldn't get to me, either. I was afraid she'd try to come back to my bed. And I'm also afraid that this is putting a strain on our relationship." I caught some movement out of the corner of my eye and turned my head to see that Natasha had slipped back in.

She looked at me with those blue eyes, a smile on her face. "Um, I didn't mean to interrupt, but I needed to ask one more teeny little favor from you, August."

I excused myself from the doctor's room and joined her in the hallway for some privacy. "What's that?" I pushed my hand through my hair, worrying that she might ask me something to get me alone. And now that she'd overheard what I'd said, I knew she'd seen an opportunity to get her claws into me. Being a wealthy man, having a woman use unconventional methods to catch my attention was nothing new to me.

"I need a ride to the lawyer's office. I don't have much gas in my car and, if you'll recall, I don't have access to any money." She looked down with a shameful expression.

Getting up, I reached into my pocket. All I had were three hundreds, and I pulled one out and handed it to her. "Here you go."

"Oh, no. I don't want your money." She looked up at me. "You've already given me so much, paying for the lawyer and all. Just a ride would be fine."

She might have been being honest, but I wasn't going to risk falling into any kind of scheme that aimed for my seduction. I'm sure she thought it would be a great way to get back at her ass of a husband. I couldn't blame her for what she wanted, but I wasn't about to mess up what I had waiting for me at home. "Natasha, I'm very much in love with my fiancé. Now take the money, and do us both a favor and stop whatever train of thought you might be on, okay? I'd like to stay on good terms with you."

A blush turned her cheeks beet red, and she nodded then left the room. I turned back into the room and saw my doctor smiling at me—clearly my attempt at privacy hadn't worked. "You handled that very well, August. So now we have the matter of figuring out how you're going to handle your nightmares and your fiancé."

That was a hell of a lot harder than what I'd just done. Taking a seat, I went back to what we'd been talking about. "I'm sure you've seen this before, Doc. What do people do when this sort of thing happens?"

"I'd like to be perfectly frank with you, August. Can you handle that?" He pulled his glasses off and looked at me with a serious expression.

Something told me that I wouldn't much like what he had to say at all.

88

CHAPTER 29

Tawny

Calum and I got home a little before August. My heart ached, but I'd resolved myself to the fact that August and I would never be able to have a normal life together. But then again, nothing had ever been normal for us.

At only eighteen, I'd found the strength to have a baby all on my own. One fiery night of passion had filled my heart with something I'd never felt before. At the time, I had no idea that it was actually love for August.

In the days that followed his leaving me, I've felt numb at times and full of pain at other times. August and I had never had a relationship at that point; we had hardly spent any time together. So, why did I miss him so damn much?

Back then, I'd talked to my best friend, Beth, about how I felt, and she'd had no idea what to say to me. Beth and I weren't alike at all—we were night and day really. She'd lost her virginity at the tender age of fifteen. In the following years, she'd had at least six different boyfriends. Attachments like love didn't come easy to her, so she didn't understand why I was crying over some guy I'd had sex with for only one night.

Somehow, with that one night, August had become a part of me. And a few months later, I realized I'd missed my period. Most girls that age would've panicked. I wasn't panicked at all. Once I thought it might be possible, I'd actually hoped that I would be pregnant.

Crazy, I know.

I'd asked Beth to pick up a pregnancy test and bring it over. With that test, I'd found out that I was going to have a baby. August Harlow's child.

At that time, his parents still lived next door; they hadn't moved away yet. I could've gone over and told them the news. They would've told August, and things would've been so different.

I didn't want to do that though. I didn't want to get in the man's way—he'd told be from the beginning it was a one-time thing, no matter the fanciful promises we made to each other. And I was happy to have a part of him that I would have forever. Our son.

Back then, I decided to take on all the responsibility, and as hard as it was, I thoroughly enjoyed every moment with Calum in my life. And when I saw how much he resembled August as he grew, it only served to make me even happier.

Though falling in love with someone overnight hardly made any sense at all, my love for August gave me strength.

Could I find that strength again?

August and I were engaged. Marriage meant sacrificing things for the sake of your spouse. Could I sacrifice sleeping with my husband so that we could have a marriage and a family?

The idea that I was short-changing myself still lingered in the back of my mind.

I knew I'd short-changed myself by keeping my pregnancy a secret from him, too. I'd lost the chance to have support throughout my pregnancy. I'd lost the chance to have help taking care of my child. But I knew I'd short-changed August and Calum with my decision as well.

My parents were great and helpful, but they couldn't replace the father that had been missing since day one. Things had been tough for me, especially once I'd started college. I was still pregnant when I began the nursing program. We had to do clinicals at one of the local nursing homes, and there were times I'd have to rush out of the patient's rooms to deal with my pregnancy-induced nausea.

My mother told me it was from the stress of having a child without any idea of how to get in contact with the father. I'd lied to my parents about who the father was, and that lie had me dancing around at times.

The truth was, I hadn't felt stressed out about having the baby. But worry had consumed me at times about August and his safety. I'd actually had nightmares about what August was going through. I hated the fact that he was in danger.

As time went on, and our son was born, that worry over August—his whereabouts, whether he was okay or even still breathing—became less and less intense. Not that I didn't care, but I just grew to accept the fact that marines live hard lives, and that was the life he'd chosen.

Now I was faced once again with having to accept a lot of new things all at once. Like the fact that I might not get to actually sleep with him for some time, or maybe never.

Again, I asked, am I short-changing myself?

The answer was that I probably was. The same way I'd done before.

Calum's voice shook me from my internal struggle. "Momma, when's Dad coming home?"

I checked my cell to see what time it was. "Should be about a half hour or so," I answered. And as I held the phone in my hand, a call rang in from August. With a swipe, I answered the call. "Hello! Were your ears ringing? Calum and I were just talking about you."

He chuckled. "No, they weren't ringing. I'm calling to let you know I'm going to be a little late. Some problems with the nightclub have come up. I've got to go over there and meet with my partners for a little while. Tell Calum I miss him and let him stay up so I can see him, will you?"

"How late are you going to be?" I asked him with a sigh, knowing this would be disappointing news to Calum.

"I really have no idea, baby. I doubt it'll be later than nine."

Calum's bedtime was eight, and he had school the next day. Keeping him up past his bedtime wasn't something I was keen on doing. "I guess I can keep him up a little past his bedtime. But can't you let them know you have a little boy who hasn't seen you in a couple of weeks and misses you pretty badly?"

"I will definitely do that. I'll do my best to get out of there as fast as I can, baby. See you in a bit. Love you. Bye now." With that, he ended the call.

Calum was staring at me when I put the phone back in my pocket. "Well?"

"Well, Dad's got a meeting to get to. He'll be a little late." I tried not to get upset about the disappointed expression on Calum's face.

"Okay," he whimpered then climbed onto the sofa, laying down and burying his face in one of the pillows.

I sat next to him, rubbing his back. "It's okay, you'll see him later. He said I should let you stay up until he gets home—even if he's really late. He'll definitely be reading you a bedtime story tonight. Even if I have to go down to that nightclub of his and drag him home."

"Promise?" Calum asked, as he moved his head to look at me.

"I promise." Pushing his hair out of his face, I kissed his cheek. "Now, come on, let's get some dinner."

The fairy tale I'd made up in my head about how life would be with August was coming to an end. I'd never been in a relationship—perhaps I should've dated at least a little to find out what relationships really were like.

Things were hitting me harder than I ever thought they would. And I knew I was being unrealistic about how things should be going for us. Even with August having PTSD, I hadn't really thought it would be like this.

I'd lied to myself, it seemed. But I had Calum to think about. What would be best for him had always been my number one priority. Having a father was what was best for our son. I'd just have to learn to deal with the reality of what being with August Harlow meant.

Tara smiled at us as we entered the kitchen. "Good evening, you two. I've got some appetizers on the bar over there, and dinner will be served at seven, as usual."

"Perfect." I went over to the tray of appetizers, finding some fresh veggies alongside a creamy white dip. "Yum. Come on, Calum, dig in."

Tara was busily preparing the meal, and everything smelled awesome as we sat in the kitchen and waited. But as busy as she was, it didn't stop her from filling me in on how the Thanksgiving plan was coming along. "The smoked turkey and ham I ordered came in this afternoon. And I made it to the farmer's market to pick up the organic vegetables and herbs for the day after tomorrow."

Calum perked up then as he realized something. "Hey, I only gotta go to school tomorrow, then I'm off for four whole days! And I get out early tomorrow."

"Yep." I ran my hand over his little head. "And you'll have lots of fun with your cousins, and Gramma and Grandpa will be here, too. Not to mention that you'll get to meet your father's parents, too—you're going to have another Gramma and Grandpa. It'll be so much fun."

With the talk of the upcoming holiday, Calum came out of his funk. In no time at all, he was dancing around, talking about what he was going to do on Thanksgiving. He was also excited to get to say what he was thankful for, practicing how he would share that he was most thankful for finding his Dad.

As bad as my heart ached over the complications between me and August, and knowing that they wouldn't get resolved any time in the foreseeable future, the joy of watching my son be so happy took over.

I could do this. I could do it for our son.

89

CHAPTER 30

August

My therapist's words echoed in my head as I came into the house at seven thirty. "You shouldn't force your fiancé to do something that hurts or upsets her, August."

In short, he thought I was wrong for making Tawny leave my bedroom. She wasn't some child; she was a grown woman and a nurse to boot. And I had to give her some credit for how she'd handled both situations. More than I'd been giving her, I supposed.

But it still gnawed at me that I might really hurt her, and that overrode anything anyone else thought.

As soon as I stepped into the central living area, I heard feet smacking the hardwood floor. "Dad!"

My little six-year-old flew through the air, the smile on his face melting my heart. "Son! My goodness, I missed you." I caught him up in my arms, hugging him as his small arms ran around my neck.

Tawny came in behind him. "We've just finished dinner. Yours has been sitting in the oven, keeping warm."

"I've already eaten." Calum still clung to me as if I was a life preserver, and he was in stormy seas. "The meeting was about the menu. We had all these samples to taste. I have no room left."

Tawny spun around. "I'll let Tara know then."

As she walked away, I sensed something off with her—there was a frigidness about her. Her eyes, usually so full of love, seemed dull. My heart thumped in my chest at the thought that she might be getting tired of dealing with me and my problems already.

Our love was new—fragile—maybe so new it was something she could easily walk away from. Maybe the doc was right. Maybe I shouldn't make her do things she didn't want to, like leaving my bed.

"Dad, am I gonna meet your parents?" Calum asked me with a wide grin on his cute little face.

"You are," I said, kissing his rosy red cheek. "They're going to love you almost as much as I do."

"I bet I'll love 'em, too, then." He was finally ready for me to put him down, and I placed him on the floor. "So, how was it in there, Dad?"

"Pretty good. Not as bad as I thought it might be. I missed you and your momma a lot though." My eyes darted to Tawny as she came back into the room. "It's nearly his bedtime."

"Yep," she said, as she came and took Calum's hand. "Bath time, then bedtime. Come on, kiddo."

As they walked away, I realized Tawny hadn't even given me a kiss hello. Now the chill was evident. There was something wrong here.

"I'll meet you guys in Calum's room at eight, then." I

shoved my hands into my pockets, rocking back and forth on my feet, feeling uneasy.

"'Kay," Tawny called back without turning to look at me.

Had I really gone too far when I'd forced her out of my room despite her protests?

Strolling to the bar, I made myself a small glass of Scotch and took a seat. All my adult life I'd been making decisions for more than just myself. Had that made me hard?

Tawny and I had a connection—that much was true. But was it strong enough to withstand this hard time? And would she be able to love a man who was used to having things his way?

The truth was that Tawny and I were great together when it came to sex. And we were doing a great job at co-parenting Calum, I'd say. But what about the rest of the stuff that came with being a couple? Relationships were hard enough to sustain; could she handle all the extra baggage that came along with me?

After finishing the drink, I headed to Calum's room, finding him dressed in some Paw Patrol pajamas and picking out a book from his bookshelf. "Hey, Dad. Here's one Momma said is called *The Princess and the Pea*. Wanna read this one to me?"

"Sure do," I said, and looked at Tawny, who seemed to be leaving the room. "Hey, you going somewhere?"

"Yeah, I'm going to my bedroom where I'm taking a long hot bath with a glass of wine, then turning in for the night. See you both tomorrow. Goodnight, sleep tight, and don't let the bedbugs bite. Love you both." She blew us a kiss before she left.

Now I knew I'd made her mad.

Gulping, I took a seat on the edge of Calum's bed as he climbed in, snuggling under the blankets. "Momma said you and I should have father-son time from now on when you read me my bedtime story."

"Hmm." I wasn't happy about that at all. She wasn't even talking to me about anything. She'd just gone and made decisions all on her own—and she'd already done that for six years where Calum was concerned.

But I swallowed my anger and read the story to our son. As soon as he'd fallen asleep, I went to her bedroom door. It was locked.

Now the anger came back, and I knocked on the door with a loud bang. 'Tawny!"

No response came, and I knocked harder, my voice louder when I called out to her. Yet still, there was no response. Pulling my cell out, I typed out a message, telling her to come to my bedroom because we needed to talk. But even that didn't get an immediate response.

I headed to my bedroom, shucked my suit and got into the shower. My head was a mess, worry mixed with anger, and I hated how I felt. I finished my shower and headed out into my bedroom, wearing nothing more than a towel around my waist, and found Tawny sitting on one of the small sofas. She was wearing a fluffy white robe and sipping a glass of red wine.

"Why aren't you in the bed waiting for me, Tawny?" I walked toward her slowly.

"I thought I'd let you get some sleep. What did you want?" She looked past me for some reason, deliberately avoiding my gaze.

"You thought you'd let me sleep?" I went to take a seat on the other sofa.

"Yeah. I'm tired. If we have sex..."

I interrupted her. "You mean, if we make love."

"Yeah, whatever," she flicked her hand in a little wave as

if there was no difference. "If we did, then I'd most likely fall asleep and you don't want that, so I'll just fall asleep in my own bed tonight." She acted like it wouldn't bother her in the least, staying apart from me all night.

"I was gone for two weeks, and you think one night together is enough for me?" I ran my hand over my stomach as I thought about her agreeing to try to get pregnant.

"I didn't say that." She pulled the glass of wine to her lips, taking a long sip. "You don't want me to sleep with you, August. I get it. I understand even. But that means that sometimes, when I feel really tired, I'll have to forgo the lovemaking. Otherwise we might fall asleep together, and you don't want that. I want to respect your wishes, that's all."

But that wasn't all. If that was all, then she'd be able to look at me as she said it, which she didn't. "Tawny, you can be truthful with me. Is something wrong?"

Finally, her eyes moved to meet mine. "August, of course, there's something wrong. I love you. I want to sleep next to you, feel your arms around me, feel your body behind mine as we spoon the night away—every night. And I can't have that. So, yes, there's something wrong. But even so, I love you, and I want this to work. So, I'm not going to fight you about it anymore. I'll sleep in my own room."

She was giving me what I wanted, and yet she wasn't. "I've missed you, Tawny. I really wanted to make love to you tonight. Or at least spend some time talking with you before you rushed off to bed."

"And I'd love that, too. Do you think I haven't missed you today? I have. But I'm just tired. It's been a rough day." She took another drink of the wine.

"And why has this day been so rough, baby?" I watched her take a bigger gulp of wine than her previous sips. She was obviously using the alcohol to cope with things.

"Okay, if you must know, I cried myself to sleep last night after you took me to my room. And I've been thinking all day about how I'd be selling myself short, living this separate kind of life with you. I even talked to your sister about moving out of here. I went so far as to call the lady I rented my apartment from and asked her if it was still available, if you must know." She downed more wine.

Even though her words hit me square in the chest, I couldn't help but notice that she was downing her drink too quickly—and relying on it too much during this conversation. I got up, walked over to her and took the glass from her hand. "No more of this. You should be clear-headed for this discussion." Placing it on the table next to her, I sat down beside her. "Are you unhappy now?"

She looked me square in the eyes. "August, I am very unhappy now."

It was never my intention to make her unhappy. But at least she was honest with me. "Do you think you'll be okay in time?"

"I have no clue." Her honesty was complete, but it was overwhelming.

Could I live with myself, knowing that she wasn't as happy as she could be?

"My doctor advised me not to make you do anything that you don't want to." I ran my hand over her shoulder then up to her chin, taking it with my fingers to make her look at me, forcing her to take her gaze off the floor. "But Tawny, I am deathly afraid of hurting you. I am a trained killer—it would be so easy for me to hurt you by accident when I'm like that. You have no idea how hard it's been for me to take you out of my bed and lock you away from me."

"I'm sure it was hard. And I know what you're afraid of." She blinked a few times, and I could tell she was holding something back. Then she said it. "I'm afraid of this sepa-rating us, August. I'm afraid that our relationship is just too new to handle this right now. And I know this isn't your fault. But it's not mine either."

Swallowing hard, I knew she was right. "Maybe I'm not meant to have a real relationship."

All she could do was nod. "Maybe not."

"I do love you." I leaned forward to kiss her, but she pressed her hand against my lips, stopping the kiss. "You don't want me to kiss you?" I asked incredulously.

"I do, but I'll want so much more if you do that." The way her brows furrowed told me she was teetering on the edge of something. "I think I'll get used to this with time. But for now, I feel hurt when you make me leave. I'm trying my best to deal with this. I'm doing everything I can."

What in the hell could I do?

"This is a thing I can't control, Tawny," I whispered, and then took her hand, holding it in mine and kissing each knuckle of her balled-up fist.

"You think I don't know that?" She watched me as I kissed her hand with soft sweet kisses.

"What I think is this, baby." Her skin felt soft beneath my hands as I ran them up her arms. "I think you and I can figure things out together. I think you and I can eventually have a normal life. So, how about we do this—you come to this bed, our bed, each night. We'll be together, either holding each other or making love until you fall asleep. I'll stay awake and carry you to your bed once you fall asleep."

The sadness that took over her expression told me that wasn't going to be enough for her. "If only that would make things better. But I know it won't. I know I'll wake up once I can't feel your body close to mine. You're a part of me; you have been since that first night. It was okay before, not to have you physically in my life, in my bed. Now that I have you, I need you like you'll never understand."

"Don't you think there's some way you can come to terms with this?" I asked her as I brushed her hair back, pinning a lock of it behind her ear. My lips yearned to graze over her neck. "For instance, if I had a job where I had to get up earlier than you did, would it bother you so much to be in the bed alone?"

"But it's not like that. You're just down the hallway, not gone." She looked away as if nothing would ever make this any better.

I may have been considered the stubborn one in our relationship, but Tawny was proving to be pretty stubborn herself. And I was at a loss as to how to help her accept things for what they were.

As hard as it was to let her go, I did it. "I guess there's nothing I can say then. Good night, Tawny. I love you." Then I got up and walked away.

It was one of the hardest things I'd ever done.

90

CHAPTER 31

Tawny

Thanksgiving came and went. At least the busy holiday season took my mind off how long it had been since August and I had been intimate.

We had gotten along alright. But with the lack of intimacy came a distance between us. When we were asked at the dinner table on Thanksgiving if we'd scheduled a date for the wedding, we'd both murmured a quiet no.

Leila took me aside, asking me how things were going. I told her what we were doing, and she told me to stay strong and give things time. I'd been doing that, but nothing was getting any better.

It began to feel as if August and I were roommates. We did things with Calum together, but I continued to let August read to him each night alone. I'd go take a bath and go to bed with a book, much the same as I'd done all the years before, when I was single. Only now, Calum wasn't coming into my bed each night. The security of knowing there was a monitor right next to him so he could reach me was enough to end that little habit he'd had.

Little by little, I got back into my old routine. Christmas was right around the corner, and another big holiday party had been planned. Everyone would come to August's house once more to spend the holiday.

Our Christmas Eve dinner—with just August, Calum, and I—proved to be a pivotal moment in our lives. When we left the dining room, August asked me to come talk to him in his room after he'd put Calum to bed.

When I went in, staying dressed in my jeans and button down, I found him to be fully dressed too. That surprised me, as I thought he might try to pull out all the stops to get me into his bed that night.

I couldn't have been more wrong.

"Please, sit down, Tawny." He gestured to one of the sofas, and I took a seat. He sat across from me on a chair. "We need to talk."

"So you said. What would you like to talk about?" I asked him as I sat back and tried in vain to get comfortable.

He pointed at me then at himself. "There's a rift between us."

All I could do was nod. "Yes, I agree."

"Do you still love me?" His hazel eyes bore into mine.

"I'll always love you, August," I admitted.

"And I, you." He looked away, trying to steel himself to tell me more. "But this isn't working."

Taking the engagement ring off my finger, I placed it on the table between us, feeling numb. "I agree. We shouldn't be getting married right now, if ever. We had a child, but that doesn't mean we have to be together forever."

"I don't want you to leave." He looked at the ring instead of me. "I want you to stay here with us."

"I'd never leave my son anyway. What should we tell Calum?" My fingers ran over my finger where the heavy ring had been. I hadn't even worn it that damn long, but I already felt its absence, and it felt horrible.

He let out a big breath. "I think we can figure that out later." He paused for a moment, looking down at his hands as if preparing himself for what he had to say next. "I've been talking to my therapist," he started. He'd progressed to doing his therapy sessions every other day now. "And to some other people, too—people who have what I have— people who've been in marriages that haven't worked out because of this. But if not being able to sleep together makes this much of a difference in our relationship, then maybe sex was the only thing holding us together in the first place." He reached across the table, taking the ring and closing his fist around it.

As I watched the ring disappear, my numbness began to fade, and it hit me. He and I were over.

"Then that's it," I said, my heart breaking as I stood up to leave. "Good night."

"Good night," he echoed.

My feet moved at a normal pace, even though I wanted to run out of the room. Tears starting pooling in my eyes as I walked toward my bedroom, the dam finally bursting as I crossed the threshold. In no time at all, I'd gone from finding true love and getting engaged, to breaking up.

Falling on my bed, I buried my face in the pillow to hide my cries. What he'd said had hurt—that there was only sex between us. I'd made him fall out of love with me. By with-holding myself from him, I'd ended what we'd found.

Pounding the bed with my fists, I tried to get the frustra-tion and anger out of my system. I'd be living under the same monstrous roof as the man, but I would never have him again.

Everything inside of me hurt—my heart, my head, my entire body.

Every time August had tried to touch me, I'd shied away, telling him I couldn't handle that yet. I wasn't ready to make love with him and be forced to leave him.

One day had turned into another and another until it led to the one that ended it all.

Life as I'd known it was over. But then again, I supposed it'd been over since the night I'd made up my mind to sleep in my own room. I had no one but myself to blame.

I knew our relationship was more than mere sex. I was the one who took everything off the table. Not just the sex, but every little act of intimacy. I didn't like to be alone with August at all, knowing I'd want him if we were alone.

I'd been cold at times, shutting myself down to avoid having any arousal for the man. My body had craved him, but I had managed to lock that craving away, telling myself that I had to get stronger before I could deal with that.

It seemed I'd waited too long.

Christmas morning came, and so did his family. My mother and father came, too. It was my mother who noticed the absence of the ring. "Tawny, you're not wearing your engagement ring."

Her words caused many sets of eyes to shift toward my hand. Before I could think of anything to say, August came to my side. Always the hero. "We might as well get this out in the open. Tawny and I won't be getting married. She will continue to live here for as long as Calum does, though. We'll continue to raise our son together. We've agreed to do what's best for him, and we do have love in our hearts for one another. We'll never hurt each other, and Calum will always be put first."

My jaw clenched, and I couldn't say a word. My brain screamed at me that this was all my fault. If I had tried to work around the problem, then we'd still be in love and getting married. Instead, we were surrounded by pitying eyes as our families learned our sad state of affairs.

Leila sighed heavily and leaned against her husband, who ran his arm around her, holding her close. Those two barely lived together with his work schedule, and yet they'd had half a dozen kids and found a way to make it all work.

Why couldn't I figure out how to make it work no matter what the obstacles were? I wasn't a dumb person. So why had I resolved myself to this?

Christmas Day was long and hard and full of awkward conversations. August's mother had slipped up and mentioned finding the perfect little mother-of-the groom dress at some shop in Napa Valley. Her eyes had gone wide as she remembered that she wouldn't need it anymore. Then her eyes went to August, who sat near Calum, before traveling to me, pity and sadness filling them once more as she apologized for saying that.

August and I stood side by side that night, saying goodbye to everyone as they left the foyer to head to their homes. Then the three of us turned around to head upstairs: me to bathe Calum, August to read to him afterward.

Was this how life would be from now on? And if so, just how long could I take it?

If I was unhappy before, I'd become completely miserable.

Calum's smile had faded as we made our way up the stairs. "So, you guys really aren't gettin' married now?"

I'd mentioned something to Calum earlier in the day,

before anyone had arrived, and he hadn't had much of a reaction—I guess it was because he didn't think it was real. This was the first time he mentioned it since. August and I exchanged looks. "Nah, not right now," August said lightly, like it wasn't a big deal at all. "But that's not going to change a thing, don't you worry, buddy."

"Do you think you might get married someday and then we could be a real family?" he asked as we reached the top of the stairs, and he stopped to turn back to look at us. "And what about the brothers and sisters you said you wanted me to have? What about them? What about all the plans?" Calum burst into tears, great heaving sobs that tore at my heart. I wished I could fix everything for him.

But there wouldn't be any fixing it. So, I stood there, frozen on the staircase as August, the hero, scooped our son up., "Things are going to be fine, Calum," he murmured softly. "Momma and Daddy will always love you, and we'll always be a family—just in a different way. You don't have to cry."

The two of them continued on to Calum's room, leaving me alone. My legs felt weak, and I sat on the top step, putting my face in my hands. It wasn't just my life that was falling apart before my eyes—it was my son's, too. Maybe not as badly as some people's do, but for us, it was bad. And then there was August, strong as hell on the outside, but ripped to shreds on the inside.

August must've seen the state I was in, because he called back to me. "I've got him, Tawny. I'll give him his bath and put him to bed. 'Night."

Instead of heading to my room, I went back downstairs. I knew I wouldn't be able to sleep. All I could do was berate myself internally for screwing everything up.

I headed out to the garage, where I got into a random car

and drove off, not wanting to see the mansion August let me live in, not wanting to be around the two people I loved more than anything. I'd failed them both immeasurably.

August had always been my hero, but I couldn't bring myself to be one to him or our son.

Selfish bitch!

That's all I kept saying to myself as I just kept driving. I didn't realize where I was heading until I'd arrived at August's nightclub, Swank. Opening night was only a week away.

Parking the car across the street, I looked at what they'd built. The building was a masterpiece even though it hadn't been lit up yet. I wondered if August still wanted me to be his date for the grand opening.

And if he did, would I go?

People usually kissed their dates as the clock struck midnight on New Year's Eve. I couldn't allow that to happen. One kiss from him now would tear me apart.

I decided to tell him to find another date. I couldn't expect him to take me when we weren't even dating anymore.

And how would I react to seeing another woman on his arm?

The thought made me sick to my stomach.

What a selfish bitch!

It was bad enough that I'd turned cold on him, but now I didn't want him to have anyone else in his life?

Heartless!

That's exactly what I was.

I'd probably never see the inside of the expensive, over-the-top club. But I bet that I'd see plenty of pictures of the man I loved inside it—probably pictures with pretty women all over him.

Even though I knew exactly who to blame for how things had fallen apart, I still had to ask myself how the hell it had all happened.

Pounding the steering wheel, I shouted and cried, screaming at myself the whole time. And once I'd gotten it all out, once I'd run out of air, I headed back home.

Back to the place I knew I had to stay until Calum was out of school. Now that we'd been living this way, the three of us together, it wouldn't be fair to take that away from him anytime soon.

Back up the stairs I trudged. Walking down the long hallway, I looked straight ahead at August's closed bedroom door. My feet carried me right to it.

I stopped just in front of it. Little sounds inside the room told me he was there, just on the other side of the door. Maybe naked, having just come from the shower. A pulse thumped deep inside of me. Wetness filled my core.

Would it be enough to let him fuck me and then leave him to go back to my room?

My body wanted to feel his, and that craving was louder than the voice in my head telling me how wrong it was for me to even ask that of him.

I gripped the doorknob in my shaking hand. But when I went to turn it, I found it locked. My jaw clenched in frustration. And then the anger set in. He'd locked me out—that's exactly why I'd shut down my feelings for him in the first place.

But those feelings were still there; I'd just buried them under fear, anger, frustration, and most of all—out of weakness. Where had that strong woman I'd been when I was just a kid of eighteen gone?

91

CHAPTER 32

August

I wasn't playing mind games with Tawny, exactly, but I was letting her see what life would be like if she couldn't come around and realistically deal with things.

She wouldn't let me touch her, made sure she was never alone with me, and had even stopped talking to me like she used to. I watched as she let her heart freeze over as she tried to force what she truly felt for me into a place where it couldn't get out.

Tawny wasn't Tawny anymore, and I knew it would take something drastic to bring her back. I hated that Calum was being hurt by this, but sometimes it takes a bit of hurt to start the healing process. Like it or not, Calum was a part of us, and when we hurt, he hurt too. That's just life in a family.

It took all I had to walk away from Tawny as she sat at the top of the stairs. But she had to be alone. She had to know what it would be like if she kept building the fortress around her heart. Tawny was hurting us all, not just me or herself, each and every one of us. Something had to give.

Sitting on the edge of my bed, I was just about to turn off the lamp and lay back when I heard the soft rattle of my doorknob. It had to be Tawny.

I didn't have anything on, and I didn't want to make her feel uncomfortable, so I pulled on a pair of pajama bottoms before going to the door. When I pulled it open, no one was there.

Taking a couple of steps to the door to her room, I found it was locked, so I went back to bed. Maybe I'd been wrong. Maybe it was wishful thinking on my part that Tawny was there, trying to come into my room.

Laying down, I looked up at the ceiling, my hands behind my head. Maybe it was still a little too soon. But a month had passed without her allowing me to so much as touch her. I felt the timing was right.

I had to admit I didn't think she'd give me the ring back. That wasn't my plan at all. But when I'd said things weren't working out, she'd shucked that ring quicker than anything I'd ever seen. The sight of that ring, sitting on the table, had made my heart stop.

When I'd picked it up, it took everything inside of me not to yell at her to just stop this shit already. I'd fisted it in my hand, hating like hell everything that was happening.

I also had no idea anyone would notice the missing ring or ask anything about it if they did. Even as I'd explained things to our families, I half expected Tawny to come around and say something to me.

She hadn't. She'd stayed quiet. But I knew she wasn't happy at all. As a matter of fact, I'd seen her growing sadder and sadder as the day went on. And when our son had started crying, she'd broken down, too. But she hadn't broken down hard enough, I guess.

What would it take to make her see that she was throwing us away, our whole family?

Calum had put it out there, asking about the brothers and sisters, asking about becoming a real family. I thought that might get to her. It sure as fuck got to me. I guess it hadn't, though.

As I lay there, thinking about everything, I wondered if I'd been wrong, too.

I could've let her stay in my bed, or tried to find some other solution before kicking her out right away. I hadn't budged a bit on that. Was I to blame, too?

Fuck, you're an asshole!

My brain turned on me. I'd been looking at Tawny for an entire month, blaming her, wanting her to see the role she'd played in creating this rift between us that grew a little more with each passing day.

My cell dinged, and I looked over at it as it lay on the nightstand next to me. There was a message, and I saw it was from Tawny.

You should find another date for Swank's opening night, it said.

That was it.

Putting the phone down, I turned over on my side. Had I really fucked things up so badly that she wasn't going to go with me to the opening night of the club I'd work so hard to build?

The truth was that I hadn't thought about that at all.

The truth was that nothing had gone the way I had thought it would.

Everything I'd hoped that conversation would accomplish had backfired on me. My intentions were to get a conversation going that would eventually lead us to a place where we could get back to what we had. But it had only served to break us completely.

I had no idea how to fix things. The only thing that did come to mind was that Tawny didn't mind seeing me with another woman. And that pissed me off.

Would she really go so far as to try to send me into another woman's arms? Because to me, that meant she didn't give a shit about me. And that pissed me off to no end.

That girl had loved me; I knew that without a doubt. It was her own stubbornness that had gotten in the way of that. But if she was serious about me taking another woman to the grand opening, then something had to have changed in her heart when she'd deliberately frozen it.

Picking up my cell, I typed in a response.

Won't be taking anyone. I hit send.

I hoped that would sink into her tenacious head, and soon she'd realize how much it would hurt her to see me with someone else. Hell, it would hurt me to take out another woman—it would have to hurt her, right?

Tossing and turning, I couldn't get comfortable. She had me irate, and all I could think about was what the hell had gotten into her head to say a thing like that to me?

She'd told me she loved me just the night before. Sure, it wasn't like she said she was in love with me, just that she'd always have love for me. I supposed that was because I was the father of her child.

I'd said it back, but I knew I didn't say it the way I meant it. I was a dumb ass then, too.

Shit, when had I turned into such a dumb ass?

Slowly, but surely, it became clear that I was just as much to blame for this shit as she was. Both so stubborn we'd cut our noses off to spite our faces.

But how to fix it...now that was the real question.

How do you fix something that's so broken?

I had to admit to myself that I didn't know the answer to that question. I could go to her and apologize, take my share of the blame, but that wouldn't change anything anyway. I still wasn't ready to let her stay the nights with me, sleeping with me.

Man, she was so damn stubborn!

Why couldn't she see that I was afraid of hurting her? Why couldn't she be okay with that shit?

Sleep wasn't coming, so I sat up, picked my laptop up off the nightstand and did a little research. It seemed that most people with violent sleep disorders ended up taking medication to ease the problem—which I'd been against.

My mind went back to Dr. Schmidt, asking me whether I'd take medication if I had high blood pressure. And I knew I would.

So, why not take something to help me save my relationship?

Blinking at the screen, I wondered if I'd waited too long to make this decision. Would Tawny give me another chance, or was she done with me?

The text told me she was damn close. The way she was so quick to take my ring off said that as well.

What if it was just too late? Would I be able to live with myself?

92

CHAPTER 33

Tawny

I'd noticed that August had been to therapy every single day the entire week between Christmas and New Year's Eve. I hadn't asked him why that was. Maybe our breakup was worsening his problems.

New Year's Eve came, and Leila showed up at the house. I had to admit I was surprised, especially since she had a garment bag in one hand and a bottle of Champagne in the other. "I'm here to help you get ready, Tawny. Why is your jaw hanging open like that?"

"What are you doing...?"

She walked past me, heading up the stairs. "I'm here to get you ready for the grand opening at Swank, of course. Come on, I've got to get this show on the road. You're to meet August at the entrance in less than three hours."

"But Calum...," I said as I moved along behind her.

"I'm taking him home with me. He'll stay the night with us." She hurried to my bedroom.

"He doesn't need to stay over. August and I don't..." I

stopped. She knew we weren't having sex. I didn't need to remind her.

"Oh, yeah, the 'we're not romantically involved' thing. Yes, he told me about that. There's no need to wake Calum up to take him home so late—that would be silly." She laid the garment bag on my bed and pointed to the bathroom. "Go in there, shower, and shave every last bit of hair off your body. This dress is quite revealing. And wash your hair, too. I'm going to put it in a fantastic up-do for you. You're going to be the most gorgeous woman there tonight." Unzipping the garment bag, I saw something shimmery and white inside.

"Leila, this is so nice of you. But you see, I've already told your brother to get another date for this. I'm not about to spend the night with him, dancing, drinking, and possibly kissing him."

"And why the hell not?" she asked as her hands moved to her hips. "I'll tell you why you don't want to do that. It's because you're in love with August. You're being foolish about this not sleeping together nonsense. I'm here to tell you that August has asked me to come get you ready. He only wants *you* as his date, and he told me to tell you that."

"He does?" I asked as a shot of heat moved through me. "He told me that he wasn't going to take anyone to the opening."

"I don't know why he said that. He's taking you, and that's that. Now hurry up, Tawny!"

With that, I hurried to the bathroom, showering, shaving, and shampooing, too. When Leila was finished with me, I looked like me, but a version of me turned way the hell up.

My hair was curled and pinned in ways that defied imagination. "Wow, you're good, Leila."

"So, I've been told." She poured me a glass of champagne. "Drink this. Take the bottle with you—Max is driving you there. It'll help you to relax and to keep an open mind this evening. See what happens."

"Nothing will happen. He's as done with me as it gets. And even if he isn't, he's not going to give me what I want. No—what I need."

"Yeah, yeah," she said, gently shoving me along. "Let's get going now."

The white heels matched the barely-there dress perfectly. A slit came up the inner thigh of my right leg, showing off much more of me than anything I'd ever worn had before. The V-neck plunged all the way to the bottom of my bellybutton, and the back did the same thing, ending just before the crack of my ass.

August had spared no expense, as diamonds dripped off my ears and hung around my neck. Even a diamond ankle bracelet accented the over-the-top get up. I felt like a movie star going to the Academy Awards.

The alcohol didn't do a lot to help my nerves as I sat anxiously in the back seat while Max drove me to the club. He stopped at the entrance, and there stood August and two other men.

I supposed they were his partners; I'd never met them before. All three of them wore matching black tuxedos, and all three of them were devastatingly handsome. August was the best-looking, though. At least to me, he was.

He came right to me as I got out of the car. "You look amazing, Tawny."

I gave him the once-over. "As do you."

"Thank you for coming." He threaded my arm through his.

"As if Leila would have allowed anything else." I tried to ignore how sexy he smelled. "Is that a new cologne?"

"It is." He leaned in so close his breath tickled my ear. "And you smell fantastic."

"Thank you." I felt my body flush at the compliment.

As we walked up to the men who were still waiting just outside the door, he introduced me. "Tawny, this is Gannon Forester, and this other gentleman is Nixon Slaughter."

I extended my hand for a shake, but they took turns kissing the top instead. It turned out they were both waiting for their significant others, so August and I headed inside.

The place was opulent—utterly fantastic. A blue light shone from nowhere and magically filled every space somehow. The entrance was phenomenal. White stone statues had been placed around the perimeter of the round room. "These came straight from Greece." August pointed over at the doorway that led to the actual club. "Wait 'til you see this."

Stepping through the door, red light echoed off sparkling waterfalls on either side of them. In the center of the large room, there looked to be a swimming pool. "You can swim in here?" Tawny asked him incredulously.

"No," he chuckled. "Come on." Leading me to it, I tried to stop when we got to the edge, but he pulled me along. "Glass covers the water. Didn't you notice that you can't hear the waterfalls?"

Looking at the water fixtures on both sides, I couldn't see the glass that covered them, but I did notice that I couldn't hear any sound coming from them. "That had to cost a lot of money."

"Everything in this place did." His arm moved around to take me by the waist. "Come on, I want to tell you something before anyone gets here." He took me to a table and sat me down as he continued to stand in front of me. "Tawny, I've spent a lot of time this past month looking deeply into myself, and I've found a selfish man in there. You told me how important it was for us to be together, always, but I didn't do a thing to try to fix that problem. I thought keeping away from you at night was the only solution. But I was wrong."

"You were?" I asked as hope filled me.

"I was. And I've been working with my doctors and have found a medication that I can take just before falling asleep that has been proven to help me with my sleeping disorder." Then he got on one knee, taking my hand. "Tawny, I want you back in our bed. And I know that there is more between us than just sex. We belong together, and I want you to sleep with me each and every night. I want you to marry me and make me the happiest man alive." He produced my engagement ring, and I didn't know what to say at all.

"I can sleep with you?" I had to ask.

He nodded. "Yes, you can. And I'm sorry it took me so damn long to figure out that I was being bull-headed. But don't worry, I'm not about to make you admit that you were being that way, too. So, will you marry me?"

I couldn't help but chuckle at his little dig at me. It made me happy that he was calling me on my shit, too. "First, let me take my share of responsibility in this. I've done a lot of soul-searching, too. I was being stubborn, and I shut myself off as well." Tears welled in my eyes as I thought about the pain I'd caused us in the past month. "You never did that. You kept trying, and I kept pushing you away. And I am so deeply sorry for doing that. But the fact that you got help with this thing makes me so happy. You have no idea."

His smile went wide. "Good. So, will you?" He wiggled the ring.

Holding out my left hand, I said, "Please put that back on my finger. I've missed it more than I care to admit."

Slipping it on, he smiled the whole time. "Thank God."

Pulling me up, he slipped his arms around me, holding me close. "After this, I'm going to take your sweet ass home and make love to you until the sun comes up. Then we'll sleep a little while before we wake up and do it all over again. That belly will be filled with our next baby before you know it."

I laughed as he began dancing with me even though no music played. "So, this is going to be one hell of a night. Not what I had in mind a few hours ago."

"Not one bit." He dipped me. "This dress looks hot as hell on you, baby. It'll look even better on our bedroom floor."

"You think?" I asked with a little giggle.

He pulled me up, slowly, his eyes trained on my mouth. "I know it will. And my cock will look great once it's slick and shiny with the juices your cunt will leave on it."

"Shit!" I hissed as he'd already gotten me hot and extremely bothered.

"Yeah, shit." His eyes never left my mouth as he came closer and closer until our lips barely touched.

A wave of heat gushed through me, my body shook, and desire took over as he kissed me. We shared a kiss that took me away from everything. People had begun to filter in, and neither of us had even noticed as we held each other and kissed like no one was watching.

No one seemed to mind though, and we continued on doing that pretty much the rest of the night.

When all the fun was over, and the club closed after a very successful opening night, we got into the backseat of the car. Max was driving, thank God, so we got to do more than we'd been able to in the crowded club.

The slit in my dress proved to be a big help, allowing

August to get to me quickly. Hiking it up only a little, he pushed the tiny bit of lace that formed the front of my thong to one side before kissing me, licking me, and sucking on my clit.

It had been too damn long, and he'd been kissing and caressing me so much in the club that I came in what felt like seconds. But that didn't seem to bother him in the least as he drank me all up.

"My turn," I said after I'd caught my breath. I was hungry for his cock and moved around to kneel on the floor as he pulled his cock out for me.

His hands on the side of my head pulled me to him, and then moved me at a slow pace. The taste of him made me groan the entire time. My tongue ran along the underside of his cock with each stroke I made. The taste of cum leaking from his tip had me growling, ready to drink him down.

But he pulled my head away, then pushed me to lie on my back on the floor. He was on top of me, tearing my panties off before slamming his cock into me. I gasped with the pleasure and wrapped my legs around him as he pumped his rock-hard dick into me.

Again, my body had wanted him so badly that it fell apart much too soon—but his had wanted me just as badly, and he came right along with me, filling me with his hot semen.

The car came to a stop as we tried to catch our breath. "We're home." August pulled me up, and we headed inside.

My heels came off at the door, and he carried me up the stairs to his bedroom. "So, this is real? I get to sleep with you?"

He nodded as he kicked the door closed behind us. "I had the staff move all your clothes into this other closet in here already. All of your personal toiletries have been put into this bathroom, too."

"You were pretty damn certain I'd say yes, weren't you?" I took his handsome face between my palms as I gazed into his hazel eyes.

"You love me. I knew that. You just needed me to give you a little bit more of myself. So, I figured out how to accomplish that. I've got you, baby. I always have. From that first night that I made you mine, I've had you. Your heart, and even part of your soul, I think. All I had to do was become more of the man you needed me to be." He kissed me long and hard before tossing me on the bed. "Now, let's get rid of these clothes."

93

CHAPTER 34

August

Only one year later, we were back again at Swank —which had become extremely popular—at midnight on New Year's Eve. I looked over as Tawny came walking toward me, her belly beautifully swollen with a little girl and a white bouquet in her hand.

It wasn't the wedding chapel back in our hometown—it was much better than that.

With Calum as my best man, we stood together watching the woman we both loved walk toward us. We were about to become a real family in Calum's eyes, and he wanted to be front and center as it happened.

"Man, Momma's so bootiful, isn't she, Dad?" he asked me as awe filled his little voice.

"She sure is, son." I patted his head, but couldn't take my eyes off my bride. "I hope when you grow up you meet a lady as good and pretty as your mother one day."

"Me too. You're lucky, Dad."

"And I know it, too." I held out my hand as her father brought Tawny to me.

She handed the bouquet to my sister, her matron of honor. Tawny's smile was wide and happy. "Hey."

"Hey." I rocked on my feet. "You're up late."

She chewed her lower lip as she looked me up and down with her pretty green eyes. "So are you."

I eyed her, taking in the pink stain of her lips, wondering how she'd taste after she became mine in name, too. "You want some company?"

Plump pink lips pulled up to one side as she turned the question back on me. "Why, you want some?"

"I do want some. I'm heading out to boot camp in the morning, and my mind's a mess about it." I took her hand, playing with her fingertips.

Her lips formed a straight line as she looked into my eyes. "So, you're really going then?"

With a nod I went on, "I'm not afraid to fight in this war. But I am afraid I'll never see home again."

At my words, she glanced up at the rising full moon through the skylight we'd built just for this momentous occasion. "If it helps at all, I think you're a hero, August."

"I'm no hero. Not yet anyway. But thanks. And I should tell you since I might never see you again, that I think you're beautiful. I've thought so ever since you turned fifteen. You and I were too far apart in age to ever do anything about that though."

Her lips quirked to one side. "Okay, if we're being honest, then I can tell you that I've always thought you were smoking hot."

The memory of everything that happened between us during our first time popped into my head, and my cock thumped in my tuxedo pants. "Well, I may never make it back, Tawny."

She looked out at her parents and winked at them as she said, "My parents aren't home. I'm here alone, August." Our guests laughed knowingly.

The last line of our little play before the actual vows had me saying, "It would be a one-night thing. You understand that don't you?"

Then she shook her head. "No, I don't understand, and neither do you. This will be an every-night thing and for the rest of our lives."

And she'd been right. We'd found our happily ever after.

The End

PREVIEW OF DIRTY LITTLE SECRET

A SECRET BABY-SECOND CHANCE ROMANCE (SONS OF SIN 1)

Michelle Love

Blurb

**Once upon a time, I was nothing more than a bad boy
seeking all the tail I could get …**

Something happened to change all that.
Suddenly, chasing women turned into chasing the dream of
becoming a doctor.
Hard work and determination had me meeting my dream a
hell of a lot sooner than most.
And with the title of doctor came ready and willing women,
set on landing themselves a wealthy physician.
Little did they know that I would readily give them some
hot, steamy memories to keep, but my heart belonged to
someone else. Someone I didn't want to share with anyone.

But then she came along, claiming what had always been
only mine.
And maybe she would claim my heart as well ...

**She was a virgin, and I was the bad boy set on getting her
gift ...**
I got it, all right.
Taking her sweet innocence, I traded her one night of
unforgettable pleasure.
Untouched skin rubbed against mine. Hot breath that had
never flowed over anyone else's lips filled my lungs.
Her body welcomed me in, and in it, I would stay for a
while.
Nine months, to be exact. Then our night of what her family
deemed sin would be born, only to be given away.
He was her secret, and he soon became mine too ...

When a young teen couple accidentally get pregnant, the
girl is forced to give the baby boy up for adoption.
Little does she realize, it's the father of the baby's aunt and
uncle who've adopted the baby.
Once the father reaches twenty-five and has made a Doctor
out of himself, the aunt and uncle give custody of his son to
him. And one fateful day, ten years after the boy's birth, the
two who conceived him meet again.
Can the three become a family after all this time?

94

CHAPTER 1

Zandra

Cold wind whipped around me as I climbed the stairs up to my apartment, which I shared with four roommates. Unfortunately, they were four of the messiest and most immature individuals I'd ever had the misfortune of meeting.

I'm met all of them while working as a cocktail waitress at Underground, a nightclub in Chicago, and we'd gotten along well enough to decide to live together. Little did I know that all four of them were very different people at home than they were while working with the public.

Being a few years older than any of them, at twenty-six I supposed I was just growing up a bit. That had to be the reason behind my budding impatience with the people I'd lived with for the last year.

It seemed like just yesterday that I was right there with them all, dumping clean laundry onto the floor instead of putting it in my closet, making a mess while trying to search for just the right thing to wear. Or even leaving dirty dishes in the sink with the hope that someone else would get disgusted enough with the mess to feel the urge to clean up. Yes, I was once just as filthy as they were, but things had changed in the last few months.

I had changed. Now all I wanted was a clean apartment to live in.

Is that too much to ask for?

Walking back into the quiet house after having a morning coffee at the small café down the street, I headed toward the one bathroom the five of us shared.

I would've loved to have been able to go to the bathroom without having to clean the damn toilet first. Two of my roommates were guys who had a habit of leaving trails of pee in places that didn't make sense. Along the edge of the tub, around the floor near the toilet, and once even by the door, for some odd reason. And they never seemed to notice their mishaps either, leaving them for someone else to deal with.

I'd begun carrying around a little container with convenient small towelettes covered in peach-scented bleach that I would use to wipe things down. It seemed I was becoming more like my mother in this regard, a realization I disliked very much, but had no clue how to push away so I could go back to not giving a hoot about cleanliness.

In retaliation to my impending maturity, I'd gone to the salon to get my dark hair done in a more fun, youthful fashion. The new dark blue streaks might just be a visual representation of my attempt to cling to my youth, but so what? I liked them.

But even as I looked into the bathroom mirror after wiping the entire room down, I could see a new maturity in my blue eyes that hadn't been there even a few months ago.

Yes, the streaks in my hair were the same color as my eyes. A girl likes to match, you know.

Staring disconnectedly into the eyes of the person looking back at me, that empty feeling I had at times started to creep in. Most of the time I could ignore the emptiness, but now and then it would find me and linger for a while before letting up and allowing me some relief once more.

Whenever it hit me, my life would temporary turn into a hellish existence. My dreams would turn into nightmares, and all I could do was drink coffee to keep me awake, trying to keep the bad dreams away. Wishing the feeling wouldn't last more than a few days this time, instead of the week-long agony that had nearly drowned me the last time it hit me, I closed my eyes.

When I opened them up again, I saw myself staring back at me once more. A young woman, no longer the girl I had been. I needed to face things instead of trying to ignore or forget about them.

I had a bad past. So what?

Lots of people had bad things happen to them in their lives. Who did I think I was?

Was I invincible? Was I too good for anything bad to ever happen to me? No, I wasn't. And I had to stop the internal berating that came along with every bout of depression.

Leaving the now-clean bathroom, I went to the bedroom I shared with the other two girls in the apartment. They were sprawled out on their little twin beds; one of them had her head at the wrong end of the bed.

I fought the urge to move her into the right position, a motherly urge that only proved to make the depressed feelings inside of me edge closer to the surface.

Tears began to sting the backs of my eyes, and I left the

room to go to the kitchen and clean some more. Cleaning was fast becoming the outlet I turned to whenever the emptiness tried to claim me.

And with this crew of slobs, there was plenty of cleaning to do. The dishes needed washing, so I did the sink full of them. The floor needed to be swept and mopped, so I did that too. The fridge needed to be cleaned out, the leftovers tossed, and the entire thing wiped down with one of my handy bleach wipes as well.

By the time the first roommate woke up and dragged his ass out of bed, the kitchen sparkled, and everything smelled peachy. Standing there in his not-so-white, tighty whiteys, Dillon rubbed his brown eyes with the back of one hand as he yawned loudly. "What the hell are you doing, making all this noise on a Sunday, Zandy? We didn't get in last night until four in the morning. Are you insane?"

Am I?

I wasn't sure how to answer that. I felt it best to ignore his question. "I'm cleaning, Dillon. A thing the rest of you must not have learned how to do yet. I'll try to be quieter, so you guys can sleep. Sorry about that." Apologizing for doing chores shouldn't be something anyone should have to worry about.

I found resentment building up inside of me. *These ungrateful kids should have to live in filth!*

As Dillon walked wearily back to the bedroom he shared with the other guy who lived with us, I looked at the clean floor and wondered what the hell I was doing there.

My parents lived just outside of town. But I would never go back to live with them. I only talked to my mother when she called incessantly, and then only for a very short amount of time. I would let her know that I was alive and fine, but nothing more than that.

She didn't deserve to know any more than that. Not after what she and my father had done to me.

Their evil deed had left a hole in my heart. A hole that I knew could never be repaired.

Going out the front door, I took a seat on the top stair outside our apartment. The wind still blew a thousand miles an hour, making my hair fly all around me. The cold air chilled me to my bones, as I'd come out once again without so much as a sweater on to keep me warm. Only an old sweatshirt and a pair of jeans covered my body. It wasn't enough to keep the cold out.

Fiddling with a hole in the knee of my jeans, I made it even bigger. The image of a baby made a brief appearance in my brain before I successfully pushed it aside.

No, I didn't ever let things like that take up any space in my head. But when I fell asleep, those thoughts and images would sneak in, taking my dreams and turning them into nightmares.

Two days had already passed with little sleep. Waking up with tears on my pillow, I would get up and do anything I could to make myself stop thinking. Thinking only made it hurt worse.

Ten years have passed. Why does it still bother me so much?

Looking down at my left arm, I still couldn't believe that I'd gotten so drunk three nights earlier that I'd gone and gotten a tattoo on the inside of my wrist.

Why did I do this to myself?

Why would I purposely do anything that would be a constant reminder of the one thing I tried desperately to forget about? Why would I put that on my body?

For the rest of my life, I'd look down and see "05/03/2008" written in baby blue ink multiple times a day. Why would I do such a hurtful thing to myself?

Only God knew why I would do such a thing, no matter what amount of alcohol I'd consumed. Or the devil. I wasn't sure which had the strongest hold on me.

At times, it sure felt like the devil was the one who'd laid out the path my life would take.

Is there a way to change my path, or is it too late? Can there be a way out of this emptiness?

If there was, I knew now that I wouldn't find the answer in Chicago. Of that much, I was sure.

I'd been dragged there against my will when I was just sixteen years old. When I left my parents' home on the day I turned eighteen, I could've gone anywhere. I had ten thousand dollars that I'd inherited from my grandmother. She'd died when I was twelve, and the money had been left in a bank account in Charleston, South Carolina, where we'd lived most of my life.

When I turned eighteen, I gained access to that money and hauled ass out of the house I'd essentially been held captive in for two long-as-hell years. Without any other plan, into the big city of Chicago I went.

The bank card from the Charleston bank had come in the mail a few days before my birthday. It had my name on it. The accompanying letter said that it would be activated on the date of my birth and would be ready to use that very day.

I used it to buy myself a birthday present—a cab ride into town and then a week in a cheap motel. I found a job that very night at Underground.

My first roommate was a girl named Sasha who'd been working at the club for a few years. At twenty-five years old, the older woman took me under her wing, teaching me everything I needed to know in order to bring in big tips by being flirtatious and sexy.

A couple of years later she met some guy and moved out to live with him. She also quit working at the nightclub. That's when I met a new friend. Taylor had come to work at the club when she was just eighteen, too. I was a little older by then and took her under my wing, letting her stay in Sasha's old room.

Taylor didn't need much coaching. She seemed to be a natural at flirting. And it didn't hurt that she had absolutely no problem sleeping with any guy who wanted her.

I had issues with sex. My past made me it very hard for me to have any kind of eagerness for the act. It was sex that had gotten me into trouble in the first place.

As sexy as I dressed and as flirty as I was, it was all a performance. An important one, that helped me keep a roof over my head, food in my stomach, and a car under my ass to keep me going to and fro on my own.

Following the same routine for nearly a decade can grow tiresome. And boy, did I feel tired. Tired of looking at the same old buildings. Tired of driving down the same old streets. Tired of living with a bunch of overgrown adolescents.

The back pocket of my jeans vibrated, so I pulled out my cell phone. A smile broke the no-doubt forlorn expression my face must have settled into. As if by magic, Taylor's name appeared on the screen.

She'd left a year ago, sparking my need to get a new roommate. I didn't recall exactly why I kept letting people move in, but I had. I hadn't heard from her in a good while.

"Hey, you," I answered the call.

"Hey yourself, girlie. What're you up to these days?" she asked me.

Shoving my hand through my hair, then holding onto it so the wind couldn't blow it around, I sighed heavily. I didn't know what to say. I had been up to the same old dreary thing. But to say that out loud seemed just too pathetic. "Not much. You?"

"Just working at this badass club in Charleston called Mynt," came her enthusiastic reply.

"Mynt?" My mind wandered back to Charleston. The home I'd had to leave when I was just sixteen. Barely sixteen, really, as my mother was constantly reminding me.

Mom would remind me far too often that I was barely above fifteen when I'd gotten myself into what she liked to refer to as "the situation." A situation, she also reminded me, that had forced her and my father to uproot our little family and move far away. Life had never been the same after that move.

"Yeah, Mynt," Taylor said, pulling me out of my reverie. "And you want to know what I think, Zandy?"

"What do you think?" I chewed on my long fake black-painted fingernail as I waited to hear what she had to say.

"I think that you should come on down here to the South and work with me." She paused to let that sink in as I thought about it. "I've got a very nice two-bedroom apartment that my roommate has just moved out of. I could use a new roomie, and who better than you to fill that role?"

Yeah, who better than me to fill that role?

Charleston sounded nice. Going back to what I had always considered my home sounded like a fantastic idea. *Why not go back there?*

Even if I saw anyone from my old life, it wasn't like anyone knew why we'd left all of a sudden anyway. What harm would it do to go back to my hometown?

"And the pay at Mynt?" I asked. "Is it pretty decent?"

"Let's just say that I make enough money to pay my bills, eat what I want, when I want, drive a nice car, and even splurge on shopping now and then with what I'm bringing home." She laughed, the pitch high and shrill but still pleasant, as only Taylor could make it. "Please tell me that you'll come. I've already talked to the boss about you. He thinks you'll fit right in with our little family at Mynt. It's lots of fun, Zandy. You'll love the atmosphere. I promise you that we'll have a great time."

She made it sound like a great idea, and it wasn't like I had anything holding me in Chicago. A change might be just what I needed to get the emptiness to go away. At least for a little while.

Another gust of frigid wind hit me, and I got up. My hand balled into a fist at my side; I was ready to make the big change. "It's a miracle that you called me right at this moment, Taylor. I've been in a funk lately. Change is exactly what I need in my life right now."

She sounded hopeful. "Does that mean you'll come?"

"Yeah, I'll come." I went back inside to get out of the cold. "When do you want me?"

"Yesterday," she said with light laughter threading her high voice. Taylor was the closest thing to a fairy a human woman could get, and it was utterly charming. People often called her Tinkerbell.

"Then I'll pack up my things and give my notice at work. Then I'll get into my car and come your way. Text me the address, and I'll be there as soon as my wheels can get me there."

Change was important. It's what I'd been missing in my life lately, and without change life could be one long, dreary existence. I wanted to leave dreary behind me. Hopefully, Charleston would see to that.

95

CHAPTER 2

Kane

The crack of the bat connecting with the baseball made my heart swell with pride. "You did it, Fox! Now run, son!"

On my feet as soon as the ball started soaring, I clapped as my ten-year-old son threw the bat down then ran to first base before anyone could get a hold of the ball. "Go to second," I called out to him, seeing that he looked a little confused about what he should do.

The coach shouted, "Go on, Fox. This could be a home run!"

My son's first home run!

Standing, watching, not daring to breathe, I crossed my fingers, hoping that he would make it. Moments later, he slid into home base. All the parents on the bench let out a cheer, as my son run had earned his team, the Bears, the one point they needed to take the lead against their biggest rivals, the Tigers. "Way to go, boy!"

Fox waved at me with the biggest grin on his face I'd

ever seen. "I did it, Dad!"

"You did!" I knew I had to be beaming.

With a nod, he headed back into the dugout where his teammates gave him high-fives and pats on the back. He'd earned them too.

Taking my seat again, I looked over at the man sitting next to me, my Uncle James. He and my Aunt Nancy, who sat on the other side of him, always joined me to watch Fox's games.

My mother and Aunt Nancy were sisters. I owed everything to Aunt Nancy and Uncle James. They'd done the biggest favor anyone could do for another person, and they'd done it for me. They'd found the girl I'd accidentally knocked up in high school and had adopted the baby.

If it hadn't been for a friend of mine, Bess Peterson, who'd lived next door to the Larkin family, I wouldn't have ever known that I'd gotten Zandra Larkin pregnant. Bess had overheard the awful shouting that had taken place when Zandra's parents had found out that she was having a baby.

Zandra and Bess weren't friends. Zandra was mostly a loner, probably because of her parents' strict religious beliefs. Those beliefs were probably what had put them into panic mode, whisking their only child away a few weeks after Zandra and I had hooked up at a party one night.

I'd always thought Zandra, who was a year younger than me, was pretty. Her long, dark hair, deep blue eyes, and pretty pink lips had caught my attention more often than they hadn't. But she was shy, reclusive, and kept to herself.

That one night at that party, which I'd found out one of her few friends had dragged her to, had given me the chance to get to know her. And boy, did I get to know her!

She didn't give me her phone number before she left me

that night in my friend's bed. I fell asleep, and she took off without waking me up. It was the end of summer, so there wasn't any school the next week. And knowing how strict her parents were, I wasn't about to just show up at her house unannounced.

Everyone knew how strict her mother and father were. I was afraid I might get her into trouble if I just showed up. I planned on catching up with her when school was back in session. But I never got that chance.

It was Bess who came to me when school started again. She'd seen Zandra and me together at that party, and she was pretty sure that I'd been the one to do the deed that had put Zandra's family in such turmoil.

It seemed that Zandra's mother kept track of her periods, and when Zandra failed to start on time, she took her to the doctor. Bess told me that she overheard Zandra's parents screaming that she wasn't going to get to keep the baby and blaming her for ruining all of their lives. They repeatedly asked Zandra for the name of the boy she'd been with, but Zandra refused to tell them a thing.

Some other boys in that position might've counted themselves lucky that they didn't have to deal with any of it. Instead, I went home and told my parents what I'd done. I told them that I knew Zandra had been a virgin before me. She'd told me so, and the fact that she'd bled told me she hadn't lied about it.

I'd gotten her pregnant the very first time she'd ever had sex. Along with that, I shared the responsibility of her being taken away from her hometown. It wasn't fair, and I knew that. I also knew it wasn't fair to give our baby to strangers.

Mom had called her sister right away, knowing she had the connections that would make tracking the baby a possibility. Aunt Nancy and Uncle James did the investigative work, and our son was given to them in a closed adoption. Neither Zandra nor her family even knew the names of the people who adopted the boy. And they would never know it was my family who took him.

"Handing custody over to you was the best thing we could've ever done for Fox," Uncle James said as he bumped his shoulder to mine. "We're damn proud of you, Kane. We're very proud of you for finishing your doctorate last year and earning that position at the clinic. Twenty-seven is pretty young to be so well established and settled down."

"Well, Fox was all the incentive I needed to grow up quick." I had to sigh as I watched my son cutting up with his teammates. "From the moment you guys brought him to see me when he was just a week old, I knew I would live my life for him. I just wanted to make sure I could be the father he deserves."

I clapped my uncle on the back. "Thanks for always letting me be there with him, you guys. I can't thank you enough for giving a seventeen-year-old kid the chance to prove that he could be a stand-up father. Letting me take custody of him and actually make him mine last year was a dream come true for me."

"And for Fox," Aunt Nancy added. "That kid has always loved you, Kane. It was only fair that he be with his biological father."

Nodding, I thought about the fact that my aunt and uncle had decided from the start to have Fox call them aunt and uncle. They'd told him I was his father right from the start. It made things easier when I finally had a home to bring him to, making the transition a smooth one.

Fox knew the whole story, now that he was old enough. We never planned on hiding the truth from him, so it was just a matter of waiting until he could understand. His mother was only sixteen when she got pregnant. Her parents made her give him up, and we jumped in to make sure we never lost him.

"He's looking more and more like his mom every day," I commented as I looked at my son. "His dark hair is the exact same shade as hers was. And those freckles across his nose come from her too."

Uncle James asked, "Do you think you'll ever try to find her, Kane?"

Shaking my head, I answered him truthfully. "No. I have no idea if she wanted to give him away or not. The fact is she went along with the adoption—and a closed one, at that. She may have wanted it that way too. I won't find her and tell her about something she may not want to hear about."

Aunt Nancy had always leaned more toward contacting Zandra one day. "He just turned ten last week. Fox is a bright boy with tons of curiosity. I know he doesn't talk to you about his mother nearly as much as he talks to me about her, but he does ask about her a lot. I think you should start thinking some more about finding her, Kane. It might be what's best for Fox."

Pushing my hand through my hair, I felt that nagging feeling coming over again. The feeling always lingered when I thought about the reality that Zandra might not want anything to do with our son, or me, for that matter.

"But what if she didn't want him? It might have started out as her parents' idea, but what if Zandra wanted to get rid of him too, in the end? How would she react then if I tried to pull her into his life when all she wanted was to be rid of him?"

Uncle James smiled at me with that expression of pure wisdom on his face. "What if she didn't want to give him up and was only doing what her parents made her do? What if she's still as shy as she was when she was sixteen and doesn't have a clue how to find her son? What if she's hurt by what she was made to do and thinks about him every day?"

God, the man knew how to pull at a person's heartstrings!

Even still, I wasn't sure about anything, other than that she had given him up in a closed adoption. No authority, other than her parents, had made her do that. "She could've told the adoption agency that her parents were making her give the baby up and that she didn't want to."

Aunt Nancy shook her head. "I was there when she gave him up, Kane. She had no idea I wasn't a nurse, Kane, and that girl was heartbroken when I took that baby away from her that day. She told him that she loved him more than anything. She told him that she was sorry for what she was doing, but that he would have a much better life without her or her parents in it."

Aunt Nancy had told me this a million times. And as many times as I'd heard the story, I had never understood why Zandra would've gone through with giving him up if she truly loved him. And I'd never understood why she'd never tried to contact me about the pregnancy.

It wasn't as if I was some lothario who had slept with countless girls. I'd never intended to just sleep with her and then drop her. I'd thought about her a lot after the party. I'd thought about how I would approach the shy girl when school was back in session, about how I would bring her out of her shell again, just as I was able to that night.

The fact that she never seemed to even try to get in touch with anyone, not even the few friends she'd had at school, had me thinking that she wanted to forget all about that part of her life.

I stayed in Charleston. With my parents' help, plus my aunt and uncle's, I raised Fox. Everyone we knew was aware that I was that boy's father and that Zandra Larkin was his mother. Everyone. Even Zandra's friends knew about it.

So why hadn't Zandra ever tried to contact any of her friends?

Each one of the girls I talked to back then told me that Zandra had their phone numbers, though Zandra's number was no longer in service after the move. And even at Fox's tenth birthday party, one of his mother's old friends stopped by to wish him a happy birthday and give him a present. She told him that if his mother were around, she'd be very proud of him. And she also told him that his mother was a very private and shy person, but she was sure that she still loved him, as she was also a very nice and loving person.

I recalled the smile that spread across my son's face that day as he and his mother's friend talked. He nodded. "I'm sure she does love me. I love her, and I don't 'member meeting her ever in my life. But Aunt Nancy said that she held me for a little while before she had to say goodbye. And that she told me that she loved me too. I know that someday I'll see her again. And then I'll be old enough to 'member her."

Most people seemed sure that one day Zandra would try to find Fox. I was one of the few who didn't think that day would come at all. And I prayed that our son wouldn't be hurt if the day he was so hopeful about never occurred.

And I wondered how I would react to her if she did come looking for him. Would I be angry with her?

As understanding as I'd tried to be about her situation, I had also been mad back then. Mad that she hadn't told me what was happening. Mad that she'd planned to give our child to strangers. Mad that her parents thought they could take my son's future into their own hands.

Zandra may have been intimidated and controlled by

her parents, but I never would've let them control me too. I would've taken care of Zandra, had she told me about the situation.

Looking at the ground, I knew my thoughts weren't healthy. I'd been a seventeen-year-old kid at that time. Zandra had been a minor; her parents had still been in control of her life.

In reality, I couldn't have taken care of her. My parents could have and would have. But only if Zandra's parents allowed that to happen. And we all knew that they would never have allowed that.

The sound of cheers pulled me out of my internal reverie, and I looked up. My son's team had won the game. The boys were jumping up and down with triumphant joy.

"Looks like we're going to get to go to a pizza party, Kane," Uncle James said. We all got up to join the kids on the field to congratulate each one of them and to tell the kids on the other team that they'd played a great game too.

"We did it, Dad!" Fox shouted as he ran to me.

"You sure did, son!" Putting my arm around his narrow shoulders, I pulled him close to my side. "Your home run was the game-winner, too."

"Hey, Fox, catch," the coach called out.

He tossed the ball to Fox, who caught it easily. The smile he'd been wearing grew even bigger. "I get to keep the game ball?"

"It's yours, kid," his coach told him. "At the pizza party, you can get everyone to sign it for you."

"I'll get you a little case to keep it in, Fox," Uncle James told him as he pulled him away from me to give him a hug.

"Man, this is like the best day ever!" Fox shouted as he held the ball up. "We won! Woohoo!"

Man, I bet his mother would love to see him like this.

96

CHAPTER 3

Zandra

"Cute outfit," the manager of Mynt said as he looked me up and down. "Nice legs. It's good to see you don't mind putting them on display." Wearing a short black leather skirt with a white button-down top, I had tied my shirt in a knot in front to show off my belly button piercing. I was the epitome of hot nightclub waitresses everywhere.

"Yeah. I've been doing this waitress thing since I turned eighteen. I've pretty much got it down pat now." I pulled the long braid I'd put my hair in over my shoulder, stroking it as I looked into Rob's gray eyes. His pupils got big, telling me he liked what he saw.

By now, I was used to having my body raked over by men's eyes, and it didn't bother me to be the center of attention. As long as the scrutiny came with a paycheck, I could suck it up.

Rob trailed his long fingers along one of my shoulders. His dark hair was parted low on the left side. Some type of product made it shiny, helping him keep it slicked back. He wasn't my type at all. He was the kind of guy most people would call a guido—maybe not to his face, though.

"And how many years have you been doing this now?" he asked.

"Eight years." Placing my hand on my hip, I defied him to say something about my age. Though I was still young and as fit as any one of the younger waitresses, I knew a lot of managers liked to stick to the under-twenty-five crowd when it came to their waitresses.

"Twenty-six," he mused as his eyes met mine. His lips pulled up to one side. "Your body might not give it away, but you can see it in your eyes, Zandy."

"Well, it's a good thing no one will be looking at my eyes, then, isn't it?" Sashaying my ass, I walked away from him, earning a wolf-whistle. The sound made me smile. That whistle meant money, and money was all I cared about.

"Does that mean she's got the job, Rob?" Taylor chimed in.

I turned around to look at him as he answered. "If she can start tonight, she does."

"I can." Hurrying back to them, I found myself grabbed up by Taylor, and the two of us jumped up and down in our sky-high heels. "Yes!"

Now I had a nice apartment with a bedroom all to myself and a job that Taylor promised would make me lots of money. More money than what I'd been making in Chicago.

On the drive back to the apartment, the two of us chatted away excitedly about being able to work together again. Taylor stopped at a light then screamed, "Yes! Together again! We're gonna rock Charleston, Zandy!"

"We rocked Chicago," I agreed. "I know we can rock this place too."

Looking to my left, I thought I recognized a guy from high school. That had been so long ago, it seemed. He looked right at me, gave me a wink, and then Taylor took off so fast that I didn't get the chance to even wink back or see if he recognized me.

I was pretty sure he hadn't. I no longer looked like the bookish, shy girl I'd been back then. Nearly eleven years had passed since I'd been in town, since I'd been that person. I didn't expect anyone to recognize me.

And I prayed that one man, in particular, wouldn't. If he was even still in the around—which I highly doubted.

The blue streaks in my hair would offer me a bit of protection, should I happen to encounter someone from my old life here. This hair choice was something I never would've done when I was a teenager. And I wore a lot of makeup now, too. It was what waitresses did. I didn't make the rules; I just followed them.

Revealing clothes, too much makeup, hair that stood out —I was dressing for the job I wanted. And I was pretty certain not one of the people I'd known back then would come to the club I'd be working at. Even if they did, no one would ever think the sexy woman who waited on them was the same mousy junior from high school who'd left town without saying a word to anyone.

"Did it piss you off when Rob said he could see your age in your eyes, Zandy?" Taylor asked me as she drove too fast down the street.

"No." I pulled a pair of dark sunglasses out of my purse and put them on. "I can see it too. There aren't many ladies in my age group who still do this sort of thing. Being twenty-six, many women my age have already hung up their heels.

And have replaced their Mustangs with minivans, yuck!" We laughed uproariously at my little joke, which wasn't too much of a joke at all.

Taylor zoomed around a corner, making us both lean to one side, laughing like hell all the way. "So why haven't you settled down, Zandy? I mean, you haven't even dated any guy seriously. What's up with you?"

Where to start?

Pain. Anguish. Guilt. Along with a healthy side of resentment and regret.

I'd never told anyone about my unexpected pregnancy, or any of the life-altering events that followed. Maybe it was time I did. Maybe talking about it would help me begin to heal from it. If anyone could truly heal from a thing like that.

Even though I wasn't sure how Taylor would take it, I decided to spill my guts to her. "Dating would mean giving someone a chance to get close to me and taking a chance of falling in love. And when two people fall in love, they eventually decide to procreate. And I've done that already. It ended badly. And I don't want to do it again."

"You had a miscarriage?" she asked as she took another hard left.

The Nissan Altima felt like it had tilted onto only two wheels, making me scream with a mix of terror and excitement. "No! Shit, girl. You're a crazy driver!"

"So I've been told." She laughed menacingly, making me smile. I loved living dangerously. Why not live that way? What did I have to live for anyway? "So, no miscarriage. Did you lose the baby after it was born?" I could hear the sympathy in her voice, mixed with caution. Taylor knew me well enough to know that revealing so much about myself wasn't easy for me.

"Kind of." I grabbed the dash as she made an abrupt stop at a stop sign that seemed to have crept up on her.

"Kind of?" She narrowed her pale blue eyes at me. Her tiny nose was pointy and turned up at the end. Taylor really did remind me of Tinkerbell. Only, her short blonde locks were pulled into spikes, and each one was dyed a different color on the ends. "How is that an appropriate answer, Zandy?"

"I had a baby. And my parents made me give him up for adoption," I clarified my answer.

"Made you?" she asked, then hit the gas hard enough to make a jackrabbit take off.

Clutching the bar above my head, the one I called an "oh-shit bar," I went on, "At barely sixteen I lost my V-card to the boy I'd had a crush on since I was about twelve. He had dirty blond hair, all-American good looks, and eventually, a killer body. The first hint of attention he gave me made me putty in his hands."

Zipping up to the parking space in front of the apartment we shared, she stopped right next to my red Mustang. Her head swiveled to look at me. "So, you gave it up to this guy who you weren't dating but you'd been crushing on for years, and you ended up preggo? On the first go?"

"Precisely." Getting out of the car, we made our way to the front door.

The whole complex was made up of ground-floor apartments, another thing that made me like this place better than the place I'd been living for the last eight years. No stairs to climb and no one living overhead, making noise all the time. The apartment was perfect.

Taking a seat on the expensive leather sofa and loveseat, Taylor asked, "Your crush didn't want to do the right thing by you, Zandy?"

Shaking my head, I said, "I never told him about it. I never told anyone about it. My mother was totally up in my personal business. She kept track of her periods on this calendar that she called the "menstruation keeper." When I got my period when I was around thirteen, she began adding mine to it. She said she did it so I would know right when I was about to start so I'd never be unprepared."

"So you'd put some tamps in your purse then, stock up on Midol," she said with a knowing grin.

"Most of the time, yeah." Chewing on my lip, I thought back to that time when my period hadn't come. "Well, anyways, suddenly, one month, my period didn't start."

"And when it didn't show up, what did you do?" Taylor asked with wide eyes. "I mean, I've never had a pregnancy scare at all. My mother trotted my ass down to the clinic right after my first period when I was fifteen. She made me start getting the shot as soon as I could, and I've been on it ever since."

"I tried to hide the fact that it hadn't started." I remembered how hysterical I felt when I was late. "I lied to my mother about having it, telling her it was right on schedule. Only I didn't think about one important thing."

Nodding, she said, "You forgot to plant evidence, didn't you?"

"Yep." My chest rose and fell with a heavy sigh.

She shook her head sadly. "Rookie mistake, Zandy."

Shrugging my shoulders, I said, "I was a rookie. And I wasn't ready to handle anything, never mind what would happen when my parents found out. I figured I'd have at least a few months to figure something out and eventually talk to the guy about it. I had no idea if he wanted anything to do with me after we'd slept together. We didn't do a hell of a lot of talking before we got naked together."

"He must've been so hot," she mused. "'Cause you're a really gorgeous girl, Zandy. You could have your pick of anyone."

"I was plain back then, and my parents were really strict. I wasn't allowed to wear any makeup at all. Everyone else was, but not me. And my mom cut my hair." I cringed, remembering the horror that was my hair. "I had these straight, very short bags. The rest of my hair was one length that went down to the middle of my back. My clothes were all purchased by my mother, too. Needless to say, they would have looked very appropriate on a teenager in, say, 1950."

"I don't suppose you've got any pictures," she said with a wry smile.

I threw a little pillow at her, smacking her in the face. "No, you jackass."

"Thought as much." She tossed the pillow back at me, and I caught it. "So, what happened next?"

"Mom took me to see our doctor. He told her I was pregnant. I was only a couple weeks along and already my parents were making decisions about the little baby I carried." The tears sprang up on cue as his tiny face made a brief appearance in my head. No matter how many years passed, I knew without a doubt that I'd never forget the sight of his perfect little face.

Taylor got up and came to sit next to me. Her arm around my shoulders was meant to comfort, but it didn't help at all. There was just no way to comfort someone who'd had their child taken away. "They made you give it up?"

Nodding my head, I let the tears flow freely. "We left that night to go stay with relatives in Chicago. Mom and Dad took me out of school. I had to finish high school online.

Dad had a cell phone, but other than that we had no other phone because they didn't want me to be able to talk to any of my friends—the few that I even had. When I was on the computer doing schoolwork, my parents would watch me, making sure I didn't get a chance to contact anyone. They never wanted anyone to know the shame of what I'd done."

"And the father of the baby never knew?" she asked as she patted my shoulder, trying to reassure me that everything would be okay. It wouldn't ever be okay. I'd already accepted that fact.

"He doesn't know a thing." I wiped my eyes with the back of my hand, seeing black smudges from my makeup. "He never will. The adoption agency arranged a closed adoption. My parents and I were never given the names of the people who adopted him. And the guy's name wasn't on anything—I never even told my parents his name. That was the one thing I refused to do. I didn't want them saying anything to him or his family about it. It was all my fault, anyway. I was the stupid girl who, when he asked, told him he didn't have to use a condom."

"Wow." Taylor sat back, looking stunned. "That was dumb."

Nodding, I had to agree. "Yeah, it was."

"All that happened a long time ago, Zandy. Why let it keep you from getting close to anyone now? Or let it stop you from having more kids when you want them?"

I rubbed my fingers over the black smudges on the back of my hand, trying to make them go away. "It wouldn't be fair to that little boy if I had more kids. I gave him away. How could I ever expect him to understand that I had to give him up and then go on and keep any other kids? Like I just replaced him like he was nothing."

"I doubt he'll ever know you, Zandy." She took me by the

chin to make me look at her. "He will never know if you get married someday and have kids. Stop thinking that way."

"I just ... I can't do." I shook my head. "And there's no way I could ever let a man into my heart anyway, Taylor. There's an enormous hole there, where my little boy is supposed to be. My heart can't hold a damn thing in it. I can't keep anyone in my heart for long before they just leak out."

"Therapy," came her answer. "You need some help, honey. And there's nothing wrong with that."

Her calling me honey just made me mad. I got up and went to the kitchen, rubbing at my eyes one last time, making sure all the tears were gone. "I'm making celebratory margaritas. I've got a new job, a slamming apartment, and I get to work with you again. Life has never been sweeter."

Taylor got up to follow me. I could feel her eyes staring a hole through me. "Zandra, seriously, you need to deal with this. It's a big deal. I'm not even smart, and I know it's a big deal."

"Yeah," I agreed. "And it always will be. Whether I talk to a shrink or not, I will never get to see my son. I will never know if he's okay or not. I will never, ever feel him in my arms. Mostly, I will never forgive my parents for what they made me do. Now, let's get wasted, take a nap, and then get up and get ready to go to work tonight."

It sounded like a solid plan at the time.

97

CHAPTER 4

Kane

My best buddy, Rocco, called to invite me to his family's traditional Italian restaurant in downtown Charleston. Seeing as it was a Saturday night, and my aunt and uncle had taken Fox to Florida to spend the weekend at their vacation home in Miami, I accepted his offer.

The vino flowed like rain, his huge family refilling the glasses all night. One long table ran along the back of the dining room, and close to closing time the family would always eat dinner together, letting the staff take over what was left of the customers.

Rocco and I had been friends since grade school, and I felt like a part of his family. His father clapped me on the back as he filled my glass with red wine. "So, what are you two handsome devils going to be doing after closing tonight, Kane?"

"Going home and getting some sleep," came my quick answer.

Rocco shook his head, his dark eyes peering into mine. "No. We are not doin' that, bro."

"I don't know about you, but that's been my plan all along. I'm stuffed and getting soused from all the wine. I think bed sounds like an amazing idea." I took another drink of the fruity wine, which had a nice, crisp finish, savoring the flavors that burst inside my mouth. "Oh, Papa, this one is delicious!"

"Glad ya like," he said with a nod. "That one came straight from my cousin Sal's vineyard in Italy. He brought me a case when he visited last month. Mama and I are taking a trip to see them all in the summer. You should bring Fox, and we can make a real trip of it."

"That sounds awesome. I might just take you up on that offer." I thought about Fox getting to see Italy and a real working winery. He'd get a kick out of it, I was sure.

"Please do, Kane." Papa jerked his head toward his son. "And we'll take the meatball there too."

Shaking his meaty fist in the air, Rocco growled, "The meatball would love to come with you, Papa." He kicked the leg of my chair as he sat across from me. "For tonight, though, I've got plans for you, my best bud."

Not in the mood to go out at all, but deciding to humor him anyway, I asked, "And what are these plans, Rocco?"

"Mynt," came his one-word statement, which told me nothing at all.

"Mint?" Crossing my arms over my chest, I leaned back to think about what mint could possibly be. "Is that like a dessert shop of some kind? Because I can tell you right now, I cannot possibly eat another bite of anything."

Loud laughter peeled through the air as he cracked up for some reason. "No! Ha!" Then he stopped laughing. "Unless you consider gorgeous females a dessert, then yes."

"Gorgeous females, huh?" I still wasn't convinced. I had no desire to hook up with anyone after the brutal week I'd had. I'd taken two shifts for another doctor who had been fighting a losing battle with his allergies. On top of that, the clinic was overflowing with sick patients each and every day. All I wanted to do was sleep.

"Very beautiful women, Kane. And God knows you could use a woman." Kicking the leg of my chair again, he wiggled his dark brows at me. "You get what I'm throwing out there, man?"

His cousin Louisa came up behind him. She'd had a crush on me for years. Her slender hands ran down her cousin's arms as she looked at me, both things seeming rather inappropriate to me. "Don't go throwing things like that at my man, Rocco."

"He ain't your man, Louisa," Rocco corrected her.

Louisa was drop-dead gorgeous—she had the face of a supermodel and her body was round in all the right places. But beauty on its own wasn't enough for me, and I'd always found that her brand of aggressive sexuality just didn't work for me.

"He ain't my man yet, Rocco. One day he'll see that I'm the woman for him, though." She licked her ruby red lips. "One day."

"Don't wait on me, honey," I told her.

"Like she's waiting," Rocco said with a chuckle. "This one here went out three times this week. Once with the guy who delivers our tomatoes, once with the man who delivers the beer, and once with the guy who comes in to ask if anyone wants their cars washed."

I couldn't help but laugh. The woman certainly liked variety!

Red cheeks blazing, she hit Rocco upside the head then turned to leave. "Idiot!"

Shaking his head, Rocco added, "I might be an idiot, but I ain't lying."

We laughed even harder. I wasn't usually a jackass, but that woman had been coming on to me forever. But then again, she came on to every man within a 10-foot radius. Either way, I was getting sick of her not being able to accept my disinterest.

"So, this place with the gorgeous women. Tell me about it," I conceded. I wasn't saying I would go, but I did want to know what the hell it was.

With a flourish of his massive arm, he told me, "Mynt is one badass nightclub. The beauties are endless, the drinks keep on flowing, and the chances of not getting any leg are slim to none."

My friend often used slang from the age of the dinosaurs, though I had a pretty good idea of what he meant. "Leg, Rocco?"

One hand came up to cover the left side of his mouth, hiding it from his mother, who sat only two chairs away from him on that side. "Sex, moron."

"Ah!" I didn't need or want any of that. "Nah. I'll pass."

"Pass?" His brows raised, his expression changing to one of absolute confusion. "Who says no to that?"

"A tired doctor," I let him know. "I told you about my week, Rocco. Don't look so stunned."

"Well, here's how my week went." He banged his fist on the table, making the wineglasses shake, "Grandmama's arthritis flared up, so I had to make meatballs every day this week. On top of that, it was my week to clean the damn fryer. That is one bitch to clean, mind you. I've worked three double-shifts this week and closed one night, then opened the next day. Now that is one hellacious week, and one that I need to end on a positive note." His hand came up to cover the left side of his mouth once again. "And that positive note is sex, my friend. As much and as nasty as I can get. And I need a wingman, if nothing else."

"And you want me to be said wingman, I suppose." My drink sloshed as I picked it up. I was just about tipsy. Maybe the rest of the wine would make my decision for me—either take me home to bed or out to play wingman for the man I considered my very best friend. Downing the rest of it, I looked at Rocco. His eyes pleaded with me. "Can I go home and change first?"

"Hell, yes, you can!" With a snap of his fingers, his young cousin Giovanni came to Rocco's side. "Give Kane a ride to his place so he can change. Then come back here and get me. I'm gonna clean up a bit in the kitchen, then I'll be ready to go. You're gonna drive us to that nightclub you were telling me about earlier."

Minutes later I was sitting in the passenger side of an old Buick as the kid drove me home. He stopped abruptly in my driveway, making me grab the dashboard. "Okay, we're here." I got out of the car then looked back. "I'll be right back."

Going into the empty house, I immediately felt the absence of my son. I hated when he wasn't home. But he'd really been looking forward to the trip to Florida, so I had let him go.

Walking past his bedroom, I stopped and pushed open the door. I hadn't stopped by the house when I left work; I'd gone right over to Rocco's restaurant. I saw that Fox had left his drawers open in his haste to pack. The maid would have to clean up his mess on Monday.

Closing his door, I pulled out my cell to call him. He answered the phone with an excited, "Hi, Dad!"

"Hey there, son. How was the trip down to Miami?" I went to my bedroom and took a seat on the bed, pulling my shoes off.

"Pretty long and mostly boring. I slept most of the way. Uncle James kept teasing me that I was farting in my sleep." I heard him laughing.

Then the voice of my uncle came in the background. "He was farting up a storm."

I couldn't help rolling my eyes. "Well, doesn't that sound like a fun trip." More like a nightmare that I was damn glad I hadn't been a part of.

"Nana and Pawpaw are coming up tomorrow, Dad," Fox said. "They wanted to surprise us. But now they're only going to be surprising Aunt Nancy, Uncle James, and me."

I'd had no idea they would be going too. And now I felt bad for not being there. "Well, dang. I wish they would've told us something. I definitely would've come with you guys if I'd known. Do me a favor and give them some kisses and hugs from me, buddy."

"Sure, Dad." He laughed. "Nana will smother me with her kisses anyway. She always does."

Mom and Dad had moved to Napa Valley, California, a couple of years back. We only got to see them once, maybe twice a year. As the newest doctor at the clinic I usually got the worst shifts, and my busy schedule made it hard for us to get out there to see them much. And they didn't like to travel, so seeing them was difficult. The fact they'd gone to Florida was odd.

"Tell them I'll call tomorrow," I said as I got up to take my pants off to put on a nice suit.

"Whatcha doin' tonight, Dad?" Fox asked.

I didn't want to tell him too much about the little outing Rocco had planned. "Not much. Just going out with Uncle Rocco for a while."

"Oh, man!" Fox laughed and shared my news with whoever else was around him, "Dad's goin' to hang out with Uncle Rocco tonight."

"Don't do anything I wouldn't do, lover boy!" Uncle James called out.

I wasn't some horny teen anymore who needed a scolding. Having a son before you turned twenty could be a real wake-up call. "I shouldn't have mentioned anything about my night. I can see that now."

"Nope, you shouldn't have," Fox told me. "Be good, Dad. And please, don't do what you did when you were in high school. I'm not ready for a little sister or brother yet."

"Gee whiz," I whined, not used to getting sex and relationship advice from a ten-year-old. "Love you, son. Be good. Mind your aunt and uncle and be careful, please."

"You too, Dad. Love ya." He ended the call as I sat back down on the bed.

Being so open and honest with my son didn't come without a bit of a backlash sometimes. It had been Rocco's party where I'd finally gotten to know young Zandra Larkin better, making my little boy in the process. And no one ever seemed to forget it.

Sitting on my bed, I found myself thinking about that night. I'd had no idea she was a virgin until she told me so. I'd been hot for her, but when I'd heard that softly-spoken confession, my cock had taken over completely.

I'd never had a virgin before. Not that I'd even had that many girls at seventeen—I'd had three, to be exact.

If I'd been more mature, I wouldn't have taken her virginity that night. I would've done things differently.

Maybe spent that night talking more and kissing less. Maybe I would've taken her on a few dates before even going past first base.

If I could go back in time, I often wondered if I would do it all over again. After all, if things had gone differently, I wouldn't have Fox, and he was my entire world. Would I have ruined that young girl's life to have my son?

Would I have taken that sweet cherry away from her if I'd known that she would get pregnant and that her parents would react as they had?

Shaking my head, I knew I wouldn't do that to her again if I could go back. If I'd only known how much that two hours of passion would take away from her, I wouldn't have done it.

My heart began to ache a bit. With no idea how Zandra had fared after all of that, I wondered from time to time what she was doing with her life.

Being a doctor, I knew what the loss of a child could do to a person. Even if she'd wanted to give our son up, that decision could've had some serious repercussions on her mental state. Every woman reacted to that decision differently.

Is she okay?

Had she moved on with her life? Had she gotten married? Had more children?

With no idea what Zandra Larkin, or whatever her name was now, was doing, I had no way of knowing how having our son had affected her. All I knew was that if I hadn't ended up with our son, then I wouldn't have been okay.

I'd gotten lucky. I had family who believed that blood ran thick. We would never give one of our own away. Come hell or high water we'd do everything we could to keep our family together and safe.

Our families were clearly very different. Hers had made her give up the baby. Mine had searched relentlessly until they found him and made him ours.

What would it do to a person to have their own blood turn on them like that—to not only not support them through a difficult time, but to actively make them give the baby they'd carried inside of them away to strangers?

I knew that some babies were better off with adoptive parents. Some people just didn't have the capacity to care for a child. And there were others who were more than capable of caring for that baby. But in those cases, the biological mother and father came to that decision.

I'd been left out of the decision. And for all I knew, Zandra had been left out of it too.

Before we knew whether we'd be able to get my son, I'd felt empty and lost. Afterward, the relief of knowing he'd be with me forever—that he'd have a loving family for the rest of his life—had been the best feeling ever. Sure, there was the underlying fear that I wouldn't be such a great father, but I knew I had great role models and that my family would help me learn along the way.

Poor Zandra clearly didn't have that same support system. How would that have made her feel? And how would she feel about that, so many years later?

And most of all: is she okay?

98

CHAPTER 5

Zandra

The doors hadn't even opened yet, and Mynt already felt electric.

"Damn, did you see that line? It goes all the way around the block!" Taylor asked me as we hurried to help the bartenders get ready for the onslaught of patrons who would soon be inside the club.

Out of the corner of my eye, I could see the manager, Rob, staring at me. I wasn't sure if that was because he wanted to see how I handled my first big crowd, or if he just liked watching me. Either way, it made me feel more than a little bit uncomfortable.

Taking a deep breath, I settled into my waitress attitude and turned to look at Rob. With a wave of my hand, I broke his silent stare. "Hey, boss. Don't worry about me. I'm used to busy Saturday nights."

Jerking his head toward the entrance, he shouted, "Let them in!" His eyes still on me, he added, "Let's see if you're up to a Charleston Saturday night, Chicago."

He'd nicknamed me that from the first night. I'd only worked three shifts so far, and they'd been easy enough. Rob got a kick out of trying to intimidate me with what he called "the largest crowds in history" that graced his club on Saturday nights.

From the line I'd seen outside when we came in, I was sure that the place would be packed, and we would have a hard night coming our way. But it wasn't anything I couldn't handle. "I've got this, boss."

With the doors finally open, the place filled up in record time. I helped people find tables and got their drinks to them before helping more patrons. It was a fast pace, but I liked to be busy rather than bored.

On the other side of the packed room, I caught sight of a couple waitresses up on the bar, dancing. People cheered as they watched the two shaking their asses.

Taylor came up behind me as I took a moment to watch. "We should show those girls a thing or two, Zandy."

Being no stranger to ass shaking, I nodded. "Okay. As soon as I get these three tables set up, I'll meet you at the bar on this side."

"It's a date," she said with a smile as she went to serve her customers.

The club had barely opened, and already I was forced to head back to my locker to put away the cash that filled my pockets. In this business, Saturdays were always the most profitable nights, but I was already on track to have one of my best nights ever.

When I left the locker room, I found Rob standing in the doorway of his office. He seemed to have been waiting for me. "How's it going so far, Chicago?"

"Not bad at all, boss." I made sure to keep calling him that, as the way he kept looking me up and down made it clear that he wouldn't mind taking our relationship into something more personal than employer and employee. And I was not interested in that at all.

Taking a step back inside his office, he offered, "You want something to help make the night go better? A little boost?"

"The night's already been pretty good so far. As a matter of fact, the tips I've already gotten tonight are enough to cover my car payment this month. I'm hoping the rest of the night will pay the rest of my bills." I laughed as I kept walking. Going into his office alone didn't seem like a great idea to me.

"Come on," he said as he reached out, taking me by the arm.

I didn't want to overreact, but the way he tugged at me had my alarms going off. Taylor's appearance did much to ease my anxiety. "Hey. They're playing our song, Zandy. Come on."

Rob's hand left my forearm. "You two going to dance on the bar?"

With a nod, I took off. 'Yep."

To my disappointment, he followed right behind me. "This, I've got to see."

Normally, tension didn't mess with me too much, and with Rob eager to watch me dance, tension had definitely settled in. By the time I got to Taylor, she had noticed my body language. "Maybe a shot first, then we dance."

Nodding, I couldn't think of a better way to help me chill out. Except if Rob would stop watching me, of course. "Yeah, how about a tequila shot?"

Rob's warm breath moved past my ear as he shuffled in close behind me. "I'll get you the good stuff," he whispered.

Slipping behind the bar, Rob poured two shots that Taylor and I downed.

My heart was pounding in my chest as Rob offered me his hand to help me up on the bar. People were already crowding around the bar, watching me and shouting words of encouragement as Taylor was helped up by one of the bartenders. She made some sign to the DJ and the music changed to something sexy and slow.

Ignoring Rob and his gray eyes that bored into me, I looked at Taylor as I moved my body in slow, sexy waves, undulating toward her then toward the crowd, who was cheering us on.

The drinks were flying as men took advantage of grabbing the alcohol-filled glasses from between our legs. The female waitresses all had to wear short black shorts with hot pink shirts that were tied up between our tits, which overflowed from the low-cut tops. Our bellybuttons were to be exposed at all times, and any customer who ordered a body-shot got one.

As the song and our dance came to an end, the men in the crowd started calling out the different shots they wanted to drink from our navels. Rob once again took my hand, this time to help me to lie on top of the bar. He filled my belly-button himself, watching closely as men took turns slurping the liquid off my body.

Body-shots were just part of the territory of serving in these kinds of clubs, and never once had I felt an ounce of the shyness that had plagued me as a teen. But tonight, that shyness seemed to be coming back, and at lightning speed, too.

My cheeks heated as one hot guy after another took their turn. Turning my head, I looked at Rob. "I think that's enough. My tables are waiting, and I bet they're thirsty."

"You're right." Rob announced the end to body-shots, much to the dismay of the men who were waiting for their turn. Groans of disappointment filled my ears as I got off the bar, once again assisted by Rob. "If you need a boost, just come to my office, and I'll make sure you get one."

Following Taylor back out to the floor, I asked her, "What's this boost that Rob keeps going on about?"

She winked at me. "Blow."

"Cocaine?" I shook my head. "I'm not doing any of that. You know I'll drink just about anything, but drugs? No way."

"I know." She bumped her shoulder against mine. "I'll tell him to leave you alone. He's just totally crushing on you, that's all."

"I can tell. And I don't like it." I looked over my shoulder to see him leaning over the bar, talking to some young girl who was making sexy eyes at him. "He's got plenty of tail available to him. He can do without mine."

"He can," Taylor agreed. "But will he? That's the real question now, isn't it?"

Squaring my jaw, I wanted to make sure Taylor knew I wasn't about to roll over for that guy. And if he even thought about pressing the issue, I'd hit him with a sexual harassment suit that would make his head spin. Since being on my own, I'd never been one to take much shit out of anyone. Not after everything I had taken from my very own parents.

"Over here, Zee," some woman called out to me. I'd made sure that only Zee appeared on my nametag. I didn't want anyone to use my real name. Zandra wasn't exactly a common name, and I didn't want anyone who knew me from before to realize who I was. I knew there would be loads of questions. And I didn't want to answer any of them.

For only a split second, that tiny baby's face filled my

head again and it stopped me dead in my tracks. "Zee?" Taylor asked as she came up behind me. "You okay?"

Am I?

Shaking my head to clear it, I said, "Yeah. Just a little lightheaded is all. I guess that tequila shot finally kicked in."

"Be careful, girl." Taylor took off to deal with her own customers as I tried to focus on the task at hand, forcing the memories as far behind as I possibly could.

Reaching out to take the empty glasses off the table full of young women who'd called me over, I asked, "Do you girls want more of the same?"

"How about we go with something different this time, ladies?" the girl who'd called me over, the apparent leader of the pack, asked her friends.

The group agreed and then they all looked at me for some suggestions. "You were drinking mojitos, so how about trying cable cars? They're both rum-based. The key to avoiding a killer hangover is to drink same-base liquor all night, but you can mix up what you drink it with."

The leader gave me a huge smile. "Aren't we lucky to have you as our guide for the night? Cable cars it is, then. Thanks, Zee. With age comes wisdom, right?"

A curt nod answered her question. As I left their table to get their drinks, it occurred to me that my twenty-six years seemed to be years apart from the early twenties of seemingly everyone else at the club.

Not even the blue streaks in my hair are making me look younger!

But did I really want to be a young twenty-one or two-year-old? I'd learned and grown a lot in the last few years, and I wouldn't go back for anything.

My expression must've given my inner thoughts away. "Feeling a little overwhelmed, Zee?" the bartender asked.

"No." I wasn't about to tell him that I was feeling old. "Five cable cars, please."

I put the dirty glasses in the washer while I waited for him to make the drinks. He eyed me while he made them up. "You're doing well tonight. I've got to admit that I thought this might be harder for you than it is."

"And why is that, exactly?" I had to ask him, thinking I already had a few ideas of what he might say. My age. A lack of experience with large crowds. The shyness I'd overcome in Chicago, but that seemed to be creeping back in now that I was back in Charleston. Any one of those things could be the reason behind his words.

Pouring some Captain Morgan into the shaker, his lips pulled up into a cocky smile. "You're new here. It takes most people about a month to get to where you are now. Impressive."

"So, it was my lack of experience that made you underestimate me," I said wryly, though truthfully I was happy to know it wasn't my age.

And when the hell did I get so caught up with my age?

It wasn't as if I was some dinosaur, after all.

"Yeah," he admitted. "I mean, I knew you'd been a waitress in Chicago, but I had no idea that you'd been such a good one." He jerked his head at the big glass jar under the bar, which was filled with cash. "Those body-shots earned us a heap of tips. We'll be splitting them at the end of the night too, like always."

Dollar signs flashed in my head, and I couldn't help but smile. "Hell, Saturday nights alone seem to be helping me meet my bills. The rest of the week will be gravy for me."

Finishing the drinks, he placed them on a tray. "And you'll get Sunday and Monday to recoup for next week's fun. Have you made any plans for your days off yet?"

"Nah. I'm gonna just play it by ear." I picked up the tray and headed off to make the girls happy.

The night just kept getting wilder and wilder with the tips coming at me left and right. Taylor came over to me as I walked up to the bar with a bunch of empties in my arms. "Hell, this is one hot night, don't you think?"

"I've made enough money to do more than pay my bills, Taylor," I said, leaning in so no one else would hear. "Thanks for calling me and asking me to come work here. This is a godsend."

"I know, right?" she asked with a huge smile. "I knew you would clean up here."

Laughing, I felt like I was on some kind of a high, knowing that the change I had made was definitely worth it. "I see a brand-new car in my future."

With an exchange of high-fives, Taylor and I parted ways to tend to the club's guests and see how much more cash we could attain.

On my third trip to the locker room to put away more cash, I passed Rob's office again. His door wasn't all the way open, just a bit ajar, but I tiptoed across anyway, hoping he wouldn't hear the sound of my heels clicking against the tile floor. Unfortunately, my attempt to go unnoticed was in vain.

"Hey, Chicago, come here, will ya?" he called out to me.

A loud sigh escaped me. As I pushed the door open, I made sure I didn't go fully into the room. Leaning on the door frame, I asked, "Yeah, boss?"

"Making bank, I see." His feet were propped up on his messy desk, his hands linked behind his head as he rested it on them. He seemed to be relaxing after doing very little at all.

Back in Chicago, when the club was busy, everyone was

busy, including the managers. But Rob didn't work that way. It seemed he liked to sit back and watch other people work.

"I'm doing well." Looking over my shoulder, I went on, "And I should get back to it. It's busy as hell out there."

"Yes, it is." He sat up, taking a more managerial position. "You can take a half-hour break now. There's a little café around the corner if you're hungry."

"I never eat when I'm working. It slows me down too much. I always eat after work." Turning to leave, I added, "Thanks, but I don't need a break, boss."

"Take one anyway. I don't want people thinking I over-work my staff. Catch some fresh air for a little while." He chuckled. "That's an order, Chicago. Take thirty and take it now. It's eleven-thirty, and we always get another surge of people at midnight."

"'K, boss." I wasn't about to argue with him.

After putting my money away and making sure it was locked up tight in my locker, I walked to the front to go outside and take in some cold night air.

Rounding a corner to go through the entrance hall, I stopped short when my eyes caught sight of a man I hadn't seen in years.

Dark blond hair, longer on top than on the sides, caught my eye. Green eyes sparkled as the large chandelier's light danced in his eyes. His tall, muscular frame moved with cat-like grace.

I faded into the wall, hiding behind several of the bouncers as I watched him walk through the hallway and into the interior of the club.

My breath caught in my throat as I whispered to myself, "Kane Price ..."

99

CHAPTER 6

Kane

The pounding bass of the music matched my heartbeat as we walked into the packed nightclub. "This is insane," I had to shout for Rocco to hear me.

"Off the chain," he shouted back at me. "Right?"

"I guess so." I wasn't in the right frame of mind to enjoy the place. To be more precise, I had full use of my mind. That made it impossible for me to just go with the flow the way everyone else seemed to be doing.

Scanning the room, which was filled with undulating bodies, I couldn't help but notice that half the girls here were hardly wearing enough to cover those moving bodies. One girl raised her arms in the air as she swayed her ass, the little bit of black material covering her nether regions flashing out, and she looked like she just didn't give a damn.

Rocco noticed it too, jabbing me in the ribs with his elbow. "Whoa, check out the barely-there underwear on the chick at two o'clock, will ya?"

"Rocco, you know that's somebody's daughter, don't you?" I asked him as he openly gawked at the girl.

"She ain't yours, so why are you even thinkin' about it, Kane? You need alcohol, and you need it stat." He led the way to the nearest bar. "Give me a couple of Godfathers, please."

So, whiskey it is, then.

It seemed my friend was going to try to dull my senses with a stout mixture of bourbon and amaretto. Unfortunately, I'd have to disappoint him. My mind wasn't into it, and my drinking would be limited.

Everywhere I looked, I imagined I saw things in a much different light than most of the other patrons. To my left, a group of four men was laughing and drinking. One of them had droopy eyes, his glass hung loosely in his hand, and he had to lean on the bar to stay upright. He'd had too much to drink, and his companions took no notice of that fact at all.

To my right, a girl who was most likely barely twenty-one danced with a man who looked like a serial killer. His hands were all over her, and he was looking down at the top of her head with a menacing stare that told me he'd like to take her outside, push her up against the side of the building, and bone her until she couldn't see straight. Then tie her up and throw her in the trunk of his car, taking her away forever.

"Drink this," came Rocco's demanding voice.

Taking the glass from his extended hand, I took a small sip. "Thanks."

With a nod, Rocco took a sip as he looked around the room. "Over there, see those two chicks dancing with each other?"

"I do." I had no idea why he would point them out. Tons

of girls were dancing with each other, some in large groups even.

"Let's cut in," he continued. "I get the blonde. I know you prefer brunettes."

I wasn't up for that at all. "You go ahead. Take them both. I'll be right here when you're done."

One heavy sigh let me know he wasn't happy with my attitude. "Come on, Kane. Loosen up, man."

"I am loose. Go on. Go dance, Rocco. I'll be fine." My attention was taken by the mass of drunken people anyway. I would be thoroughly entertained just watching them.

Finally, he seemed to accept that I wasn't going to get out on that dancefloor and we parted ways. Now I could focus my attention on people-watching.

When I saw a girl stumbling off the dancefloor, heading to the bar, I couldn't hold the doctor inside of me back any longer. I reached out, taking her by the arm. "Hey, where you headed?"

Her blue eyes were glazed over, and she had trouble focusing on me as she wobbled in her high heels. "The bar. I need a drink. Care to buy me one?" she slurred.

"How about I pay for your cab ride home, instead?" I offered as I put my drink down on the bar.

"What?" She shook her head then stopped. "Whoa. I'm kinda dizzy."

"So, how about that cab?" I slipped my arm around her narrow shoulders, moving her toward the exit instead of the bar.

"Are you trying to take me home?" she slurred, then her head bobbed. "'Cause that's okay if you are. I'm up for it."

"Good to know." She wasn't up for shit. "But I'm not taking you home. I'm sending you to your home. You do know your address, right?"

"Fifteen fifteen, um ..." she hummed as she tried to recall where she lived. "Blue Ridge Trail. Yeah, that's it." Pride filled her eyes as she looked up at me. "See, I knew it."

"Great job. Do you know how many drinks you've had?" I pushed the door open and we stepped outside, the cool air hitting us in the face. It didn't seem to affect her much at all.

"I didn't count them," she said, and then hiccupped. Looking over her shoulder, she looked lost for a second. "Um, I should go back and tell my friends I'm leaving."

Her cell phone was in her hand, and I took her by the wrist, raising her hand so she could see it. "Why don't you send them texts while you're riding in the cab?"

"You're smart," she said with a giggle before another hiccup popped out of her mouth. "Has anyone ever told you that?"

"Yep." Snapping my fingers, a cab pulled to the curb, and I helped her get inside. "Fifteen fifteen, Blue Ridge Trail please." Handing the driver two twenty-dollar bills, I added, "Please see this young lady gets there safe and sound, will you?" The fact that the driver was a woman in her fifties gave me confidence that the drunk girl would meet no harm in her vulnerable condition.

"Will do," the driver said with a smile.

The girl reached out, trailing her hand over my cheek. "You're, like, my hero. I should get your number."

"Nah. But do yourself a favor and drink some water when you get home. And watch your intake of alcohol next time—it's time to stop when your head gets light. And if your words start to slur, you're already drunk. Got it?" I knew she probably wouldn't retain a word I said, but I had to say them anyway.

"'K." She kissed the palm of her hand and then blew it

my way. She had no idea how terrible her breath smelled. "Thanks, hero."

Closing the door, I waved goodbye before heading back inside. One of the bouncers nodded at me as I went back in. "That was nice. Don't see a lot of good deeds like that going on in my line of work."

"Yeah, well, I'm a doctor, and I couldn't just watch that poor girl get another drink." With a shrug, I went back inside. I didn't feel like a hero at all. I just felt like that had been the right thing to do.

Maybe it was the fact that I had a ten-year-old at home, but suddenly all the people around me just seemed like kids to me. At twenty-seven, I wasn't much older than the majority of them, but I felt eons older—and wiser as well.

Some rambunctious shouting drew my attention to another bar. A waitress lay on the bar, a line of men waiting to take shots out of her navel. Not one of them cared about the fact that their lips were touching the same place another man's had been just seconds earlier. On top of being disgusting, it wasn't sanitary either. "Yuck."

Rocco came up behind me, clapping me on the shoulder. Jerking his head toward the men I watched, he asked, "Thinkin' about getting in that line, lover-boy?"

"There's not a chance in hell that that's what I was thinking, Rocco. And as your physician and best friend, I can't allow you to even think about doing that either. Do you have any idea how many germs are now on that poor woman's body?"

Shaking his head, he said, "The alcohol kills all the germs, Doctor Price. It's perfectly safe, and it's sexy too."

"You're as crazy as the rest of them." I shoved my hands into my pockets before looking elsewhere, as that scene made my stomach uneasy. "I could use a drink. And not the kind you gave me. I wonder what kinds of wine they serve here."

"You've got to be kidding me." Rocco huffed. "At least have a beer, Kane. Shit, you can act like such an old geezer sometimes."

He was probably right, and I knew it. But it wasn't something I particularly wanted to change about myself. I was a father first and foremost, and prided myself on acting like one. But he was right about ordering wine in such an establishment. "I'll get a beer then. I don't want to spoil your bad boy rep by acting like a geezer." Spotting a waitress not too far ahead of me, I called out, "Can I get a beer over here, please?"

She paused for only a moment before hurrying through the crowd. I knew she had to have heard me—she had stopped, after all. Following after her to get her attention, I noticed the swell of her hips, the dip of her waist, and the way her long dark hair was twisted into one braid that hung down her back. Dark blue streaks ran through it. Normally, I didn't particularly care for unnatural colors in a woman's hair. For some reason, I liked it on her.

Just as I was about to catch up to her, she placed the tray of empty glasses she carried on the edge of the bar and then disappeared behind it, going straight through a door into the back.

Disappointment welled within me. I just wanted to see her face.

"What can I get ya?" the bartender asked me.

"A beer," I said, my eyes still glued to the door she'd gone through. I crossed my fingers, hoping she'd pop back out of it before I walked away.

"What kind?" he asked me, taking my attention away from the door.

I looked at the names on tap. "Michelob Ultra."

Another waitress came up next to me, putting empties on the bar as she rattled off, "Two gin and tonics, a blue spruce, and three bloody Marys."

The waiter placed the beer on the bar in front of me. "That'll be seven fifty." He looked at the blonde waitress with a frown. "What the fuck is a blue spruce, Taylor?"

"Fuck if I know." She shrugged. "This guy said he wanted one. I figured you knew what it was."

"I'll have to look that one up, I guess." The bartender got to work making the drinks, and the waitress looked at me.

Raising my glass to her, I said, "Here's to you, and every other hard-working woman in this bar."

"Thanks." Her smile was sexy as she asked, "You having yourself a good time tonight?"

"Would it offend you if I said I wasn't?" I took a sip of the cold beer as I looked the little thing over. With pale blue eyes that sparkled with good humor and pixie-cut blonde hair that was pulled into spikes that were each dyed a different color at the tips, she reminded me of a fairy— small, with a fiery look in her eyes.

"Not me personally." She put her hand on her hip. "But can I ask you what might make your night more enjoyable?"

With a chuckle, I answered, "Being at home with my son, watching cartoons or playing video games with him."

She cocked her head to one side. "Then why aren't you doing that?"

"He's out of town this weekend." I found Rocco and nodded in his direction. "My friend made me come out with him tonight. I'm not very good company though."

She looked over at Rocco just as a girl approached him. "Looks like he'd be fine on his own." Her eyes came back to mine. "I've got a break coming up. Maybe I could make your night more pleasurable. Say, in the back room, where no one would see us."

Now ain't this some shit!

Nearly choking on the beer I'd taken a drink of, I shook my head. "No, thank you."

"You married?" she asked with one dark brow cocked.

"No." I couldn't believe she'd think the only reason I'd turned down her generous offer was because of a prior commitment. "I just don't make a habit of screwing women I don't know, is all."

"Shame." She picked up the tray of drinks and gave me a wink.

"There's no drink called a blue spruce, so I made up something blue for the idiot." The bartended watched her go. "Good call not picking up what she put down."

"You think so?" I asked as I took another drink, watching her as she swayed her ass on purpose, trying to entice me into changing my mind.

"Yeah. She's a sweet girl, but she gets around." He got back to work, and I nodded.

Yeah, I can tell!

Waiting at the bar until I finished my beer, I was disappointed that the woman I'd been after hadn't come back out. Placing the empty mug on the bar, the bartender came back. "Want another one?"

"No. What I'd really like is to know when that waitress who went through that door a few minutes ago is coming back." I couldn't believe I'd said that. It wasn't like me to stalk women. But there I was, stalking away.

He looked back at the door then shook his head. "I've got no idea who went back there. I can tell you this, though. If she's been back there since you came up to this bar, then she's with the boss. If you know what I mean."

"Oh." Now I really felt disappointed. "I'll be heading out now, then. She's the only one her who's snagged my interest, and if she's not available, then I think I'm just wasting my time here."

With a nod, he said, "Yeah, if she's been back there that long, chances are she isn't available."

Hands back in my pockets, I had to fight myself from letting my head hang as I went to tell Rocco that I was leaving.

I must've had an even worse week than I'd realized if I was getting down in the dumps over not getting to, at the very least, see that waitress's face.

What the hell is wrong with me, anyway?

100

CHAPTER 7

Zandra

Watching Kane through the two-way mirror behind the bar, I couldn't understand why he was waiting there instead of going back to the guy he'd come in with. I recognized that man as his friend from high school, Rocco. The way he kept looking at the door I'd gone through gave me chills.

Does he know it's me?

After Kane left the bar, with what I thought looked like a dejected expression, I came out. "Did that guy say anything to you?" I asked Patrick, the bartender.

With a smartass tone, he answered, "Which one, Zee? There're tons of guys here tonight."

"The guy with the dark blond hair. Black suit, green eyes." I sighed quietly, thinking that he looked even better than he had the last time I'd seen him.

"Ah, the beer drinker who asked about the waitress that went to the back. That guy. I see it much more clearly now.

Were you the one who went back there, Zee?" He handed change back to some woman, who stuffed it in her bra.

"Yeah, that was me. Did he ask about me or what?" My heart began to pound with the idea that after all this time, he'd recognized me.

It hadn't crossed my mind at all that Kane and I might meet up. I didn't know why that was. He and I had both lived in Charleston growing up. I guess I just assumed he'd be on to bigger and better things than our small hometown.

Boy, was that a mistake.

And now he's found me.

"He did ask about you, as a matter of fact."

My heart stopped. "Did he know me by name?"

A slight laugh left his mouth. "No."

"Good," I sighed with relief. "So, what did he ask?"

"He wanted to know when you were coming back out." He went to help a customer. "What'll you have, partner?"

"Jack and Coke."

I went with Patrick as he started making the drink, so I could hear more. "Did he say why?"

"He said you were the only one who'd made his juices run or some shit like that. He told me he was leaving." He smiled at me with a wicked grin. "I told him that if you were back there that long, then you were with the boss. Like— with the boss. You know what I'm saying, Zee?"

"He thinks I was back there with Rob?" I was horrified. "God, no!"

He looked confused by my exclamation. "So, you weren't back there with the boss then?"

"Hell, no!" With long strides, I left Patrick behind and went to see to my customers. With the news that Kane had left, I could finally get back to work. Hiding from him had set me back, and I was sure the tips wouldn't be nearly what they had been.

Not only had I hidden from him, but I'd also spent a good chunk of time before that watching him from afar. When he put his arm around that drunk girl, my insides had gone hot with jealousy. I hadn't experienced anything like that before.

Sneaking along through the crowd, I followed them all the way to the exit. I couldn't believe he would just randomly grab a girl out of the crowd and so easily take her home. She looked like she was all for it, too.

I couldn't hear what they said because the music was too loud. But I could see that he was taking her outside. Then he snapped his fingers and a cab pulled up.

I couldn't even breathe as he opened that cab door. When the cab pulled away without him, I understood that he'd simply made sure that the drunk girl would get home safely.

Hell, maybe she was the sister of a friend of his. There had to be some rational explanation. I mean, no one was that damn nice, to make sure a drunken stranger got out of a club and back home safely for no reason at all.

Unless he's some kind of a saint.

Taylor saw me then and came up to me. "And where the hell have you been?"

"Hiding." I kept walking to get to my customers. "There was a guy here. You talked to him at the bar. I know him from the past."

"I've talked to a lot of guys here." She grinned at me. "You'll have to be more specific."

"Dark blond, green eyes, rocking body." I picked up the empties from the table full of girls. "More of the same, ladies?"

"Yes," came their enthusiastic answers. "More!"

"Oh, that guy." The way her eyes twinkled gave me a sinking feeling in my chest. "You know him?"

"Yes." Making my way back to the bar, I found a few more people holding up empty drinks and grabbed them as I went. "I'll be right back with refills, guys."

"I'm on break right now," Taylor told me. "I'll help you play catchup."

"Thank you." I needed the help at that moment. My head wasn't in the game after my unexpected reminder of my past.

She picked up more empties as she walked around with me. "He wasn't in his element here. He wanted to be back home with his son, who he said is out of town right now. I didn't spot a ring on his finger, and he even said he wasn't married, but my bets are that he is. Maybe he just didn't want it getting back to the old ball and chain that he was out, I bet."

"He's got a son?" I felt that stab of jealousy again.

"That's what he said. And when I offered to liven up his night while on break, he didn't take me up on it." She placed the empties on the bar as I got behind it to load them in the washer while spouting out what I needed to Patrick.

"Liven up his night, huh?" I mumbled. I knew what that meant. Taylor was still as forward as she'd always been. I should've expected as much. "It would please me very much, if you ever see him again, if you don't offer him any of your favors, Taylor. He's special to me in a way."

"Wait a minute." She stared a hole in me. "Is he?"

I didn't want a soul to know that Kane was the father of the boy I'd given up. "No. That's not him. He was just this guy who I messed around with once, that's all. And if you and he did anything, it would upset me." The lie came out so easily that it scared me.

"I see." She didn't seem completely sure of what I'd said. "He wasn't into me anyway. And I doubt he'll ever come in here again."

I prayed he wouldn't. "That would be nice. If he is married with kids, then I don't really want to know that anyway."

"I don't see why not." Taylor took one of the trays full of drinks while I took the other.

Going to serve the drinks, I said, "It's just better to leave him the way he's been in my memories all these years. Single, young, and still hot as hell."

Placing the girls' drinks on the table, I felt the tray slipping on the palm of my hand. "Oh, shit!" one of them shouted as she shot up to get out of the way.

Three of the glasses hit the table, splashing liquid and shards of glass everywhere. It all happened so fast that it stunned me. Taylor pointed at me. "Your hand!"

Looking down, I found a few small cuts and one big one on my palm. Blood poured from it. My head went light, and then all I saw was black.

"Hey, wake up, Zandy," Taylor's voice came to me. There wasn't any noise in the background, so I had no idea where I was.

Opening my eyes, I saw Taylor and Rob looking down at me. "What happened?"

"You fainted when you saw the blood," Taylor told me.

"You should go get stitches," Rob added. "That's a pretty deep cut. The club will pay the bill. Don't worry about that."

Picking up my left hand, I saw a white bar towel had

been wrapped around it. There was only a little bit of pink color to it. "I'll be okay."

With a sigh, Rob walked away. "Well, I can't make you go to the ER, but I can make you go home. See you on Monday. Hopefully with stitches on that hand."

"You're making me leave?" I sat up, then felt woozy, so I laid my head on the back of the sofa they'd put me on.

"Yes," he said with a nod. "Go home. Come back on Monday."

Taylor looked a little concerned. "Do you need me to drive you?"

"Nah. I can make it." I got up. It was easy to do when I thought about what kind of crap might be on Rob's sofa. "I'll see you at home later, Taylor. See you on Monday, boss."

The ride home passed in a blur as all my thoughts were focused on one man.

Kane Price.

He was there. In Charleston. And he was most likely married. He also had a son—that much I knew for sure.

A son.

What would he do if I told him that he had more than one son? He had a son that I had had to give away. He had a son, and I had no idea where that son might be. He had a son, but I couldn't tell him if that son was okay—because I didn't know the answer to that myself.

No. If I ever did run into Kane, I would never tell him about the other son he had.

The apartment was dark as I walked in. I left it that way as I walked past the light switch, heading straight to my bedroom then to the attached bath. A nice bath would help soothe my sore hand and jagged nerves.

After putting a bandage on my hand, I soaked in the tub.

And as I soaked, the memory of that night so long ago filled my mind ...

"HEY, aren't you in my chemistry class?" Kane asked me with a sexy grin on his gorgeous face. His dark blond hair hung in waves to his broad shoulders. His green eyes danced, making me weak in the knees.

"I am." I looked away to find the girl I'd come to the party with. "Have you seen Ann around?"

"Nope." His index finger trailed along my bare arm, leaving the oddest sensation behind. Heat mixed with cold —it was outstanding. And the way it made my bottom half pulse excited me.

"I should go look for her." Slowly, I looked up at him, and his index finger moved up to trace a line along my jaw.

"Why?" he asked as he looked into my eyes. "What's wrong with talking to me for a while?"

Everything.

"Nothing, I guess." Shyly, I looked off to one side.

With just that one finger, he drew my head back to look at him. "I've always thought you were pretty, Zandra. Did you know that?"

I tried to speak past the shock clogging my throat. "How could I?" He'd never said more than a couple of words to me the whole time we'd been in high school together.

The smile he wore faded. "Yeah, how could you have known I thought that?" He brushed my hair back, away from my face. "I haven't exactly been upfront with you, now have I?"

I shook my head. "No, you've never been upfront with me." I had never been upfront with him, either. I'd had a crush on the guy since I was in seventh grade and he was in eighth.

"So now I'm being upfront." His hand moved down to rest on my shoulder. "I like you."

"You don't know me, Kane." I looked down at my feet, biting my lip. I wasn't sure why that had come out of my mouth, but it had.

"Not well." He nodded then leaned in close to whisper the rest. "But I'd like to."

"I'd like that too." I thought in that moment that I'd never like anything more than that.

When his lips touched mine, I felt my whole world change. No more shyness. No more inhibitions. Nothing.

When he ended the kiss, which had taken me away to a place I hadn't known existed, he took me by the hand and led me up the stairs to a bedroom. I didn't ask any questions; I just let him touch me, kiss me, make me crave him.

My clothes came off without me realizing it. Then his did too. Naked, we lay on the bed, facing each other. When he ran one hand between my breasts, over my stomach, down to my pulsing sex, my body became tense. "It's okay, Zandra." His lips pressed against mine again, our tongues tangled, and I let him explore me more intimately.

One finger slid into me, and I gasped at the odd feeling. It didn't hurt at all, but it felt good—very good. I didn't know anything could feel as good as his finger pumped into me over and over again. His thumb rolled in circles over my clit, which I could feel swelling with arousal.

My body heated as he played with it. Moans came out of my mouth involuntarily as he moved his finger inside of me. His lips left mine and he smiled at me. "Can I kiss you down there?" he whispered.

My body got even hotter, and I couldn't believe what

came out of my mouth. "Yes." It was too late to take the word back, not that I wanted to, deep down.

Our eyes locked then a smile curved his lips. "You won't be sorry, Zandra." His eyes stayed on mine as he kissed one nipple then bit it playfully.

"Kane?" I bit my lower lip as I thought about what I was going to say.

"Yeah?" He went back to nibbling my tit.

"I'm a virgin. I just wanted you to know that about me." For some reason, shame filled me. I felt my cheeks go red with embarrassment.

Moving back up my body, his lips met mine again. "Thank you for telling me that." He kissed the side of my neck as he played with one tit, guiding my body so I lay underneath him. "Do you want to give your virginity to me, Zandra?"

"I do." I couldn't believe what I'd said. But I meant it.

He made a sexy groan then bit my neck. "Good."

Gripping his biceps, I arched up to him, feeling his hard dick press against my sex. I just wanted to feel it inside of me —feel him inside me. I couldn't think of anything else.

"Easy, baby. I want to make sure this is something you'll always remember with fondness." He pulled his head up to look me in the eyes. "You just relax and let me do all the work, 'k?"

I nodded. "'K."

His green eyes grew serious for a moment. "Should I use a condom?"

I shook my head. "No."

One word was all it took to change my life. One damn word that would change me forever. What a goddamned fool I was.

101

CHAPTER 8

Kane

"Hello?" I sat up when I heard my cell go off. "Shit." It was five in the morning, the Sunday after my night out, and even though I'd gone home relatively early, I was a bit out of it. Picking up the phone, I saw that it was another doctor from the hospital I worked at. "Hey, Jack. What's up?"

"Me. With my sick daughter. She's puking everywhere, and her mother's out of town. I've got the day shift at the ER today, but I'm going to need to stay here to take care of her. Do you think you can go in for me today?"

"Yeah." I was always one to help out others. "I'll do it. You just take care of your little girl, Jack."

"Thanks. You're the best." He hung up, and I rolled out of bed.

One hot shower, a cold blueberry muffin, and a hot cup of coffee later and I was on my way to the hospital. There weren't any cars in the ER parking lot. Most Sundays were easy. I wasn't worried about being swamped.

Heading in through the sliding glass door, I walked past the nurse's station, calling out to the blonde who sat at the desk. "Buzz me in, please."

"Good morning, Dr. Price. I thought Dr. Friday was scheduled for today," she said just before I got to the door.

Grabbing the handle and pulling it open, I nodded. "Yeah, he was. His kid got sick, and he asked me to take this shift. How's it been so far?"

"Quiet. A typical Sunday." She went back to reading a book, and I went into the back.

An office had been set up for the doctors on duty. I went to it, using my key to open it. The smell of cleaning products stung my nose. I should've been used to it by now, but I didn't think it'd ever be easier to smell. The scents were just so pungent.

Going straight to the coffee machine, I started up a pot before opening the computer to see what had happened the night before. "Gunshot. Stab wound. Rabies?" I had to look at that entry again. "You've got to be shitting me."

Pulling up the results, I found that a man had come in with a bite from his pet bat.

Who the hell owns a pet bat?

I found there were a few patients who'd been admitted to the hospital for their conditions, and the man with possible rabies was one of them. I had to go meet this guy.

Heading out of the ER to go up to the rooms, I crossed paths with one of the men who worked in laundry as he was pushing his heavy cart along the hallway. "Hey, Gerald. How's it going today?"

"It's going, doc. How're things with you?" He stopped as he got to the staff elevator. I decided to ride up with him.

"Well, I'm on my way up to see a man who was bitten by

his own pet bat," I answered after stepping on the elevator with him. "He's worried about rabies."

"No shit?" he laughed as he shook his head. "The things people do, huh?"

"Yep." The patient was set up on the third floor. "Here's my stop."

"I think I'll get off here too and go on ahead and pick up the dirty linen on this floor," Gerald said with a grin. "I've got to take a gander at this gentleman."

Heading to room 352, I tried to gain control over my expression. I didn't want to bust out laughing or anything like that. A light tap on his door and Mr. Jim Jones croaked, "I'm up. Come in."

Pushing the door open all the way, I was ready to see some kind of character. Imagine my surprise when a normal-looking older man sat up in the bed to welcome me in. Gerald was right behind me with his laundry cart. "Well, I'll be. You ain't what I was expecting."

The old guy laughed. "Yeah, I know. Who owns a bat as a pet? And a vampire bat, at that."

"A vampire bat?" I asked as I wondered how one even acquired such a thing. "Is that even legal?"

The old guy shrugged. "Not sure about that. You don't suppose your hospital will tell on me, do ya?"

I truly had no idea. "Let's hope not. Imagine the fine for owning a vampire bat. Well, let's move past that. Was the bat —um." I had no idea how to put it. The thing was the man's pet, after all.

"Murdered?" he asked me with a straight face.

"For lack of a better word, yes," I said.

"Yes. I had to kill Herman." He raised his hand up high, then it came down swiftly. "I took my shoe and WAP! Right on the head. It was quick."

I didn't see a bandage anywhere that was visible. "And the bite is where?"

When his cheeks went red, I began to wonder. When he threw back the blanket, I really had to wonder. When I saw the lump underneath his hospital gown, I knew this wasn't going to be easy to take. "On my junk, doc." He pulled up the gown and there he was, stark naked except for the bandage wrapped around the end of his penis. "I know how this looks."

"Yep," Gerald said. "You were letting that bat lick your cock, weren't ya? And he bit it, didn't he?"

The old man shook his head. "It ain't like that. And it wasn't a he-bat. It was a she-bat. But it's not what you're thinking. You see, I'd fallen asleep in my lounger." He might've look like an unassuming old guy, but it turned out he was a bit of a character after all. Seemed he wasn't shy about sharing all this with a stranger—I could understand him telling me, a doctor, all this, but he seemed more than happy to tell Gerald all about it too.

"And what's a lounger?" Gerald asked. "Is that some kind of a bat/man sex chair or something like that?"

A laugh came right out of my mouth before I could stop it. "Gerald! Please refrain from asking my patient any more questions." I clapped him on the back. "Let me do that, 'k?"

With a nod, he said, "Sure, doc. Go on. Ask him about the lounger and what it's for."

Mr. Jones ran his old wrinkled hand over his face. "A lounger is what I call my old recliner rocking chair that I sit in when I watch television in the living room. You see, I was doing laundry. Now, when I do laundry, I like to do it all of it at one time. That means I strip down to nothing while it washes."

"I get it now," Gerald said. "So, there you was, just sittin' there mindin' your own business when this lady bat came at ya and started biting your junk. So you're not some kind of freak after all!" He looked at me. "Thank goodness. I was startin' to get real worried there for a minute or two."

Mr. Jones looked right at me. "I feel asleep in the chair, and the door on Herman's cage must not have been shut right. She got out and bit the tip of my junk for some reason. I woke up, found her there, licking up the blood, and jumped up, grabbed my shoe and murdered her right then and there." He pulled his gown down and the blanket back up to cover himself. "It wasn't easy taking old Herman's life. But she'd never done anything like bite me before, so I thought she might've gotten rabies or something."

Nodding in agreement, I had no idea what to say. But Gerald did. "If she was a girl, why'd you name her Herman?" He put his hands on his hips, still looking a bit skeptical about the whole story. Despite what he'd said, it was becoming clear to me that Gerald still thought the old guy was some kind of a weirdo.

Mr. Jones clarified things for the laundry man. "When I first found the bat, I thought it was a male. I named it Herman after that guy on that old television show, *The Munsters*. You know, the vampire?"

"Ah hah!" came Gerald's quick reply as his finger shot up into the air. "Herman Munster was no vampire. He was a Frankenstein. It was Grandpa who was the vampire, and so was Herman's lovely wife, Lily. Their son, Eddie was a were-wolf, and their niece Marilyn was the only one who was left out of the monstrous pack."

Things were getting out of hand. "Okay, Gerald. Get the dirty laundry and get going while I check Mr. Jones' bandages and his wound."

I'd been curious about the story but had had no idea just how crazy this rabies case would be.

The wound was small and clean, without a hint of infection. "So you've received the vaccine and now we're waiting on the results of the test. The vaccine should do its job, and you should be able to go home once we get them, Mr. Jones. It's a good thing you came in right away. Tell me, do you have any more bats at home?"

"Nope," he said with a toothy grin. "But I did find myself a little snake out back. I call it Thelma and keep her in the house too. She stays in the bathtub. I don't ever use it. I shower outside, the way God intended."

"A word of advice, sir," I offered, "maybe don't take anymore wild animals into your home. And that snake isn't going to stay put in that tub either, I bet."

"Shit!" he sat up and shouted.

"What?" I asked, not having any clue what he was going to say next.

"You're right, doc!" He wore a worried expression. "I bet it was Thelma who let Herman out of her cage."

And with that, I started making my way out of his room. "Yeah, probably. See ya, Mr. Jones."

As I walked down the hallway, back to the ER, my cell rang. I saw that it was Aunt Nancy and answered it. "Hello."

"Hi, Kane. We're almost there. Just wanted to let you know," she told me.

"Ah. I took the dayshift at the ER. I forgot to text you guys." I felt bad about forgetting that Fox would be coming home.

"Dad, can I come up there and hang out with you today?" I heard him ask in the background.

"Seems he heard me." I loved when he came to work

with me. "Sure can, buddy. Can you drop him off here, Aunt Nancy?"

"Yeah," she said. "We're a few minutes away. I'll call you when we send him in, so you can meet him in the lobby."

"'K." I heard my name called over the speaker system and ended the call.

Hurrying to the ER, I found a nurse waiting in my office. "Hey, Dr. Price. We've got a twenty-six-year-old female in room one. She's got a laceration on her left palm. It's approximately one inch in length and fairly deep. She said she got it at work last night."

"Last night?" I asked.

"Yes, sir," she replied with a nod. "She wants stitches, but I told her that we probably couldn't do them now. It's just too late."

"So, what's the problem?" I took a seat in my chair, thinking there wasn't any reason for me to see this patient at all.

Her hands went to her hips, clearly annoyed. "The problem is that she wanted me to ask a real doctor."

"And you looked at the laceration, right? If you think it's too late, then go back there and tell her that a real doctor has told you that stitches can only be done within a few hours. After that, all we can do is use butterfly bandages on the wound." I opened the computer to get back to seeing what had happened the night before.

"Will do, Dr. Price." She left the office, and I went back to checking things out.

Not five minutes had passed when my aunt called me back, telling me to go to the lobby to meet Fox. Hopping up, I went to get my son, happy that he was back and would be spending the day with me.

When he spotted me, he ran my way. "Dad!"

"Hey, you!" I went to him, grabbing him up and hugging him before putting him back on the ground. "Boy, you got some sun." More small freckles peppered the top of his nose, and there were some on his cheeks now too.

"Yeah, I did. We played at the beach all day yesterday. It was fun." He followed me as we headed to the office. "And I saw a shark too."

"You did?" I asked with enthusiasm. "Up close?"

"Nah," he said as he waved his hand in the air. "It was really far away. And it was just the fin. Uncle James said it was probably a dolphin, but I was pretty sure it was a shark. I got out of the water to be on the safe side."

"Good thinking. Better safe than sorry, I always say." We turned the corner to the ER wing, and I pushed the double doors open.

"I know that." He laughed. "That's what I told everyone when they laughed at me. I said, better safe than sorry. What if it had been a shark? Bet no one would've been laughing then!"

"Smart thinking." I noticed a young woman up ahead at the nurses' desk. Bent over, she looked like she was signing papers. "So, what else happened in Florida, Fox?" I couldn't seem to take my eyes off the woman.

"Well, I walked on the beach and found lots of seashells." He tugged at my white jacket to make me look at him. "Don't worry. I brought them all home to put in our shell collection outside."

"Great." I looked away from him to look at the woman again. "We can add them to the garden outside when we get back home this evening. Doesn't that sound like fun?"

"Yeah, it does." He tugged my jacket again, and I looked down at him. "Can we maybe cook some hotdogs outside too? I really wanted a hotdog this whole weekend, and Aunt

Nancy wouldn't let me. She says they're nasty and she won't feed me nasty food."

"Well, some of them are. But the ones I buy aren't. We can make some hotdogs on the outdoor grill." I looked back at the woman, who had by now straightened up and shook out her hair.

Long dark hair cascaded down her back. Dark blue streaks ran through it.

It's her.

It had to be the waitress from the bar.

She was talking to the nurse and raised her hands as she said something. There was a bandage wrapped around her left one.

The patient with the cut. The hand she'd cut at work the night before.

It has to be her.

"Dad, the door's right here!" Fox shouted, as I walked right past it in my distracted state.

The woman turned around at the sound of Fox's shouting. The world around me seemed to stop as our eyes met.

Zandra Larkin!

102

CHAPTER 8

Zandra

Like a deer in the headlights, I stared at Kane Price. *This cannot be happening!*

It had to be a dream. Or more precisely, a nightmare.

I had never, ever wanted to see this man again. Not after what I'd gone through because of him.

Not that it was his fault, really. I'd been the one who'd told him there wasn't any need for him to use a condom, even though I hadn't been on any type of birth control. I'd never faulted Kane, or myself, for that matter, for what had happened to that baby boy we'd made.

Seeing him again, with his muscular body that showed just how much he'd grown up, sent chills through my veins. I knew that body rippled with every little movement he made.

Kane Price is standing perfectly still, staring into my eyes, and I can't move or even blink.

My mind went back to the night he'd changed my life.

His eyes had been glued to mine as he pushed his hard cock into my virgin pussy. Gasping with the intrusion, pain ripped through me. And that pain would stay with me—not in my pulsing body, but in my heart—forever.

A few small tears fell down my cheeks. He kissed them away, soothing me with his body and his whispered word. "Hush now, Zandra. The hard part will be over soon. It'll feel good in a minute, you'll see. You can trust me, baby."

No one had ever called me baby before. The way he said it stirred something inside of me. "I trust you, Kane."

"Good girl." He moved slowly, pulling his cock almost all the way out before pushing it back in with one smooth stroke.

Biting my lip as I tried not to think about the white-hot fire that blazed in my most sensitive parts, I got lost in the green depths of his gorgeous eyes. "Kane, has anyone ever told you that you're really beautiful?"

The way his lips curved into a sexy smile made my heart pound. "No. No one has ever used that word to describe me. How about you? Has anyone ever told you just how beautiful you are?"

"No." I ran one hand across his back, feeling the tight muscles there. "Are you telling me that you think I'm beautiful, Kane Price?"

His lips barely touched mine as he whispered, "You are more than beautiful. I'm finding it hard to find the right words to describe the way I think about you, baby."

I didn't want to think about Kane and how many girls he'd been with before, but the fact was, he was kind of known as a flirt. "I bet you say that to all the girls."

Pulling his head up, his lips pressed together, forming a

straight line. He moved his cock with ease now, and I was feeling more pleasure than pain. "Zandra, I don't think about you the way I think about anyone else. You're different."

Feeling embarrassed, I closed my eyes. "I know I am."

Brushing his lips across my cheek, he said, "In a good way. A great way." He gave me one long kiss that sent electricity through me. Somehow, my body heated up even more, and we moved together now, my body finally having adjusted to his size.

Although I had never been intimate with anyone before, I found myself moving in ways I didn't know I could. My body just knew what to do. My legs moved to wrap around him, holding him close to me. My hands wandered to every place I could touch.

Moving his mouth away from mine, he kissed a line straight up my neck before finding the spot just behind my ear. His teeth grazed my soft flesh before biting down, gently at first and then harder as he moved faster.

With no idea how just a little bite in that place could affect me so much, all I could do was moan with how wonderful it all felt as he moved his hard cock in and out of me.

"Kane!" I gasped as my body began to shudder. "I think I'm about to ..."

"Do it, baby," came his growled words. "I want to feel you come all over my cock. I'm aching to feel your tight pussy clenching all around my hard dick. Give it all to me, baby. Just like you did when I ate your sweet pussy. Give me all you've got, Zandra. I want it all. Every last drop. And then I'll give you mine."

Shrieking with the release—the second orgasm he'd given me that night—I let it all loose, just like he'd told me to. At that moment, I would have given him anything he wanted. I was his for the taking. As long as he wanted me, I would belong to him. He'd owned me then.

I had no idea just how much he actually would own me —or how much of my past would belong to him, at least. No idea of what was to come for me and the little boy we were in the middle of creating.

WITH THE THOUGHT of the baby I'd given away, my memory faded quickly.

On Kane's left stood a boy. Dark hair covered his head, and green eyes looked at me.

Kane's eyes.

I watched as the two came closer to me as I stood there frozen in place.

"Is that really you?" Kane asked me.

All I could do was nod. A lump had formed in my throat that made it impossible for me to say a single word. My eyes turned to the boy who walked next to him.

"Hi, I'm Fox." He waved at me as they came my way.

Light freckles spread across the bridge of his nose, much the same way mine had back before I started using sunscreen every day to keep my skin freckle-free and hopefully wrinkle-free. The boy reminded me of someone, but I couldn't quite place him.

Swallowing the lump down so I didn't seem like such a freaking idiot, I tried to smile at the boy, who looked to be about the same age as the one I'd had to give up.

"Hi there, Fox. That's a cool name." I looked at Kane. "And is he yours?"

He nodded. "He is."

Well, wasn't he just a procreation machine. He must've

gotten another girl pregnant about the same time he'd knocked me up. And by the looks of Fox, the mother must've looked a bit like me too. Seemed I hadn't been as special as he'd said I was that night—clearly, he just had a type.

Before Kane had fallen asleep that night, he'd held me in his arms. He'd told me he wasn't about to let me get away from him. But when he'd fallen asleep, I'd gotten up, dressed, and left him there on the bed he'd told me was his best friend Rocco's. The bed we'd made our son on. The son he had no idea existed.

"Leave it to you to come up with such a cool name, Kane." I thought better about what I'd said. "Or perhaps it was your wife's creative thinking?"

"My dad's not married. He's never been married." Fox looked up at his father. "It's just him and me. That's the way it's been for a while now."

Kane put his hand on his little boy's shoulder. "Well, it's not exactly just you and me, Fox. We've got Aunt Nancy and Uncle James too, you know."

"But they don't live with us," Fox said as he shook his head.

Kane looked back at me. "I saw you at Mynt last night. The back of you, anyway. The blue streaks in your hair gave you away today."

"You did?" I asked, acting like I didn't know. "Why didn't you come say hello?" I felt a little guilty for lying, but I didn't know what else to do. I couldn't tell him that I'd seen him too and had hidden from him.

"First of all, I had no idea it was you." Kane shifted his weight then crossed his arms over his chest. I could see the outline of some pretty massive biceps and felt wet heat pooling in my nether regions.

"You didn't?" I asked, as if I hadn't known that already either. "Well, then no wonder you didn't say anything to me."

"But I wanted to." He smiled at me, and I nearly swooned with desire for him.

Oh, if I could only have one more night with this man!

"You did?" I asked as I clasped my hands in front of me to keep them from shaking. "And why is that?"

That smile turned from charming to sexy with one easy move that I was certain he could make millions off of if he knew how to teach it. "There was just something about you that piqued my interest. But you walked into the back, behind the bar, and never came out. I waited and waited, and then I finally asked the bartender where you'd gone. He told me if you were still back there, then you were with the manager. Like, *with* the manager." He paused for a second, looking me up and down, and I felt that look from the tips of my toes to the roots of my hair. "So, are you?"

"Am I what?" I'd gotten a little lost in his eyes while he talked.

That heartbreaking smile got wider. "With the manager?"

"Oh, God, no." I shook my head. "He's not my type."

You know my type, Kane. My type is you.

"No?" he asked, then nodded. "Good to know. So, what brought you back in Charleston? Better yet, where have you been all this time? And why did you leave in the first place?"

I knew he would ask the hard questions!

"Long story." My brain hurt as I tried to think of what to say. "Another time, maybe."

"Definitely," he said with a nod. "Come back to my office with us. I want to catch up. And you're not getting out of here without giving me your number, either."

He wants my number!

"I don't know." I looked at the clear glass sliding doors that would lead me outside.

I should really get away from him before I blurt out the secret I've kept from him and everyone else for nearly eleven years.

"I do." In typical Kane fashion, he reached out and took my hand, tugging me along with him. "You're not getting away from me as easily this time."

Fox trotted right along with us on the other side of his father. "So, how do you know my dad?"

With no idea how to answer that question, I looked at Kane, who helped me out. "School, Fox."

"Oh, I get it now. You went to school with Dad." Fox nodded, looking much older and wiser than his young years. "Did you know my mom?"

Kane patted his son on the back. "Let's not go there, Fox. Not right now."

Kane had to have gotten another girl pregnant right around the time he'd gotten me that way. I knew that now without a single doubt. And she'd gone to the same school as us too, apparently.

Now I really didn't want him to know about the son we'd made.

How humiliating!

"Is his mother still in the picture?" I whispered to Kane as we went through a door that took us to a long hallway.

Shaking his head, Kane said, "Nah."

I found his answer pretty vague. But how could I say anything about that when I was being so vague too? "Oh."

Fox opened one of the many doors that lined the hallway. "Here's the office the doctors use when they work here. Dad really works at the clinic next door."

"I can't believe you're a doctor, Kane. That's such an

amazing accomplishment. And you're still so young, too." I was thoroughly impressed, and a bit envious, too.

What could I have become had I not been shamed by my own parents, called an evil sinner every day for two hellish years, and made to give up our son?

Kane gestured to a chair, and I took the seat he'd offered. "Well, I found motivation in my son here. He came into my life at a young age, and all I wanted to do was accomplish my career aspirations as fast as I could. That way I could take care of him the way I thought he deserved."

"I had no idea you were on becoming a doctor." I crossed my legs, bouncing my foot to help release some of the nervous tension that had built up with our meeting.

This was never supposed to happen. Yet there I was, sitting in his office, looking at the little boy he'd made with someone else—and had been able to keep and raise, too.

He could've been a father to our son. But my fucking parents had taken it all away from him and me both. He had been a standup guy. He had taken on the responsibility of having a baby. And he'd made something of himself too.

We had both been robbed, and so had our son. And all because my godforsaken parents thought what we'd done was evil, impure, and one of the biggest sins one could commit.

It only served to make me hate them even more than I already did.

"Do you have any kids?" his son asked me as he sat on a sofa, smiling away at me.

"No," came my quick reply.

Kane took over the questioning, "Married?"

"No." I shrugged. "No one has ever asked."

"So, never married." Kane nodded as he leaned back on

the desk, not six inches away from me. My body craved his. Every last part of me wanted him.

"No. And have you ever gotten close to getting married?" I asked as I tried not to look him up and down, very aware that I shouldn't be looking at him with so much lust in front of his young son.

"Nope." His reply filled me with the hope that I might get to feel his body all over mine again. How would he feel against me now that he had the body of a man?

"Never?" I asked as I went ahead and let my eyes wander over him.

My God, I want him!

"Not ever." He reached out, taking my chin in his large hand. "Will you be staying in Charleston long?"

Now that I knew he still lived here, I had no idea if staying in Charleston was a smart thing to do. "I'm not sure. I'm kind of a drifter."

Furrowed brows only served to make him look even hotter. "And why's that?"

Because if I'm around you, I might spill the beans and you'll end up hating me, that's why not.

But there was no way in hell I'd say such a thing. "Can't say. I just like to see new places, I guess," I said instead.

The drifter thing wasn't true at all. I'd spent my adulthood in one place—Chicago. I'd worked in one club, Underground. I had no idea why I'd told him that lie.

But the truth sounded so pitiful; I couldn't bring myself to tell him about the sorry existence I'd lived for the last eight years. An existence that had been caused by that one fiery night when I'd given him my virginity, and he'd given me a baby that I'd never had a chance of getting to know.

I should've run away from my parents. Straight to Kane Price.

103

CHAPTER 9

Kane

Zandra Larkin sat half a foot in front of me, and I couldn't believe it.

Our son looked at us from his seat on the couch, completely unaware that the woman I had yet to call by name was his mother. Unsure of what to do if she told Fox her name, I decided to wait and see what happened.

Fox knew the name of his mother. But how would he react if he found out this woman was her?

With his wellbeing at the front of my mind, I asked, "As a drifter, where have you lived?" I wanted to know if Zandra Larkin had become a person that shouldn't be in Fox's life. I was praying that she hadn't changed too much, that she'd be exactly right for his life.

I knew the attraction that I'd felt for her all those years ago was still there. It was simmering under the surface, urging me to hurry up and grab her, to pull her into my arms and get her into my bed. The way she looked me over told me she felt pretty much the same way I did.

Her blue eyes darted back and forth, telling me she was having a hard time coming up with the answer to my question, which I found odd. Finally, she said, "I've only lived in Chicago. I don't know why I said I was a drifter. I'm not. I guess you make me nervous, Kane."

The answer reminded me so much of the Zandra from my memory that my mind went back to that night.

WATCHING her from across the room filled with wild teenagers, I liked the way Zandra sipped from the red Solo cup filled with beer. Her cute little nose wrinkled with each tiny drink she took. I knew she would never finish that cup of alcohol.

Two other girls stood with her, talking quietly as they looked around at the others now and then. One of them said something that made them all laugh. Zandra's laugh sounded melodic and magical. Her sweet smile made my pulse speed up.

I didn't know a lot about the girl, except that her parents were the strictest people on the planet, supposedly. But Zandra was out for the night. I'd overheard that she'd gotten to come to the party only because her friend had told her parents that they were going to some kind of a lock-in at her grandma's church in Beaufort, a town a couple of hours away from us.

Apparently Zandra wasn't opposed to telling a little lie so she could have some fun, and that told me she just might not be opposed to what I wanted either.

Taking notice that Bobby Franklin was coming up to the girl I'd already pegged as mine for the night, I was shocked by the spark of jealousy that shot through me.

"Hey, Zandy, how'd you escape?"

Her pretty blue eyes went straight to the floor, her shyness taking over again. "I'd rather not say, Bobby."

But her friend didn't mind letting him in on the secret. "She lied to her parents for the first time ever!"

Zandra's cheeks turned beet red. "Hush, Stacy." She pulled the cup to her lips and took another sip, wrinkling her nose again. "I don't want anyone thinking I'm a liar."

Bobby nudged her shoulder with his, and I saw red for a second or two.

My girl.

He whispered something in her ear, so I had no idea what he said. But the blush on her cheeks went a shade deeper, and the red haze of jealousy came back to cloud my vision.

Time to make your move, Kane.

A TUG on my white coat pulled me out of my reverie.

"Hey, Dad. Can I run down to the nurses' station to see if they've got anything good to eat? They always have cake or something down there."

"Yeah." I looked at Zandra. "You want him to bring you anything back? The cake is always good."

She shook her head. "No, thank you." Her eyes went to Fox and followed him as he walked out of the office, leaving us alone. She looked back at me after he closed the door behind him. "It's good to see you, Kane."

"You too." My hands itched to touch her. But I didn't dare, not here. "I would really like to take you out sometime."

"No." Her answer came way too quickly. Her hair flew around her shoulders as she shook her head, adamant. "I can't."

"Why is that?" Purposely, I reached out, taking her hands into mine. "You'll have to come up with something good, you know. You did take off on me that night. I think you owe me a date or two. Or I owe them to you, rather. I've never forgotten you—I want you to know that." It wasn't a lie. She came into my head pretty often.

"Kane, things are different now." She tried to pull her hands away, but I held onto them. "I'm different now." Her eyes bored into mine. "I'm not that same little shy girl you knew back then. I've grown up. I have all the baggage that comes along with being a grown woman now. You could say that I'm damaged goods."

With a chuckle, I pulled her up. Having her standing in front of me, facing me, our bodies only inches apart, had my dick getting hard.

"I'm a doctor. I fix damaged people for a living. If you've got problems, I'm the perfect guy to help you get rid of them." Pulling her right hand to my mouth, I watched her lips quiver as I kissed her palm. "Give me a chance, Zandra."

There had always been a part of me that was mad at her for running away, for never telling me she was pregnant with my baby, and for giving him away. But the biggest part of me simply wanted her. I would get to the whys of that later on.

For now, I only wanted her again. In my arms, in my bed, in my life. And that meant in Fox's life too.

I would have to say her name some time, after all. She didn't know who he was, but he would know who she was right away, and he would definitely say something.

For now, I wanted to keep the cat in the bag. I knew next to nothing about Zandra's life, or her state of mind. I had no idea how she would take the news that I had our son and had had him since he was born.

How will she take that?

As I looked into her eyes, I saw a lot more strength there than I had seen eleven years earlier. She wasn't a girl anymore; she was a woman. A mature woman who'd been through a lot and had come out the other side of it a stronger person.

"I do not want to be fixed, Kane. I'm not willing to become your patient."

The idea of playing doctor with her began to fill my head, and it made my dick grow harder. "Oh, but I could make that a lot of fun, Zandra." I pulled her into my arms, brushing the hair off her face as I stared deeply into her eyes. "Come on, give me what I want. Say yes. You know I can talk you into it. Don't make me beg, baby."

Her body shook as I held her. My cock pulsed against her cunt, making her cheeks flush. "Kane, please," she moaned.

Moving my mouth closer to hers, I gave her my demand. "Give me what I want, and I'll let you go."

"I can't," she muttered. "Please."

"No." My lips grazed hers, teasing. "I still want you."

"Oh, God," she whispered, and then leaned in to meet me halfway.

The kiss sent me back in time to that one magical night when I'd had her underneath me. To when I'd been panting with such intense passion that I thought I might pass out. The sex had been off the charts that night. We'd fucked like wild animals after our first soft session when I'd introduced her to making love for the first time.

If I hadn't been expecting Fox to come back to the office at any moment, I would've put her ass on that desk and taken her nine ways to Sunday. But he was going to be back, and most likely soon.

He couldn't catch us like that. Pulling my mouth away from hers, I had to smile when I saw the raw desire on her beautiful face. "So, that date I want. Can I get it now?"

Her chest rose and fell against mine. "I really can't."

"Wrong answer, Zandra." Grabbing the back of her head, I grabbed a fistful of her silky hair, pulling it back, then kissing her again. Harder, more demanding this time. I wanted her to give into me the way she had when we were young.

I could feel her heart pounding in her chest. Her tongue danced with mine. Her hands gripped my arms. When I took my mouth off hers, I was panting too. "Tell me what I want to hear."

"He'll be coming back soon, Kane. You don't want your little boy to see us like this." She searched my eyes as she went on. "I can't go out with you. I'm sorry."

"I'm not the kind of man who takes no for an answer when I know damn good and well that you want exactly what I want too." My blood boiled as it raced through my veins. "Tell me that you don't want me, and I'll leave you alone."

Staring into her eyes, I defied her to lie to me. "You know I do. But I just can't get involved with you."

Letting her go, I walked away from her in frustration. I could've just spit it all out—let her know that I knew her secret. Let her in on the secret I was keeping from her, too.

You're the mother of my son!

It would be out in the open, and we could see where things would take us. I could tell her that I forgave her for never telling me the truth. And she could tell me what the hell had happened back then.

Why had she let her parents force her to put our son up for adoption? Had she wanted that too? And why in the hell had none of them seen fit to let my family know a thing about the baby she carried?

Instead, I took a deep breath to control myself as Fox came back into the office, holding up a brownie. "See, they did have something!"

Zandra ran her hands over her shirt to make sure it was straight, looking down as she did so. "Well, I guess I should be going. You've got work to do, Kane. It was nice to see you again after all these years. Being that we're both living in Charleston, I'm sure we'll run into each other now and then. It was a pleasure to meet you, Fox." She rattled on as she made her way to the door.

Fox took a seat on the sofa again, munching on his sweet treat, basically giving it all of his attention as he virtually ignored us. While he was distracted, I headed to the door, placing myself between it and her. "I'm not busy at all. Please stay a bit longer. Let's catch up."

One brow cocked as she gave me a sly smile. "Haven't we already done that?"

"Verbally," I whispered. "I don't want you to go yet."

"I know what you want." She winked. "Sorry, Kane. I can't."

"You can." I leaned back on the door. "And you will."

It had been a very long time since I'd craved anyone like this. But now that I had her, I felt a hunger for her that rivaled anything I'd ever felt. I would have her obstinate ass under me again if it was the last thing I did.

Fox got up to toss the napkin, now empty of brownie, into the trashcan. "What are you guys doing anyway?" He walked up to my side, looking at me with a confused expression. "It sounds like you two are fighting about something."

"We're not fighting," Zandra said as she looked down at him, running her hand over his head. The maternal action made me catch my breath, and I wondered if she had any idea that this was the boy she'd grown in her belly for nine months. "Your dad's just being silly, is all."

Fox looked at me, his tone surprised, "You're being silly?"

It wasn't like me to be silly, and Fox knew it. "No, I'm not being silly. I've just asked her on a date."

Now his eyes grew big. "A date?" He looked at Zandra. "You should say yes, 'cause my dad never goes on dates." Then he looked back at me. "You must really love her, Dad." He tried to whisper that little bit, but I was sure people on the other side of the hospital could have heard him.

Zandra choked a little as she backed up, holding her throat as she looked down at the floor. "I just can't. I really can't."

Patting my son on the top of his head, I said, "Grownups don't talk about love so soon, son. But I would like to take this nice young woman out for dinner and maybe some drinks and dancing, if she's not opposed to it, of course. Gentlemen never force themselves on a lady. You remember that, Fox."

Zandra suddenly found herself with the upper hand as she saw that I wasn't about to teach my son to bend a female to his will the way I'd been trying with her earlier—and fully planned on doing again. "Glad to hear you think that way, Kane. So you do understand that I just can't go out with you on any kind of a date. Sorry about that."

"Aw, man, Dad. She don't love you back." Fox shook his head. "Sorry, Dad. That's gotta hurt."

"Oh, it does." I held my hand over my heart. "Just one little date is all I'm asking for."

Fox turned to look at her. "Please, lady. I've never seen my dad like this. He's so, so—um—acting so weird, is what he is. It's just dinner, drinks, and dancing. Come on. Please." Then my son put on his most pitiful pleading face as he tried one last time. "Please. Can you do it for me?"

The way Zandra looked at him made my heart stop. Her eyes shimmered a bit, and I could tell she was holding back tears. Maybe she was thinking about the boy she had given away.

She had no idea she was looking at that same child.

"You two are making this very hard." She looked up at me. "Kane, if I thought it would be a good idea, I would say yes. I'm sure nearly every woman in this city would love to go on a date with you. I know that's how it was back when we were in high school."

"But I'm not asking any of them out—I'm asking you out." I crossed my arms over my chest and looked at her with a sexy grin. "Come on, just say yes already."

Fox walked over and put his hand on her arm. "Come on, please? Just tell him you'll go on at least one date with him. I've never seen him this way."

Reaching out with her left hand, the one with the bandage wrapped around it, she said, "I just can't, Fox."

He caught her by the wrist, looking at something on the inside of it. "Hey, you've got my birthday tattooed on you."

Holy hell!

If you want to continue reading this story, you can get your copy here:

Dirty Little Secret: A Secret Baby-Second Chance Romance

https://books2read.com/u/38EWpL

OTHER BOOKS BY THIS AUTHOR

His Beautiful Revenge

So, you think I have it all? Yes, I'm Giacomo Conti, the
billionaire. Dark Italian good looks,
sex appeal, and every woman I meet practically begging to get
me into bed? That's my world, yes.

So why am I in a loveless relationship with a gold-digging woman
who cheats on me every chance she gets?

Click here to get your copy from your favorite bookstore

https://books2read.com/u/3J8NaP

The Orphan Next Door

Emily is too young for me, but I can't shake how much I
want her.

I want to rescue her from her isolation.
I certainly want to rescue her from that gold-digging little creep
James.

I want to love her and be loved by her, and wake up to her face
every morning.

Click here to get your copy from your favorite bookstore

https://books2read.com/u/bWBlN1

~

Hot Nights in Sturgis

Intrigue. Lust. Passion.

Blaze is a member of a motorcycle gang on their way to Sturgis, South Dakota for the huge biker rally held there every year. He's single and wants to keep it that way, but plans on taking as many females as he can to his bed while in the rowdy town.

Click here to get your copy from your favorite bookstore

https://books2read.com/u/boZKd1

~

The Billionaire's Lighthouse Series

Hope. Chemistry. Heat.

Elizabeth Cook is a conservationist trying to save a lighthouse on the northern side of Chesapeake City, Rhode Island.

Zane White is the billionaire who just bought the real estate it sets on and plans on tearing it down to build condos that overlook the Atlantic Ocean.

Click here to get your copy from your favorite bookstore

https://books2read.com/u/mlY5z7

~

Stormfronts

When billionaire property mogul Theo Storm gives the Commencement address at her college,

grad student Jess Wood initially dismisses him as a rich, bland businessman.

When he notices her in the audience however, his blatant admiration for her attracts whispers

amongst her friends and colleagues and an embarrassed Jess escapes from the throng,

Click here to get your copy from your favorite bookstore

https://books2read.com/u/31xzjl

A Billion Dollar Arrangement

Angela Hayes is a beautiful city girl who longs for some excitement and fulfillment in her love life.

She has a great job at a huge marketing company and she just learned that the

company's billionaire CEO will be making an appearance at her branch.

Click here to get your copy from your favorite bookstore

https://books2read.com/u/4NGMk9

The Dirty Doctor's Touch: A Doctor's Romance

Dirk

I am a master. An elitist. I am at the top of my field, and I know what I am doing.

Women want me. They worship me. They come to me to fulfill all their needs—all of them.

I can have any one of them I want. But I only want her.

A goddess with a perfect body. So pure, so vulnerable.

The Reconstruction of Cyprian: A Bad Boy Billionaire Series

Look, I'm no Prince Charming.

I like my life exactly the way I've designed it,

Billions in the bank,

And my fair share of beautiful women in my bed.

I don't have the time or interest in the chase,

I'm always honest with my intentions.

Dangerous Kiss: A Billionaire Romance

I never thought I would ever feel this way again...

Losing my wife was bad enough, but now I've fallen for someone so vulnerable and half my age.

Even her name makes me smile. Her spirit, her laugh, the way her dark eyes look at me...she makes me weak.

https://books2read.com/u/bpODnq

The Surgeon's Secrets: A Bad Boy Billionaire Romance

Dr. Damon Chase just saved my life, going over my doctor's head to perform a life-saving surgery.

He's taken me from wondering if I'll die soon to looking forward to my life,

and I'm falling for him fast and hard. There are just two problems.

Click here to get your copy from your favorite bookstore

https://books2read.com/u/3nvn15

SIGN UP TO RECEIVE FREE BOOKS

Would you like to read **The Unexpected Nanny, Dirty Little Virgin** and other romance books for free?
Click here to read The Unexpected Nanny for FREE

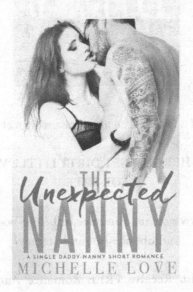

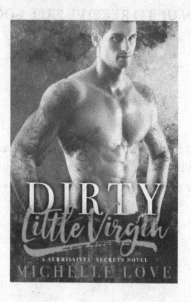

ABOUT THE AUTHOR

Mrs. Love writes about smart, sexy women and the hot alpha billionaires who love them. She has found her own happily ever after with her dream husband and adorable 6 and 2 year old kids.

Currently, Michelle is hard at work on the next book in the series, and trying to stay off the Internet.

"Thank you for supporting an indie author. Anything you can do, whether it be writing a review, or even simply telling a fellow reader that you enjoyed this. Thanks

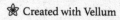 Created with Vellum